Praise for
IN FEAST OR FAMINE

"Mesu's talent for intertwining extensive research with riveting storytelling breathes freshness into the ancient and beloved story of Joseph. I highly recommend this fascinating glimpse into his life and faith journey, along with that of Asenath, the often overlooked Egyptian woman at his side."

—CONNILYN COSSETTE,
Christy Award–winning and ECPA bestselling author

"In the pages of *In Feast or Famine,* Mesu Andrews shines light on the little-known but beloved wife of Joseph. With deftness and deep insight, she brings her characters to vivid life, lifting Asenath from obscurity to multifaceted daughter, wife, future mother, and ultimately a believer in Elohim. Well researched and richly presented, this latest offering is a literary feast!"

—LAURA FRANTZ,
Christy Award–winning author of *The Rose and the Thistle*

"Mesu Andrews possesses the ability to pull aside the curtain to the past and bring biblical characters to life. Although long familiar with the biblical story of Joseph and his transition from slave to powerful leader, I was mesmerized by the journey this story laid out for him. My deepest takeaway can be found in a single line of dialogue: "Elohim meets us in our pain." Truth indeed, painted eloquently by this author's gifted pen. I highly recommend this novel."

—KIM VOGEL SAWYER, bestselling author of *Freedom's Song*

"The second half of Joseph's story comes to life in this exciting sequel to *Potiphar's Wife*. The spotlight shines on Asenath, Joseph's Egyptian wife, giving us a firsthand look at her journey. Palace intrigue, political drama, romance, and inspiration are all woven together in this inspiring story. Those who are looking for well-written biblical fiction with exceptional research will be delighted with this new novel from bestselling author Mesu Andrews."

—CARRIE TURANSKY, award-winning author of *The Legacy of Longdale Manor* and *No Journey Too Far*

"*In Feast or Famine* invites us to experience a familiar story come to life. As an unlikely romance blooms amid political machinations and ruthless ambition, one woman learns to trust the God who has a plan for her life, even when the future is uncertain. This novel is a treat for all those who are fascinated by ancient Egypt, love the rags-to-riches story of Joseph, and are ready to step into experiencing the faithfulness of God to every nation."

—TRACY HIGLEY, author of *A Time to Seek*

"Imagine if the entire foundation of your life turned out to be a lie. That's the essence of Egyptian priestess Asenath's story in *In Feast or Famine* by Mesu Andrews. Forced into an arranged marriage, Asenath tries to remain true to her beliefs until Elohim, her husband Joseph's one true God, reveals His worthiness to her. The author's thoughtful research moves this fascinating slice of biblical history along like a fast-moving river. A riveting page-turner!"

—SUZANNE WOODS FISHER, author of the bestselling book *The Moonlight School*

IN FEAST OR FAMINE

IN FEAST OR FAMINE

A Novel

THE EGYPTIAN CHRONICLES

Mesu Andrews

WATERBROOK

In Feast or Famine

In Feast or Famine is a work of historical fiction based closely on people and events depicted in the Bible. Details that cannot be historically verified are purely products of the author's imagination. Any resulting resemblance to persons, living or dead, is entirely coincidental and unintentional.

Published in the United States by WaterBrook, an imprint of Random House, a division of Penguin Random House LLC.

WATERBROOK® and its deer colophon are registered trademarks of Penguin Random House LLC.

Interior map created by Stanford Campbell

Library of Congress Cataloging-in-Publication Data
Names: Andrews, Mesu, author.
Title: In feast or famine / Mesu Andrews.
Description: First Edition. | Colorado Springs: WaterBrook, [2023]
Identifiers: LCCN 2022048778 | ISBN 9780593193785 (Trade paperback) | ISBN 9780593193792 (Ebook)
Classification: LCC PS3601.N55274 I48 2023 | DDC 813/.6—dc23
LC record available at https://lccn.loc.gov/2022048778

Printed in the United States of America on acid-free paper

waterbrookmultnomah.com

1st Printing

First Edition

Book design by Diane Hobbing

To Lissa Halls-Johnson, my precious friend and tenacious writing partner. You see my words at their worst and then help shape them into a pleasing offering to our God. "Thank you" is never enough.

NOTE TO READER

Pharaoh gave Joseph the name Zaphenath-
Paneah and gave him Asenath daughter of
Potiphera, priest of On, to be his wife. And
Joseph went throughout the land of Egypt.
Joseph was thirty years old when he entered
the service of Pharaoh.

GENESIS 41:45–46

From Broadway to children's books, the biblical story of Joseph, his colorful coat, and his rags-to-riches journey in Egypt has fascinated people of all ages. But most of the focus remains on Joseph and his brothers, their reunion, and the overwhelming forgiveness he musters for the family who betrayed him. Granted, it's a great testimony of integrity and grace. But what about his wife? Have you ever wondered how Joseph, a man so committed to Elohim, could remain faithful to his God and offer such grace while married to Asenath, the daughter of Potiphera, priest of On (see Genesis 41:45)? And why did Pharaoh choose this woman to marry his second highest official—the "savior" of Egypt?

Before we can understand the heights to which Joseph rose, we must understand the mountain he climbed. After studying the political climate in which Joseph navigated his years of leadership during both feast and famine, I believe Asenath and her priestly father were as perilous to Joseph's climb as were the years he spent in prison.

I also believe his wife may have become one of his greatest blessings. Why? I've used historical findings to build on the truth of Genesis 40–50, then used creative fiction as mortar to create Joseph and Asenath's world. Come. Experience ancient Egypt and meet a woman too few have ever considered.

THE GREAT SEA

NILE DELTA

AVARIS

LOWER
EGYPT

BUBASTIS

ON

MEMPHIS

FAIYUM

MAGIC LAKE

SHEDET
HAWARA
GUROB PALACE

TEBTUNIS

MEYDUM

BAHR YUSSEF

UPPER
EGYPT

ABYDOS

THEBES

NEKHEN

EDFU FORTRESS

CUSH

CHARACTERS

Ahira	Hebrew maid; Joseph's first love; Pushpa's assistant cook
Apophis	co-regent of Lower Egypt with Pharaoh Yanassi; Queen Tani's brother
Asenath	Potiphera's daughter; priestess; Isis Incarnate; Joseph's wife
Esi	Asenath's maid
Fadil	old Ra priest in Memphis
Hami	vizier until he is assigned to be captain of the guard for Zaphenath-Paneah (Joseph)
Hodari	captain of the guard for Pharaoh Yanassi
Hotep	Asenath's cautious, introverted handmaid; becomes King Apophis's wife/queen
Jendayi	Asenath's guenon monkey (female)
Joseph/Zaphenath-Paneah	vizier of Egypt; Asenath's husband
Katesch	chantress known as the Songbird of Memphis; beloved deceased wife of Potiphera

Maahir	Vizier Pancah's steward
Medjays	Cushite warriors who serve as bodyguards for Egypt's high-ranking officials
Mentuhotepi	Queen Sitmut's firstborn son; half brother of Neferhotep; a madman
Nebiriraw	one of Upper Egypt's pharaohs
Neferhotep	young son of Queen Sitmut and Pharoah Sobekhotep; half brother of Mentuhotepi
Nuru	captain of On's temple guard; Potiphera's bodyguard and faithful spy
Potiphar	captain of the guard for King Apophis
Potiphera/Potabi	high priest of Ra (later Amun-Ra); father of Asenath
Pushpa	"Ommi" to Pharaoh Khyan and Potiphar; chief cook for Apophis's army
Shu	Shedet's high priest
Sitmut	scarred wife of Pharoah Sobekhotep; mother of Neferhotep and Mentuhotepi
Sobekhotep	Queen Sitmut's husband and brother; Neferhotep's father; Mentuhotepi's stepfather
Tani	Pharaoh Khyan's widow; Pharaoh Yanassi's mother; Pharaoh Apophis's sister
Tau	Potiphera's steward
Ubaid	warden of the prison underneath Potiphar's (Joseph's) villa

Yanassi	co-regent of Lower Egypt with Pharaoh Apophis; Queen Tani's son
Zahra	Asenath's bubbly, bold, adventurous, and outspoken handmaid

A captain of the guard is assigned to each person of high importance. There are three who play a role in this story: one for each of the co-regents—Yanassi (Hodari) and Apophis (Potiphar)—and one for the vizier (Hami).

GLOSSARY

ABBA	(Hebrew) father
ABI	(Egyptian) father
AKH	a spirit or ghost
AMU	Egyptian term for Canaanites or those from Canaanite ancestry
BARQUE	a large, flat-bottomed ship made for navigating the Nile
BAHR YUSSEF	River of Joseph
CHANTRESS	a woman who served in the temple; though their duties were unclear, chantresses of Amun were highly esteemed
EYE OF HORUS	a symbol derived from a mythical conflict between the gods Horus and Seth and used in art and cosmetics to signify well-being, healing, and protection
FAIENCE	earthenware embellished with opaque colored glazes

FAIYUM	an area of varied topography in northern Egypt, west of the Nile, watered by a channel initially constructed by Pharaoh Amenemhat
FELUCCA	sturdy reed or wooden boats with triangular sails
GIDETY	(Egyptian) grandmother
GIDY	(Egyptian) grandfather
GREAT-SABA	(Hebrew) great-grandfather
GREAT-SAVTA	(Hebrew) great-grandmother
HIGH PRIEST	the highest-ranking priest of a particular temple who held authority over all his priests
HYKSOS	Amorite tribes that Bedouins forced from Canaan and that were relocated to Egypt; from approximately 1800 to 1550 B.C. they rose to a ruling dynasty
IMA	(Hebrew) mother
INUNDATION	ancient Egypt's first of three seasons; marked the new year with the akhet festival and measuring the Nile's floodwaters
ISIS	Egyptian goddess of healing, rebirth, and motherhood
KA	a person's soul
LECTOR PRIEST	second to the high priest; his responsibilities included instructing other clergy and maintaining and reading from the sacred writings during festivals and sacrifices

MA'AT	describes both the ancient Egyptian goddess of truth, justice, harmony, and peace (Ma'at) and the goal of every human to achieve those qualities in daily life
MAMMISI	the place in a temple where the goddess would give birth to the son of the god
OMMI	(Egyptian) mother
PHYLE	a month-long term that gave community members the opportunity to serve as priests (and priestesses)
PROPHET	the administrative priest in a temple
SABA	(Hebrew) grandfather
SCHENTI	a single strip of linen wrapped around the hips and secured with a belt
SENET	an ancient Egyptian board game
SOBEK	Egyptian god associated with a crocodile; manifested as a crocodile or man with a crocodile head
VIZIER	a vice-regent; second to the Egyptian king or pharaoh
WAB PRIEST	the lowest order of temple servants who performed the most mundane tasks with little recognition or reward

Abundance doesn't always come with feasting—nor
famine in times of drought.

PROLOGUE

*So the chief cupbearer told Joseph his dream. . . .
"This is what it means," Joseph said to
him. . . . "Within three days Pharaoh will lift
up your head and restore you to your position,
and you will put Pharaoh's cup in his hand, just
as you used to do. . . . But when all goes well
with you, remember me and show me kindness;
mention me to Pharaoh and get me out of this
prison."*

GENESIS 40:9, 12–14

AVARIS, LOWER EGYPT
CIRCA 1693 B.C.
Ahira

I was a prisoner of time, awaiting word of a baker's death, a cupbearer's favor, and Joseph's release.

My handsome husband-to-be emerged from the cell he was
cleaning. "You must let me leave the prison, Joseph, just long
enough to ensure the cupbearer honors his promise."

He took the broom from my hands and drew me close. "Are you
trying to shirk your duties, Ahira bat Enoch?"

How could a man clean filthy cells all morning and still smell of cloves and honey? "You make my head swim," I whispered.

"Will you be so enamored when I am your husband?" He raised a single brow, mischief in the challenge. "Because I plan to make you my wife the moment I'm freed."

I nodded toward the torture tables behind me. "I'm not sure you can outshine these romantic surroundings once you're free, but I'm anxious to see you try."

His laughter was pure joy and ended with a tender kiss. We'd waited nearly four years for Elohim to right the injustices done to my beloved. After an especially dark series of events, Master Potiphar's wife had accused Joseph of attempted rape. Though the master knew his wife had lied, he imprisoned Joseph and kept the whole matter secret from Pharaoh Khyan—adding another brick to the wall between our master and the king, his childhood friend. If the cupbearer revealed Joseph's imprisonment, would Potiphar be angry? Would Pharaoh? Would Joseph be forgotten in a renewed battle between the two most powerful men in Lower Egypt?

"Joseph, I—" Pleading, I looked up. "Let me go upstairs. I'll slip quietly into the throne room and see what's taking so long. If the cupbearer mentioned you as he promised, Pharaoh should have sent someone to free you by now."

"They'll come." He tucked a strand of hair behind my ear. "Elohim gave the dreams, gave me the interpretations, and arranged the timing of today's feast. It's all too perfect not to happen."

But the slight tremor in his smile told me he was nervous, too. I laid my head against his chest and heard the pounding of his heart. *Elohim, please let our hopes become reality!*

Two Medjays had come at dawn to escort the chosen prisoners upstairs, just after I'd arrived with Pushpa's basket of food for Joseph and the warden, Ubaid, to break their fast. The water clock had run out long ago, and our bellies confirmed it was well past midday. When I was chosen as the freedom prisoner years ago—in celebration of both Pharaoh's birth and Inundation, the Nile's annual rebirth—I'd been presented to Pharaoh and finished the feast and parade by early afternoon.

"I must go!" I broke away, nearly knocking over the prison warden in my mad dash toward the stairs.

"Don't run off on my account!" he called up the steps, cackling. "I finished my nap and hoped for a game of senet."

"Later, Ubaid!" I shouted. Reaching the ground floor landing, I darted through the villa door and closed it behind me. The hallway was deserted, and the sounds of distant screams sent gooseflesh over my body. Panic launched me toward the kitchen across the hall. *Empty.* Pushpa, my dearest friend and the master's ommi, must have gone to the throne room for the festivities.

My legs turned to water as distant sounds of turmoil grew. Shrieks surrounded the villa from all sides—the kitchen courtyards and even from the streets beyond the palace walls. I had to find Pushpa. She'd likely be among the nobility in the throne room. Though she hated the pomp, she endured it to be with her sons. She'd adopted Pharaoh Khyan and Captain Potiphar when they were mere boys, having no idea they'd one day rule the nation.

I burst into the hallway and raced through the dining room and into the walkway connecting the palace to my master's home. When I was barely halfway to the entrance, the throne room's door flung wide. Two Medjays flanked hysterical Pushpa, her grief at full volume.

"Ahira!" she cried when she spotted me. The warriors released her, and she ran into my arms, sobbing incoherent news. I looked over her shoulder for an interpretation.

"Pharaoh Khyan is dead," Hami said without conciliation. Though he'd been Egypt's vizier for years, he dealt with urgency like the impassive Medjay he once was. "We cleared the throne room as soon as the king fell, but panic at his death will be seen as an ill omen for this year's akhet festival and will spread like a plague. Take Mistress Pushpa to her chamber and wait there for Captain Potiphar. Go. Now." Though never unkind, Hami always put duty before courtesy.

Pushpa looped her arm in mine and started without dispute. "Pharaoh's death changes everything. When power shifts in Egypt, the wise remain close to the truest of heart."

Of course, we would gain a new pharaoh, but . . . "What do you mean 'it changes everything'?"

"General Apophis immediately assumed Khyan died from poisoning and accused Potiphar of lagging in his protection. In Potiphar's defense, Queen Tani affirmed Khyan had complained of chest pains for two weeks but wouldn't let anyone call for his physicians. Had she not spoken on his behalf, I might have lost both my sons this day."

"Oh, Pushpa, I'm so sorry." Always horrified at Egyptian politics, I silently praised Elohim I was but a slave.

She glanced over her shoulder. The Medjays had returned to the throne room. We were alone in the connecting hall, but she still whispered, "The queen's gracious act was followed almost immediately by a foolish one. She appointed Apophis as her son's co-regent."

"How can the queen appoint the next king—and a six-year-old pharaoh?"

She shushed me as we entered the villa. "Tani is well respected by Khyan's counselors. They won't challenge the grieving widow when she appoints her own brother to rule alongside her son. But Apophis has always been ambitious. Placing him on the throne beside Yanassi is inviting conspiracy."

"He wouldn't kill his own nephew . . . would he?"

"I don't know. But anything's possible when a man hungry for power catches its scent. Potiphar has never trusted General Apo—I suppose *King Apophis* is more appropriate now."

We entered the villa's residence hall in silence, my mind whirring with how to broach the subject of Joseph's release. Before we reached the kitchen, I whispered, "Perhaps Joseph could be released now that . . ." The horror on Pushpa's face bowed my head in shame. How callous of me to think of Joseph's release when our pharaoh had died only moments ago.

"I know it seems unfair that Potiphar sent Joseph to prison, but you must realize that if Khyan believed Potiphar deceived him in even the smallest detail, it would have been reason for dismissal—or even execution. Potiphar risked his life to return Zuleika to Crete, and Joseph is well cared for in the prison as Ubaid's assistant. You two will be married someday, but—" Her eyes filled with tears, and she looked away.

We'd avoided this topic for three years. I hadn't even told her that Joseph interpreted the cupbearer's and baker's dreams, fearing she might warn Master Potiphar and somehow ruin Joseph's chance to be free. But with Pharaoh Khyan dead, there was no reason to keep Joseph hidden.

"Did Pharaoh Khyan restore the cupbearer to his position before he died?" I asked.

Pushpa's brow wrinkled. "He did. And he chose a second freedom prisoner—the baker—but deemed him unworthy for some reason. It was so strange. The moment after Khyan ordered the royal baker taken away and hanged, Khyan fell to his knees and grasped his chest." Her face twisted with emotion. "Potiphar ordered his guards to surround Khyan, but how could they hide a giant? Everyone in the courtroom saw their god-king gasp for his last breath before clearing the courtroom. When people are frightened, they become unpredictable—"

I pulled Pushpa into my arms to hide my devastation. *The cupbearer didn't have time to mention Joseph.* "For safety's sake, we should remain inside the villa, or ask Hodari to escort us."

She broke away. "We're leaving Avaris. Pack what you can carry in a shoulder bag."

The floor felt as if it had shifted. "Why?" I could barely form the word.

"Queen Tani appointed Potiphar to the position of captain of King Apophis's bodyguard. She reasoned that spending all day every day with her brother would relieve Potiphar's misgivings about his character." Pushpa scoffed. "King Apophis revealed his character with his first act as co-regent. He plans to march Lower Egypt's troops into our southern nomes and quash any rebellion that stirs when news of Khyan's death travels." She gripped my shoulders. "Remember what I said, Ahira. When Egypt's power shifts, the wise remain close to the truest of heart. My Potiphar is the truest heart I know. We leave at dawn with him and his regiment of Medjays who will guard King Apophis. We will be the official cooks for the king and his royal guards."

"No!" I shrugged her off. "I can't leave Joseph!"

She stared at me, utterly calm. "We can, and we must. I love Joseph, too. You know I do. But he is safer in that prison than we are in these halls. Khyan's death will ripple conflict throughout Egypt, and it will begin here in Avaris—the likes of which you can't imagine, my sweet Hebrew. In every nome, in Abydos, and even farther south—in Upper Egypt—pure-blooded Egyptians will see Khyan's death as an opportunity to advance north and seize his throne. Coups and conspiracies will bloom like lotus at dawn. Rebels will separate the Egyptians from so-called Hyksos—the dividing lines Khyan worked so hard to erase."

"If we must leave, then ask Master Potiphar to release Joseph. Take him with us. We can't abandon him—"

"No!" she shouted. Her sudden harshness sobered me. She raised her chin and straightened her shoulders. "I'm the cook for Potiphar's royal guard, and you're my assistant. We have much to prepare. Visit Joseph if you must, but be quick with your goodbye." Her chin quivered slightly, the lone crack in her unfeeling demeanor. "You must believe me. Joseph is safe. And he'll be exactly where we left him when we return."

IN FEAST OR FAMINE

ONE

*The foreigner residing among you must be
treated as your native-born. Love them as
yourself, for you were foreigners in Egypt.
I am the LORD your God.*

LEVITICUS 19:34

If raising a monkey was intended to train me as the Great Ommi of
Egypt, I was failing miserably. "Jendayi, naughty girl. Give me that
mirror!" I lunged at my furry-faced guenon as she scurried up the
slanted branch in her corner of my audience chamber. She was the
size of a water pitcher, and her brown speckled fur was softer than
lamb's wool. She was the joy of my life but as unruly as a spoiled
child.

"I'll get the mirror this time." Zahra, my adventurous handmaid,
raced after her. Jendayi scampered up more dead branches, with a
squeal like laughter, then settled into her favorite hiding place.
Potabi had constructed a web of hemp ropes like vines hanging
from my gilded ceiling. My mischievous monkey had picked off

nearly all the gold sheeting, exposing the limestone blocks of my tower's ceiling.

"Be careful, Zahra." Hotep chewed her nails. "Don't corner her. She'll bite you."

Instantly defensive, I glared at my overly cautious maid. "Jendayi doesn't bite."

Hotep glared back at me and pointed to the scar on her forearm.

I rolled my eyes. "That was one time—when we were thirteen. Jendayi was a baby. Will you ever forgive her?"

"I've forgiven her, but I don't repeat mistakes, and I try to help others learn from them."

"Here, little Jendayi." Zahra's sing-song tone stole our attention. Balancing precariously on one of the dead branches, she slowly reached for the mirror. "Come, little girl. Give me—"

Jendayi squealed, jumped on Zahra's shoulder, and skittered down the branch—running straight into my arms. The little scamp pressed her lips against my face, then looked over her shoulder and puffed her cheeks at Zahra.

My maid hung from the branch like an overgrown ape, growled, and began her descent. "I daresay your new husband won't endure Jendayi's little pranks. Did your abi inform King Webenre that your 'child' was part of the dowry traveling with us to Abydos?"

A flutter stirred in my belly every time I thought of my upcoming wedding to a man I'd never even seen. "I'm sure Potabi told him whatever was needed to seal our union as divine Abi and Ommi of Egypt."

When Zahra's feet landed on solid ground, she straightened her sheer white robe and glared at me. "Have you considered how Jendayi will react to a child from your womb?"

"What a strange question." Yet inwardly I winced, adding this to my forbidden thoughts. "Jendayi will love my children as she loves me—as I love her."

Hotep left her perch by the east window, where she'd been watching On's activity below, and held out one hand to Jendayi. The monkey gave her the mirror and then curled her arms around my neck. "You see?" Hotep said. "Jendayi loves no one as she loves you, and she grows jealous when anyone steals your attention. She could harm an infant if—"

"Quiet!" I heard the scuffing of sandals on the stairs. "Potabi's coming." It could only be him since no one else climbed our steps. He usually conquered the 375 steps on the first day of each week to teach us a new chant. Any other day, he used the tray attached to ropes and pulleys to send up messages or meals. I lowered my voice. "And don't ask Potabi anything about marriage and children. I'm nervous enough."

My maids exchanged an uneasy glance. They were anxious about moving to the Abydos palace, too. Zahra, Hotep, and I had never been in the same room with a man other than Potabi since we were four years old. How could I let a man—even a king—touch me? *Mother Isis, give me courage.* For fifteen years Potabi had kept us in secluded safety on the upper level of Ra's temple tower, separated from the world below. We were the chantresses of On, serving the great sun god, Ra. We sang from the east window at dawn, midday, and dusk, filling the city with chants of warning, blessing, and grief to glorify our god. Our education came from Potabi, who taught us history, geography, sums, and the hieroglyphs. Above all, he'd emphasized we must be chaste in body, mind, and ka, but he left my wedding night a complete mystery.

Trying to calm myself, I stroked Jendayi's soft fur and said to my maids, "Isis will give us wisdom for the wedding and the marriage after."

"I'm happy to hear you say that, Daughter," Potabi said from the top step, leaning heavily on the railing.

Jendayi gripped my neck a little tighter, always nervous when he came to visit.

"Are you ill, Potabi?" I hurried over and wrapped my arm around his ample waist, guiding him toward our gathering area.

"Leave us." He waved my maids away.

Dread raised the hairs on my arms. "Is the news so dreadful that my sisters can't hear—"

"I will speak with my daughter alone." He glared at me, crankier than normal in summer's heat.

I bowed in obeisance and then transferred Jendayi to Hotep. She placed my little one in the rope vining corner. Zahra mouthed the words *We'll be listening* and retreated soundlessly across the purple tiles to their adjoining chamber.

Potabi arranged himself on a cushion. I sat across from him and offered the cloth I kept tucked in my belt for him. He wiped the steady stream of sweat seeping from beneath his priestly skullcap. His face and neck were crimson.

"Tell me what's troubled you, Abi."

He looked at me, startled. I called him "Abi" only when we were alone or at times like these, when I sensed he was upset.

His kohl-darkened brows drew together, forming a canal for the sweat to race down his nose. "The gods have taken King Webenre from you, Asenath." He removed his skullcap, smearing sweat and kohl over his head and face.

"Have I done something to offend the gods?"

"Of course not." He waved off the question. "A stronger king took his throne, my girl. An Egyptian more worthy of the throne— and of you."

Years of practiced calm helped me maintain a placid façade. "I'm disappointed that my divine birth as Isis Incarnate may be delayed, but I always defer to the gods' wisdom—and to yours, Potabi." I bowed my head, relief overshadowing every other emotion. How could I feel grief for King Webenre, a man I'd never met? "Who is the worthy Egyptian that the gods have chosen for me instead?" I met his eyes, careful to reflect calm. Potabi had taught me that each emotion triggered a reaction in a person's eyes, brows, lips, hands, and shoulders. To control and sculpt those reactions meant to reflect the elegance and grace of my mother goddess.

"King Apophis." He watched me as he spoke the name. Measuring me. Daring me to react.

"How could . . . I can't . . ." I exhaled to gain composure. "Apophis is co-regent with the half-breed son of the dead Hyksos, Khyan." My voice wobbled, and I fought for control. "Why would the gods couple Isis Incarnate with the co-regent who served as general of the Hyksos king? How could you even suggest such a thing when my single purpose for life and breath is to reunite the Two Lands under a pure-blooded Egyptian king and purge our nation of the Hyksos pestilence?" My voice rose despite my efforts to remain calm.

Jendayi squawked. She bared her teeth at Potabi and bounced on the branch—a warning to the perceived threat.

"You will calm yourself, or I'll leave." Potabi wiped more sweat from his face while maintaining his infuriating reserve.

I snapped my fingers and called Jendayi from her perch. She skittered over the vines, down the dead branches, and over the purple tiles to leap onto my shoulder, then peeked at Potabi from behind my long dark hair.

In those few moments of silence, Isis gave me wisdom. "I'm trained as Isis's high priestess. Take me to King Webenre and let me use the powers of Egypt's Great Ommi and healer to raise him from the dead."

"No."

"But don't you see? Webenre's death could be a test from the gods. If the high priestess of Isis raises him from the dead, no one could deny we are the *true* king and queen of Egypt, destined to unite the Two Lands and rule from Abydos."

He humiliated me with a condescending smile. "Don't be a fool. You're not Isis yet, and your failure would ruin any other marriage prospect."

"Where is your faith?" Indignation stoked my anger. "How do we know what power flows through us if we never trust the gods to work beyond our control?"

"You're mine to control!"

Jendayi squawked, preparing to lunge, but Potabi's backhand sailed past my cheek and sent her flying across the purple tiles.

"No!" I shrieked, darting after her. Thankfully, she landed in a pile of cushions, but she was terribly shaken. I cradled her, shocked at the man who had once been so kind.

"Keep that animal away from me, or I'll have it stuffed by morning."

Shaking like Jendayi, I met Potabi's angry stare. "You should be relieved Jendayi protects me. You can know I'll be safe no matter who I marry."

The harsh lines on his features softened. "You won't need a protector when you marry Apophis, and I would never let anyone harm you, my girl. Surely you know that by now."

I wanted to believe it, but when he'd started seeking the gods' choice for my husband without my input, he treated me more like the high priestess I was becoming instead of the daughter I'd always been. "You've always said Ommi's death meant something, that fulfilling her last wish for me could redeem it." I inhaled a sustaining breath and grasped at reason. "How can you ask me to marry a soldier who fought for the Hyksos, who destroyed our Songbird of Memphis? Apophis was among the troops who divided Egypt . . ." Tears strangled me, and shame bowed my head. I buried my face in Jendayi's fur. Potabi would think me nothing but a silly girl. Perhaps I didn't deserve the calling of incarnate goddess.

"Come, my girl. Sit with me while I explain." Reluctantly, I accepted the outstretched hand that called me to trust him—the same way he'd coaxed me from beneath the altar that awful night in Memphis when we lost the one we held most dear.

I slipped my hand into his, feeling again the security of his protection. Jendayi hid beneath my hair at the back of my neck while I sat across from him again. Squaring my shoulders, I tried to assume the persona of the goddess while he explained.

"Though Apophis was Pharaoh Khyan's general, both he and Queen Tani have a unique connection to the Memphite kings."

"Unique connection?" I choked on his word choice. "Their abi was the Egyptian vizier who betrayed the pharaoh in Memphis and ushered in the first Hyksos king."

Potabi's momentary tenderness fled. "Yes, and for nearly two years Apophis has raided villages from Avaris to Abydos killing zealots like us who seek to purge the Hyksos from Egypt."

"Why would you give Isis Incarnate to a man who kills the very rebels you send silver to support?"

"Because Apophis, misguided though he may be, is ultimately fighting for what we seek—unity for the Two Lands." He raised a single brow, letting his words tumble in my mind. "Apophis made sure I was appointed to Yanassi's royal council because Ra is his patron god and I'm the high priest of Ra's largest temple. Before he began his quest to unify Lower Egypt, he entrusted his sister and his nephew to my god's care. Queen Tani trusts me implicitly, and Pharaoh Yanassi believes I secure Ra's favor for both him and his uncle Apophis. But one royal alone possesses unwavering devotion to Ra and the willingness to fight for a united Egypt." Potabi paused. "When the young pharaoh dies unexpectedly—"

"He's a little boy. Why must he die?"

"He's a Hyksos half-breed."

I agreed with the words. It was his tone that chilled my blood.

"When Yanassi has been removed, King Apophis will rise to Lower Egypt's throne as a pure-blooded Egyptian. He's powerful. He's ruthless. And he trusts his sister, Queen Tani, who will treat you as the daughter she's always longed for." He rolled to his knees, struggling to stand. "Besides, it was Apophis who killed King Webenre. He'll understand his obligation to take you as his bride."

I tried to swallow my fear as I steadied Potabi on his feet. "Apophis sounds more like a soldier than a king." Haunting memories came unbidden. Another soldier. Ommi's last gasp. Her final words. I swiped tears from my cheeks, offended by the weakness they proved.

"I vowed you would marry a king, and you shall." His harsh features softened again. "When you marry Apophis, you'll fulfill your destiny as the Great Ommi and healer of Egypt. You must trust me. King Apophis is who the gods and I have chosen for you."

He'd said the same thing about King Webenre. "If I'm the high priestess of Isis, why haven't the gods shown *me* who they've chosen?"

His eyes grew dead with an emotion worse than anger. "You disappoint me, Priestess."

Like a millstone around my neck, his words bowed my head in shame. "Forgive me, Highness. I will obey your loving command and the gods' good wisdom."

He tipped up my chin. "I forgive you and bless your obedience, Daughter. I sail to Avaris next month to celebrate the Nile's rebirth. Hopefully, Apophis will return to the capital to celebrate young Yanassi's eighth akhet festival. If Apophis is a true Egyptian, worthy to marry a goddess, you'll be his queen before your twentieth Inundation."

TWO

Pharaoh had a dream. . . .
So he sent for all the magicians and wise men
of Egypt. Pharaoh told them his dreams, but no
one could interpret them for him.
Then the chief cupbearer said to Pharaoh,
". . . Pharaoh was once angry with his servants,
and he imprisoned me and the chief baker in the
house of the captain of the guard. Each of us had
a dream the same night, and . . . a young Hebrew
was there with us, a servant of the captain of the
guard. . . . And he interpreted them for us. . . ."
So Pharaoh sent for Joseph, and he was
quickly brought from the dungeon.
GENESIS 41:1, 8–12, 14

AVARIS, LOWER EGYPT
ONE MONTH LATER
Joseph

Joseph climbed the prison steps toward the villa's door, praise con-
quering fear. For the first time in five years, he'd be guided by daylight, not a torch's harsh glow. He'd walk on tiled floors rather than
the prison's packed dirt. He'd inhale the fresh scent of lotus blos-

soms instead of the stench of human despair. And he'd enter a throne room governed by Pharaoh Khyan's son rather than the giant who died so suddenly two years ago, on this very date.

Elohim, what is Your plan for me? Am I to be freed today? Or will I interpret Pharaoh Yanassi's dreams simply to be returned to prison? The thought of resuming his role as assistant warden knotted his stomach. *Please, Elohim. Ahira and I have waited so long to be married.*

She'd written him faithfully for two years, but her scrolls had suddenly stopped two months ago. "Hodari," Joseph said to his Medjay escort, "have you heard from Master Potiphar?"

The broad-shouldered captain paused at the top of the stairs, one eyebrow slightly higher than the other. "Perhaps you're more interested in the cooks of King Apophis's camp."

Joseph grinned and joined the man on the landing. When Joseph had served as Potiphar's villa chamberlain, Hodari had been one of his favorite guards. "Is Apophis still camped at Abydos?"

The Medjay's humor faded, stirring Joseph's concern.

"Tell me, Hodari. Is Ahira safe? Are Pushpa and Master Potiphar well?"

He led Joseph through the door and into Potiphar's former villa—Hodari's home now. "I can say that they are well, and it may be months before you receive more correspondence from Ahira." Hodari was captain of Pharaoh Yanassi's bodyguard and undoubtedly knew every detail of Lower Egypt's military plans.

"What would keep Ahira from sending a message? Is she still at Abydos?"

"If I tell you," Hodari said, "will I gain favor from your god as Potiphar did when you managed his villa?" Before Joseph could explain that Elohim wasn't like the pagan gods, manipulated by human whim or bribery, Hodari leaned close. "If you betray my confidence, Joseph, I will kill you." He waited for a nod to signal understanding.

Joseph gulped and agreed.

"After Pharaoh Khyan's death," Hodari began, "the southern

nomes raised fierce resistance against the young pharaoh—as King Apophis anticipated. It's taken two years for his troops to gain control and finally conquer the greatest stronghold of rebels in Abydos. He killed Webenre, the pure-blooded Egyptian zealot, and has now marched south to offer peace to Pharaoh Sobekhotep in Thebes."

"King Apophis offered peace with an army?" Even a Hebrew slave with no military experience noted the irony.

"Peace is more attractive when your army stands behind you in bloody armor." Hodari's logic was surprisingly sound. "Now come. We must prepare you to interpret Pharaoh Yanassi's nightmares. The boy king has suffered much torture from them."

Joseph followed the Medjay into the villa's main hall and stepped into a colorless memory of life before his imprisonment. A few torches burned, revealing signs of neglect—once-vibrant wall reliefs faded, floor tiles chipped, and ceiling paint peeling—that would never have been tolerated by Potiphar's Minoan wife.

"Come, Joseph. My steward will prepare you." Hodari passed two chamber guards and entered his chamber.

An Egyptian servant bowed to his master and then scowled at Joseph, examining his prison robe. "What am I to do with him?"

"Bathe, shave, lotion, and paint him like a nobleman. He's to appear before Pharaoh."

The Egyptian sneered at Joseph the same way Potiphar's old steward had done years ago. Evidently, some things in Egypt hadn't changed. Egyptians still hated Hebrews, and—from the sound of Hodari's report—those considered rebels still labeled Khyan and his descendants *Hyksos,* a derogatory term for foreign usurpers of Egypt's throne.

Joseph submitted to the slave's ministrations while probing Hodari on other changes in the world above the prison. "Who's your chamberlain, Captain?"

"My steward manages the villa." He motioned to the man applying Joseph's lotion. "And your shepherd friend, Maahir, manages the few fields and livestock I own."

The steward pointed toward the cosmetics couch where Joseph had prepared Master Potiphar each morning. Obeying the silent command, Joseph lay back, closed his eyes, and remembered the daily reports he'd recited as Potiphar's Overseer of Livestock. His master had soon promoted him to steward and, eventually, to chamberlain of the whole estate. By that time, Elohim had multiplied the master's wealth beyond any estate in Lower Egypt—second only to Potiphar's best friend, Pharaoh Khyan.

"Perhaps if you interpret the king's dreams, he'll allow you to oversee my estate." Hodari invaded his thoughts. "Since Pushpa left, I don't even have a cook. The palace provides meals for me." He released a regretful sigh. "Our lives would have been very different had Mistress Zully been happy in Egypt."

The familiar resentment rose like bile in Joseph's throat, but he swallowed hard and prayed again for Elohim's grace to forgive. He had forgiven Potiphar's wife—a million times—and would continue to do so every time feelings of injustice threatened his peace. Though he shared Hodari's loss of an unrealized future, he let silence answer, encouraging the painful memories to fall away.

"You may sit up," the steward said when he'd finished. "I've turned a pig's ear into a fine-looking belt."

Hodari wasted no time with pleasantries. He rushed Joseph from the chamber, down the hall, across the private dining room, and into the walkway connecting the captain's home with the palace. It all felt so familiar, yet strange due to the subtle changes that came with time.

Joseph didn't recognize the two Medjays at the throne room entrance, but their expressionless features were familiar. The warriors nodded at their captain, then opened the doors and stepped aside. Joseph and his escort entered an eerily calm throne room.

Joseph leaned over to whisper, "Shouldn't they be celebrating akhet?"

"Pharaoh Yanassi postponed all festivities until he gains clarity on his nightmares."

They walked in silence to the back of the room, where they

would then proceed down the center aisle. Upon reaching the edge of the crimson carpet, Joseph surveyed the small golden throne on the dais and found the biggest change of all.

No longer was there a giant king—the height of two men, one stacked on the other's shoulders—seated on the throne. Instead, an eight-year-old child stared back at Joseph, looking like any other frightened boy. A braided sidelock hung on the right side of the pharaoh's shaved head. The kohl-drawn Eye of Horus was smeared from tears. His ima, Queen Tani, watched Joseph with the eyes of a hawk and the regal bearing of an eagle. She'd never been one of the silly noblewomen who ogled him like a lioness hunting prey.

Pushpa loved the queen and had proudly told Ahira about her political acumen after Khyan's tragic death. Queen Tani had protected her son by promptly returning Ziwat—Khyan's second wife—to Cush, ensuring Pharaoh Yanassi was safe from any power grabs within the palace. Today, however, the queen looked more like a worried ommi than a political advisor. She sat stiffly beside her son on a matching gold throne, deep worry lines marring her lovely features.

The Medjay vizier, Hami, stood between the queen mother and king. He wore the emotionless mask of his countrymen, though he'd been Joseph's closest friend while they both served in Potiphar's household. Hami had been the villa's chief Medjay, but when he uncovered a treasonous plot to kill Khyan, the king promoted him to the second highest rank in the nation. Now Joseph's friend wore the long white schenti as the boy king's chief counselor instead of the loincloth and weapons of the nation's fiercest warriors.

"Quickly, Joseph." Queen Tani's tone was sharp, words clipped. "My son was awake most of the night and has endured inept wise men all morning."

Hodari lengthened his strides, and Joseph kept pace. The pharaoh's royal counselors glared as he approached. Joseph recognized three who had served Pharaoh Khyan as physician, magician, and priest. Their palpable hate ushered Joseph to the front edge of the carpet, where he halted and bowed before Pharaoh Yanassi. Hodari ascended the dais steps and took his protective position at the boy's right shoulder.

"I fear no one can interpret my dreams." Pharaoh Yanassi's desperate voice brought Joseph upright. The boy had moved to the edge of the dais, his chin quivering. "But the cupbearer said you can interpret any dream."

Joseph opened his mouth, but no words came. *Elohim, will You give me the interpretation?* "*I* cannot interpret your dream, my king."

Elohim's assurance came like a breeze. *I will interpret.*

The boy shot a panicked look at his ommi.

"But my God will give the interpretation," Joseph clarified.

Relief washed over the queen's features and her son's. "In my dream," the boy began without preamble, "I was standing on the bank of the Nile. Seven cows, fat and sleek, came up out of the river, and they grazed among the reeds. After them, seven other cows came up—scrawny and ugly. I've never seen such ugly cows in Egypt. The lean, ugly cows devoured the seven fat cows, but even after they ate them, they were as skinny and ugly as before. Then I woke."

Joseph prayed silently for wisdom as Pharaoh continued, "In my second dream there were seven heads of grain, full and good, that grew on a single stalk. Seven more heads sprouted quickly, but they were withered and thin, scorched by the hot east wind. The thin heads of grain swallowed up the seven good heads. And then I woke."

Agitated, he went back to his throne and plopped down as if exhausted by the telling. "Ommi said you used to serve Captain Potiphar, and the favor of your god spilled over on your master. Will your god help me?" Desperation laced his tone.

Joseph felt both the peace and certainty of Elohim's interpretation. "Mighty Pharaoh, the God of my ancestors has already helped you by giving you these dreams, and He's the Revealer of Mysteries. He sent you the same dream in two forms to ensure your understanding and reveal what He's about to do." Joseph cast a pleading look at the queen, hoping she'd remember the integrity he showed while serving Potiphar and extend favor to Joseph when he revealed the hard truth about Egypt's future.

Returning his attention to Pharaoh, Joseph began, "The seven good cows and good heads of grain are seven years of abundant harvests. The seven scrawny cows and scorched ears of grain are seven years of famine unlike any the world has seen before. Elohim has shown you what He is about to do, my king. Seven years of great abundance are about to bless Egypt, but they will be swallowed up and forgotten when seven years of famine ravage the land and its people. The dream was given twice because it's firmly decided and will happen soon." Joseph fell silent, respectfully conceding to those in authority.

Both Vizier Hami and Captain Hodari's distant expressions were unreadable. The huddle of Pharaoh's counselors stood unusually still. No one met Joseph's eyes or even looked his direction. No one offered hope or provisions in the face of certain disaster.

Elohim, I know Your solution as surely as I knew the interpretation—but dare a slave offer advice to Pharaoh?

The tender voice came as before: *Speak, Joseph.*

With a deep breath fueling his courage, Joseph exhaled wisdom that could only have come from God alone. "Perhaps Pharaoh could search out a discerning and wise man to oversee the whole land—both Lower and Upper Egypt. This overseer would work in harmony with all three pharaohs—the co-regents of Avaris and the Theban king—to appoint agricultural officials in each nome to collect a fifth of their seven abundant harvests under the authority of their respective pharaohs."

"Ridiculous!" One of the officials scoffed. A short man, dressed in a white robe and skullcap, stepped forward. "How can a slave know the inner workings of Egypt's complex governmental systems well enough to propose a solution?"

Queen Tani arched a single brow. "This *slave* interpreted Pharaoh's dreams—something neither you nor Egypt's magicians could do—and Potiphar's estate prospered under this man's wise management. We will hear his proposal without further interruption."

The priest bowed. "Of course, my queen, forgive me." He straightened and returned to his roost.

"Proceed, Joseph."

Strangely, the interchange bolstered Joseph's courage, rather than weakened it. "Thank you, my queen. As I mentioned, each nome would store their own harvest in local granaries and the overseer appointed by Pharaoh Yanassi would monitor all grain distribution during the seven famine years. Thus, Egypt's central power would be strengthened as well as cooperation between the Two Lands. Pharaoh Yanassi will have brought peace to the Two Lands in a time that would have otherwise been in great turmoil."

A slight smile curved the queen's lips. "What say you to Joseph's counsel, Pharaoh Yanassi?"

The boy shot off his throne. "The wisdom of the gods dwells in this man!"

Queen Tani stood beside her son. "I, too, see a divine spark in him, Great Pharaoh. I wish Apophis were here to witness how powerfully the gods have anointed your rule by speaking through your dreams. He'd be very proud of you—as am I." She affectionately drew his sidelock through her hand, then looked at Joseph with a smile both kind and concerning. "Vizier Hami speaks highly of you, Joseph. Everything I know about your service to Captain Potiphar confirms your imprisonment was unjust. You were—and are—a man who lives for your god. On behalf of Pharaoh's household and our friend Potiphar, let me publicly exonerate you of all charges made against you."

Joseph opened his mouth to thank her but was consumed with praise. *Elohim, You've done this!* He dropped to one knee, gathering his thoughts. "Thank you, my queen. Your favor is an answer to many prayers."

"What you've done today has given us hope. Stand and face the men of Pharaoh's royal council so they may thank you properly."

Joseph obeyed, feeling every counselor's eye like a fiery brand as the queen introduced them one by one. Their feigned smiles looked more like the bared teeth of growling jackals. The last introduction was Potiphera, the priest who had objected to a slave's opinions. He was high priest of Ra—King Apophis's patron god—at the temple of On.

"What do you think of a slave's advice now, my friend?" The queen watched Potiphera with the intensity of a hawk flying over a freshly harvested field. Master Potiphar always said she was the most discerning woman in Egypt. Would she notice Potiphera's discomfit? His feigned smile? His refusal to meet Joseph's eyes?

"I had no idea this man was more than a common slave," Potiphera conceded. "As high priest of the great sun god, Ra, and well connected with the families of Upper Egypt's pharaohs, I could be a vital part of Egypt's survival when we seek Ra's favor during the famine."

The priest's crafty words stirred a fierce protectiveness inside Joseph. Potiphera had effectively avoided the queen's question and blatantly volunteered to become Pharaoh's chosen overseer. *Elohim, protect the young pharaoh against all who would manipulate and deceive him.*

The boy king whispered something to Hodari, who exited through a door hidden behind curtains on the dais, and then addressed his counselors. "Is there any among you with a better solution than Joseph's to manage the fourteen years prophesied about our nation?"

The ten men whispered amid their huddle before answering. Ra's high priest glanced at Joseph with a wry grin and acted as spokesman. "Ra gives me wisdom to speak over every Egyptian who makes a pilgrimage to the city of On, my king. Given time, Egypt's gods will give your council a better plan than the hasty rantings of this Hebrew slave."

"Given time?" Pharaoh Yanassi scowled at the priest. "The council had all night to interpret my dreams and failed. Who better than Joseph to implement the wise plan he suggested immediately after the interpretation his god provided?" The decision struck every counselor like a slap.

"He's a slave!" one man shouted.

"He's Hebrew!" said another.

Pharaoh's hand shot into the air, silencing his frantic council members.

But Joseph, too, had objections. "Please, Mighty Pharaoh, why not make Vizier Hami the overseer to manage Egypt's granaries and taxation? He's more than capable and already—"

In a rare break from Medjay stoicism, Hami subtly signaled a *no* at the same time Pharaoh said, "You are my new vizier, Joseph, and Hami will be captain of your bodyguard."

"What? No, my king."

Queen Tani's brows shot upward. "Never say no to your king, Joseph."

He turned to Hami, hoping for rescue, but the Medjay bowed to the boy. "Though you are young, my king, you already possess a heart of wisdom, and you're quickly becoming a great man. I'm honored to return to a warrior's duties and guard someone matching your integrity." He grinned unashamedly at the eight-year-old. "Your gods have given you a worthy man with whom to share the heavy burdens of Lower Egypt's throne."

Queen Tani's eyes glistened, but her son shoved the big Medjay playfully. "You think I'm smart solely because I often beat you at senet." He turned a wry grin toward Joseph. "The truth is, he's terrible at the game."

Joseph laughed despite the significance of the moment. This pharaoh was likable. *And he's made me vizier of Egypt.* As the weight settled on his shoulders, Elohim's peace came with it. "I'm honored to serve you, Pharaoh Yanassi—and my God—in whatever way best serves Egypt." Joseph's freedom and instant rise to power had been too miraculous to believe his own knowledge or skill had anything to do with it. *Elohim, remind me of that if I try to wrest control from Your hands.*

Pharaoh Yanassi descended the dais, while removing his signet ring. "You must have an Egyptian name to gain respect from officials in Egypt's Two Lands, Lord Vizier." He unwound a measure of hemp string from his ring, revealing its size twice that of any other.

"My abi gave me this scarab ring days before he died. He said I'd grow into it and Egypt's throne someday. You must help me."

He slipped the ring onto Joseph's first finger, eyes misty. "You will be called, *Zaphenath-Paneah—the god speaks, and you live.* Wear this ring as my representative and return it to me when my dreams have been fulfilled. You will travel through Egypt in my chariot while heralds proclaim, 'Make way! Make way!' For only in regard to the throne will I have more power than you, Paneah. No one will lift a hand or foot except by your command—so that we may live and not die in the coming years of feast and famine."

Speechless, Joseph met the young pharaoh's eyes. He could have been any innocent boy asking for help. Joseph looked down at the ring, dangling on his finger. He'd need more than some hemp string to grow into Pharaoh Khyan's ring and serve Egypt in the coming years.

Before Joseph could voice his gratitude, Captain Hodari reentered through the hidden door, carrying a purple robe and gold chains. Joseph silenced a groan but started shaking his head. "Please, my king, I'd rather dress simply in—"

"Nonsense!" Queen Tani silenced his objections. "You must look like the reigning vizier of Egypt's Two Lands."

The king took the items from Captain Hodari and placed the gold chains around Joseph's neck. When Hodari slipped the purple robe around his shoulders, the memory of Joseph's first ornate robe flashed in his mind. Abba Jacob had given him the special offering to show his love and his favor. Joseph's brothers had stripped off the robe before they sold him to the Midianites. What had happened to his treasured robe? Had it been sold—as he'd been—or destroyed like Joseph's hope of ever seeing his beloved abba again?

"Come, Potiphera." Queen Tani's bright tone jolted Joseph. "Give Ra's blessing to Egypt's new vizier."

The portly man strode to Joseph's side, a practiced smile in place. "My, my. No one would even guess you're Hebrew." The cavernous room fell awkwardly silent. He reached into the pouch at his belt and sprinkled ashes on Joseph's head. "May all-powerful Ra live and all poison die through the secret name known exclusively to Aset, his divine mistress, given the name above all gods and goddesses—Isis, the healer. May Ra and his consort Isis use you, Zaphenath-Paneah, to restore Egypt's unity."

The priest's eyes locked with Joseph's. The air crackled with tension. *Elohim, protect me.*

"Ra gave me a thought." Pharaoh turned to Queen Tani. "Didn't Abi say you were his best advisor? Paneah needs a wife!"

"I have someone in mind," Joseph said.

Hami started down the dais steps, head moving with an almost imperceptible *no.*

"Could it be the lovely Hebrew maid who accompanied Pushpa to cook for Apophis's men?" Queen Tani's tone held a measure of sadness—foreboding even.

"Yes, my queen—Ahira. We've known each other since we were children. She was my sister's friend and the daughter of Abba's chief shepherd." He recognized hesitation in her furrowed brow and rushed to add, "She wasn't always a slave, my queen. She was betrayed by one of my brothers and sold to the Midianites—as happened to me."

"Filthy Hebrews," Potiphera mumbled.

"That's enough." The queen shot him a harsh glare and returned her attention to Joseph. "We can change your name, Paneah, but we can't change your heritage. Though my son is as committed as his abi to unity among all people in Egypt, there are many in the Two Lands who would not eat at the same table with a Hebrew. As Egypt's vizier, you must marry an Egyptian woman. Pure-blooded and of highly respected birth."

"But Ahira—"

"You could make Ahira a concubine or second wife, if your first wife is aware and amenable."

"I would never . . ." Joseph couldn't even finish the sentence. Every eye in the throne room bored into him.

Despair and confusion bowed his head. *Elohim, Ahira and I have waited for my freedom to be married. Please—*

"Potiphera, you called on Isis and Ra to assist Paneah with his new role," Pharaoh said. "Your daughter, Asenath, was named after Aset and serves as Isis's high priestess. Who better to become Paneah's wife?"

Joseph snapped to attention.

"Yes!" Queen Tani clapped her hands.

"No!" the priest said. He bowed at the queen's quick disapproval. "I mean, I've already offered sacrifices to the gods to gain their approval for Asenath's marriage to King Apophis. We dare not renege on that plan before inquiring of Ra for his final decision."

"I am a god," said the young pharaoh, "and I say your daughter is better suited for Paneah than for my uncle—who is more than twice her age and married to his sword."

Potiphera straightened and met Joseph's eyes for the first time. Silently pleading, Joseph tried to reassure the man he didn't want the marriage either. *Elohim, please.* Marrying Ahira had been the one hope that kept him alive in the tiny, dark prison cell before Ubaid made him assistant warden.

"My daughter will make a fine wife for you," Potiphera said flatly.

No! Panic tore through Joseph. He could never marry the daughter of a pagan priest. "But my queen, I love Ahira."

"You can learn to love anyone, Paneah." Her sad smile brought little comfort. "Do this for Egypt. Do it for your king."

Joseph closed his eyes, hoping for Elohim's wisdom. A way out. A wise plan—like He'd given for the famine. Absolute silence answered.

"You see?" Startled by Potiphera's voice, Joseph opened his eyes and saw him speaking to Pharaoh. "This Hebrew understands nothing—neither the gravity of his disobedience to the god on the throne nor the precious gift of my virgin daughter. He'll paw at her on their wedding night and frighten her beyond her wits."

Queen Tani's smile became a thin, pale line, her eyes hard as obsidian beads. "Lord Paneah, my son has set before you life or death. Splendor or an afterlife in the jaws of the heart eater, Ammut. Take Asenath as your bride, a devout woman who has been saved for a king, or die for disobeying the wishes of your pharaoh."

"Ommi." Pharaoh Yanassi's quiet plea went ignored. He paused, then faced Joseph. "Accept Asenath, Paneah. I don't wish to kill you, but I will order it if you refuse." He raised his chin, blinking away tears to maintain the dignity of a god.

Joseph glimpsed desperation on Hami's features. No doubt, his friend would be the one ordered to carry out his execution. Death. Joseph had faced it before. He'd begged for it in the empty cistern before his brothers sold him. He'd thought Master Potiphar would certainly kill him when Mistress Zully accused him of rape. Now the choice was truly in Joseph's hands. Would he prefer death to a lifetime bound in marriage to a pagan woman he didn't love?

Do this for Egypt, the queen had said. No. He wouldn't do it for a nation. He stared into the eyes of an eight-year-old boy, pleading silently for his help. *Do it for your pharaoh,* his ommi had asked. Elohim had given this boy dreams and Joseph their interpretations. Moments ago, Joseph had recognized the miracles of his God and His undeniable control over the coming events. How could he now deny this situation that was equally beyond Joseph's control and in Elohim's hands?

Bowing to one knee, he submitted to Elohim while vowing to Pharaoh, "I'll obey you, my king, and accept the gift of Asenath, daughter of Potiphera, priest of On's temple of Ra. I will serve as vizier of Egypt's Two Lands and embrace her people as my own."

The young pharaoh patted his shoulder and leaned close to whisper. "I'm so relieved, and I know you'll like Asenath. I've heard rumors that she's the most beautiful woman in Egypt. Now rise."

The queen nodded at Joseph, pleased but sober. "We'll divide Hami's vizier duties between Avaris's palace administrator and Lower Egypt's nome governors since your position will focus on preparing all of Egypt for the next fourteen years. You'll need some training before you tour both Lower and Upper Egypt, and you must take an escort who knows 'the inner workings of Egypt's complex governmental systems.'" She turned her attention to Potiphera, having used the exact words of his objection to Joseph. "You will accompany Paneah on his tour of the Two Lands, Potiphera."

"I'm honored, my queen, but how could I leave my temple unattended so long when—"

"Pharaoh can appoint another high priest if no lector priest at On is capable of overseeing the temple in your absence." Her veiled threat brought a compliant smile to his face.

"My lector is quite capable, my queen."

She lingered in a knowing smile. "You'll spend the next month with Paneah here, in Avaris, introducing him as our new vizier to every important nobleman. If the Nile brings the abundance my son's dreams foretold, you should be able to leave for On within the month. Take Joseph with you. Introduce him to your daughter."

Pharaoh Yanassi interrupted. "On's summer harvest begins next month. You can plan for fruit storage before sowing season begins for the first abundance."

"Potiphera will introduce the vizier to all the nobility in his region as well." Queen Tani still held the priest's gaze, communicating something deeper. "Do you know why I'm sending you with our new vizier, Potiphera?"

"I hope it's because you know I'm eager to serve Egypt." He chuckled nervously.

"It's for the same reason I made Potiphar the captain of my brother's royal guard. Potiphar didn't trust Apophis—as you mistrust Lord Paneah. I believe as you spend more time with him, you'll find him to be a man of wisdom and integrity—as Potiphar has found my brother to be."

Potiphera forced a smile. "I bow to your wisdom, my queen."

"Indeed," she said flatly, then returned her attention to Joseph. "Tour On and its surrounding nomes. Prepare for the abundance, meet with the governors, and return to Avaris with your bride for a royal wedding before you tour the Two Lands." She placed her hand on his forearm, features softening. "I was married to Khyan for almost a year before I could say 'I love you' and mean it. Perhaps after you meet Asenath, you'll be so smitten you'll forget about your Hebrew maid."

THREE

So when the Midianite merchants came by, his brothers pulled Joseph up out of the cistern and sold him for twenty shekels of silver to the Ishmaelites, who took him to Egypt.

GENESIS 37:28

Potabi left for Avaris four weeks ago to arrange a marriage I didn't want to a king I didn't respect. Each year, he traveled to the capital to celebrate Inundation, but he'd never stayed so long. Had negotiations with Apophis gone badly?

The squeak of the pulley system caught my attention, and Zahra rushed toward the rising tray. Someone below was delivering our midday meal. The sick gnawing in my belly continued. Deepened. *Mother Goddess, what becomes of Zahra, Hotep, and me if Potabi doesn't return?* We were the chantresses of On, but who would protect us from a temple complex full of priests and temple guards? Who would ensure my destiny was fulfilled?

I sat on the ledge of my west window, watching multitudes

churning in the streets beyond temple walls. Surely, he'd return today, the first day of On's famed fruit harvest. People had slept in the streets, waiting for the lector priest and this month's phyle of prophets to begin the harvest festival at dawn. They marched through the city while the lector proclaimed Ra's blessing from the sacred book. Potabi had never missed the summer harvest processional or opening celebration.

"Sitting in that window won't make him appear." Zahra shoved a plate of dried figs and cheese into my hand. "You must eat something."

"I can't."

Jendayi leaned down from my shoulder and stole a dried fig, then blew bubbles against my cheek. A giggle escaped without my permission.

"At least Jendayi can still make you smile," Hotep said as she looked up from her weaving. "Zahra and I will call the physician if you don't eat your midday meal."

Zahra rolled her eyes. "I don't think we'll call a physician, but if Highness returns and finds you ill, he'll punish us for neglecting your care."

I sighed and shoved a fig into my mouth, lowering my voice to a whisper. "I need to know Potabi is safe, Zahra, but is it terrible that I also dread his return a little? I wish he would send word of King Apophis's decision." Glancing toward the temple quay, I hid my burning cheeks and changed the subject. "The crowds of pilgrims have grown larger as our voices have become more confident with the familiar songs."

Zahra knelt beside me. "I'm anxious to hear King Apophis's decision, too." She glanced over her shoulder to be sure Hotep was consumed with her weaving. "I've also enjoyed repeating the familiar chants. Perhaps you could talk to Highness when he returns about—"

"Priestess Asenath?" The lector priest's resonant voice boomed from the base of our stairs.

I jumped to my feet. "You're not to climb the stairs, Lector." My maids and I pulled our veils over our faces in case he dared break Potabi's rule.

"Of course, Priestess, I would never. A message has arrived. The courier said it was urgent and must be immediately delivered to you."

Fear clogged my throat like a handful of wool.

"Place it on the tray." Zahra removed the remainder of our midday meal and used the ropes to lower the tray.

We waited a few moments and heard, "I've placed the message on the tray. Would you like me to wait for your reply?"

"You may go, Lector," Hotep answered for me.

"As you wish," he said. "The guards will remain outside the door. Simply ring your bell to—"

"Thank you, Lector. We know the system."

We waited beside the circular stairway for the familiar squeaking of the outer door's leather hinges as they opened, then closed. Zahra lunged toward the ropes and started pulling. "Who would send you a message directly?"

"It must be from Potabi." I tugged Jendayi from my shoulder, needing the comfort of her in my arms. "But why would he wait four weeks to send it?"

Hotep chewed her nails. "If it doesn't bear the high priest's seal, we should wait until he returns to open it in his presence."

Zahra's final pull on the hemp ropes brought the tray even with the railing. My curiosity felt like a living thing, crawling up my arms and into my chest like ants on a discarded honey cake. "Well?" I said. "Is it Potabi's seal?"

Zahra gave me an impish grin. "If it's not his seal, can I read the message?"

"No!" I grabbed at the scroll, but Hotep snatched it from Zahra's hand.

"Wait!" Hotep held it behind her back and lowered her voice. "What if it's a trick? What if the lector or temple guards are waiting until we're engrossed in reading to rush up the stairs? Highness Potiphera isn't here to protect us."

"Stop it, Hotep. They've had weeks to rush up the stairs." I extended my hand, demanding the scroll. I'd never admit I fought the same fear of my first encounter with a man face-to-face. Other than Potabi, we'd seen men exclusively from our tower windows. "Give me the scroll. The lector said whoever sent it meant for me to read it immediately."

My cautious maid held my gaze. "Whatever it says, we'll face it together."

I realized then that her hesitation was more about protecting my ma'at—peace, justice, and truth—than fearing for my physical safety. My maids were more than servants. They were sisters of my heart, born the same night as I. My earliest memories were of playing with them in the streets of Memphis—until the night tragedy stole our naivety, our childhood.

She handed me the scroll, and I marched toward our cushions in the audience chamber.

I sat down, and Zahra clapped impatiently. "Do you recognize the seal? Who's it from? Can you tell?"

I studied the imprinted red wax and realized with a sudden sinking feeling—

"King Apophis!" Hotep gasped. Even Zahra quieted as both settled onto their cushions beside me.

"Don't read it!" Hotep reached for the scroll, but I pulled it away.

"Why not?"

"No man should send a message directly to a maiden."

I turned the scroll in my hands, considering her warning. I descended the tower twice a year, alone, to celebrate fall and summer harvests in Potabi's private villa. He cleared every priest and guard from the path, and we ate in his dining room without servants. The last time my sister-maids and I had been within a man's reach, we were four years old and hiding with Potabi beneath the altar of Memphis's temple, while Hyksos soldiers killed Ra's priests and my ommi, the Chantress of Ra. I wasn't interested in *any* man—especially a soldier-turned-king who pledged his allegiance to Hyksos.

My hands began to tremble, then my whole body. Hotep and

Zahra wrapped their arms around me, as they'd done our whole lives, and we began singing Ommi's favorite chant. Our unified voices always calmed me. This song beckoned the goddess closer and reminded me Ommi was well cared for, waiting for me in the life beyond.

Zahra's chanting changed to a hum, and together we fell silent. She straightened and pointed to the scroll. "Apophis is the rightful Egyptian king, Asenath. Born of nobility and honorable in his quest for Egypt's unity. He's the true Pharaoh, the incarnate Son of Ra, with more right to the throne than the young Hyksos, Yanassi." Her eyes widened. "And what if King Apophis wishes to convey something to the gods? Since Highness isn't here and Isis's high priestess would preside over Ra's temple in the high priest's absence, it would be your duty to read the message." The glint in her eyes seemed more sassy than sacred, but her argument was valid. I'd be considered a high priestess as soon as I married. Who knew when Potabi would return?

With the same determination I used to swallow noxious fish oil, I broke the seal and unrolled the papyrus, sating my curiosity with the words. Each word felt more forbidden, and dread slithered down my spine, while regret soured in my belly.

"Read it aloud!" Zahra bounced on her pillow.

I swallowed hard and started at the beginning . . .

Life, ma'at, and health to you, sacred Chantress of Ra and daughter of Potiphera, the greatest seer and high priest of On.

From the perfect god, Apophis Nebkhepeshre, I bless you with truth: Though I would have made you my wife, I chose instead to honor my family, the queen mother, and Pharaoh Yanassi, entrusting you to Ra's protection.

One day after Potiphera sent his proposal that requested you and I unite as husband and wife, I received a second message—this one from Pharaoh Yanassi and the queen mother—informing me that a new vizier had been appointed and you are betrothed as his wife. The vizier is a Hebrew shepherd from Canaan, sold as a slave by a family who despised him, imprisoned for raping his Egyptian master's wife, and wholly unworthy of your sacred purity.

I covered a sob, unable to read the rest. Hotep gathered me into her arms, while Zahra finished the final lines aloud:

Though I honor the queen mother and Pharaoh Yanassi's wisdom, I write to you directly, Daughter of Isis, to warn you about Zaphenath-Paneah, the man to whom you are betrothed. He broke his vow to marry a woman in my camp. He cannot be trusted. Deal with the jackal as you see fit.

I have provided this information as a powerful weapon for the high priestess of Isis. Use it to heal Egypt's wounds as the instrument of our mother goddess.

So says your king, your god, and Ra's sacred son.

Zahra let the papyrus fall to the purple tiles. "He used your ommi's dying words, 'Heal Egypt's wounds.'"

"He said you're betrothed to a Hebrew rapist," Hotep said, isolating the single most terrifying fact.

I saw all my emotions reflected on their faces. "Why would King Apophis tell me those horrible things?"

"He said he told you the *truth*." Zahra's eyes filled with tears. "We don't always get that from Highness."

"Zahra!" Hotep looked over her shoulder as if Potabi might have somehow heard. Then she leaned close and took my hand. "But Zahra is right. King Apophis respects the gods and his role as Ra's divine son. He's a true pharaoh."

Agreement emerged in a low groan. "I asked the gods to show me who to marry, and they have." He'd written ommi's words, the destiny of Isis Incarnate that had molded every waking moment in this tower for fifteen years. "How can I marry anyone but King Apophis?"

"We should have waited and let Highness read the scroll." Regret shrouded Hotep's countenance.

"No!" Zahra said. "Asenath needed to know. That was the king's point. Truth gives power."

"How do we know King Apophis truly sent this message?" Hotep asked.

Zahra rolled her eyes. "It had Apophis's seal. Who else could have sent it?"

"The message said the Hebrew broke his marriage vow to a woman in the king's camp. What if she somehow—"

"Stop it. Both of you." I buried my face in my hands, weary of their inane reasoning. "How could Potabi go to Avaris to arrange my marriage to King Apophis and four weeks later give me to a Hebrew vizier?" I truly didn't understand, yet something deep inside me said the scroll was authentic and its contents true.

A gentle hand rested on my back. "What can we do to help?" Hotep—always first to comfort.

I let my tears fall, leaning into their silent acceptance. With them, I could simply be Asenath—not a high priestess or goddess—and didn't need all the answers in this moment. Their voices blended without mine this time, melody and harmony swelling and softening. They sang praise and lament, reflecting my swirling tangle of emotions. Peace began to trickle in.

Suddenly, temple trumpets sounded, startling us all to our feet. We rushed to the west window, searching the temple quay.

"It's Potabi." My words came in a whisper, my greatest hope now my deepest fear.

"At least you'll soon know what happened in Avaris." Zahra slipped her hand into mine as we watched eight strong slaves carry Potabi's curtained palanquin on their shoulders. They marched toward the temple, cheering pilgrims lining both sides of the grand Avenue of Sphinxes.

"I must speak with him right away." But the thought of it tightened my belly into a knot.

"He's just arrived," Hotep said. "He'll be tired after the two-day trip from Avaris. Perhaps you should wait to tell—"

"Could *you* wait, Hotep?"

My friend released a sigh. "No, but if you're going to confess to reading the scroll, you must look your best." She looked at Zahra. "We'll dress her in the purple robe, all the jewelry, and exquisite cosmetics."

Zahra twirled me to face her. "You mustn't say anything about the king's message until Highness divulges his version of what happened in Avaris."

I nodded, too nervous to string together two coherent words. I submitted to my sister-maids' ministrations, trying to relax my body while my mind whirred like it was spinning wool. The sun nearly touched the western horizon by the time they'd finished applying scented lotions, henna stains, and cosmetics. I stood before the full-length, polished-bronze mirror and saw the goddess, not Asenath. "Potabi will be pleased, Sisters. Thank you."

"We must hurry, or we'll be late with the evening chant." Hotep scurried toward the chest Potabi brought with us from Memphis and chose one of the sacred scrolls. Zahra and I met her at the west window, and she placed the scroll in my hand. "I thought this one fitting for us to sing tonight."

It was the song Ommi sang when the Hyksos soldiers stole her breath.

Zahra gasped. "Why would you choose that, Hotep?"

I tried to contain the same horrified response.

Hotep's pride dissolved into instant defense. "Because we received the Great Chantress's ka when it left her body, her voice lives through us to bless others."

"Oh, Hotep . . ." I embraced my sisters in a hug too fierce for Zahra to protest. *Thank you, Mother Goddess, for two women who share my heart, my breath, my life.*

We began the sacred chant, lifting our voices with a profound confidence in all the gods had done for us. Surely, they wouldn't have brought us this far to deliver me into the hands of a Hyksos rapist.

FOUR

They served [Joseph] by himself . . . because
Egyptians could not eat with Hebrews, for
that is detestable to Egyptians.

GENESIS 43:32

Potiphera

"Welcome to my humble home, Lord Paneah." Potiphera escorted his unwelcome guest into the spacious audience chamber of his private villa.

The Hebrew meandered through the entry, hands clasped behind his back, eyes traveling up and around every grand detail of the high priest's inner sanctuary. "You have worked very hard, Potiphera, to make On's temple to Ra the largest in Egypt."

"It is also the destination where all truly devoted followers come and make at least one sacrifice a year."

The Hebrew halted three steps inside the room, his imposing Medjay like a shadow behind him. "Your priests seem very dedicated to you, a sign of strong leadership."

What does a slave know of leadership? Potiphera bowed, hiding his revulsion. "Wise words, Lord Vizier." Forcing his face into pleasantry, he straightened and swept his hand toward the waiting tables. "My wab priests have prepared a delightful meal, and if it suits you,

Paneah—may I call you Paneah?—Lord Hami may sit at your table with you."

The Hebrew's amiability dropped like a stone in the Nile. "Do your guest's bodyguards usually dine at the table with them?"

"Well, no, but . . ." I detected a slight grimace on the Medjay's face. "I simply thought since Lord Hami was vizier before you, he—"

"I am *Captain* Hami, Highness." The Medjay spoke, a rarity, then fixed his eyes on a distant nothing above Potiphera's head.

A sudden clap made Potiphera jump. The Hebrew rubbed his hands together and started toward his table, where a place setting had been laid for him and his captain. "The fresh fruit looks enticing—grapes, pomegranates, figs. Were they all harvested from On's temple gardens?"

Paneah's forced gaiety was worse than his own ire. "Yes. I'm told the wab priests harvested them this morning."

"Who are these wab priests you've mentioned?" The vizier reached for a grape and popped it into his mouth as he lowered himself to the embroidered cushion and stretched out his long legs. "They seem quite important."

Potiphera chuckled. "The antithesis, actually. They're the lowliest priests of all, responsible for cleaning, serving, and anything else the important servants of Ra wish to avoid."

"So, they're your temple slaves." Paneah's tone held challenge.

"Have you come to learn or to teach, Vizier?" Potiphera leaned forward, resting both elbows on his private table. "I have wisdom that I can share and see you prosper or withhold and watch you flounder. Which would you prefer?"

"I command you to obey your pharaoh." He leaned forward on his elbows, too. "That means you show me the respect I deserve and help me prepare Egypt for the tragedy that's already begun. The Nile's abundance is flooding villages. Destroying homes. We can't fight each other and save Egypt, Potiphera. We must work together, you and me, or I'll request another escort after I marry your daughter, and you'll remain in On while Asenath and I get acquainted."

"No, my lord. That won't be necessary." He chuckled and reached for his goblet of dark beer. "I apologize. The summer heat makes me tired and cranky. When you meet Asenath, she will attest to it." He took a long draw on the warm liquid, watching the power-drunk Hebrew's satisfied nod.

"I'm glad to hear you're not always going to oppose me. Your daughter will need you with her. I'm sure her transition from life in a tower to the real world won't be easy."

Anger stirred, but Potiphera swallowed another gulp of beer before responding. "Perhaps when you meet her, you'll realize what a fulfilling life she's experienced as a chantress in Ra's temple. On her wedding day, she'll become Isis Incarnate, high priestess of the mother goddess, and begin fulfilling her destiny as ommi and healer of Egypt. She's been well trained to raise your children and—"

"There will be no children."

Potiphera set his goblet down slowly, hand shaking with pent-up fury. "What . . . Why ever not?" Had Potiphar made him a eunuch after he attacked the captain's wife?

"I will always treat your daughter with kindness and respect. I've made that vow to you, to Queen Tani, and to my pharaoh. But Asenath and I serve different gods. I'm sure she would be as committed to raising a child for Ra or Isis as I would be to teaching my children of Elohim. Our child would become a prize to be fought for—as I was in my family. I would never inflict that sort of pain when it's within my power to withhold it."

"*Your* power?" They were the only words Potiphera could speak without committing treason. He reached for the bell on his table and called for the wab priests to begin serving the trays of stew, fish, and roast meats. "You've given me much to consider, Lord Vizier. Perhaps we should eat in silence, and then I'll take you to meet my lovely daughter."

"Silence would be refreshing, Potiphera. Thank you." He exchanged a glance with his Medjay, in an unspoken language of their own.

Potiphera had already sent a message to Asenath, alerting her to the imminent visit of her betrothed to her tower. She would, of course, be expecting King Apophis. Better she faced her shock in the vizier's presence than having time to brood over what the gods intended by the strange turn of events. Potiphera had spent more than three weeks with the Hebrew and still couldn't imagine why the gods had betrayed them.

FIVE

Asenath

I stood at the window with Zahra and Hotep, watching the temple
grounds for any sign of the Hebrew monster. Guards remained at
the four corners of Ra's altar in the courtyard separating our tower
from the priests' residence complex. Torches lined the outer courts,
illuminating the world I'd considered safe until Potabi's message
arrived with our evening meal.

"Read it to me again," I said.

Hotep unfurled the scroll in her hands.

> *Your betrothed traveled with me from Avaris, anxious to meet you.*
> *He and I will share a meal in my private villa before I bring him to*
> *the tower. The betrothal has been sealed by Pharaoh Yanassi and*
> *approved by the gods. Be at peace, Nathy. The power of Isis sustains*
> *you.*

"He hasn't called me Nathy in years."

Zahra scoffed. "He used your pet name to soften your heart before he shatters it."

"Zahra!" Hotep scolded. "Highness loves her. He loves all of us. I'm sure there's a reasonable explanation—"

"A reasonable explanation for Potabi to lie to me?" I stifled a sob.

Hotep shot a burning glare at Zahra. "See what you've done?"

"He didn't actually lie." Zahra wrapped me in her arms. "Your abi loves you. Never doubt that. We'll soon find out why the gods have allowed this test to come. You are still the goddess and will become Isis Incarnate when you marry the Hebrew. Her power will surge through you, and you'll overcome whatever obstacles lie ahead."

"Here they come!" Hotep's panicked whisper sent all three of us leaning out the window. Two shadowy figures walked through the priests' courtyard, past the summer fruit trees still heavy with fruit. We lost sight of them amid the rows of grape arbors that ran parallel to the wall separating the consecrated areas from the common public grounds.

The two figures emerged from the gardens and climbed the steps toward Ra's altar, and I caught a glimpse of the most handsome man I'd ever seen. I turned away, feeling exposed and unprepared. "My cosmetics. Is the kohl smeared?"

"No, we fixed it."

"Fix it again!" I ran to my chamber, knowing they'd follow. I'd felt cheated when Potabi's missive said I must meet the Hebrew in the tower. I so looked forward to my summer-harvest venture down the tower steps, but my sister-maids helped me see it would be best to face the stranger in our safe tower. Closing my eyes, I lay back on my cosmetics couch and swallowed my raging fear. "You two must remain hidden in your private chamber when he arrives. I don't want him to see your beauty and be disappointed in mine."

After a long pause, Zahra spoke quietly. "We'll gladly remain in our chamber, but no man could ever be disappointed by your beauty."

The sound of men's voices in the audience chamber silenced us. I sat up on my couch, listening hard. A deep baritone laugh filled the air like sweet perfume. How could a Hyksos sound so delightful?

"Asenath, come and meet your groom." Potabi's voice drew near my chamber door. The latch clicked and he peeked inside. A tentative smile crossed his face, and he entered my chamber, closing the door behind him. He hadn't taken his eyes off me. "Asenath, my girl . . ." His lips trembled as he visibly fought for control. "You've never looked more like your ommi."

"Abi." I ran into his arms, hanging on to his neck like a lifeline. "You stayed away so long, I feared you weren't coming back."

"I'll never leave you, Nathy." He unlocked my arms to meet my eyes. "You know I always do what's best for you, and I would never endanger your destiny—the gift Katesch gave us with her dying breath."

Ommi's name on his lips undid me. "Then how could you promise me to a *Hebrew?*"

His hands tightened on my wrists. "How could you know—"

"King Apophis wrote . . ." Rather than explain, I broke from his grasp and produced the scroll tucked in my belt.

He snatched it away and started reading. A slow, terrifying smile curved his lips. "The gods have surely been at work without my knowledge or assistance."

"How can any of that message mean help from the gods?"

"Are you blind?" He gaped at me. "It's obvious King Apophis disagrees with his sister's and nephew's decision to give you to Paneah. King Apophis never responded to my messages about making you his wife, which means he won't openly defy his co-regent. But he's a military man, a strategist. He'll wait for an opportunity to discredit the Hebrew and then the gods will reveal you as Apophis's true wife." Potabi patted my cheek. "For now, you must marry the Hyksos. Come." Without giving me a moment to think, he opened the door to the audience chamber. "Lord Paneah, let me introduce my daughter, Asenath."

The man, looking out the west window, turned toward Potabi.

His eyes landed on me, and he stood silent—mouth agape. He shook his head and laughed. "Forgive me," he said, starting toward us. "I—"

I yelped and skittered back. He halted.

"Asenath," Potabi scolded, capturing my elbow.

My cheeks burned, but I dared not bow my head. Potabi had always said the Hyksos were as clever as they were cruel. I'd watch the vizier's tics and twitches, discern his habits and moods. I'd learn to know my enemy—and right now, his humor had fled.

"I didn't mean to frighten you." His voice was as soft as Jendayi's fur. I'd seen many men from my tower window, but none like him. Why had the gods wasted such beauty on a *Hebrew*?

The thought cleared my head. "I'm not afraid of you," I lied. I wrenched my arm from Potabi's grasp. "I know you were a Hebrew shepherd, sold by your family, and imprisoned for raping your master's wife. I don't know why the gods have condemned me to become your wife, but I'll pass whatever test they give me and emerge stronger."

Potabi patted my arm, chuckling. "Lord Paneah, as I've mentioned many times, my daughter hasn't been close to a man other than me since she was a child, so she's predictably unsettled in your presence."

"It is quite reasonable that she would be unsettled—even frightened—in the presence of a prodigal Hebrew rapist." He took three steps, towering over Potabi. "Where would she have heard such skewed information?"

Potabi produced King Apophis's scroll from his belt.

"No!" I lunged for it, but the Hebrew was quicker. My hand brushed his, and I shied away, hiding behind Potabi again.

"She'll become the Great Ommi of Egypt when you two marry," Potabi said, guiding me closer to the vizier. "I'm sure she'll acclimate once—"

"No!" I pulled away.

"It's all right, Asenath." The Hebrew's voice was gentle, but his smile was as tight as spun linen. "Of this you can be certain. I will never harm you."

He turned his attention to the scroll, reading a missive from a powerful king meant strictly for me. Apophis might harm me if he discovered I'd let the Hebrew read his message. I shot a withering glance at Potabi, feeling betrayed.

"As I told you in Avaris," Potabi said as the vizier tucked the message in his own belt, "I had already sent a proposal to King Apophis of marriage to my daughter but immediately rescinded the offer when Pharaoh Yanassi and the queen mother made their wish clear that you marry Asenath. I discovered King Apophis's message moments ago upon greeting my daughter. I hope you see by my immediate transparency that there will be no secrets between us," Potabi added, betraying my secret to the Hebrew.

I looked away. "I don't wish to marry you, Vizier."

"Asenath!" Potabi whirled on me.

"Potiphera, I will speak with Asenath alone." The Hebrew motioned Potabi toward the stairs.

Potabi appeared astonished. "Lord Paneah, I cannot leave you alone with a virgin priestess—"

The vizier lifted a hand, silencing Ra's high priest. "You will leave us, Potiphera. Asenath will be my wife in less than a month."

Potabi actually bowed to a Hyksos, and my courage drained with his retreat. "Potabi, wait!" I wanted to flee when he disappeared into my chamber.

"Be at peace, Asenath." The vizier remained two steps away, hands clasped behind his back. "Much of what Apophis told you has been misunderstood. Yes, I'm Hebrew, and my family are Bedouin shepherds, but the truth is my brothers despised me because they were jealous of my abba's love for me. I never treated Master Potiphar's wife inappropriately, and Queen Tani has exonerated me of all charges—though my reputation will undoubtedly always carry the stain." He let his hands fall to his sides. "Are there other reasons you don't wish to marry me?"

I forced my feet to stay planted and studied my enemy. Gold and green flecks sparkled in light brown eyes, and his bottom lashes were nearly as long as those on top. "You broke your vow to marry another. Who was she?"

He flinched, and I considered myself the victor. "I . . . I don't wish to say." Avoidance. Potabi never allowed it.

"Are you a coward as well?"

The softness around his eyes tightened into something that felt dark and dangerous. "I should have known you play games as well as your abi." He turned away, combing his fingers through wavy brown hair. "If it's any comfort, I don't want this marriage any more than you do. It's true. I'm still in love with—" He cleared his throat. "With someone else."

I flinched at the confession, raw and vulnerable. "Then tell Pharaoh Yanassi you refuse to marry me."

He turned and scoffed. "I tried. Believe me. But one ultimately does not 'refuse' Pharaoh or the queen mother and live long enough to explain why."

So. This Hebrew was locked in his own tower—made of royal expectations and impossible demands. He held my gaze, silent and searching. I felt drawn; something sad and pleading beckoned me. "Lord Paneah—"

"If you're the Chantress of Ra, why does your jewelry bear the symbols of many gods?" He pointed at my necklace, armbands, and crown, his smile tentative.

"I thought all Hebrews had beards."

"You didn't answer my question."

"You didn't answer mine."

Our eyes locked in playful battle. "How do you know the symbols of our gods? I've heard Hebrews worship a single desert god."

"I know about Egypt's gods." He pointed to the wheel of gods on my necklace and named the twelve most powerful. "But you are correct that I serve Elohim alone—God of all creation. He's not merely a desert god. He guides my every thought, word, and deed. He is the God who interpreted Pharaoh Yanassi's dreams and will heal the Two Lands in feast or famine."

"Heal the Two Lands?" My throat constricted. I turned away, remembering Potabi's training and the goddess who called me. *Mother Goddess, how could this Hyksos recite Ommi's last words?*

"Have I upset you again?" His voice was soft.

Too confused to face him, I kept my back turned but felt the goddess's courage. "I was named after the goddess Isis, who guides my destiny."

"Your destiny?" His voice was smooth as butter.

"My destiny is to heal Egypt, as Isis heals the family of Egypt's gods. I wear all the gods' names because I'm destined to marry a man who will help me unite the Two Lands and heal Egypt's greatest wound."

"I see." In the silence, I listened to his slow, steady breaths. "Asenath, can you face me? I won't touch you or come any closer. I promise."

Slowly, I turned to look at this man with the face and body of a god. His smile made me ache from head to toe. Did he hold some strange power over women, or would all men have this effect on me?

"*We* will unite Egypt. Together. Elohim revealed through Pharaoh Yanassi's dreams that Egypt will experience seven years of great abundance followed by seven years of famine beyond anything the world has known. Elohim then revealed to me a plan to prepare Egypt during the abundance for the years of famine. I believe my God has given you the passion to help me save your nation." He stared at my armband intently and began naming the gods there as well. "Seth, the god of chaos. There's the Eye of Horus." He scanned Hathor's crown on my head. "We will marry, Asenath, because we dare not refuse the command of Pharaoh Yanassi and the queen mother. But make no mistake. I serve Elohim only, and I will not share my body with a woman who shares herself with imaginary gods. I bid you good night." He started toward the stairs. "Tell Potiphera I've returned to the villa."

"Wait!"

He paused to face me.

"You must understand. My destiny is everything to me. It cannot be fulfilled without children."

"I do understand. It's a woman's privilege to teach her children about her faith." An inner battle played on his features. "But your gods are merely stories, and your faith is based on lies. So, unless you deny your gods and worship Elohim alone, I cannot—I will not—give you children." He disappeared down the tower stairs—leaving me gasping.

Stories? Lies? My neck and cheeks burned as I watched him go. Was it worse to be forced into marrying a Hyksos or to be rejected by one? No children? What tricks were the gods playing? I was tired of their games. If the boy pharaoh commanded me to marry his pet Hebrew, so be it. Divorce was simple enough—as long as there were no children. Perhaps in this way, the gods were protecting me. Hadn't Potabi said King Apophis would wait for an opportunity to discredit the new vizier and then the gods would reveal me as Apophis's true wife? Shame subsided as relief began to rise. Perhaps remaining chaste in marriage with a vile Hebrew was the best I could hope for in my vexing situation.

"You did well, Daughter." I turned and found Potabi leaning against the open doorway of my chamber, my sisters behind him. "We heard every word. Our new vizier is a mere slave greedy for control. He knows your desire is to have children, so that's how he'll manipulate you." He scoffed and walked toward me. "But it's you who holds real power in the bedchamber. That Hebrew will beg for your body on the wedding night."

"Stop!" I pressed my palms against flaming cheeks. "Don't talk to me like I'm a common prostitute." Jendayi leapt from Hotep's shoulder, skittered across the tiles, and bounded into my arms. "I know nothing about a wedding night, but I'll never give myself to that Hebrew vizier, Potabi."

His extended silence screamed disapproval. "You're letting emotions rule you. You will gain control of yourself, or—"

"Or what?" I choked on a cynical laugh. "You'll marry me to a Hyksos? You were supposed to protect me, Potabi. Make me a queen. Instead, you've given me to a Hebrew shepherd!"

Hotep ran to me. "Asenath, calm down. Please!" She took Jendayi, and I turned away.

"She's tired, Highness," Zahra said. "She doesn't mean it." My sisters stood beside me like twin shields.

"None of you know anything about the world outside this tower."

"That's not true," I said, still defiant. "You've given us the education of kings. We speak four languages and write the hieroglyphs. We've raised a guenon monkey since her infancy to learn how to care for others before ourselves. I think I can discern the will of the gods about whose children I'll bear."

He glared at me, as expected, but I felt empowered by my rebellion. Was I building my tomb or a barque to sail free? My next words would likely reveal the results. "Do you remember from our studies that guenons like Jendayi recognize their own species of monkey by distinctive facial features? Do you realize why this is important should we ever decide to breed Jendayi?"

"Who cares?" Potabi hissed.

"Because mingling two species produces an infertile race like mules that result from breeding horses with donkeys. The gods gave even *guenons* the sense not to interbreed. Shouldn't I exercise the same animal instinct and spare the world some subspecies of non-Egyptian urchins?"

Potabi's momentary shock turned to seething, and even my maids couldn't protect me. "Zahra, Hotep, descend the stairs. Take the monkey with you." His icy calm was more frightening than fury. I didn't dare look at my sisters when they whimpered and moved reluctantly toward the tower stairway. "Wait at the bottom!" His shout made us all jump.

Jendayi's screech shot through me like a spear. "I'm sorry, Potabi. Please don't punish them for my disrespect. I'm confused and frightened, but if you'll listen, I can explain. Divorcing the Hebrew will be easier if—"

He lifted a hand. I flinched, expecting a blow. "You deserve more than a slap, but I dare not leave a mark. "Paneah and I leave tomorrow to tour neighboring nomes. You will spend the next eight days alone. No maids and no monkey. You seek independence? You shall have it. You'll receive food, water, and nothing else." He scoffed. "Welcome to the real world."

"Potabi, wait!" He ignored me as he started down the stairway. "Potabi, please! I've apologized. Let them come back." I looked over the rail and heard a stream of questions from Hotep and Zahra. Jendayi squawked and then screamed. "Jendayi!" I rushed to the window, hoping to see where they went, but Potabi walked the torchlit path to his villa alone. "Where are they?" I shouted from the window. "What have you done?" I slid to the cool tiles, pressed my cheek to the floor, and wept. *What have I done?*

SIX

Joseph had a dream, and when he told it to his brothers, they hated him all the more.

GENESIS 37:5

Joseph dismissed the wab priest assigned as his steward, then turned to Hami—concern high, voice low. "Will Asenath remain unattended in the tower for the full eight days Potiphera and I are away?"

Hami gave a single nod. "It was Potiphera's instruction to his temple guards."

"How can he be sure they'll protect her, now that they know she's betrothed to a Hebrew?" Joseph had noted the razor-sharp stares pointed his direction since he'd debarked at On's quay. Gaining Potiphar's favor as his slave had been far easier than winning Egypt's respect as its vizier. "You must leave a small contingent of Medjays at the base of Asenath's tower to protect her."

Hami slightly raised one brow. "I answer to the pharaohs for your protection alone, Lord Vizier. And my men heard the temple guards setting up watch shifts for the priestess and her maids. Though Potiphera's emotional attachments can't be trusted, he wouldn't allow anything to threaten his chantresses of On. His daughter's circumstance is . . . regrettable, but I don't believe she's in danger."

Regrettable. Joseph's decision to leave the tower so soon was also regrettable. What had gone so terribly wrong after he left? He'd barely entered his chamber when he heard women's screams. He and Hami charged toward the sound—six Medjays with them—and happened upon Asenath's terrified maids with an equally frightened monkey. Temple guards coaxed them toward the villa without touching them. Potiphera had marched toward them soon after but refused to answer Joseph's questions.

Closing his eyes to focus his thoughts, Joseph recalled the single truth that explained both the triumphs and tragedies of his life. *Elohim, only You can protect those I love and fit this moment into the good future You've promised me.*

Refreshed by the truth, Joseph opened his eyes. "Hami, dawn has come, and we visit Egypt's first nome today. Any advice?"

A slight grin curved his lips. "Don't turn your back on Ra's high priest."

"Point taken." Joseph chuckled. "I was referring more to dealings with governors and village noblemen."

The Medjay sobered. "You're not the slave anymore, Joseph. I'm honored that you would ask me for advice, but I'm no longer Vizier Hami. I'm your protector, your captain. I can offer suggestions, but you are Lord Zaphenath-Paneah, vizier of the Two Lands. You have the authority to make every decision in both lands, my lord. Your god proved through the interpretation and the famine plan that he gives you wisdom above all others. Consider advice, but make your own decisions, Lord Paneah—my friend."

Joseph touched Hami's shoulder, his throat too tight to speak, and left his chamber with newfound courage. After his emotions calmed, he'd tell the Medjay how Elohim had spoken through his words straight to Joseph's deepest insecurities. Right now, however, Potiphera awaited their arrival at the temple quay.

"Ma'at has returned to On, Lord Vizier." The portly high priest bowed as they approached.

"Would your daughter and her maids boast the same peace, Potiphera?" Joseph walked past him, Hami following close behind, and boarded a medium-sized felucca. Potiphera deemed the sturdy reed boats, smaller than the king's barque, easier to navigate in and out of village ports.

"The chantresses are well cared for, Paneah." Potiphera climbed into the boat awkwardly, bracing himself on Joseph's shoulder and then plopping down on a cushion. The boat wobbled, making him chuckle. He motioned to the helmsman, who hoisted a small triangular sail, and the Nile's rushing current swept them away. "Hotep and Zahra are young," he said, returning his attention to Joseph. "This separation will help them adjust to life without Asenath."

He turned his face to the sky with a satisfied sigh—far too chipper after last night's events. "Ra has emerged victorious from the underworld again, Paneah, and his sailing journey across the sky promises scorching heat. We should visit as many villages as possible this morning and plan to rest through midday."

Joseph cast an infuriated glance at Hami. Would the pompous priest guide every decision for the whole tour?

"I agree with Highness Potiphera," Hami said. "But the decision is yours, Lord Vizier." His subtle reminder recharged Joseph's confidence and garnered Potiphera's attention.

"It's good advice, indeed." Joseph produced the scroll he'd worked on late into the night. "I've planned four villages on the eastern shore for this morning, letting the strong current push us quickly north. We'll rest at midday, visit two more villages this evening, and overnight at the last one."

* * *

At the end of two days, Joseph and Potiphera had visited ten villages—four fewer than planned. Joseph had accounted for slower southbound travel—rowing against the tide—while visiting villages on the western shoreline, but he hadn't expected Potiphera to purposely hinder their progress.

Joseph traversed the ten paces between his reed hut and Potiphera's and faced his temple guard. "I would speak with your high priest."

The guard didn't move or acknowledge him, but a voice from inside called, "Paneah?" Potiphera pushed open the woven reed door, dressed in his tunic.

He looked tired, and Joseph's temper cooled. "Did I wake you?"

"No, I was checking the figures for this village's requests."

"Requests?"

Potiphera waved away the comment. "You said you wished to speak to me?"

"May I come in?" Joseph noted the hesitation before the priest pushed the door open wider to allow him entry. Potiphera's hut was as small as Joseph's, barely enough room for two grown men to stand with a comfortable distance between them. An unfurled scroll sat atop an overturned basket, held in place by two rocks and flanked by small oil lamps.

Drawn to the open scroll, Joseph knelt beside them.

Potiphera explained, "Each village in the fifteenth nome can request part of our temple's harvest of both fruit and grain. I keep detailed records."

He tried to deftly move it away, but Joseph snatched it first. He'd noticed something interesting. "It seems this village gave back to the temple more than double the amount they received in fruit and grain." *No wonder On's temple is so prosperous.* "What makes the fruit and grain from On's temple worth more than double their own crops?"

Potiphera extended his hand, silently demanding Joseph return the scroll, which he did. The priest rolled it up while he answered. "The temple's crops are blessed by Ra, Lord Vizier, and shared freely with any village that sends a representative to gather from our store-house. The relationships and system I've already established will work perfectly when the famine comes. There's no need for you—"

"Your system is not Elohim's system." Joseph swallowed his rising indignation. "Have I not made it clear there will be one official distributing grain vouchers during the famine and one location from which all grain will be allocated? It will be me—only me—in Avaris."

"Then what is the reason for the villages to build such large storehouses? Why not—"

"Because both the abundance and famine will be beyond anything experienced in the past." They locked eyes like rams lock horns, neither willing to relent. Joseph twirled Pharaoh's ring on his finger, reminding himself he need not even raise his voice. "Each village must be ready with its own storehouse."

"So you've said at each stop, Lord Vizier," the priest said with a smirk.

Indeed, at every location, Joseph had informed village elders that the Nile's record flooding was the beginning of the abundance. Pharaoh's dreams were real, and building storehouses was vital—an immediate need. Then, before any real plans were made, Potiphera digressed to town gossip and frivolous distractions.

Potiphera raised his chin. "If that's all, Lord Paneah, I'm an old man who needs my rest."

"You're an influential high priest who can either help me or hurt me. If you refuse to support Elohim's plan, I'll find someone else to introduce me to the elders and nome governors."

His black eyes bored into Joseph's. "May I speak freely, Lord Vizier?"

"I wish you would, Highness."

"You really must converse more with the people. You may *look* Egyptian, but with the first word out of your mouth, they know you're Hebrew." His tone was wicked with delight, his condescension a well-aimed blow.

Joseph had been beaten, imprisoned, mocked, and insulted but never so offended. "I speak Egyptian, Swahili, and Akkadian with perfect diction and—"

"It's not *how* you speak our language, Paneah. People know when someone truly cares about them—and you don't. Why does On's temple give villages part of our harvest? So we can know the people.

Yes, they give much of their own harvest right back, but it's the relationships we build in the process that matter." Eyes narrowed, he glared at Joseph. "How do you think On's temple became the largest in Egypt? When I arrived fifteen years ago, I was a lowly prophet—one level higher than a wab priest—trying to protect three little girls in a chamber no larger than our reed felucca."

"Three? Are Hotep and Zahra also your daughters?"

"I rescued them on the same night Asenath and I fled from Memphis."

Joseph softened. There was far more to this man than the preconceived image he'd sculpted. "So, you fled Memphis when General Salitis killed the Egyptian pharaoh and moved the capital Avaris to become king?"

Potiphera offered a single solemn nod. "The two girls had been born on the same night as Asenath and lived in the same mudbrick complex near the temple. The gods wove their destinies together from the beginning. As soon as we arrived in On, I began teaching them chantress duties, and their voices blended more beautifully than morning larks. People make their pilgrimage to On's temple from every village in Lower Egypt to receive Ra's sacred blessing, present their offerings, and hear the famed chantresses of On."

Joseph recognized an abi's pride—the same spark he'd seen in Abba Jacob's eyes when he spoke of Joseph to passing merchants—and better understood why the prestigious high priest was reticent to offer his daughter to a despised Hebrew. "Thank you, Potiphera," Joseph said. "I understand you and your harvest record a little better now."

Even in dim lamplight, Joseph noticed Potiphera's features soften. "When I began visiting the villages and encouraging people to experience the greatness of our sun god, Ra, our temple coffers overflowed. Perhaps we should have built storehouses, like you're suggesting, but we built the Avenue of Sphinxes instead. We expanded the public court and altar, and—"

"And the high priest's opulent villa," Joseph added with a wry smile.

A slight twitch in his cheek showed offense, and Potiphera's trained pleasantness returned. "I was appointed high priest by the thirteenth nome's governor—whom you'll meet tomorrow—with the people's overwhelming support. Egyptians are loyal unto death, Paneah. They love their high priest because he loves them well." He paused slightly and added, "Perhaps they'll even love a Hebrew vizier if he loves them well."

"You remind me of my abba in many ways." Joseph loved Prince Jacob of Hebron, but he'd never do business with a man—even his abba—who'd proven deceitful. Potiphera was also a spider spinning webs. Though he sounded willing to support Joseph's relationships with Egyptian leaders, Ra's high priest would never endorse a Hebrew vizier. "Good night, Potiphera."

Joseph turned to go, but the priest halted him with a single declaration. "You realize your Elohim is simply Ra by a different name."

Joseph kept walking. "We'll save that discussion for another day, Highness."

"Will we discuss it tomorrow?" he asked. "Or will we rush through our village visits as we've done for two days?"

Joseph faced the high priest in the moonlight. "Introduce me to the *people*, Potiphera, not exclusively the town's elders. Then I'll be satisfied to visit two villages each day and mention to the elders at the end of each visit their need to build a storehouse. Will you begin that plan with me tomorrow?"

Potiphera's eyes narrowed, and his smile reminded Joseph of a crocodile before it opened its jaws. "I'll work with you, Lord Vizier, if you'll discuss the gods and Asenath with me between villages."

Weary to the bone, Joseph respected the man's tenacity. "We'll discuss whatever you like, but I ask that you remember one thing."

"Anything for Zaphenath-Paneah, the one to whom the god speaks, and all live."

"Remember, it was Elohim who gave me the interpretations." Joseph paused, letting a slow grin soften his next words. "And Elohim gave us two ears and one mouth, my friend. Let's consider how we might use the double portion more and the single portion less."

Without waiting for an answer, Joseph nodded his thanks to Hami at his open door and ducked into his own hut.

After removing his jewelry, leather belt, and schenti, Joseph lay on his mat wearing only his loincloth. He tossed and turned in the sweltering heat of Egypt's breezeless night. How he missed the prison's cooler subterranean temperatures! He even missed Ubaid, the odorous, foul-humored warden. With a deep sigh, he repositioned his lamb's wool headrest and tuned out the village's strange sounds. He looked forward to sleeping on the stuffed mattresses in Potiphera's villa and his new home in Avaris. The vizier's villa was larger than Potiphar's home and even more elegantly furnished. Ubaid would say he'd already grown soft. He grinned, then sobered. *Where would Asenath sleep?* Potiphar and his wife had hoped for children but still slept in separate chambers.

Thoughts of the past always conjured memories of Ahira. Her tenderness toward their mistress had given him strength to forgive Zully after she'd betrayed them both. *Ubaid set you free from your cell, Joseph, but your bitterness toward Zully is eating you alive.* When Joseph closed his eyes, Ahira's lovely features were still as vibrant as they were on the day they parted. In his eyes, she was more beautiful than any other woman on earth. *Forgive me, Elohim. I know I must free Ahira to marry another, but in my heart, she'll always be mine.*

But he wasn't hers anymore. He winced, remembering the fiery priestess. His cheeks flamed with memories of every soft curve beneath her sheer linen robe. He rolled to his side, frustrated by his body's unwelcome desire. Many noblewomen wore linen as sheer as butterflies' wings, but none had ever been chosen as Joseph's wife. Queen Tani's assessment of Asenath's beauty was like a crow's caw repeating in his mind.

Joseph turned over again and shoved his shoulder into the packed dirt at another grating memory. "My destiny is to heal Egypt," she'd said, eyes glistening with both compassion and zeal. Hadn't he felt the same passion to unite the Two Lands once the shock of becoming Egypt's vizier became determination? "But she'll never . . ." He finished with a groan and turned over again, surrendering to the hopeless conclusion. Though he and Asenath shared the same exhilarating call to save the world's greatest nation, she could never replace Ahira—the woman who'd possessed him so completely for nearly nine years.

And yet. Pharaoh Yanassi had spoken. Elohim hadn't stopped the match. And Joseph agreed to implement God's plan for the famine with a pagan wife by his side—which meant he must release his dearest love to the will of Elohim. Could Ahira find love again? The thought twisted his gut into a knot. *Ahira with another man?* He couldn't bear it. A future with Asenath pulled the knot tighter. How could the high priestess of Isis ever relinquish the gods she served so passionately?

I can't fix this, Elohim. Please. Give me peace so I can rest and start to love the people of Egypt well. He began humming Ahira's favorite shepherd's tune and prayed silently to the God who heard men's thoughts. Slowly, steadily, he fell into a restful half consciousness.

He imagined Abba Jacob greeting him in a lush green pasture. He looked older. Stooped. But his face radiated joy. He pointed at something behind Joseph, so he turned. A boat approached, large and ornate—Pharaoh's barque. Joseph shaded his eyes from the midday sun to identify the three people standing on the bow. His chest nearly exploded when he saw Ahira. With her stood Potiphar and Pushpa.

"Welcome her, Joseph," said the woman who appeared at Joseph's side.

Asenath?

"Show Ahira our love is secure enough to welcome her home."

Joseph bolted upright. He searched his surroundings and found dawn peeking through the hut's window. His mind still foggy from exhaustion and the dream, he whispered, "Was the dream from You, Elohim, or simply a fantasy?"

Abba had said his boyhood dreams that predicted his brothers would someday bow before him were prideful hopes and vain imaginings. *Were they, Elohim?* As a boy, Joseph hadn't wanted his brothers to bow. He'd wanted their friendship, but they hated him more after he told them his dreams. He no longer wanted their friendship. Now, especially after prison, he'd *make* them bow. He felt the familiar hatred rising.

Show Ahira our love is secure enough to welcome her home.

Elohim, what are You saying to me? He didn't understand. He didn't love Asenath, nor could he imagine a future in which he did. But the dream was as profound as those of his childhood.

"Wake up, Lord Vizier!" Potiphera shouted outside his hut, grating his frazzled nerves.

He quickly donned his schenti, placed his wool headrest at the edge of his mat, and rolled the two together. "I'm ready," he said. "I'll eat something on our way to the first village." When he ducked under the low doorway, he met Potiphera's strained expression and dark circles beneath his eyes.

"I've had the strangest dream all night, Paneah. Each time I went back to sleep, the same vision came again." They started toward the quay, but Joseph didn't probe. He was weary of hearing the dreams of others. Potiphera explained anyway. "A white-haired old man with a long white beard stood in a green pasture pointing toward the Nile."

Joseph stopped, dread rising in his belly.

"I looked where the man was pointing . . ." Potiphera stopped, clearly disturbed. "Pharaoh's barque was approaching. There were three people on the bow. I recognized only two."

Joseph's eyes slid shut. "The two you recognized were Captain Potiphar and his ommi, Pushpa."

"Yes." Potiphera considered Joseph. "Asenath stood beside you on the shore and identified the young woman I didn't recognize as Ahira." The high priest's tone grew sharp. "I assume *Ahira* was your Hebrew—"

"Careful, priest." Joseph's glare was enough to silence him.

"Forgive me, Lord Vizier." His shoulders stiffened.

"What else happened?" Joseph both dreaded and needed to know.

"Asenath stood beside you and said, 'Ahira can come home

because our love is so strong.' Or something like that." He waved away the words as if they were unimportant.

Joseph recited them as the hallowed message they'd become. "Show Ahira our love is secure enough to welcome her home."

The high priest regarded him with suspicion. "How did you—" he sputtered. Then realization dawned. "You had the same dream! What sort of spell have you cast on me, Hebrew?"

"Elohim needs no spells," Joseph said. "Don't soil the sacred with pettiness."

Both men stood in silent awe, their guards scurrying around them, packing the feluccas that would carry them to more villages. All Joseph could think of, however, was the utter impossibility of a loving marriage with Asenath. The dream, like Pharaoh's, had come twice, but this one was given to separate people—making its message even more undeniable. Joseph was to marry Asenath, and Elohim had promised them love. *How can it be, El Shaddai?* Even trusting *Almighty* God, he couldn't imagine that Isis Incarnate would ever relinquish her gods or the destiny she so vehemently attributed to their calling. But neither would Joseph have imagined himself as the vizier of Egypt.

"Let's go, Potiphera!" He started toward the quay again. "We have villagers to care for and elders to meet."

The priest caught up to Joseph's long strides. "Don't worry about anything. I'll tell Asenath about the dreams, and she'll comply. She always does."

"I'll tell her," Joseph said. "I'll visit her tower as soon as we return to On. I want her to know what Elohim has promised for our lives together."

SEVEN

Mockers stir up a city,
but the wise turn away anger.

PROVERBS 29:8

ON

Asenath

The sound of my maids' chanting began the second dawn of my seclusion. Zahra's high notes wafted on the air. Hotep's harmony glided beneath it, mournful and haunting. I shivered, though Ra already taunted with unbearable heat. Having fallen asleep beside the window, I sat up and scanned On's busy temple grounds. Did no one care that my perfectly planned life was ruined? Had no one heard of the great injustice done to me?

"Prove yourself!" I shouted to the mother goddess. Could she hear me, or had Potabi taken the power of the gods with him when he and the vizier sailed away?

I'd watched them from my window yesterday at dawn, strolling from villa to quay. Potabi had laughed when he landed hard in the felucca. *How could he laugh when he'd been so cruel to me?*

I shook my head, disgusted with my self-pity. Why couldn't I focus on the miracles I'd witnessed—the sure sign of the gods at work? Vizier Paneah had spoken the exact words of Ommi's destiny for me. *Heal Egypt's wounds.* But King Apophis had written the same miraculous words in his message. Were the gods playing tricks on me?

If so, which gods?

Something frightening stirred inside. Doubt? No. Passion? Not exactly. Though I couldn't define the emotions, I knew one thing for certain: *I must know which gods are real.*

I smoothed my sackcloth robe, determined to set aside my disdain, and scanned the empty chamber. With a cleansing breath, I resolved to embrace simplicity. I had cowered in a corner when Potabi sent guards before dawn to strip my chamber bare. My furniture, my robes, my jewelry, my cosmetics—all gone. Potabi wanted me to experience true need.

"Does Isis Incarnate ever need?" I whispered.

Yesterday the lector priest had brought me three plentiful meals, delivering each one on the tray with ropes and pulleys. I'd refused them all, stubborn and angry. Sleep had been slow to come, my stomach rumbling like thunder. I whispered to the empty chamber, "If I'm truly Isis and have power over life and death, why not prove my power to Potabi and the vizier? What if I ate and drank nothing but the food and drink offerings normally given to the goddess?"

My cheeks felt prickly, nervous, like they had when I'd challenged Potabi, asking him why the gods hadn't spoken to me about whom I should marry. I wished Hotep and Zahra were here to give me counsel.

Did I believe in Isis's power or didn't I? If Isis was real, I would thrive on devotion to my singular destiny. *Mother Goddess, if I'm truly to become Isis Incarnate when I marry a king, sustain me on the kernels of wheat and swallows of wine the priests provide for your offerings and give me your power to heal Egypt's wounds.*

I shook away all doubt and returned to the altar beside my west window. After placing some kernels of wheat on the tray with a few pieces of straw for kindling, I struck flint stones together, and the straw flared. Smoke rose to the mother goddess and my prayer with it. "Adoration to you, Isis, divine ommi and queen of all gods and goddesses. Even as you gained power over almighty Ra—creator of heaven, earth, and everything therein—so I beseech you now to imbue me with your power to prove a life worthy of your incarnate hands and feet to heal our land." I poured a drop of wine to quench the flame, and a breeze blew in, swirling the smoke and my untethered hair.

A breeze in the dead heat of summer? A sign. I knew my prayer would be answered.

Zahra and Hotep's chanting had stopped, but another sound emerged from the constant noise in my familiar world. "Please, masters. A scrap for my child." Other similar pleas rose through the south tower window, and I rushed to see the source. Gazing down, I saw hundreds of beggars congregated at the temple storehouse and bakery, pleading for scraps from the priests. Temple guards stood outside the buildings, ignoring them, while priests came and went without acknowledgment, comment, or aid.

I suddenly realized the beggars had always been there. My maids and I hadn't known because we never went to the south window. Our attention always faced west, so their need had simply become temple noise to which we'd dulled our senses. We sang our chants over the pilgrims arriving at the quay and strolling on the Avenue of Sphinxes. And I, the Great Ommi of Egypt, had ignored her hurting children. But in this moment, I heard the beggars as I imagined an ommi might hear her child's first cry. Hundreds of them weeping. Yearning for help.

Why wait any longer to heal Egypt?

I marched to the single room Potabi hadn't emptied. Gathering as many gold and silver statues of the gods as I could carry, I returned to the south window and shouted to my children below, "Clear the way! Don't let these fall on you!" I heaved the gods, one at a time, and gained the attention of the starving poor. The temple guards paid attention, too. With my second and third armloads of silver-and-gold rain, the priests dispensed moldy bread to the beggars. By the time I'd emptied Potabi's treasure chamber—plus everything personal from our private chambers—the poor had become rich, and the priests had disappeared.

And then I was alone. No more gods. No jewelry. No belts or robes or scrolls. And none of the gods had stopped me.

When my meals came, I tossed them out the window as well. The crowd of beggars swelled and chanted. "Isis! Priestess! Isis! Priestess!"

Each time I gave life and healing, I felt the goddess's power surge through me—until the third day when I could barely walk to the window. Still the crowd below shouted, "Isis! Priestess! Isis! Priestess!"

After all Isis had given them, still . . . it wasn't enough.

EIGHT

God is strong and always wins.
He controls those who fool others and those who are fooled.
JOB 12:16, ERV

EIGHT DAYS AFTER POTABI'S DEPARTURE
Asenath

A new day pierced my interminable darkness. Squinting, I raised
my head from the ash-covered tiles, my tears having mingled with
the ashes from my overturned altar to form a thin layer of clay on
my cheek. I thought to scrub it away, but I was too weak to lift my
hand. As light poured through the tower windows, I tried to order
my jumbled thoughts.

How many dawns had passed since Potabi took Zahra, Hotep,
and Jendayi from me? How long since more than Isis's portion of
food or wine passed my lips? My lips were cracked, tongue swollen.
I glanced at the swallow of wine I'd saved for today's offering to Isis.
Would the great healer allow her high priestess to die? Were the
gods real, or had Potabi used their stories to manipulate?

Zahra's and Hotep's chants floated on the edges of my awareness
like a dream. They sang the blessings of the dead—mournful dirges.

Soon, my friends. Perhaps today I'd enter the Hall of Ma'at to be judged.

I rolled on my back, sprawled on my purple tiles. The gold ceiling reflected the morning sun and nearly blinded me. Every gemstone mortared into my wall—amethyst, carnelian, lapis lazuli, and more—mocked me with its splendor. I'd considered luxury my right, my destiny. Now the baubles peered down on the pitiable, destitute wraith I'd become.

Would Potabi return in time to say goodbye? Would he be angry that I'd emptied his treasure chamber of all the wealth he'd hidden for years from Egypt's royalty? Yes, he'd be furious and think it was retribution for matching me with a Hebrew and for leaving me alone. There may have been a seed of vengeance within, but my true motives were purer. I had become Egypt's ommi and healer.

Whether I live or die, Mother Goddess, my life has healed this land in some small way. Perhaps with a few trinkets tossed to beggars and as one of On's three chantresses, but I have helped bring peace and joy to pure-blooded Egyptians. *Peace and joy . . .*

The internal wrestling exhausted me. Dark shadows imposed their presence. Then silence.

Asenath. A whisper. A dream. *Asenath.*

I tried to sit up but could barely roll to my side. Vision blurred, I closed my eyes. Something tickled my face. I swatted at it and opened my eyes to see dung beetles crawling over my hands. I screamed, bolted upright, swiped them away. Suddenly, they were gone. I was sitting on my tiles, ashes at my feet. I marveled at the energy summoned by fear.

The beggars' chanting faded into silence. All sound ceased—except I could hear myself breathing. Was I dreaming? Was I dying? I shook my head, slapped my ears, and then screamed. Still no sound. Gulping air, I fought for sanity and skittered to a corner. Had I angered the gods by tossing them out the window? Would Osiris come for me? Seth? Or Anubis to weigh my heart against his feather on the scale. Would my heart still weigh lighter, at peace with my destiny and the gods?

"Don't be afraid, Asenath."

I searched my audience chamber. Empty. The hairs on my arms stood at attention. Where had the voice come from? Were the guards marching up the stairs? "Don't come near me!"

No answer.

My voice echoed inside my head. Was I already dead?

Brilliant light surrounded me. I covered my face but peeked through slatted fingers. A radiant figure stood five paces from me. Human in appearance but taller than any man and built like a warrior. He certainly wasn't the jackal-faced Anubis.

"Who are you?"

"I've come to strengthen you, Asenath."

"I don't believe you." If Isis wasn't helping me, why would any other god care? "I'm not even sure you're real."

He knelt before me, tipping a wooden cup to my lips. "Drink."

The water tasted of honey and felt cool all the way to my belly. When he pulled it away, he sat opposite me, his radiance enfolding us both.

"Are you a god?"

He seemed startled. "Oh, no! There is but one God, Asenath. He is all-powerful. All-knowing. The Creator of all things."

"Potabi says all nations serve the same gods but call them by different names."

The messenger stared into me. "There is but one God, Asenath." The voice rumbled like thunder. Terrifying and loud.

I pressed myself harder into the corner. *One god?* "Which one is . . . I can't reject . . ." The consequences of such a truth tightened my throat, cutting off the explanation. I could easily toss Egypt's minor gods to the beggars, but to reject either Ra or Isis meant Potabi would reject me. As it was, I would certainly bear his wrath for dispensing his wealth to the poor. In time, he might forgive that deed as noble. He would *never* forgive the public shame I'd bring upon him if I relinquished the honor of high priestess.

"I can't lose Potabi." I dared to meet the eyes of fire. "Abi is my only family."

He placed his hand over my heart. Flashes of my childhood came to mind, and I clutched at the ache inside. I saw myself as a child, Potabi playing senet with me and the first day he placed Jendayi in my arms. Feeling so deeply loved, I moaned. "Why show me what I've lost?"

He removed his hand and the aching ceased. "I've shown you imperfect attempts at love, dim reflections of the Creator's perfect heart for you, Asenath. *He* is your true Abi. He will never abandon or betray you."

The sole abi among the gods was Osiris, and Isis had killed him, sending him to rule the underworld. This radiant being must have been referring to Ra—the one Upper Egypt called Amun—who birthed a new day each dawn. "I willingly submit to a creator," I said, "but will he make me choose between the abi who saved me and a god who can't embrace me? With Potabi comes the certainty of my destiny, the single purpose that's enabled me to survive this tower." I covered my mouth, appalled at the confession. I had never before grumbled about my confinement. I'd understood it fully— even recognized its necessity—yet secretly longed to live in the city below.

Tears came unbidden, and I sensed compassion intensified in the being's radiance. Without a touch, warmth and comfort wrapped and soothed me, calmed and strengthened me. When I reached up to wipe my cheeks, they were already dry. It was an embrace—of sorts. Amazed, I looked into his smiling face.

"You will marry Joseph, Asenath."

"Who is Joseph?" *I had a third suitor?*

"He is Zaphenath-Paneah, and his Egyptian name applies to you as well—*God speaks, and you live.* You will bear his children and partake of an ancient promise. Your descendants will bless not only Egypt but every nation of the world."

"But I must—" I shook my head and looked down at my hands, confused and uncertain. "If I marry Zaphenath-Paneah, I must relinquish every foundation of my life. My gods. My family. My very reason for life."

He offered no reply, but his light remained. It was clear. The decision was mine.

My arguments chased in circles. Finally, I focused again on this being—what might be a vision borne of starvation and thirst. "My ommi had the most beautiful voice in Egypt, but Hyksos soldiers killed her when they attacked Memphis. They spared one priest to dispose of the dead. A soldier returned after the killing and took Ommi's body. In exchange, he gave the priest safe passage to On. The priest escaped Memphis that night, hiding Potabi, me, and my two friends in his skiff. I don't remember anything about the priest who saved us, but the soldier who took Ommi's body visits my nightmares—as do Ommi's dying words: 'Heal Egypt's wounds.'" I swallowed hard. "I don't care about blessing other nations. If I can't *heal Egypt,* then surviving that night means nothing."

"*You* can't heal anyone," he said, undeterred. "But the one God can heal—you *and* Egypt. Go into your chamber. You'll find a new robe and embroidered belt. Remove your sackcloth. Grieve your ommi no longer. You're a bride now— a virgin bride—prepared for your groom. Return to me for nourishment after you're dressed."

"But I—" My protest stopped when I realized my legs sustained me with each step of obedience. I crossed the threshold of my chamber and found the white robe hanging on a wall peg with the embroidered belt hanging beside it—as the messenger promised. I untied my hemp belt and removed the scratchy sackcloth robe, littering the floor with ashes. Looking down at my nakedness, I was startled at the frailty of my flesh. This was no goddess. Bony. Splotchy. Eight days with scarcely any food or drink. I'd wasted away to something no lotions or henna could mask to prepare for a groom. Yet I obeyed the messenger and donned the white linen and colorful belt, then returned as he'd commanded.

The moment he saw me, the glow surrounding him brightened, and his smile sent a surge of warmth through my veins. "You are pleasing to the Creator, Asenath." As he extended his hand, a honeycomb appeared in it. "Eat. Strengthen yourself. Joseph arrives today."

I reached for the comb, its golden goodness dripping all over my hands. The radiant creature disappeared, but the sweet nourishment remained. A simple clay pitcher and a wooden cup filled with water in his place. I ate. I drank. And I waited for my groom, the man called *Joseph*.

NINE

So Jacob served seven years to get Rachel, but
they seemed like only a few days to him because
of his love for her. . . .
    Laban brought together all the people of the
place and gave a feast. But when evening came,
he took his daughter Leah and brought her to
Jacob, and Jacob made love to her. . . .
    When morning came, there was Leah! So
Jacob said to Laban, "What is this you have
done to me? I served you for Rachel, didn't I?
Why have you deceived me?"

GENESIS 29:20, 22–23, 25

Joseph

After eight days of exhausting travel and unrelenting conflict with
Potiphera, Joseph had promised the oarsmen a full wineskin each
and extra portions of meat if they'd row at full speed to On. Perhaps
the overbearing priest would accept Joseph more readily after he
married Asenath. He'd thought their simultaneous dream would
have proven Elohim's will—or even Ra's will—to On's high priest,
but Potiphera had seemed barely affected.

   Joseph, on the other hand, searched for Ahira's face in every village they visited. Each night on his bed, when he'd closed his eyes, it was Ahira who appeared in his mind. *Elohim, You must help me forget her.* His best efforts to not think of the woman who had consumed him for nine years caused him to miss her more desperately. How could he ever stop loving her—and love another?

The well-muscled sailors rowed hard for their extra rations and made the half day's journey a breezy morning's sail. Sliding the felucca onto On's temple quay, Joseph felt suddenly and profoundly unprepared to face the fiery priestess.

Potiphera hurried ashore. "Come, Paneah. You can ride with me in the palanquin."

But Joseph had already started jogging toward the temple complex. "I'll meet you at your villa's entrance."

He needed time alone with Elohim before the conversations that would likely change his life and Asenath's. The sun poured out its unrelenting heat as Joseph prayed with equal intensity. *I can explain to this priestess the logical arguments that You're the only God, Elohim, but You alone can help her believe. I can recount the dream, El Shaddai, but it is You who must lead us into love.*

The thought of forcing any marriage turned his stomach. He'd seen the devastating effects in Abba Jacob's life with four wives. If Saba Laban hadn't deceived Abba into marrying his older daughter before giving him the woman he'd loved, how would Joseph's life— and others—have been different?

Perhaps my ten older brothers wouldn't have been born.

The thought sobered him but quickened his pace. Elohim showed Ima Leah *His* love for her though she was unloved by her husband. God closed Abba's beloved wife Ima Rachel's womb, while blessing his other three wives with ten sons. Finally, Elohim showed favor to Ima Rachel, too, and gave Joseph life—birthing the favoritism that cultivated his brothers' hatred. The rancor of a loveless marriage had been the seedbed that resulted in Joseph becoming a slave in Egypt. *Elohim, I beg You. If I must marry Asenath, let us be united in peace until the love You've promised fills us.*

Sweat soaked Joseph's short schenti when he arrived at the Avenue of Sphinxes. He reached its end and greeted eighteen guards at the temple's lone entrance. They ignored him until Potiphera's palanquin arrived.

When the eight strong slaves lowered his gilded coach, the high priest drew back the curtains. "Open the gate for the vizier of all Egypt!" he shouted. "How dare you make the great Zaphenath-Paneah wait in this heat!" Potiphera rushed toward Joseph, his face as red as Canaan's wine. "Come, Lord Vizier! We'll freshen ourselves before greeting your bride." He gave a withering glare to each of the sentries as he passed. Four prophets and two servants met their high priest at the villa's entrance, arms full of correspondence that had arrived in his absence.

Grateful for Potiphera's distraction, Joseph started toward the guest chamber he'd occupied before they left, hoping for more time alone before meeting with Asenath.

"Paneah!" Joseph halted as Potiphera scurried toward him. "I should be the one to speak with Asenath about our matching dreams. My priests report that she's acted rather impulsively during our absence. I fear—"

"Then I'll speak with her." Joseph faced him and locked eyes. "Alone."

Potiphera's red cheeks deepened to the color of Abba's Hebron grapes. "She's my daughter, Lord Vizier."

"She'll soon be my wife, Highness. I alone can look into her eyes and tell her Elohim has promised us a loving marriage."

"At least let me escort you."

"No!" Joseph immediately regretted his impatience. "Forgive me, Potiphera, but I wish to see her alone."

"You must have an escor—" A wry smile replaced Potiphera's hard features. "I'll send someone with you who she trusts even more than me." He hurried away, leaving Joseph to refresh his cosmetics and clothing before he met with his bride.

He entered his chamber and dismissed the steward assigned to him. A splash of cool water from the basin was as refreshing as the elegant surroundings. The eight days of dusty villages, reed huts, and Potiphera's political maneuvering had been worth the hardship. Though he and the high priest were like two striking flint stones—causing sparks and sometimes flames—Potiphera had been right to challenge Joseph's leadership methods. When Pharaoh changed Joseph's name, he'd tried to become Zaphenath-Paneah and deny his Hebrew heritage. Hami's wisdom had once again proven the key to Joseph's success. "Why hide what you cannot change?" he'd asked. So, acting on Potiphera's example of loving the people well, Joseph had resumed his shepherding skills with the people of Egypt and won the villagers' favor by simply caring about them.

Joseph looked into the polished bronze mirror mounted above the washbasin. He'd experienced enough austerity to appreciate finery. He'd felt the sting of betrayal and knew the peace of true belonging. Today, he'd forego cosmetics, choosing instead to acquaint his bride with *Joseph*—neither Hebrew nor Egyptian but simply the husband she'd wake beside each morning.

After washing away the travel grit, Joseph reapplied scented oils and chose a long white schenti with a simple gold belt. He emerged from his chamber and nearly ran headlong into Potiphera, who stood barely two paces outside his door with two lovely young women—one of them holding a monkey no larger than a clay pitcher.

The monkey squeaked. The women scuttled back a few steps, pale as goat's milk. Joseph realized they must be Asenath's maids and averted his gaze. They were likely as uncomfortable around men as Asenath had been.

"Lord Paneah," Potiphera began, "I'd like you to meet—"

The monkey squawked again; then chaos ensued. The little beast lunged from the maid's arms—directly at Joseph!

"Capture it!" Potiphera shouted.

A servant ran toward them, but Joseph cried, "Wait!" as the furry creature settled on his shoulder. "I think it's friendly," he said. The little monkey began stroking his cheek and made a throaty sound—almost like a cat's purr.

One of the maids whispered too softly to be heard. She was the taller of the two and wore a long-braided wig with gold beads.

"I'm sorry, I couldn't hear you," Joseph said softly. "You may call me Lord Paneah. What is your name?"

"My name is Zahra, Lord Paneah." The maid showed him a shy smile, then looked at her sandals again. "Jendayi likes you, which is miraculous since she doesn't like anyone but Asenath and Hotep. We've heard the spirit of the gods lives in you. Perhaps she senses it."

"Thank you, Zahra. I'm honored to finally meet you and Hotep." Joseph offered his finger to the little monkey. She curled her hand around it. "And I'm honored to meet you as well, Jendayi. Will you accompany me to speak with your mistress?"

"That's the escort I'd intended," Potiphera said, still seeming shaken. "Though I'm not sure the monkey will leave Hotep. Surely, Asenath's maids could accompany you, Lord—"

"Jendayi and I will be fine." Joseph turned to go.

"Wait!" Hotep offered him a small basket.

"What's this?"

With her head bowed, he could see only the top of her short-braided wig and silver beads. She seemed to shrink as all attention focused on her. The bolder maid looked up, even met Joseph's eyes for a moment. "Hotep is quiet but very thoughtful. She cut fruit and vegetables into small pieces to feed Jendayi during the tower visit. In a monkey's world, the one who holds the food holds the power and wins its favor."

Joseph pulled out a piece of cucumber and offered it to his new little friend. Jendayi received it gladly, and Joseph chuckled, offering thanks to both maids. "I'll remember your advice, Zahra: 'The one who holds the food holds the power and wins the favor.'" He offered goodbyes and pondered the concept that would likely hold true for his position as vizier as well. When famine struck the Two Lands, Joseph would control every granary in the divided nation, and with that control he'd wield great power. *Elohim, help me to win Egyptian hearts for You in the process.*

Skirting the edges of Potiphera's courtyard, Joseph walked in the shade of an avenue of fruit trees to avoid the afternoon's unbearable sun. He approached the overshadowing tower and tilted his head back to marvel at another of Egypt's building feats. The shutters were opened on the top-floor window. "I wish your mistress would look down and see our approach," he whispered to the monkey. "It might help her feel more prepared for my arrival." He suddenly wondered whether he should have listened to Potiphera and allowed him to come along.

The door in the lower tower level opened, and four guards spilled out. "Welcome, Lord Paneah." They bowed and motioned him inside, where four more guards pointed toward circular stairs leading up the tower. Evidently, Potiphera had given them notice of his coming. Had he secretly prepared Asenath as well?

Suspicion stirred, but he forced a calm nod toward the guards, lest they misinterpret that his displeasure was aimed at them. Jendayi wasn't as polite and screeched as Joseph passed. "Shh, little one." He offered her a grape, and she calmed. *The one who holds the food* . . .

His heart was racing even before the climb up the circular stairs began. Who would think to carve a rock staircase into the curvature of the rounded tower wall? *Elohim, You make some minds more brilliant than others.*

"Potabi?" A frail voice, barely audible, echoed from above. Jendayi perked her ears and dropped the half-eaten grape.

"Shh." Joseph stroked the monkey's soft fur, calming himself and the monkey. A strange thought struck him. Why didn't Asenath call Potiphera *Abi*? Why add a portion of his first name before the familial relationship? He continued the climb, pondering their complex kinship.

With fewer than twenty steps to go, Jendayi leapt from his shoulder and scampered to the tower's top level. "Jendayi, my lovey!" Asenath's delighted welcome was quickly followed by "Zahra? Hotep?"

Joseph rushed up the final steps. "No, it's me, Asenath."

The woman leaning against the wall was not the woman he'd met eight days ago. She was wraith-like. No cosmetics. No jewelry. Dressed in a simple white linen robe, she wore nothing ornate except an embroidered belt. Her chamber had been stripped bare of all furnishings and comfort. Fury propelled Joseph toward his bride. "Asenath, what happened?"

She stumbled back, fear-filled eyes sunken and dark. "Don't come any closer!" Pale as the moon, she looked as if she might faint. He halted two steps away, close enough to catch her if needed, but didn't dare touch her otherwise.

Sunlight streamed in on her gaunt features. The sharp lines of her cheekbones were like jagged edges of broken pottery.

"Are you ill? I'll call Pharaoh's physician—"

"I'm not ill." She looked down at Jendayi, nestled in her arms.

The monkey suddenly jumped to Joseph's shoulder and began patting his arm, begging for more treats from the basket.

Asenath squelched a chuckle, her pallor brightening. "She likes you?"

"Don't be so surprised." Joseph smiled.

To his amazement, Asenath seemed calmer. "I might like you someday, too—*Joseph*."

Who was this friendly stranger? Wait . . . "Who told you my Hebrew name?"

"A messenger told me."

"Someone your abi sent?"

"No." She grinned.

"Someone from the palace?"

She shook her head.

"Did King Apophis contact you again?" Pharaoh and the queen would be furious.

"May we sit down? I feel—" She swayed.

Joseph lunged to catch her, and Jendayi jumped to the floor. He dropped the monkey's basket of food but caught Asenath. "Are you all right?"

Her eyes fluttered and then widened. "Put me down!" Her violent attempt to escape his touch nearly sent her to the tiles. They both landed on their knees, facing each other. Sweat beaded on her forehead. "A messenger visited me," she said, breathless.

"You said that."

"He was kind."

Joseph's chest ached. She'd obviously endured something traumatic. It had kept her from eating—perhaps even from drinking. Or had she been ill-treated? Her lips were cracked and swollen, her speech slurred. He sat cross-legged, hoping to put her at ease. "You can tell me what happened, Asenath. I won't be angry." At least, he'd attempt to save his anger for those who deserved it.

"At first, I thought the messenger was a dream," she whispered. "He said he'd come from the one god. The all-powerful creator. He told me your name was Joseph and that I'd bear your children." Her eyes fluttered, and she swayed again. Joseph caught her and this time lowered her to her side. He stretched out next to her, and Jendayi nestled between them.

The monkey was a welcome distraction as Asenath's words registered into understanding. *The one God. The all-powerful Creator.* Elohim had sent an angel to convince her of His faithfulness, as He'd done decades ago for Great-Savta Sarah; Hagar, Sarah's Egyptian maid; and Savta Rebekah. He marveled that Asenath had received the same mercy as the women in Great-Saba Abraham's recited histories. *But her story will never be told among our family.* Joseph could never return to Abba's camp to tell it.

Swallowing a sudden wave of grief, he rolled to his back. When Joseph obeyed Pharaoh and Elohim to marry this Egyptian high priestess, Ahira would be lost to him, and Jacob ben Isaac would disown him. Only a wife from the promised lineage was good enough for Prince Jacob's favored son. Joseph's brothers had been allowed to marry women from Shechem, but Abba had vowed that Joseph would have a wife from the household of Rachel and Leah—the daughters of Terah.

Joseph would marry Asenath and save Egypt, but he would lose Abba forever.

Joseph pressed the moisture from his eyes, determined to overcome regret. Elohim had done the impossible and proved His existence to the daughter of Ra's high priest. He should be filled with praise, awed at his Creator. *But letting go of Ahira feels like losing part of myself.* Who was he without the shepherd girl he'd known all his life? Who was he without the woman he'd discovered in Avaris's slave market on Potiphar's wedding day? Who was Joseph without the faithful partner who constantly recounted Elohim's promises during his years in prison? *Elohim, I know I'm to marry Asenath, but knowing it's right doesn't make it easy.*

"Joseph, you're crying." Asenath's voice was barely a whisper. "Is the thought of marrying me so repugnant?"

Her sudden trepidation shamed him. "No, Asenath." He sat up and wiped his face, determined to share the hope of Elohim's proof. "On the contrary. The mighty Creator gave your abi and me a dream—an *identical* dream—that you and I will be married."

"Potabi had the same dream?" Her eyes widened. "Did he accept the revelation, or will he try to change the will of the gods?"

"There is only one God." Then Joseph set aside his concern about her beliefs to reassure her. "Potiphera accepted the dream."

"What did you see in the dream?"

He'd hoped she wouldn't ask. "You and I stood on a shore together as my friends sailed toward us on the king's barque."

"Your friends were on the king's barque? Hebrew friends?"

"One was Hebrew. The others were Captain Potiphar and his ommi, Mistress Pushpa."

"You and I were together on a shore—where? Which port?" She searched his features, probing for more. "Was anyone else with us?"

"I don't know the location. My abba was with us."

"I'd like to meet your abba someday." She laughed awkwardly. "Did anyone *do* anything in this dream? Did they speak?"

A lie would have been so easy. "You spoke." Fighting to keep his features impassive, Joseph revealed the promise that broke his heart. "You said, 'Show Ahira our love is secure enough to welcome her home.'"

She paused a moment, then whispered, "Is Ahira the Hebrew friend you mentioned?"

"Yes."

She looked away, then struggled to sit up. Joseph reached out to help her. "Don't touch me!" she shouted.

Awkward silence fell between them.

"Was Potabi's dream *exactly* the same?" she asked quietly.

"Yes. This is Elohim's confirmation that we will have a loving marriage."

More silence.

Asenath watched him. "What makes you sure it's a confirmation we'll love each other? It sounds more like confirmation you still love this Ahira. Do you? Still love Ahira?"

"I do." He quickly added, "But if Elohim can prove to you He's the one true God, He can change my heart as well." Couldn't He?

"Jendayi, no!" Asenath tried to stand.

"I'll get her." Joseph dashed toward the window, realizing the little scamp had found something else to eat. "Jendayi, what— Is that honeycomb?"

When he bent to take it from her, she screeched and skittered away, knocking over a water pitcher and the wooden cup beside it. *A wooden cup for Potiphera's daughter?* Joseph picked up the cup and the simple pitcher. It was an exact match of the items used in Abba's camp—quite a paradox in the expansive chamber with a gold ceiling and gemstone-flecked walls. Had Potiphera purchased the items to taunt Asenath about her Hebrew groom? Quiet fury started to rise. Or had Potiphera nearly starved his daughter for some other reason?

Returning to his bride, Joseph showed her the cup and pitcher. "Why did your abi strip away your furnishings and give you a single pitcher and cup?"

"He didn't . . ." She appeared dazed, the skin beneath her eyes translucent, almost bruised. Her gray-toned complexion made him want to weep.

He threw the items aside and gently grasped her arms. "Asenath, little one, can you hear me?"

"I hear you." Her voice was weak, but she met his gaze and didn't pull away. "Potabi took away my furnishings because I refused to bear your children."

She must have been delirious. She hadn't refused to bear his children. In fact, she'd been despondent when Joseph had told her they'd be married in name alone. "Come. You must lie down." Then he'd call for a physician.

"I told Potabi I refused to lie with a Hebrew and produce a subspecies of non-Egyptian urchins." A slight grin curved her lips. "But the messenger brought the promise of our descendants when he gave me honeycomb and water," she said. "Potabi didn't give me that pitcher and cup. It was Ra's messenger."

Ra's messenger? "Asenath?" He braced her shoulders, feeling an ethereal stirring of confusion and awe. "This pitcher and cup are exactly like the ones my family uses." He wanted to shout, "It wasn't Ra!"

"Your family? But how . . ."

"You said the messenger came from Elohim, the one true God, the all-powerful Creator."

"Yes. To me, he's Ra. To you, he's Elohim. Potabi said all nations worship the same gods but call them different names. In ancient Mesopotamia, the creator is named Ea."

"I know, but—"

"Ra is the all-powerful creator, Joseph." She blinked, struggling to focus. "May I call you Joseph? You can call me Nathy."

He sighed. "Are you sure your 'messenger' wasn't a temple guard you didn't recognize from the complex below? A man who brought you honeycomb and water for the past eight days?" Perhaps that was Potiphera's punishment.

"The priests brought me three meals a day that I refused."

That was unexpected. "Why did you starve yourself?"

"I fasted to test Isis's healing power. I started healing Egypt myself by giving everything to the beggars—including all Potabi's hidden wealth. But Isis failed the test."

"How did you help beggars if you never left the tower?"

"I tossed everything out the south window. Gold. Silver. Gods. All of it." Her satisfied smile sent Joseph to the window, where a crowd of people expectantly waited below.

"Isis heal us!" they shouted. "Isis! Priestess!"

It seemed her relationship with Potiphera was as convoluted as Joseph's with his family. When he turned to probe further, his bride had tried to stand and reached for him. "Jos—"

"Asenath!" She went down hard, striking her head on the tiles. "Little one?" Joseph jostled her. No response. "Nathy!"

"Joseph?" Potiphera appeared at the top of the stairs. "The prophets said she hadn't eaten—"

"Get a physician!" Joseph shouted.

He approached slowly, horror twisting his features. "I didn't know, Nathy, my girl."

When he bent to kiss her, Joseph grabbed his collar. "If you want to help, get a physician and send up some broth—now!"

"Yes. Yes, I'll do it." Potiphera hurried toward the steps. "And I'll send the maids."

"I'll tend her."

The priest paused at the first step. "You can't—"

"Priest, I wear Pharaoh's ring," Joseph seethed. "Do as I command!"

Potiphera glared at him. "You wear Pharaoh Yanassi's ring, but Asenath has King Apophis's favor. Remember, only one god chose you as her husband." He started down the steps and shouted, "Asenath's maids will tend her, Lord Paneah!"

Joseph cradled his unconscious bride, willing her to live. "It doesn't matter what kings or priests or even our hearts decide or desire. Elohim said we're to be married." He laid her on her reed mat—the lone furnishing in the chamber—and Jendayi nestled against the bend of her neck. Joseph lay on his side next to them.

Potiphera would undoubtedly send the best physician, the two maids, and plenty of broth. Joseph would fight more battles with the headstrong priest, and Asenath would recover. Elohim wouldn't have sent a messenger and dreams if the matter wasn't final. Peace settled over him like a wool blanket in a Hebron pasture. He studied the woman who would soon become his wife, asking thoughts of Ahira to step aside and allow room for this woman. If Elohim had chosen her, He could prepare Joseph's heart for her.

Something stirred within. It became clear that Joseph's love would be a conscious choice. He must choose every day to believe Asenath was Elohim's will for him.

Pillowing his arm beneath his head, he reached over to brush a few hairs from her cheek. This woman would need a patient and gentle husband, a man who made few demands. A man who sought to understand her past and how it shaped her present. "I will be that man, Elohim."

She stirred, blinked rapidly, gasped—then calmed when she turned her head and saw him. "I was afraid you'd left me."

"I won't leave you." He inhaled a fortifying breath as she closed her eyes again. Somehow, they'd clarify the truth about Elohim—but later, after her body and their bond were stronger. Why rush? They would have a lifetime together.

TEN

Joseph was thirty years old when he entered the
service of Pharaoh king of Egypt.
GENESIS 41:46

NEXT MORNING
Asenath

I woke to the foreign sound of a man's soft snoring. A slow smile greeted my day before I opened my eyes. Zahra and Hotep lay on my left and right, still sound asleep—and silent. I propped myself on an elbow and peered over Hotep, finding Joseph curled up on a tapestry by the window. Jendayi was already awake. Huddled beneath another window, she was licking at remnants of honeycomb that remained on the tiles.

I relaxed onto my back and stared at the ceiling. The one god sent a messenger to *me*. My breath caught, remembering his size, the light that shone around him, emanated from within. Why was he sent to me? Why not send Ra's messenger to Potabi, his own high priest? I served Isis. Perhaps he'd come because I asked the gods for proof. But how many pilgrims had begged for proof yet never received a visitation?

Movement near the window drew my attention, and Joseph was

suddenly kneeling near my head. "How do you feel this morning, little one?"

I drew a tapestry around me like a blanket and sat up. "Yesterday's abundance of bone broth restored my strength, but if I never ate another bowl, it would be too soon."

He chuckled, waking my maids. They straightened their skewed wigs and wiped at smeared cosmetics. Self-conscious with a handsome man in our tower, they were determined to hide their shaved heads beneath their lovely wigs. Truth be told, I'd never been happier than at this moment that Potabi had insisted I maintain my natural hair.

Joseph stood, walked a few paces away, and then stretched his bronzed, sinewy arms to the ceiling. "You're young, Asenath. Your body will heal quickly."

My maids looked away. I stared, openly curious, at the man who would be mine.

"I'm thirty years old now, and this body feels the difference between sleeping on a soft mattress and faience tiles." He caught me staring and grinned. "May I ask how old you are?"

Though my cheeks flushed, I didn't look away. After a full day of his tender care, he'd earned a measure of trust—and even a little mischief. "Lord Vizier, isn't it rude to ask a woman her age?"

"We've seen nineteen Inundations," Zahra answered for me.

Joseph's brows shot up. "Potiphera told me you three were born on the same night."

What else had Potabi told him about me?

"Under the sign of Isis," Hotep added. Even my cautious sister trusted the Hebrew who'd stooped low enough to feed me broth.

"Each of you is quite remarkable. Now, if you'll excuse me for a moment . . ." He retreated to the private chamber where Zahra and Hotep had placed the waste pot. The only times Joseph and I had been separated since he'd climbed my tower stairs yesterday was when either of us needed to care for our personal needs.

Zahra rushed over the moment he left. "He's the most stunning man I've ever seen," she whispered.

"He's a Hyksos!" Hotep protested.

Zahra waved away the objection. "He's kind and gentle, and he'll be a wonderful abi to your children."

You will bear his children and partake of an ancient promise. The messenger's words echoed in Asenath's mind. What ancient promise had Ra made that their children would fulfill? And if Ra favored Joseph—a Hyksos—must she and Potabi now bow to the will of Hyksos kings?

ELEVEN

Stern discipline awaits anyone who leaves the path;
the one who hates correction will die.

PROVERBS: 15:10

Potiphera

Potiphera raised his hand in farewell to Zaphenath-Paneah and four of Ra's most loyal prophets. The four priests aboard the king's barque would sail with Asenath's groom to Avaris and replace Potiphera's current palace spies. Unbeknownst to Egypt's vizier, one of the priests on his boat carried a message to Pharaoh Yanassi, reporting Paneah's indecent behavior with the virgin high priest of Isis. He'd remained the only man in the tower with Asenath and her two maids for the past two days and denied Potiphera any privacy with his own daughter. Zahra and Hotep had seen to Asenath's personal hygiene.

Still, Egypt's vizier should never compromise the purity of a priestess nor stoop to the mundane tasks of tending the sick or weak. Never had there been a man so hungry for both power and affection. He'd revealed the weaknesses that would prove his downfall.

"Shall I alert the others yet, Highness?" Potiphera's steward anxiously waited on the dock beside him.

"Not until Lord Paneah moves to the bow of the barque."

When the vizier left the stern and ventured toward Pharaoh's couches, Potiphera initiated his second step toward unifying the Two Lands. "All right, bring the other prophets while I speak with the captain who will take them to King Apophis."

His steward hurried away as an oily-looking man approached Potiphera. The experienced seaman was eager to earn a little silver and sail in the opposite direction of the vizier's barque. "Good morning, Highness." The captain offered a quick bow.

Potiphar sprinkled a few ashes over his shoulder and began his instructions. "When you arrive at King Apophis's camp in Edfu, you're to explain to his guards that you've brought four priests of Ra as a gift from Potiphera, the high priest of On, the same gift given to Co-Regent Yanassi. You must repeat this message exactly as I am telling you: 'These priests have been sent to you, King Apophis— Great Son of Ra, Divine of Birth, Healer of the Two Lands—to make daily sacrifices in order that Ra will show his favor and secure for you the most beautiful woman in Egypt as your wife.' Will you remember?"

"Ya, ya."

"*Exactly* as I said—is that understood?"

"Yes!" He opened his palm. "Four priests. Same gift to Co-Regent Yanassi. Daily sacrifices. Win Ra's favor to get the most beautiful wife." He mumbled, "I'd say I was a purple crocodile for the silver you're paying."

"Take three extra, Captain." Potiphera counted out the silver pieces into his outstretched hand. "Buy something nice for your wife and children."

The man cradled Potiphera's hand and kissed the scarab ring on his index finger. "May Ra smile on your descendants, Highness."

The steward arrived with four more prophets, all breathless from their hurried journey from the villa. Potiphera removed a small scroll from his belt and handed it to the priest he'd known the longest, the man who'd brought him and the girls from Memphis to

On fifteen years ago. "I'm trusting you to place this message in King Apophis's hand. No one else must see it, Tau. Understand?"

"I won't fail you, Highness." Tau scurried onto the boat with the other three spies, the captain, and the eight oarsmen who would row against the tide to the Edfu Fortress. These priests would likely receive a warmer welcome in Edfu than those who went to Avaris. King Apophis had, at least, incorporated Ra into his throne name— Apophis Nebkhepeshre, Ra is Lord of Strength—and he'd clearly identified himself as Ra's son in his marriage proposal to Asenath.

Why hadn't Ra given the dreams of feast and famine to Apophis? Why reveal the future to a Hyksos pharaoh who adopted Seth as his patron god—and then give the interpretation to a Hebrew? Ah, but who was he to question? The gods seldom made sense to human minds.

As Potiphera watched the oarsmen straining against the current, he wondered if his message to Apophis was straining against the gods' current. In the scroll Tau carried, he'd confided his disappointment that King Apophis—Ra's bright son—would not be united to Asenath, the daughter of Isis. And he'd added a vow that could prove dangerous: "Know that I am not only Ra's loyal servant but yours as well."

Had he overstepped? Would Apophis see his offer of Asenath in marriage and Potiphera's loyalty as the sedition he himself felt to the marrow of his bones? Hopefully not. Potiphera raised his face to the unforgiving sun. *Great and almighty Ra, let my unrest plant a seed in King Apophis that grows into rebellion against his Hyksos nephew.*

Ra's heat encouraged him to take shelter in his palanquin. A moment later, his slaves had started toward the villa. Now that the Hebrew was gone, he'd visit the tower and calm Asenath—whom he imagined was either hysterical at Paneah's forced visitation or entirely deceived by his charm. When Paneah had first arrived in On, she'd cast aside her training and become overly emotional. *Refusing to bear Paneah's children, indeed.* Of course, it was the right decision, but to make it without Potiphera's approval was unacceptable.

Oh, Katesch, I hope you didn't see our daughter's tantrum. She'll make us proud—eventually. The familiar ache came, as it always did when he yearned for his lovely wife to offer their daughter an ommi's advice. Would the longing for her ever end? Katesch was the only woman he'd ever loved. *Can you hear me from the underworld, my love?* Had she made it safely to her resting place—or had Potiphera's cowardice sent her akh wandering? *What sort of husband hides beneath an altar while his wife is brutally murdered?*

One of his slaves pulled back the palanquin curtain. "Highness? Are you well?"

When had they stopped and lowered him to the ground? "I'm fine. Fine." Potiphera scooted out and rushed toward the residence, bypassing a bevy of prophets clamoring for his attention. "I must check on my daughter." He entered the tower door and paused at the bottom of the stairs. How would he make the climb when he was already winded?

Voices wafted from above him. Quieter than usual. Indecipherable. His daughter and her maids lacked the joyful tittering of women's gossip or serious tone of reciting lessons. His chest ached. *Am I losing my little girl?* He'd worked too hard all these years, preparing her for greatness, to now surrender her to a charming Hebrew. Had Paneah stolen her allegiance so quickly?

With a determined sigh, he started up the stairs. Offering Asenath gold or jewelry wouldn't sway her. She'd already tossed her wealth—and some of his—out her window. A grin came unbidden. Isis was waking within her, demanding she heal the hurting and hungry. How could he begrudge his daughter's zeal? But, to maintain control, he must remind her of Katesch's words—their shared destiny—and bridle her independence with what she held most dear.

Being a parent was no different than being a high priest. When prophets obeyed, he rewarded them handsomely. When they disobeyed, the sting of discipline righted their path.

The voices above stilled. They'd undoubtedly heard his footsteps and labored breaths.

"Highness?" Zahra called.

"Yes . . . I'm . . . coming . . . up." Hopefully, they'd have honeyed water for him.

After the examining physician reported that Asenath had merely sustained a nasty bump to the head—and would recover with rest and proper nourishment—Potiphera had allowed her maids to return to the tower. Within moments, they'd reappeared, saying Paneah demanded the high priest replace the tower furnishings. Potiphera had sent the girls back up with as many pillows as they could carry and a message explaining there was no need to furnish a chamber that would soon be empty. Paneah then sent two guards to gather rugs and a tapestry from his own guest chamber. The stubborn Hebrew had remained in the tower until he met Potiphera this morning at the quay.

"The physician said Asenath could travel to Avaris tomorrow," Paneah had said. "I already sent a message to Pharaoh Yanassi that you and my bride will arrive by midday tomorrow for an evening wedding banquet." He'd nodded a curt goodbye and boarded the king's barque.

Potiphera paused to rest on the tower stairs, the memory stoking his fury. "Good riddance," he seethed. With a few more steps to climb, he leaned heavily on the rail. Putting his daughter in a tower had definitely kept her safe from old, fat men. But it hadn't kept her safe from the one man who'd proven most dangerous to his plans for her future.

Steadying his breathing, he scanned his daughter's stark chamber. The changes sobered him. The opulent gold ceiling and gem-studded walls overlooked three huddled figures gathered around the simple altar he'd provided before his eight-day tour. A single tapestry wrapped each chantress, and individual pillows separated them from the chilly faience floor tiles. *They aren't little girls anymore, Potiphera.*

The monkey screeched at his appearance and peeked out from Asenath's wrap. None of the others greeted him. Potiphera's face flushed from more than exertion. But why should he feel ashamed?

Squaring his shoulders, he said through clenched teeth, "I will speak with my daughter alone. Get out."

Hotep stood immediately, but Zahra scooted closer to Asenath. "She's still weak, Highness. May I stay to help—"

"I said go! And take that monkey!"

The creature screeched when Hotep took her from Asenath.

Both maids scurried away without a bow or any sign of respect. Had Paneah's presence ruined the maids' training, too? Potiphera huffed and waited until the adjoining chamber's door clicked shut. Asenath kept her head down.

"Look at me," Potiphera snapped. When he saw her haunted eyes, frustration drowned in concern. Was it the crimson tapestry around her shoulders that made her appear lifeless? "How do you feel, Daughter?"

"Much stronger this morning." She forced a smile. Her dry lips cracked and bled, so she looked away again. "Did Joseph tell you I had a visitor the morning you returned?"

"A visitor?" Silent warnings roused his temper, but he worked to control it. "Surely, the guards didn't—"

"It was a messenger from Ra." Meeting his eyes, she didn't appear delirious.

"He brought me honeycomb and water to strengthen me for Joseph's return and—"

"You will call him Zaphenath-Paneah, his Egyptian name."

She smiled—more like a sneer—and he nearly slapped away the condescension.

"Ra's messenger told me Joseph's Hebrew name to prove it had been a divine visitation. It should be proof for you, Potabi, if you'll accept it. Joseph and I also decided—"

"Joseph and you decided?" Potiphera scoffed. "You don't decide anything without me, Asenath."

Her features remained pleasant—and hard as granite. "*Joseph* and I decided we would use our familiar names in private, but I'll call him *Paneah* in public." A little color filled her cheeks.

"By the gods! You've given your heart to him!" He couldn't fathom it, and she didn't deny it. He longed for Katesch's wisdom now more than ever. "He's Hyksos. Because of him and his clans, your ommi isn't here to guide you, so you must listen to *me*." Forcing calm, he knelt beside her. "We have one day to prepare you for the sail to Avaris and wedding ceremony tomorrow evening. You'll stand before Pharaoh Yanassi and sign a binding wedding contract. This marriage will consummate your role as Isis's high priestess but will *not* transform you into the goddess incarnate—the Great Ommi of Egypt. Since your singular calling is to marry an Egyptian king who can fulfill your destiny, we'll find a way to release you from this so-called marriage."

"I've already begun healing Egypt by sharing the treasure we don't need."

"How much treasure *do* we need?" He met her defiant whims with reality. "How carefully did you study the temple ledgers before you tossed all that gold and silver to On's beggars? Did you consider the expenses of maintenance, supplies, offerings, and meals for the temple servants? Do you know how many were killed in the last week because of the rampant greed among those who had no idea how to manage sudden wealth?"

"I simply . . ." Her color waned. "Summer harvest generates On's greatest profit. Won't the temple be able to replenish—"

"And summer is the season of our greatest expense. We pay harvesters a fair wage, house, and feed them. Admit it, Asenath. Distributing my treasure and starving yourself was an emotional tantrum because I disciplined you for the disrespectful way you spoke to me." His eyes narrowed, daring her. "How could the high priestess of Isis let her emotions so completely disarm her?"

"I've told you plainly, Highness." She raised her chin. "I knew Egypt's wounds needed immediate attention, so I dispersed your *personal* treasure as the first act of healing. If you'll show me the temple ledgers, I'm more than capable of helping you make the other decisions you mentioned." Her pallor had turned rosy, and her stony features remained. Her shoulders squared and her spine straightened. She had the regal bearing of a queen—but would marry a filthy Hebrew.

In less than two days, Zaphenath-Paneah had ruined fifteen years of careful training. White-hot fury simmered beneath Potiphera's own calm demeanor. He'd hoped to gently guide Asenath back to the loyal, compliant daughter she'd been, but clearly harsher measures were needed to restore his control and her focus. *Katesch, forgive me.*

"I have been angry with you before," he said tenderly, "but I've never been disappointed in you."

She winced. *Good.* She still valued his opinion.

He stood and moved toward the window. "Tomorrow, I'll send temple guards to escort you to the quay. Zahra and Hotep must remain here to continue their duties as chantresses, so only you and I will travel to Avaris. I'll choose relatively handsome sailors for our felucca. They'll set sail and let wind and current carry us. Then I'll give them permission to acquaint you with a man's touch so you won't embarrass yourself on the wedding night."

"Potabi, no." She crawled to his feet, sobbed, and wrapped his ankles. "Please, no more punishment. I'm sorry I shared your treasure."

He coaxed her to release him and to stand. "It's not about the treasure, my girl. It's about the speed with which the Hebrew turned you against me."

"But I'm not against you."

He raised his hand for silence. "You interrupted me, yet another sign you've allowed emotion to control you." *Instead of my careful training.* "Immediately after your wedding night, Zaphenath-Paneah will begin his tour of the Two Lands. Most men would leave their wives behind. The Hebrew has decided to take you with him."

"He mentioned last night that I'd accompany him on the tour." Her features brightened. "The messenger of Ra promised I would bear Joseph's children."

No wonder Paneah had so quickly charmed her. "I thought you

wanted to spare the world some subspecies of non-Egyptian urchins." He could barely repeat her witty defiance without grinning. At least when she'd said it, she still recognized Paneah as the enemy.

"Joseph said—"

"Asenath, you will call him *Paneah.*"

She bowed her head. "Yes, Potabi. Paneah said that Ra gave you and him the same dream—one in which a loving marriage is affirmed—and you accepted the dream as affirmation from the gods. I, too, received affirmation in the visit from Ra's messenger. He said I'd bear Joseph's children." She wore a tentative smile. "How can I refuse the gods, Potabi—even if I must bear non-Egyptian brats?"

His chest ached. Asenath's first beloved toy had been a cloth doll swaddled like a baby—from Katesch. She'd always wanted children of her own, and the Great Ommi of Egypt demanded it of her. He stared into the pleading eyes of the little girl he'd loved since the moment he glimpsed her at Katesch's breast. "If the Hebrew gives you a baby, he'll take you and the child away from me." There. His fear exposed.

"Potabi, no!" She hugged him fiercely. "Never!"

Awkward at first, he patted her back. It had been a long time since they'd embraced. But she held on, and his defenses fell. "I love you," he whispered. "You must know that."

"I know," she whispered, "and I love you."

He knew, but the facts remained. If she bore children with the Hebrew, divorce would be messy and marriage to a king nearly impossible. Gently, he helped her sit on a cushion. She was trembling from head to toe, still very weak. Regardless, he needed to ensure Paneah couldn't steal her away.

He knelt on one knee, above her in authority, yet speaking softly to show compassion. "I've raised an intelligent young woman. My intention in asking you the coming question isn't to manipulate you but to remind you of truth." Of course, he would also manipulate the truth, but it was for her own welfare, their shared future, and the future of Egypt. "Paneah is a driven man. I watched him work all day and night for eight days because he aims to please Pharaoh Yanassi."

She nodded. "Isn't that a good thing?"

"It's a very good thing." He watched the expected smile bloom on her pale features and then delivered the sour news. "What will you do when your husband leaves you to meet with governors and work on granaries?" He waited, watching as his daughter considered her answer carefully.

"I would go with my husband as the Healer of Egypt."

He let a pregnant pause prepare her for the blow. "You disappoint me. My intelligent daughter would recognize that Egypt's nobility will more likely obey a Hebrew vizier who is accompanied by a well-connected Egyptian official, not merely his wife. Your emotions have blinded you, causing you to hope instead of think."

She remained silent until he nodded, giving her permission to speak. "Hasn't Queen Tani and the young pharaoh already assigned you to accompany Paneah on his tour of Egypt? Why torment me about going along? Do you want Joseph all to yourself?"

Rebellion tinged her tone with mocking and proved his work wasn't yet done. "Perhaps I'll return to On after the wedding and you'll be completely alone again—this time because your husband has no time for you. You'll have no maids. No Jendayi. And a barque full of soldiers and sailors to make sure you don't get lonely while your husband stays away for days."

"Joseph would make sure I was safe." She said the words, but fear glistened in her eyes.

"What if I no longer protect Zahra and Hotep at On's temple?" He let the question hang between them—then added, "And Jendayi. Poor little thing is so wily. What if she wandered away from them, got too close to the Nile, and became a crocodile snack?"

The reality of his threats settled on Asenath's features. "Tell me what you want, Potabi." She bent to kiss his feet.

By the gods, if only Apophis would kill Yanassi and Paneah and take Asenath as his wife! But he dared not speak it aloud nor let sympathy conquer wisdom. "I want to change the will of the gods," he said finally. Asenath's startled look fueled his determination. "I watched Paneah use his charm and intelligence to win the people of our nome. He used the same favor of the gods to steal your devotion, and if we don't stop him, he'll overtake Upper Egypt as well. The gods are for him, but we can't allow a Hyksos to rule a united Egypt." He helped his daughter to her feet and braced her shoulders. "Paneah knows I'm set against him, and he'll try to keep me from accompanying him on the tour of the Two Lands. You must insist I come along. Together, we will find a way to stop this Hyksos who has charmed our gods."

She gazed at him, panicked and pleading, like a doe in a hunter's bow sight. He showed no weakness. No hesitation or remorse. He recognized the moment of surrender—like the doe with the glint of the arrow in its eye, the moment before the piercing. "I'll do whatever you ask of me, Potabi." All emotion gone, she was his once more.

"Remember this moment," he said, grasping her chin, forcing her to meet his gaze. "The next time *Joseph* wishes to decide something without my approval, remind him you were my daughter before you became his wife." He released her, and the sound of her quiet weeping crawled up his arms like an army of fire ants. He had to escape. On his way to the stairs, he called over his shoulder, "Take courage, my girl. You must endure the Hebrew for a time, but you'll always be my daughter."

TWELVE

*The LORD was with Joseph and gave him success
in whatever he did.*

GENESIS 39:23

Asenath

Since I'd lived secluded in a tower, I'd said very few goodbyes.
Ommi left me without one. Watching Potabi leave for Avaris was
always painful. My chest had ached yesterday when I watched
Joseph sail from On's quay. Today, I stood with my sister-maids,
certain our goodbye would shatter me.

We tightened our embrace, with Jendayi cradled between us.
"You must write to us every day." Zahra's tearful demand was impossible, of course.

"I'll try."

"Jendayi will be fine," Hotep promised. "I'll spoil her like you
do." We tried to laugh but it came out as sobs.

"Enough!" Potabi shouted. "Ra has already sailed above the eastern horizon." Jendayi screeched, signaling his approach, but I
couldn't see anything through the opaque veil he insisted I wear.

Hotep pulled a squealing Jendayi from my arms, and the three
who'd been my life and breath moved away. Potabi gripped my arm

and guided me. Head down, I saw the sandy shore beneath my sandaled feet, my world now limited to the diameter of my veil. We marched up a wooden plank to board the ornate barque I'd seen from the tower window this morning.

"You'll sit and remain here for the journey," Potabi said, forcing me onto a cushioned seat. "Because you've agreed to obey me, you'll be safe. The veil is for your peace and protection. You won't see the men around you, and they won't be tempted by your beauty."

At least he'd protect me. "Thank you." Since the day Potabi had returned from Avaris, he'd displayed a part of himself he'd never revealed before. When I was young, he'd been a demanding teacher but also my savior and loving abi. Though his demands grew with my training and duties as high priestess, I'd never experienced his cruelty until he began his search for a husband to fulfill my destiny. That's when he stopped hiding his manipulation and I started to suspect the search was as much to advance his position as mine. But I never realized I'd always be his captive—even after he released me from the tower. Although no longer imprisoned above people and priests, I was forever entrapped by my own fear and his threats.

I leaned back, feeling the sun's harsh rays beating down. "Potabi?" I ventured quietly.

"Yes, Asenath." He sounded distracted.

"Is there no shelter? Perhaps a covered area—"

"You must learn to face adversity and conquer it, my girl. A little discomfort will ensure you'll happily leave the barque despite the large crowd waiting at the Avaris quay."

It would also ensure I'd vomit on my groom. My veil, intended as protection, intensified the heat. "May I remove the veil while we pass deserted shorelines?" I begged.

He patted my hand while crushing my hope. "The mystery of your appearance will ensure the warmest welcome at the capital."

I didn't dare argue. Instead, I leaned back, feeling every rise and jolt of the Nile's rushing current. My hands gripped the sides of the couch. I hadn't entrusted myself to Hapi, the Nile god, since that awful night when I was four years old. My stomach churned with every sway. I tried to rest, but sailors' bawdy songs about crocodiles, women, and death clashed with the sacred chants I tried reciting.

"Potabi, get a bowl!" But it was too late. I doused the deck and his left foot with the scant remains of the few dates I'd eaten before leaving the tower at dawn. I was too sick to care about his anger. Perhaps I'd die before we reached Avaris and I wouldn't have to face the crowd. Potabi had kept our temple grounds cleared for me, but there would be no such consideration when the vizier's bride arrived for the wedding celebration. According to Potabi, Queen Tani had planned an event to rival her own wedding.

The sound of a trumpet in the distance brought both relief and sheer terror.

"We're almost there." The excitement in Potabi's voice was palpable. "You must drink a little honeyed wine to freshen your breath." He maneuvered a wineskin under my veil.

I took a drink and choked as the boat slammed into the dock.

"Drink, Asenath! You need strength for the walk to the palace."

I swallowed another long draw. Perhaps the wine would calm my nerves—or make me forget them altogether.

"That's enough." Potabi took it and leaned close. "Paneah is coming for you." He grabbed me by the arm to stand, his grip like a vise. I nearly cried out.

"Let me help."

Joseph. The sound of his voice caused a stirring inside—not nausea like the sail, but more like butterflies' wings.

"Are you strong enough to walk?" he asked quietly. I felt the warmth of his breath against my cheek through the veil.

"Potabi wants me to—"

"She's much improved, Lord Vizier," Potabi interrupted. "Let her greet the people she's destined to serve."

A strong arm circled my waist, supporting me against a body as mighty as my tower and smelling of cloves and mint. "She'll serve the people after she's healthy enough to do so, *Highness.* Until then, my bride will receive care from more compassionate healers."

Unable to stop a grin, I was grateful for my veil. When Joseph hoisted me from the dock to Avaris's sandstone-tiled street, I felt weightless. A great cheer rose. I covered one ear and pressed the other against Joseph's side to muffle the racket.

"Are you all right?" Joseph shouted over the noise.

"She's fine!" Potabi shouted back. "Allow the people to greet Isis Incarnate, Lord Vizier." Joseph's arm tensed around me. "Asenath." Potabi's voice was quieter, close now. "Remember what *improvements* we made together yesterday. Tell the vizier you're fine." The subtle reminder of his threat was louder than the chaos.

"Potabi is right." I swallowed disappointment when Joseph's hand fell from my waist. "You'll see how much stronger I am when we stand before Pharaoh and sign our wedding contract."

"Very well." Joseph's tone was taut. "Queen Tani waits for you in the harem to prepare you for the wedding." He placed his hand at the small of my back and with gentle pressure guided me across sandstone tiles. The roar of the crowd became muffled when we walked through a darkened, cooler space. "Where are we?" I asked.

"We've passed through the temple complex gate."

The sun greeted us when we emerged on the other side, as did renewed shouts of welcome and jubilation. I focused on three pairs of jeweled sandals: mine in the middle, Joseph's on my right, and Potabi's keeping pace on the left. The tiles beneath our feet in the temple complex were faience artistry, unlike anything I'd seen— even in Potabi's elegant villa.

The sound of splashing drew my attention. "Does the Nile run through the palace complex?"

"No." Joseph laughed, the sound more refreshing than the splashing. "We're passing Pharaoh's central fountain. It's like a giant pond that separates the palace from our home, the vizier's villa."

Our home. A thrill rushed through me. Then we were suddenly climbing an expansive stairway, wider than my veil could reveal. Though I'd told the truth about feeling much improved, my legs were now shaking, still weak from my ordeal. "How much farther, Joseph?"

"Almost there." He slipped his arms around my waist and lifted my feet off the ground as he continued the hurried pace. Did we appear to the crowd as silly as I felt? But I was too weary to complain. He conquered the final steps across an intricate marble mosaic amid the muffled roar of an indoor crowd.

"Lord Vizier." Two unfamiliar voices offered respectful greetings.

"Is Hodari in the king's residence hall?" Joseph asked.

"He's waiting to escort your bride at the harem entrance."

I wriggled from his grasp. "Let me try to walk."

I heard the familiar sound of Potabi's labored breathing and saw his jeweled sandals appear beside mine. "Lord Vizier, you can't simply take my daughter and—"

"Yes, Potiphera, I can." Joseph's tone was kind but firm. "The mystery of Asenath's beauty stirred unhealthy curiosity amid an unpredictable crowd. You suggested your daughter greet the people, but I chose to bring her immediately into the safety of the palace where Queen Tani is waiting for Asenath in the harem."

"You could have explained why you—"

"There was no time for conversation," Joseph said. "You may say goodbye to your daughter here, Highness."

"Why can't Potabi stay with me?" My words slipped out on an exhausted plea. I'd never met the queen.

"Only Pharaoh and I are allowed to enter the harem, little one. I'll introduce you to Hodari, Pharaoh Yanassi's captain of the guard, and he'll escort you to Queen Tani." Joseph's hand cradled mine. "Hodari is a Medjay who looks big and terrifying, but my captain, Hami, is even bigger and more terrifying. Hami will protect you as Hodari protects the queen, so we're all safe in the Medjays' care."

Wine churned in my belly. I swallowed hard and submitted to Joseph's slight tug.

"I'll see you at the ceremony," Potabi called out behind me.

Fear robbed my voice, and my body trembled as the vizier led me away from the noise. Within moments, I heard only the echo of our sandals in the silence. My hand grew sweaty in his grasp.

"Queen Tani has been looking forward to meeting you," he said. "You need not be nervous."

Nervous? I would have scoffed if I could have uttered a sound. How could anyone know what I felt? *Alone.* The word screamed inside me. My tower, my maids, Jendayi—even Potabi—had been my shields. Without them I was worse than alone . . . *I'm exposed.*

Joseph halted. "Hodari," he murmured, "take good care of my bride."

He transferred my hand to a dark black hand, waiting palm down. "You are safe with me, Priestess." I felt the rumble of Hodari's voice in my chest. I followed him a few steps before I heard a loud knock—metal on wood.

"Come. Come!" A woman's excited voice spurred our march. We crossed a gilded threshold, and my escort halted two steps inside. "You may leave us, Hodari." It must have been the queen.

The queen! I swayed.

"She appears somewhat unstable, my queen."

"So she does." My cheeks burned at the humor in her voice. Strong arms whisked me to a cushioned couch. "Now you may leave us, Hodari."

Silence magnified the sound of the door's latch falling into place. Then I heard the scuff of sandals approaching. "Are you strong enough to remove your veil, most beautiful Asenath, or should I help?"

I took a breath to clear my head. "Thank you, Queen Tani, but I can—" What if I removed the veil and wasn't *most beautiful Asenath*? "Perhaps I should leave the veil on. Potabi is known to exaggerate, and after all this fuss, I could be a grave disappointment."

The sound of her laughter was soothing balm, infusing me with courage. I slowly removed the heavy cloth while protecting the intricate braids Zahra and Hotep had worked so hard to perfect. I was mortified when her laughter faded to silence. "Forgive me, my queen. I chose to forego cosmetics, certain the heat would melt away kohl and other paints. I should have—"

"Potiphera did not exaggerate." She tipped up my chin, and I met her approving smile. "Your hair alone will make Egypt's noble-women claw at their mirrors tomorrow morning." Frowning, she touched the fragile skin beneath my eyes. "The shadows here affirm Paneah's report that you and your abi had a—" She raised a perfectly drawn eyebrow. "A difference of opinion?"

What else had Joseph told her? I looked away, fearing anything I said could risk the safety of those I'd left behind. "It wasn't Potabi's fault. I was stubborn and—"

"It's difficult for a parent when your child declares independence." She stepped away to look out her window at a beautiful view of a courtyard overlooking the Nile. The queen drew a breath, as if to speak, but shook her head.

"Have I offended you, my queen?"

She faced me, melancholy darkening her countenance. "I've crossed political swords with many counselors before my husband's death and after. To most, I talk in riddles, but to you I will speak plainly. Trust Paneah over anyone else. Before his unjust imprisonment, I knew him as a faithful servant of my husband's friend Potiphar. Since my son appointed him vizier, I've worked with him closely and discovered he's honest to a fault and speaks with wisdom from the gods." She ducked her head, cheeks flushing. "If anyone were listening, they might think I'd succumbed to his overwhelming good looks."

"Have you?" I asked without thinking.

She grinned at me, though her eyes misted. "No, my dear. I still ache for Khyan, and Joseph is too loyal for such antics. Before he vowed to marry you, there was another. Now there is you alone."

Her gaze was so intent, I looked away. "He sounds *too* perfect."

"I've found one flaw in our new vizier." Her tone had grown serious. "Paneah refutes the existence of Egypt's gods and trusts none but the ancient god of his ancestors. How will Isis Incarnate heal Egypt when her husband demands loyalty to his god?"

Feeling stronger, I left my couch to face her. This woman had honored me with honesty and questions of substance. I would honor her with the portions of truth that wouldn't endanger my friends. "Since I was a child, Potabi has taught me about the deities of all nations. The ancient gods of Sumer spread to Akkad, Syria, Egypt, and beyond. We share the same gods but gave them different names as legends and nations evolved. Joseph's Elohim is simply Ra by another name, and I'm inclined to agree there's one real god."

The queen appeared skeptical.

"Potabi and Joseph are both right. Ra sent his messenger to me directly."

The queen's features softened into a placating smile as she took my hand and led me to her cosmetics couch. She sat on the stool and helped me lie back. "Listen well, little Asenath. Zaphenath-Paneah does not serve Ra, and Potiphera will say anything to control you." She leaned over me, her kohl-lined eyes a handbreadth from my face. "Trust no one except your husband, for he alone can protect you in this world of hungry lions—no matter which god he serves."

Was she threatening me? Helping me? Why was she telling me not to trust Potabi?

"Let's make you look like a bride." She straightened and clapped her hands, and a line of maids entered with armloads of robes, jewelry, lotions, and wigs. "Well, we won't need the wigs." She chuckled as if our past conversation hadn't happened. "Your hair is exquisite. How do you keep the lice out of it?"

"My maids treat my scalp daily with a special solution."

The queen snapped her fingers, and a servant appeared with a papyrus, reed, and pigments. "If you're willing to share, my scribe will take notes."

The shock on my face must have been humorous because she burst out laughing and even apologized. "After living in the palace for so many years, I suppose I've grown accustomed to recording even the smallest of details. But if kings record what they ate to break their fast, surely queens should record the remedy for lice!"

We laughed together, and I ensured her scribe recorded the exact proportions of vinegar and water with cinnamon, rosemary, and terebinth oils. Queen Tani relinquished the stool to one of the maids, who primped and painted me while the queen filled me with beauty secrets, wine, and bread. Night had fallen when I finally stood before her, refreshed in body and ka.

"You are stunning." She traced the curve of my jaw, her thoughts much farther away. "I'd celebrated twenty Inundations when my abi gave me to Khyan as a war prize."

Her comment drained my joy, and I stepped away from her touch. Looking at my hands, I nervously spun the borrowed rings she'd placed on my fingers.

"Leave us," the queen ordered her maids.

I blinked fast to stave off tears.

The latch clicked, and the queen spoke again. "When Memphis was still Egypt's capital, my abi was Pharaoh Monthhotep's vizier. I remember growing up in the opulent palace, playing with the king's daughters in the harem. Every day, my ommi took me to Ra's temple to hear the exquisite voice of the famed chantress, Katesch."

I gasped at my ommi's name and met the queen's expectant eyes. "Yes, I know your story, Asenath. You have your ommi's beauty, and from the reports I've heard of On's chantresses, you have her talent for song as well."

"Thank you, my queen."

"My abi was the Egyptian vizier who betrayed the Egyptian pharaoh and put the first Amu king on Lower Egypt's throne. I was the prize for the new pharaoh's grandson."

Amu king. Why not call them Hyksos—foreign rulers—that they are? Anger stirred hot in my belly. "Why are you telling me—"

"Women have few choices in political games. We must use our wits and instincts to protect those we love."

Nodding, I said cautiously, "You were forced to marry a Hyksos, but now—"

"Don't *ever* use that term again." Her offense was immediate and intense. "I adored my husband—" Her voice broke. She turned her back to me. I waited in silence, wondering if I'd made a critical error. When the queen faced me again, her regal bearing was set like stone. "You've been taught to distrust the Amu and the way they came to power, but there are good men among them—as there are bad men among our Egyptian race. My abi was a betrayer, who sold his ka and his daughter to gain wealth and more power. But Pharaoh Khyan was the greatest king to rule Egypt since Amenemhat-Nimaatra—that is, until our son, Pharaoh Yanassi." She grinned like the proud ommi she was. "And it's time for you to meet him."

Without giving time for a reply, she reached for a bronze bell. An immediate knock followed. "Come!" Her powerful word brought an equally powerful guard through her door.

A large dark-skinned man filled the doorway. He wore an animal-skin schenti and an elaborate headdress of feathers. His weaponry was equally impressive: a sword, a spear, a bow, a full quiver, a dagger at his waist, and a smaller blade strapped to his thigh.

The queen reached over and tapped my chin. "You're gaping, dear." She chuckled and made introductions. "Asenath, daughter of Potiphera, meet our escort, Hodari, Medjay warrior and captain of my son's royal guard."

I almost took shelter behind the queen. "You're the one who escorted me here to the harem?"

His expression remained unchanged. "I am."

"You're far more impressive when I'm not wearing a veil."

His lips twitched—almost a smile—and the queen cackled. "Asenath, you've done it!" She looped her arm with mine and started out the door. "You've been in Avaris less than a day and almost made a Medjay smile."

"Hmph," Hodari grunted as we passed.

I fell in step with the queen, my grip tightening around her arm as we approached three more guards who waited in the secluded hallway. They ushered us no more than twenty paces, then paused at a closed door. On the other side I heard the roar of a large gathering, and prickly flesh rose on my arms.

Queen Tani picked at a loose thread on my robe and swiped at invisible imperfections. "All right," she said with a deep sigh. "I believe you are, indeed, the most beautiful woman in Egypt."

Hodari opened the door, and the queen preceded me through it, onto the royal dais. A cheer rose at our arrival. In the throne room, hundreds of guests stood beside long tables, where it appeared they'd been feasting while the queen had been preparing me for this moment.

My cheeks flushed instantly when I saw Joseph climb the dais steps with the eight-year-old king. The pair crossed the elevated platform with a single Medjay between them. This guard was dressed more simply than Hodari, wearing a long white schenti and gold belt. He, too, bore the weaponry of a royal guardian. He was no doubt Hami, Joseph's protector—and mine.

"This is Asenath, my king." Joseph's voice drew me, and all else fell away. My groom wore a purple robe interwoven with gold, a long white schenti beneath. A golden wreath encircled his head, each leaf accented at its base with an inlaid gemstone. I looked into his eyes and could barely breathe.

"Daughter!" Potabi startled me from the spell.

When had he arrived at my side? "Potabi, I didn't see you—"

"Your king gave you a compliment," he said, implying I should offer a polite reply.

If only I heard what he said. The boy's eyes were bright, his smile as kind as his ommi's. "I'm honored by your warm welcome, Pharaoh Yanassi." I bowed and reached for his hand, pressing it to my forehead as a sign of fealty. I'd never planned such a thing. Not to a Hyk— To an Amu king.

When I straightened, the boy elbowed Joseph. "Perhaps *I* will marry her, Paneah."

"She belongs to Paneah," Queen Tani whispered, giving him an arched-eyebrow of silent correction. "And a king's integrity is measured by his word."

"I was speaking man to man, Ommi. You don't understand these things." The boy rolled his eyes. "You're a lucky man, Zaphenath-Paneah. I'm happy for you."

"I am indeed." The vizier looked at me and smiled. My knees felt like water.

A scribe ascended the dais with a podium, papyrus, reeds, and pigments, presenting the official contract to Potabi first. He scanned it quickly but lowered the scroll, leaning into the huddle to speak privately. "I stand as Asenath's witness, my king, but who will stand for the vizier since he has no relatives in Egypt?"

"I stand as witness to Paneah's character," Queen Tani said.

Potabi's eyebrows shot up.

Queen Tani leaned toward him and whispered, "Are you surprised a woman will be recorded as Paneah's witness, Potiphera? Isn't it a pity the four priests you sent as spies on Paneah's barque didn't inform you of that little detail. You must remember they can't know everything that happens in the palace."

Potabi had no words, his conniving squelched like a torch in the sand. *We must use our wits and instincts,* the queen had told me, and she'd proven her skill.

I found Joseph's hazel eyes waiting. He was a good man like the Amu king Queen Tani had loved. With Ra's power to guide me, I'd persuade Joseph to keep Potabi on our tour and thereby ensure my friends' protection in On.

THIRTEEN

*That is why it was called Babel—because there
the LORD confused the language of the whole
world. From there the LORD scattered them over
the face of the whole earth.*

GENESIS 11:9

NEXT MORNING
Joseph

The wedding feast continued all night with no sign of reprieve.
Musicians played a constant flow of lively tunes with harp, lyre,
flute, pipe, bells, and tambourines. Pharaoh's favorite jugglers had
provided the early entertainment, but Queen Tani insisted the scant-
ily clad dancers wait to roam the aisles until after the young king
retired to his chamber. Pharaoh Yanassi ruled Egypt, but his ommi
still decided his bedtime.

Dawn's rays peeked through the narrow windows high above the
gathering in the expansive throne hall. Positioned to release heat
and capture light, the tall and slender windows also created their
own dancing show as dust sparkled in morning's first light. Asenath
leaned on Joseph's shoulder, her head bobbing like a piece of drift-
wood on the turbulent Nile. He placed his arm around her, then

looked away, aching for Ahira. *Elohim, forgive me. Will I ever see my wife and not think of my first love?*

"Take your wife to the wedding chamber, Lord Vizier," Queen Tani said, seated at the table on his right. "She is a great prize."

"Indeed, she is." Potiphera lifted his goblet, drained it, and immediately raised it to be filled again. The wine keeper had stationed one of the stewards beside the bride's abi to quench his insatiable thirst. Potiphera leaned across the divide that separated him from Joseph. "My daughter would rather die alone than give you children."

Joseph glanced around the large hall to see who heard. One head turned—Queen Tani's. The other guests had ignored Potiphera after he'd finished his second wineskin. "She'll never die alone," he mumbled. "I'll never leave her." After a loud belch, Potiphera fell forward, his face landing in his plate.

"Lovely." Queen Tani sneered and then motioned toward two Medjays. "Take Ra's high priest to his guest chamber." Then she grinned at Joseph. "Parting with one's only child must be devastating, but now you can be sure the bride's abi won't disturb you—at least for a while."

"Thank you for hosting us in the palace, my queen." Truth be told, Joseph would have preferred a quiet affair in his villa, but the queen had insisted they celebrate their first days as husband and wife in the palace. "Our wedding banquet and your kindness to Asenath has meant more than I can express."

"Your wedding chamber awaits," she said. "May your god bless you with a long life of love, Paneah." With the elegance of a swaying willow, she inclined her head and turned to converse with a nobleman's wife.

Joseph tried to wake Asenath, but with wine added to her exhaustion, she was nearly unconscious. He stood and hoisted her into his arms, and she startled awake. He feared she might struggle as she had in the tower. "Let me carry you, wife," he whispered. She glanced at the well-entertained crowd and laid her head on his chest. It felt like a victory, a step of trust.

Hami led them toward the back of the dais, and the wedding guests stood to applaud. Another guard pulled back a tapestry, revealing the hidden door to the palace residence chambers. As Joseph followed Hami, he studied the woman in his arms, so small and frail. *My wife.* When they'd been in the tower together, she'd asked him to call her Nathy. That had seemed forced, but "little one" came naturally. It fit. She was small but mighty yet chafed at the implications. Tonight, no matter what he called her, she had become his. To protect. To support. To understand. And somehow—to love.

Hami greeted the two Medjays guarding the wedding chamber. He entered first, as was protocol, while Joseph waited to receive his signal that the room was safe to enter. After Hami's short, shrill whistle, Joseph crossed the threshold into another world. With every footstep, his sandaled feet crushed hundreds of colorful flower petals strewn across the faience tiles, releasing myriad lavish scents that swirled around him. An ornately carved cedar bed perched on an elevated platform in the center of the chamber, its wool-stuffed mattress nearly as thick as the frame was tall. Heavy tapestries hung floor to ceiling across an adjoining outdoor courtyard, fighting the light of a new day to create a romantic dimness lit solely with a few oil lamps.

"Congratulations, Lord Vizier," Hami said from the threshold. "The queen suggested you receive no interruptions for a week except meals when you request them. Is this your command?"

Lack of sleep almost made Joseph agree. "No, Hami. This day we sleep; tomorrow, we rest; and the next day we begin our tour of the Two Lands." He looked at Asenath and wished many things could be different for them. "We've set our itinerary, and we'll follow it."

"As you wish, Lord Vizier." The door clicked shut behind his captain.

Asenath stirred in his arms and nestled closer against him. His chest ached with an overwhelming urge to protect her. Protecting her meant removing her from Potiphera's influence—but how? He'd requested that Pharaoh Yanassi and the queen mother send an alternate member of the royal council with them on the tour. They'd refused, citing two reasons. The first was true and difficult to argue against. Potiphera was Lower Egypt's most respected high priest, serving at its largest temple a deity most Egyptians believed to be the most powerful of their gods.

Their second reason for refusing still grated. He whispered to Asenath, "Your abi is a viper." Her eyes fluttered. Had she heard? Would she agree?

He gently placed her on the bed, hoping she'd sleep so he could consider how to manage Ra's deceptive high priest. Pharaoh Yanassi and the queen mother told Joseph that Potiphera had sent a secret missive, accusing the vizier of "inappropriate" contact with Asenath in the tower. Joseph was angry, of course, but the betrayal wasn't the entire reason he wanted Potiphera replaced on their tour of Egypt. Although Joseph understood the royals' reasoning, allowing Potiphera's deception to go undisciplined set a dangerous precedent.

"If Potiphera hurts me, he hurts you as well. Can't he see that?"

Asenath rolled to her side, her long, steady breaths continuing. Joseph lay down beside her, leaving plenty of room between them, and finally allowed his weary eyelids to close. *I pray someday, Elohim, I'll share a bed with this woman without thinking of her abi or Ahira.*

* * *

Joseph heard an owl's hoot and opened his eyes in darkness. The oil lamps had burned out, and the tapestries blocked most light from the moon and stars. He slid off the bed, hands outstretched, and felt his way toward the dim glow of the courtyard. When he reached thick woven cloth, he pulled back a curtain. Moonlight streamed into the chamber, casting striking shadows over the elegantly simple room.

Beside each oil lamp in the wall niches, he found a small pitcher of oil, a fresh piece of wicking, and flint stones to relight the lamps.

He carried a lamp to a low-lying table, where he found blank papyrus and reeds for writing. Queen Tani had thought of everything.

He'd thought of a few more things he'd need for the tour's first stop in Bubastis and wanted to write them down.

"Joseph?" Asenath bolted upright in bed. She looked toward the courtyard, braids and gemstones falling across her face. "We slept all day?"

"You even snored."

"I did not!" She threw her fleece headrest at him.

"I see you've regained your strength." He tossed the fleece back to her, but their smiles faded into awkward silence.

A noticeable protest erupted from his new wife's belly. She gasped and covered her face.

"Evidently, your appetite has returned as well." He laughed, and his stomach rumbled, too. "I'll send Hami for a meal."

"So this is your protector?"

"That's right. You haven't officially met my captain." Joseph opened the door, and Hami appeared. "Come in and meet my wife." *My wife.* It sounded so strange.

The Medjay stopped two paces inside the chamber, leaving the door ajar. "I'm honored to meet you, Mistress Asenath. Are you hungry?"

Her stomach growled before she could speak, but Hami pretended not to hear.

"I am," she said, giggling. "And I'm honored to meet you, Hami."

The Medjay gave Joseph a sidelong glance and slight grin—practically a shout of praise from the stoic warrior. He looked into the hallway and said, "You may enter."

A line of servants streamed into the chamber, carrying trays full of food. Medjays stationed at the door inspected each servant as he entered, and Hami examined every tray. Joseph gestured toward the courtyard. "You may set the trays outside. We'll enjoy the fresh air."

Asenath rolled off the overstuffed mattress. "Hami, how did you know we were ready to eat?" She snagged a cluster of grapes from the first tray and turned to the Medjay, who maintained his focus on the servants and trays, ignoring her completely.

Asenath started toward Joseph. "Why are your guards so interested in our food?"

Joseph, too, ignored her question. "Would you like honeyed water or watered wine with the meal?" Surely, she'd understand the subtlety of his avoidance and stop asking questions.

"Joseph!" She stabbed both fists at her hips. "Did you hear me?"

Hami hurried the last servant from the room, while Joseph glared at his wife's untimely return to her feisty demeanor.

"Why did you ignore me? And your captain was unforgivably rude. I demand—"

He lifted his hand to quiet her.

"Don't you dare silence me." Her cheeks turned crimson. "You did the same thing to Potabi. We're not slaves to be commanded, *Lord Vizier*," she spat.

Joseph took a step toward her. "Nor do you comprehend the danger we face in this city, *Priestess*."

"What danger? You have the power of Pharaoh. Who would dare—"

"*Many* would dare!"

She stepped back. He feared he'd frightened her, but her eyes still boldly met his.

"Did you know your abi sent Pharaoh a secret message to defame my character?" he asked.

Her breath caught. "Joseph, no!" Her surprise proved her innocence, but her guilty expression said she wasn't surprised. "I'm sorry. Potabi can be unkind."

"Families betray." Bile rose in his throat. "Sometimes, we must let them go."

"Let them go? No. Please. He'll—" She lowered her head.

"He'll what?" Joseph reached for her hand.

She pulled away and looked at him with unnatural calm. "I'll talk to him. He'll do as I ask. Please, don't take him from me. He's all I have." Her voice broke on the final words, but she sniffed, visibly fighting for control.

He's all I have. As Joseph needed time to embrace Asenath, so she needed time to fully trust him. Though he hated to admit it, Potiphera was still a part of Asenath's security.

"He's no longer all you have," Joseph said. "And I hope you never experience betrayal from Potiphera like I endured from my family."

Her features softened. "I know very little about your family or their betrayal."

Could she fully grasp the betrayal without knowing Elohim or understanding Great-Saba Abraham's covenant? "I thought they were all I had—all I'd ever need."

"Tell me."

"We should eat." Joseph started toward the courtyard, but she snagged his arm.

"Tell me about your family first. It will be sort of like taking fish oil." She grinned. "Do it quickly and then we move to more pleasant things."

"Ima Rachel said the same thing, but I gagged every time." He sighed but couldn't deny the need for disclosure. "Elohim spoke to me through dreams at a very young age," he began. "When I shared the dreams with my brothers, hoping they'd think I was special and deserved their respect, they hated me even more."

"What were the dreams?"

His cheeks warmed. Would she think him arrogant, too? "The first dream was about sheaves of grain. My brothers' sheaves bowed down to mine. In a second dream, eleven stars plus the sun and moon bowed to me. My abba rebuked me for my arrogance." He looked away, shaking his head. "So, my brothers sold me to Egypt, where everyone but Pharaoh bows to me—and my family never will."

"Perhaps the dreams from your god meant Egypt would bow—not your family. When we're children, our worlds are quite small. Mine was a tower, yours a Bedouin camp. You knew your family exclusively and interpreted the dreams in that context. Through slavery and hardship, your world expanded. Egypt is your family now, Joseph."

The profound truth of her words was too painful to bear. "Yes. Now I have more 'brothers' to hate me." Joseph studied Pharaoh's signet ring on his finger and then showed it to his wife. "This ring gives me power to command but also makes me the target of power-hungry men. I can implement God's plan, but I can't dissolve hate." He nearly choked on emotion. "My Egyptian 'brothers' can't sell me, but do you understand why you and I sat alone at a table on the dais last night? Not because it was our wedding banquet, but because I'm Hebrew. You bore my humiliation because some who attended our wedding still blame my wealthy Bedouin family for driving the Amu out of Canaan and into Egypt. They blame Hebrews for the Amu's rise to power and will blame young Pharaoh Yanassi for wisely listening to a Hebrew vizier and his God."

When reality replaced vain hope in her eyes, Joseph knew it was time to ask the question standing between them. "Why do you believe it was Ra, not Elohim, who sent the messenger to you?"

She straightened. "Why must you insist it wasn't Ra?" Her head barely reached his shoulder, yet she stood like a Medjay in battle.

Would she always answer his questions with more questions? He squelched a sigh. This was the woman Elohim had chosen for him. She was stubborn, passionate, and intelligent—not the frail and weak *little one* in the tower. "You believe there are many gods, Asenath. I *know* there is only one."

"You can't know that." Her eyes narrowed. "Every great civilization shares the same gods. How can you know better than me—a priestess who dedicated her whole life to study and serve the gods?"

"I think you're very intelligent, but you've never been taught the truth."

"I know the truth. If you knew the history of ancient Sumer and how their pantheon—"

"In ancient Sumer, men built a tower, thinking humans could become equal to Elohim." Her eyes widened as he began the story he'd heard since his earliest memories. "Saddened by their pride and willfulness, Elohim confused their languages and scattered them across the earth. Angered by His righteous discipline, every tribe and nation created their own false gods. Mesopotamia created violent gods to explain the unpredictable forces of nature throughout their territories. In Egypt, where nature is more predictable and less destructive, their gods are generally kinder and more generous. I don't believe in Elohim because I'm ignorant. I believe because the one true God has proven Himself real and active in my life. But He has never sent His personal messenger to me as He did to you."

Her lips parted in quiet awe. Two heartbeats filled the silence. "Is that some new teaching Potabi imparted while on your nome tour?"

"No. Abba Jacob taught me. His abba, Isaac, taught him. Great-Saba Abraham learned the stories before he left Sumer—Ur of the Chaldeans."

"The Bedouin prince Abraham lived in Sumer? Why did he leave?"

"Because Elohim, the one God, spoke to him. He promised to give his descendants the land of Canaan."

"And bless all nations through his descendants," she said.

"*Elohim's* messenger—not Ra's—promised you this because you're a part of *my* family now. Each generation after Great-Saba Abraham bears Elohim's covenant to the next and passes down the promise to bless all nations someday, somehow."

She took a shuddering breath. "Ea is Sumer's all-powerful god. Ra is the same god in Egypt's family of gods. They're the same . . ." She studied her trembling hands. "Your god is the same, merely called by a different—"

"Asenath." Joseph cradled her hands. "Elohim isn't simply my God anymore. He spoke to *you*."

"No!" She broke from his grasp and rushed to the courtyard.

Joseph massaged the back of his neck. *Elohim, give me patience and compassion while her foundation of sand is swept away.* He followed her and waited. Watching.

Silhouetted in moonlight, she faced the night sky glittering on the Nile. Crickets sang. Frogs croaked a slow cadence. "If I accepted your story of Elohim's tower, Potabi would reject me." She turned, hugging her waist as if holding herself together. "If Potabi rejects me and I lose him, my whole life has been merely a nightmare without meaning or purpose. I could perhaps make Ra my sole god, rejecting all others. But to reject Ra himself, the all-powerful creator, would mean I reject everything and everyone I've ever known and loved—including Potabi."

Her words were like a dagger to Joseph's belly. He'd offered life-giving wine, and Asenath chose Egypt's cesspool. Intelligence ignored. Logic forsaken. She'd willfully rejected truth for the lie and liar. Joseph inclined his head. "Then we remain married in name alone."

"Joseph, please don't be angry with me." Her tone was pleading. "All of this is my decision. Don't blame Potabi. And he didn't mean any of those awful things he said at the banquet. He was drunk. Please, Joseph. He must accompany us on the tour."

Something more than insecurity glistened behind her dark brown eyes. "Pharaoh Yanassi informed me this morning that Potiphera will be our escort for the entirety of the yearlong tour." Joseph covered her hands, holding her in place. "Is there another reason your abi must accompany us?"

A battle raged behind her eyes before she broke away and hurried toward their trays of food. "Potabi will be an invaluable help on your tour." Reaching for a silver plate, she began inspecting the bountiful food. "Come, Joseph. We can talk while we eat."

Each of them filled a plate and bowl with delicacies, then settled side by side on cushions facing the river. They started with goat cheese on dark brown bread and fresh pomegranates. She reached for a boiled quail egg. Her delicate fingers and wrists were so unlike Ahira's work-worn hands, but it was Asenath's faith that was the most troubling difference. *Elohim, how can I love a woman who rejects You?*

"I've known my destiny since hearing Ommi's last words," Asenath whispered, "but now I'm not sure what 'healing Egypt' really means." It wasn't a question, and her gaze never left the river.

Joseph felt her words like a chisel in Sinai's turquoise mines. She searched for something more valuable than wealth. Asenath needed her life to mean something.

"Trust the promises we've received from the all-powerful Creator." Joseph spoke of Elohim, but perhaps they could agree on generalities for now.

Relief brightened her features. "I'm willing to trust the all-powerful creator." She popped a grape into her mouth. "Tell me more about our yearlong journey. Where will we go?" Her eyes widened. "May we stop at On and visit my sister-maids and Jendayi first?"

"I wish we could." He felt almost cruel causing the sadness that darkened her features, but if all went as planned, her beloved maids and monkey would be waiting in Bubastis tomorrow to surprise her. "We must focus on cities and villages I haven't visited yet," he said with feigned sadness. "You can write to them as often as you like, using the same messenger that takes my reports to Avaris."

"That's very kind, Joseph. Thank you." She looked up at the sky, leaving most of her food untouched. "I'm still rather tired. I'm going to sleep a little more if you don't mind."

She returned to the chamber, leaving a chilly silence between them. Something thrashed in the river, ending quickly, proving a crocodile had found easy prey. The morbid image portrayed Potiphera rather well—a crocodile, hungry for power. *Please, Elohim, keep Asenath and me from becoming his next meal.*

FOURTEEN

The wise fear the LORD and shun evil,
but a fool is hotheaded and yet feels secure.
PROVERBS 14:16

Asenath

Joseph and his Medjays left at dawn to prepare the vizier's new barque for our yearlong tour. Seated on the cushioned couch beside me, Queen Tani waited with Potabi and me in the wedding chamber. "Don't be nervous, my dear." The queen patted my hand. "Captain Hami is the best Medjay the Cushites ever sent to Egypt."

"He's a eunuch, Asenath."

The queen's glare could have smelted iron. "How is that relevant, Potiphera?"

"Well, I . . . I, uh . . ." His features hardened. "My daughter has lived in a tower for fifteen years, my queen, and fears the presence of any man except me. She'll be comforted to know her sworn protector can't harm her."

"I told Asenath he was the fiercest warrior in Egypt," she said. "Of course, he *could* harm her, Potiphera, but he *won't.*" She released a disgusted sigh. "What has happened to you, Highness? Apophis appointed you to the royal council because he respected and trusted your judgment. You've been loyal and invaluable to my son's reign during the past two years. But since your daughter was chosen as Paneah's wife, you've been nothing short of hysterical. I'm beginning to wonder if Paneah was right to suggest we replace you on this tour."

"My queen, please don't even speak of it." I bowed my head and grasped her hand, pressing it against my forehead. "I couldn't bear being separated—"

"Quiet, my dear." She stilled me, placing her other hand on my head. "The decision is made, and Pharaoh won't change his mind. Sit up now," she said. "You're not a beggar. You're the second highest noblewoman in the kingdom."

I straightened, glimpsing Potabi's relief before meeting the queen's stern gaze. "Remember what I told you during our first meeting, Asenath. Wit and instincts. You're not in your tower anymore. Potiphera isn't your sole protector. Paneah and Hami are good men you can trust."

"Asenath doesn't need good men. She has me." Potabi struggled to his feet, seeming oblivious to the irony.

Queen Tani stood to face him, grinning. "Yes, Potiphera, why have good men nearby when Asenath has you?"

Lips pursed tight, his head wobbled as if trying to shake free a witty reply. None came. He extended his hand to me. "Come, Asenath. I'm sure Pharaoh is waiting to escort us to the quay."

I stood but refused Potabi's hand, caught between his glaring foolishness and the queen I deeply admired.

"You may have a few moments alone with your daughter," the queen said on her way out. "I'll have one of the Medjays alert you when Pharaoh Yanassi is ready." She left us without a backward glance.

My cheeks could have warmed the room on a winter's night. "How can I ensure your presence on this tour if you make us appear as fools to Queen Tani and my husband?"

The slap came too quickly to defend myself. I stumbled and stared at Potabi's equally shocked gaze. "Asenath, forgive me. I . . ." But his words died as his features hardened. "No. You're the one who will apologize. I'm the Great Seer of On. Highness of Ra. How dare you speak to me with such disrespect? Remember your training."

I regained my balance and my wits. "Forgive me, Highness. How foolish of me to think I had any influence over your placement on the vizier's tour. From this day forward, I'll speak neither in favor nor against your presence on the journey."

By speaking so frankly to him, I'd gambled my friends' safety. But the odds were in my favor. Queen Tani seemed to favor me over Potabi—at least for the moment. Was he desperate enough to win back her favor by showing me some respect?

"Mistress Asenath, Pharaoh Yanassi is ready to escort you to the quay."

Potabi motioned toward the door. "After you, *Mistress* Asenath." The disdain with which he spoke my new title proved continued disrespect.

I preceded him through the chamber door, and we bowed to the young pharaoh. Potabi added a honeyed greeting. "Ra's blessing upon you, Pharaoh Yanassi, as my all-powerful god brings yet another rising sun from the defeated underworld."

"You may rise, Highness, and answer one question before boarding the vizier's barque." The young pharaoh's regal manners exceeded his age. "Vizier Paneah is both the gods' choice and mine to save Egypt. Will you accept him as such, or will I choose another to become his honored escort?"

Potabi bowed again. "I accept Lord Paneah, Pharaoh Yanassi."

Before Potabi's lie had grown cold, Pharaoh spoke to me, his cheeks flushed. "Mistress Asenath, if I were a few years older, you would have been my wife."

"Yanassi!" The queen's scolding made his grin bolder.

I bowed to hide my own smile. "I'm deeply honored to be pleasing in your sight, Mighty Pharaoh."

Queen Tani walked arm in arm with her son, Hodari leading the way. Potabi and I followed, and a host of Medjay surrounded us all. Another layer of Medjays circled when we emerged into the main palace hallway, holding back the swell of human chaos.

Unnerved, I squeezed Potabi's arm tighter. "It's all right, my girl."
He leaned close for my ears alone. "Now you understand why I
insisted you wear a veil when we arrived."

We hurried down the palace stairs, then past Pharaoh's public
pond. Noblemen and their families clamored for our attention as
we crossed the faience-tiled palace complex.

Finally, we reached the complex gate, and Hodari halted us inside
its wide, dark tunnel that separated the noble well-wishers in the
palace complex on one side from the curious commoners of the city
on the other. "Wait here, Mistress Asenath. My men have alerted
Hami and your husband. They'll escort you from here to the docks."
Queen Tani faced me while Potabi spoke quietly to the young pharaoh. "Wit and instinct," she said, then kissed my cheek. "Yanassi
and I must say goodbye here. We'll keep in touch through messages,
and I'll see you for Yanassi's next akhet celebration."

Joseph appeared with Hami and his men. He bowed to Pharaoh
and the queen, waving farewell as Hodari and his men escorted
them back into a much calmer palace complex.

"Good morning, Wife."

My husband started toward me, but Potabi pinned my arm to his
side and leaned down to whisper, "I'll escort you, and we'll sit
together during the sail. We have much to discuss."

"Asenath?" Joseph stopped, glancing first at Potabi, then me.
"What's going on here?"

"Can't you see she's terrified?" Potabi hissed. "Get us on the
barque, Paneah. She's never faced this kind of chaos. Have you no
consideration for your wife?"

I wanted to disappear between the cracks in the mudbricks.

"Hami, more men!" Joseph shouted at his captain. And suddenly
I was rushed through the insanity. More precautions for the priestess who'd been locked in a tower. Potabi was right. I'd never experienced the overwhelming crush of human curiosity. I'd never been so
close to poverty, to dirty hands clawing at me, to rotted teeth and
fetid breath. By the time we crossed the narrow plank to board the
elegant barque, I was shaking uncontrollably.

Potabi guided me toward three covered couches and forced me onto the one farthest from shore. "Turn away. Don't look at the people."

I did as I was told, too rattled to protest.

"Asenath, forgive me." Joseph's breathless appeal drew me, but Potabi stood between us like a shield.

"Lord Vizier, I beg you, if you have any feelings for my daughter at all, leave her alone with me today." His tone was suddenly pleading and tender. "It's not you she fears, Paneah. Asenath is brave, but she's still adjusting to this world outside her tower. Try to understand. I've been her protector. She'll turn to you soon, but for now, she needs a more familiar face." A slight pause, and then he hovered over me. "Tell him, Asenath."

Wit and instinct; wit and instinct. I had no wit in the moment, and my limited instincts were formed by fifteen years of seclusion. "Yes, Potabi," I said and curled into a ball on my couch, still shaking. Peering over my hands, I let the tears fall as my husband walked away. *Don't give up on me, Joseph.*

Potabi pulled his couch closer to mine and reclined beneath the heavy linen covering, lacing fingers behind his head. "Well done, my girl. I doubt he'll bother us until we arrive in Bubastis." The pride in his voice made my stomach churn.

"How long will we stay in Bubastis?"

"Not long. I've seen the vizier's itinerary. Some would say it's ambitious." He scoffed. "I'd say it's ridiculous."

Did I want to know why? I sat back on the couch, pulling knees to my chest. Should I wait to hear Joseph's reasons for the route and timeline?

"The vizier ignored my advice to visit trade cities exclusively," Potabi began without prompting. "He also intends to waste time on smaller villages—locations that add little wealth to temples or Pharaoh's treasury."

"Shouldn't you be pleased he's taking the advice you gave on the nome tour and 'loving people well'?"

He looked surprised. "He's confiding in you. That's fine. Just make sure you're not sharing our secrets with him. Remember, my girl. You're Isis Incarnate."

"I'm not Isis Incarnate!" I looked away, hiding my instant tears.

Silence fell between us, and I distracted myself by watching the helmsman ascend his perch near our couches on the stern. The sailors' oars splashed into the water, and the helmsman called out, "Pull . . . and . . . pull . . . and . . . pull!" The giant barque slid south against the tide with each rhythmic heave.

"You're Isis Incarnate, and you'll heal Egypt's wounds." Potabi was suddenly a handbreadth from my face. "Your ommi foretold it, and you will—"

I pulled away. "I know what ommi foretold, and my destiny remains unchanged. But one god, the all-powerful Ra, sent his messenger to confirm my calling. It is Ra who shines on all of Egypt— trade cities and poor villages alike—or so you said when you rescued three little girls from Memphis."

He couldn't have looked more wounded had I bludgeoned him. He turned away without speaking. His chin quivered while he focused on the wake from our sailors' rowing. "Forgive me." He paused. "I've been so afraid of losing you. I've driven you away, haven't I?"

Had he? I was angry with him, yes, but a deeper part of me clung to him regardless of his foolishness and pride. "You haven't, but I need you to trust me." Then I added, "And trust Jo— Paneah. Even Queen Tani assured me. He's a good man."

The tender moment was shattered. "You foolish, foolish child. The queen loved Khyan, a Hyksos traitor. Of course she would be snared by another charming Hyksos." He shook his head, sneering. "We must be far more cautious about the time you spend alone with him."

"He's my husband, Potabi." I lay back on my couch, weary of the fight. "Leave me be." I closed my eyes, hoping for silence all the way to Bubastis.

I left my couch a few times but never far and always under Potabi's overzealous scrutiny. The silence between us continued and, with it, my nerves frayed. We passed noisy villages with curious onlookers waving from shore. Crocodiles swam alongside the barque, and one even chomped at an oar. Terrifying sights and sounds mingled with the wonder of this new life, my new reality. I'd always wondered what it was like to be *normal*. And here it was. This was life outside a tower. Life with messy people. Scary crocodiles. And a grumpy Potabi.

FIFTEEN

Know therefore that the LORD your God is God;
he is the faithful God, keeping his covenant of
love to a thousand generations of those who love
him and keep his commandments.

DEUTERONOMY 7:9

Joseph

Hami joined Joseph at the bow. "You should come away from the railing, Lord Vizier. If you're within sight of a city, you're also within an archer's sights. I don't want an arrow finding your heart."

"What if I wish for an arrow to pierce both our hearts?" Joseph nodded toward his wife. "I want us to *feel* something for each other, but she hasn't even spoken to me today."

"She watched you when the oarsmen gave you a turn at rowing."

"She did?" He glanced at Asenath again, but she was focused on Bubastis, the city of the cat goddess. He sighed. "She didn't cheer for me."

"Even I—a eunuch for fifteen years—recognize longing in a woman's eyes, Lord Vizier." He leaned closer, lowering his voice. "Potiphera seems preoccupied with voices from the grave."

"Is he mad?" Joseph whispered. It might explain his rash behavior.

"I'll keep my opinion to myself, Lord Vizier." Hami's smirk was equal to other men's belly laughs. "One of my men heard Potiphera whispering prayers to his dead wife, Katesch, last night. Then he harassed Mistress Asenath about her destiny again this morning."

"He uses her destiny like a leather strap to do his bidding." Joseph gripped the rail and searched the Bubastis shore. "She needs her friends."

"Your wife's gift will be waiting at the quay." He laid a large hand on Joseph's shoulder. "You can trust my men, Jos— I mean, Lord Viz—"

"You can call me Joseph when we're alone, you know."

"No, Lord Vizier, I cannot." Hami slid between Joseph and the rail. "If you were *Joseph,* Pharaoh wouldn't have sent his chariot in the ship ahead of us for you to ride through Bubastis with heralds declaring your authority. You are Zaphenath-Paneah, the second most powerful man in Egypt, who my men will risk their lives to protect." He inclined his head slightly. "Now, Lord Vizier, if you would, please join your wife at the stern so my men can gather in one place to protect you both."

"No, Hami. She hasn't spoken to me all day, and—"

With a sharp whistle, Hami motioned his guards toward Asenath and Potiphera. Every Medjay rushed toward Asenath, and Potiphera's temple guards separated him from his daughter.

Her features twisted with fear. "Potabi!" she shouted.

Joseph ran toward her, anger kindled that his captain would use his guards to manipulate him. "You should have let me prepare her," he shouted over his shoulder. Hami knew Joseph would rush to Asenath if she was frightened.

When he drew near, she reached out for him. "What's happening?" she cried. "Why are your guards surrounding us?"

"It's a precaution." Awkwardly, he grasped her hand.

"Is this how you'll meet the priests and noblemen of Bubastis?"

Potiphera sneered. "Like a frightened lamb? As if you're preparing for attack?"

"Merely precautions," Joseph shouted over the protection between them.

Asenath squeezed his hand, drawing his attention. "Tell me the truth, Husband." Suspicion darkened her features. "Please."

Her emotions seemed so fragile, yet honesty about the rising danger might curb Potiphera's ability to twist the truth. "We've had reports that some in Egypt's larger cities fear their new Hebrew vizier will take the people's grain like my family took the Amu's land in Canaan." He shifted his attention to Ra's high priest. "Your presence, Potiphera, will be helpful to allay the people's doubts. In addition, Pharaoh has insisted I demonstrate the authority he's given me as soon as we dock."

Joseph leaned down to whisper to his wife. "I must leave you for a while after we dock, but Hami and my Medjays will see you safely to the king's villa. I've arranged for a surprise to meet us there."

"A surprise?" Her head shot up. It was the first time he'd seen her smile today. And to his own surprise, it was the first time he wanted to kiss her.

"Brace!" Hami shouted as the crowd on Bubastis's shoreline welcomed Egypt's vizier.

The barque's angled bow slid onto Bubastis's sandy shore, jarring its passengers to a sudden and safe halt. Joseph and Asenath were held steady by the faithful Medjays pressed between them and the rail. Celebration erupted on shore while those on deck breathed a sigh of relief.

Hami barely let two heartbeats pass before he reminded Joseph, "Pharaoh's chariot awaits, my lord."

Joseph squeezed Asenath's hand. "I'll see you at the villa."

He met Hami mid-deck at the plank with a wry grin. "Don't ever use your guards to frighten my wife again, Captain."

"Forgive me," Hami said with a slight bow. "Surely, the need for such maneuvers will soon be over." His captain handed him the newly crafted crook and flail, much like Pharaoh Yanassi's, except Joseph's were made of olive wood. He felt like a fraud—the son of a Bedouin shepherd from Hebron—debarking a fine ship, carrying the signs of royalty, preparing to ride in Pharaoh's chariot pulled by four white stallions. But the small voice inside reminded him it was Elohim who had taken him from Canaan to the palace halls.

After he'd shared with Pharaoh Yanassi the similarity of a shepherd's tools—a crook and staff—to Egypt's royal crook and flail, the young king had commissioned the olive wood gift to be made for Joseph's tour. He'd been waiting in the throne room to present the gift before Joseph went to the quay. *The great Pharaoh Khyan said a good leader must both guide and discipline,* he'd said—wise words from the abi he idolized.

With the memory, Joseph proudly crossed the symbols over his chest. *Thank You, Elohim, for making me a shepherd of many flocks in my lifetime.*

The crowd's applause dwindled as he approached the king's chariot. The four horses pawed the sandy ground, anxious to run. His Medjays hurried their pace, still in tight formation.

Then a horrendous sound rent the air. A high-pitched wail. A screech that halted Joseph and silenced other sound. "Nooo! Not the chariots! Nooo!"

Joseph whirled toward the barque. "Asenath?"

"They killed her!" she shrieked.

"Get out of my way!" Potiphera clawed at the Medjays.

Joseph ran toward the barque.

"Wait for your escort!" Hami shouted behind him.

But Joseph had already made it to the boat. "Leave her!" He shoved everyone away and reached to gently control his tortured wife's flailing. Holding her, he lowered himself to the ship's deck, Medjays surrounding them like a shield to avoid unwelcome onlookers. Her wailing calmed to a low whine as he pressed her face against his chest and whispered, "Shh, my wife. You're safe." Rocking, he began humming a shepherd's tune—the one Ahira sang when he despaired in that dark prison cell. Slowly, eventually, Asenath began to calm. Her moan became a whimper, and the whimper turned to silence.

Potiphera leaned over them. "Asenath, you must stop this."

She covered her head. "Do you remember the chariots, Potabi? The soldiers in Memphis. Zahra and Hotep's maids were in the street. The Hyksos ran them down in chariots."

Horrified, Joseph asked Potiphera, "Did you know this?"

"I had no idea she remembered it." The priest's pallor proved he spoke truth. "Come, Asenath, I'll take you—"

When he reached for her arm, she flailed again. "No! I want Joseph! Leave me be, Potabi!" Her nails dug into Joseph's arms.

He saw the devastation on Potiphera's face and actually pitied him. "Hami, give Highness Potiphera an escort ashore, and make sure he's comfortable in our villa for the night."

One of the temple guards faced Hami. "We'll escort his Highness." Hami gave a quick nod of permission.

"There will be no chariot tonight, my wife. We'll go ashore together." Joseph looked at Hami. "Elohim knew she'd need the comfort of friends tonight. Let's get her to the villa." Humming, low and steady, he carried her to a palanquin that had quickly been arranged for them. Joseph joined her in the curtained litter, cradling her under his arm.

She was no longer whimpering or crying.

"Can you look at me, Asenath?"

She shook her head and stifled a sob.

"The chariot is gone. We're on our way to the king's villa now."

"I'm ashamed," she said. "Word will spread. The vizier's wife suffers hysteria."

"Of course not." He kissed her head. "We'll say you saw a mouse." She poked his ribs, a good sign. "People will be too busy hating me to worry about your fear. They'll love you, Asenath. I have a suspicion you're easy to love."

She fell silent for several moments. "Joseph?"

"Yes?"

"I'd forgotten they attacked us with chariots in Memphis until I saw you approaching . . ." She covered her eyes. "I can't bear to see you in a chariot."

Pharaoh Yanassi had said Joseph must ride in the king's chariot in *every* city they visited. How could he honor his wife's request yet obey Pharaoh's command? One painful solution made sense. "Perhaps you should return to Avaris and stay with Queen Tani—"

"No, please." She sat up, cosmetics smeared by her tears. "I'll try harder, Joseph. I'm sorry."

"It's not punishment." He cradled her face. "Our next stop is Memphis. If the sight of a chariot brought on such traumatic memories, what will happen—"

His words faded when she spoke. "I don't know what will happen, but the thought of leaving you is worse than facing my memories. I think facing my past is the path for you and me to have a future."

The palanquin stopped, and Joseph peeked through the curtain. Relief washed over him at the sight of two women waiting at the villa's courtyard gate. "Tomorrow I'll meet with the city elders while your past heals you. The next day, we'll embrace the future together."

Someone yanked the litter's curtain aside, and Asenath startled. "Zahra?" She gasped. "Hotep and Jendayi, too?" Skittering out of the palanquin, Joseph's wife wept again—joyful now. Potiphera stood three paces away, six temple guards around him, glaring at Joseph.

When the women's giggles and squeals abated, Asenath released her maids and approached Potiphera. "Potabi, did you . . ."

But his rancid stare drained her excitement. "The pilgrims who journey to On's temple will be cheated of the chantresses' blessing, Asenath, because your husband thought your little reunion was more important than their worship." He turned a seething glance at Joseph. "And didn't consult me about the decision."

Even in torchlight, Joseph saw his wife's cheeks drain of color. She glanced at Joseph and back to Potiphera, panicked. "I didn't ask him to bring them, Potabi. Joseph, tell him. I didn't—"

Joseph had stepped out of the palanquin and glared at the manipulative priest. "I understand now why Asenath's friends remained in On. Holding them captive there makes Asenath your captive anywhere."

"Asenath and I are both captives, Lord Vizier, to her ommi's last wish. All that matters is that we heal Egypt." One brow rose in challenge. "Isn't Egypt all that matters, Zaphenath-Paneah?"

"*People* matter, Highness. That's why—"

"That's why you'll return my two chantresses to On's temple tomorrow morning." The priest's face flushed crimson.

"You may command your guards and priests, Highness, but I command all of Egypt! The maids stay." Joseph advanced on the little man, but his temple guards collapsed around him.

"Joseph!" Asenath's coarse whisper stopped him. "Please, don't be cross."

"Cross?" Joseph almost laughed. If only she'd seen Abba Jacob when Saba Laban accused him of stealing household gods. Or his brothers Levi and Simeon, who murdered every man in Shechem because their prince raped their sister. That was *cross* and much like the fury Joseph fought now. Before he erupted, Hami appeared at his side.

"Take your wife into the villa," the Medjay whispered. "A crowd has started to gather, and you need not fight more gossip."

Asenath touched Joseph's shoulder. "I'm grateful for your thoughtfulness—truly—but Zahra and Hotep should return to On in the morning. The people who travel to On for their pilgrimage need their blessings."

Joseph faced her. "What about your needs? And your maids' needs? You experienced something significant when you saw that chariot that involves their loss, too. Share it with them. Grieve with them. Don't let your abi's control of the past rob your futures."

Her chin quivered as she nodded, but he sensed her mind had already locked on the decision. "It hurts me when you and Potabi are angry with each other. I *need* to be at peace with him, Joseph. I'll visit with Zahra and Hotep tonight, and they'll return to On tomorrow."

Joseph recognized her fear but felt helpless to break the invisible shackles Potiphera had placed on his daughter. She alone held the key to her freedom.

"We'll allow Zahra and Hotep to return to their temple service, but Jendayi remains with us for the tour."

Sheer joy replaced the disappointment she'd tried to hide. "Thank you, Joseph!" She kissed his cheek and hurried into the villa with her sister-maids. The unexpected affection got a smattering of applause from those who had gathered to watch the newlyweds and judge the Hebrew vizier.

Joseph lifted his hand for silence and shouted to the crowd, "A peck on the cheek is a victory for a new husband who made a slight error on the first night of a long journey!"

Potiphera gave a disapproving huff and started walking toward the villa, but Joseph meandered toward the people who had lined the street. Medjays surrounded him. Hami's eyes roamed like a hawk on the hunt. But Potiphera's advice still burned in Joseph's memory. *Perhaps they'll even love a Hebrew vizier if he loves them well.*

"Lord Vizier, perhaps you could greet more Bubastis citizens on your way to tomorrow's early meetings." Hami spoke loud enough for the growing crowd to hear his not-so-subtle suggestion to curtail the impromptu town meeting.

Joseph waved goodbye as his Medjays whisked him toward the king's villa. They entered the courtyard gate, passed the lotus pond in the garden, and found Potiphera waiting at the villa door.

"You're making decisions for me without my approval, Paneah."

"I won't stop making decisions that affect you and your daughter. I'm your vizier and Asenath's husband." He clasped his hands behind his back to portray a calm he didn't feel. "If you'd like to remain a part of Asenath's life—which I hope you will—my decisions will also affect you. I'm sure I'll make decisions for Egypt that you'll be uncomfortable with as well, but you must respect me—"

Joseph stopped himself. "No. You must respect the God who used me to interpret Pharaoh's dreams and devise the plan that will save Egypt from disaster in the coming years of feast and famine. He is the same God who confirmed my marriage to your daughter while we toured your nome. Have you completely forgotten, Potiphera, or are you willing to ignore such signs from a powerful God?"

Potiphera nodded toward Hami. "Must he always be near?"

"Yes. Whatever you say to me, you'll say to Hami. He's closer than a brother."

"He's annoying." Potiphera continued to the villa.

Two Medjays escorted the grouchy priest down the left hallway toward his chamber. Potiphera's vexation ran deeper than Hami's presence or Joseph's room assignment.

"He will betray you," Hami said.

"He has already betrayed me." The priest entered his room. "Hami, there's little I can do when Pharaoh and the queen command his presence. So, I pray Potiphera's sincere desire to help Egypt will overshadow his hatred for me."

"I hope his sincerity grows to loyalty before he hires an assassin."

Joseph gave him a sidelong grin. "It's your job to save me from assassins." The Medjay growled as Joseph turned down the hallway on their right. Two Medjays waited at the lone chamber on the king's wing and opened the door as he approached. He expected the greeting of three women. Instead, he heard the joyful squealing of a guenon. Jendayi bounded across the tiles, bounced on his shoulder, and wrapped her arms around his head.

His eyes completely covered, Joseph heard three women giggling.

"Jendayi is happy to see you, Lord Vizier."

He moved the little creature's arm aside and saw Zahra looking his way. Hotep, the shy maid, stared at her hands but smiled broadly.

"I'm so happy you're here." He strode toward them, the monkey perched on his shoulder.

Asenath met him and reached for Jendayi. "Thank you for bringing my friends back to me." She stepped closer, cradling the monkey between them. Jendayi patted his cheek, and Asenath chuckled. "My monkey has fallen in love with you. I think I'm a little jealous."

"Based on my dream, we'll feel that way about each other some-day." The words had come from an unknown place. The surprise on Asenath's face mirrored his own.

"I can see that day coming." She held his gaze. "Even if we must remain married in name alone." Though she spoke softly, he was certain her maids heard. Glancing over her shoulder, he noted their bowed heads.

"May I ask yet another favor, Lord Vizier?"

"Of course."

"Since Zahra and Hotep must leave in the morning, would you mind if we moved to a guest chamber so we could spend the night talking? I think you were right about needing to share our memories about Memphis."

Joseph surveyed the elegant furnishings of the king's private chamber. Bubastis had been a favorite trade city of previous pharaohs, so the chamber was filled with Persian pottery, Tyrian tapestries, ivory, and ebony sculptures. "You and your maids should stay in the king's chamber tonight."

"No, Joseph, we couldn't."

He kissed her forehead—without thinking—and stepped back quickly. "Goodnight, Wife." He waved to Zahra and Hotep. "I'll bid you farewell at the quay in the morning." He rushed out the door, closed it behind himself, and pressed his back against it as if narrowly escaping a chase.

Hami's brows lifted, a clear but unspoken inquiry.

"Remember when I said I wished the arrows would pierce our hearts?" Joseph shook his head. "I should be more cautious with my wishes."

SIXTEEN

*People who show no respect for anything must be
brought to justice.*

Potiphera

Nuru, captain of Potiphera's temple guards, waited with him
between the temple quay and the large crowd gathered on the streets
of Bubastis. They watched Asenath's tearful farewell to her friends
while Egypt's vizier hovered over her like a domineering ommi.

The quay buzzed with life and trade, so Potiphera kept his voice
low. "Do our two guards understand how to sufficiently express my
displeasure to Zahra and Hotep?"

"I've trained them myself, Highness." He leaned closer. "The
guards will impress the importance of loyalty to you above all others
with a single meal of moldy bread and fetid water for two weeks and
repeated applications of the strap. They'll never allow you to be
surprised again, most worthy Highness and Greatest Seer of Ra's
high priests." He inclined his head, showing the respect Potiphera
deserved.

"You'll be rewarded, Nuru, in this life and the next for your faithfulness." Potiphera reached into the pouch at his waist and tossed

ashes over the guard's shoulders. "Did you also deliver the scrolls last night to the Bubastis elders and priests?"

"I did, Highness."

"Well done."

As the chantresses sailed away, Paneah and Asenath strolled toward Potiphera. He offered a pleasant smile—not too friendly, lest they sense his pretense. "I owe you both an apology," he said before they reached the crowd assembled on the city street.

"You do, indeed," the pompous vizier said. "But you've wronged your daughter most, Potiphera, by robbing her of time with her friends."

He bowed to hide the fury in his flaming cheeks. "I'm sure when you become parents, you'll realize there are many grave things for which we should apologize to our children, Lord Vizier. Perhaps my greatest wrong was believing Asenath was too young to remember some of the details of her ommi's death." He straightened. "Asenath, we should speak at length before we reach Memphis to be sure you're ready for what we'll see there."

"Your consideration is very kind, Potabi, but after talking with Zahra and Hotep through the night, I think I'm much more prepared for what I'll face." She turned to Paneah. "But I'm exhausted. Would you mind if I went back to the villa and slept today while you meet with the engineers and builders?"

"Engineers?" Potiphera asked. "What builders?"

Paneah met and held his gaze. "I've invited local engineers and builders to today's meeting, men—and women—who built the temples and other large structures in Bubastis."

"Why would you do that?" Potiphera realized his tone had grown shrill, so he cleared his throat and added, "It's the nome governor, elders, and priests who make the final decisions."

"No, Potiphera." Paneah's brows drew together. "The governor, elders, and priests offer valuable insight into their region, harvest schedules, and citizenry. Engineers and builders consult on the most efficient design for granaries and how Bubastis soil affects the mudbrick building materials. But make no mistake, Potiphera—it is *I* who make the decisions." He entwined Asenath's arm with his and looked at her with too much familiarity. "I'll walk you back to the villa before I go to the meeting."

Potiphera watched them go, trembling with rage.

"Arrogant Hyksos." Nuru breathed the words churning in the high priest's mind.

"And we'll let his own arrogance destroy him." He watched as the citizens of Bubastis welcomed the handsome vizier as he and Asenath entered the crowd. Paneah had learned to manipulate people nearly as well as Potiphera himself. What if the young pharaoh and Queen Tani realized their precious vizier was manipulating them? King Apophis already mistrusted the Hebrew. "I allowed my emotions to distract me at my daughter's wedding, Nuru."

"She's your only child, Highness, stripped from a glorious future to stand in a Hyksos's shadow."

"Not for long, Nuru. Have one of our guards take a yearling lamb to Ra's temple at the center of the city. We'll convene there tonight after the meeting."

"Yes, Highness."

They began walking toward the crowd. "While this city sacrifices to their meager goddess, I'll offer the yearling as a sacrifice to all-powerful Ra and read our future in its liver. We'll repeat the offering in every city on this tour, seeking wisdom and reminding the great god to make my daughter King Apophis's bride." He'd been so concerned about Asenath's loyalty to him that he'd lost focus on the most important loyalty of all. "King Apophis is Ra's choice to unite Egypt and heal her wounds, Nuru. Even he may not realize it yet, but I am certain."

SEVENTEEN

[Pharaoh] had [Joseph] ride in a chariot as his second-in-command.

GENESIS 41:43

TWO DAYS LATER
Asenath

With Memphis in sight, Joseph escorted me to the barque's stern. "Are you sure you'll be all right?" He cradled my elbow, standing so close his musky scent dulled my senses.

"Yes," I said, glancing beyond his shoulder where Potabi waited like a vulture. "I've seen your chariot, Joseph. Touched it. Even helped groom the horses. I'll be fine."

"I'm very proud of you." Joseph leaned down to kiss my cheek.

My whole body tingled. I savored the sensation as I watched his lanky strides, admiring the sinewy muscles in his back. I was fully entranced until Jendayi screeched and hid beneath my hair.

Potabi stood before me. "Don't you dare say you have feelings for that Hyksos."

I linked my arm in his and pulled him aside, fearing he'd be heard. "You can't defame my husband, Potabi. I won't defend you—"

"You'll defend him but not me?"

I inhaled slowly, exasperated, hoping to reason with a man who once taught me logic. "What more could Joseph do to prove Ra's favor? We left Bubastis with the people's support for granary construction in the city as well as surrounding villages. Joseph won the favor of both commoners and nobility. Because of his example, even our temple guards are helping relieve the oarsmen so we can reach Memphis by midday instead of dusk."

"Your emotions are leading you astray." Potabi's features tensed as we approached the Memphis quay. "We need to be united when we return to the true capital of Egypt."

I sighed. No matter what I said to Potabi and other zealots, Memphis would always be the capital—as it had been before the Hyksos invasion.

Standing side by side, we leaned against the railing as the helmsman shouted to his oarsmen. "Port oars, down! Starboard, pull!" The barque swung to the right, and he urged, "Full oars—pull, pull, pull!"

Then Hami shouted, "Brace!" He and Joseph were cocooned at the bow amid a circle of Medjays.

On's temple guards surrounded Potabi and me at the stern. I cradled Jendayi like a baby in my arms. "It's all right, little one." But it was I who needed consolation when the grand barque slid onto the Memphis shore. Head down, I dreaded my first glimpse of the city that had so thoroughly changed my world.

Our sailors celebrated docking, and more shouts erupted on shore.

"It's completely different." Potabi breathed the words.

The horror in his whisper drew my attention—not to shore but to him. "Potabi, are you all right?" He stared at buildings beyond the quay. "They've rebuilt what was burned."

Joseph appeared at my side. "Hami has a contingent of Medjays ready to escort you from the dock to the palace. I'll ride Pharaoh's chariot after—"

"I need to see Ra's temple," I said. Before he could deny me, I turned to Potabi. "Please. I must see if more memories surface."

"Can't you wait until we've prepared a sacrifice?"

"I want to see the mudbrick building where we lived and walk to the temple next door—as we did that night with Zahra and Hotep."

Potabi paled. "You remember where we lived?"

"I remember bits and pieces." Did he think my memories began and ended under that altar? "There's so much I don't recall, Potabi. That's why—" Emotion strangling my words, I bent my head, brushing Jendayi's fur with my cheek. The morning farewell to Zahra and Hotep had been painful, made more so by not knowing when we'd meet again, but our time together had been healing. Each of us had remembered something about that awful night we'd never been brave enough to discuss. "If I could piece together more of what happened on the night of the invasion, perhaps my nightmares could end."

"We'll go to the mudbrick building first and see if our one-room home still stands." Potabi sighed heavily. "Then the temple."

"Thank you, Potabi." My stomach clenched with too much dread to rejoice in the victory.

Our oarsmen had already leapt into the water and tied large hemp ropes around palm trees to keep the barque moored for the month we would remain in Memphis.

"Asenath . . ." Joseph blocked my path, concern written on his features. "I must ride the chariot from the quay."

"I'll be fine."

He looked toward the ship's bow, and I caught my first glimpse of the city's busy docks. "I'll find the mudbrick building nearest Ra's temple and wait for you there." He drew to within a handbreadth and whispered, "Are you sure you're all right?"

Jendayi leapt to his shoulder and took the golden wreath off his head. He snatched it back and tickled her belly. "You little thief. I need that." She pressed her lips to his cheek and made a bubbling sound, then returned to my shoulder. My baby had become quite comfortable with her two human perches during our sail from Bubastis.

Hami handed my husband the olive wood crook and flail as

Joseph started down the wooden plank. His long strides were that of royalty, not a Canaanite shepherd. The gathered crowd applauded weakly as his contingent of Medjay escorted him toward the chariot I'd so feared in Bubastis. My heart skipped as I watched my gentle, kind husband mount the weapon of war that killed my sisters' beloved nursemaids. I turned away and swallowed the fear, reminding myself that Ra's destiny had brought me this far and would continue to protect me.

Jendayi perched on my left shoulder, as far from Potabi as she could get. I inhaled a deep breath of courage and reached for Potabi's arm. "You must lead us. I don't remember where the temple is."

He pursed his lips. "I remember every brick and stone." Unusually somber, we followed his temple guards off the barque, through the busy docks, and onto the dirty streets of a once-great city. Eyes forward, Potabi spoke not a word.

Although I'd grown more accustomed to people, noise, and dirt, I was still not completely comfortable outside my tower. "Is there a route we could take that doesn't involve so many people?"

"Nuru, stop!" Potabi halted in the bustling street as his guards formed a shield around us. "Let me take you to the palace first," he said. "Please don't go to the temple, Nathy. I can send one of the guards to tell Paneah you changed your mind."

Startled, I spoke around strangled emotions. "You call me Nathy when you're concerned about me."

He swept tears from his cheeks. "A visit to that temple will prove how completely I failed you."

Always focused on my own insecurities, I sometimes forgot Potabi fought his own. Bracing my hands against his crossed arms, I challenged his inner doubts. "Your daughter is married to the second most powerful man in Egypt. A *good* man, by the queen's own decree. Let yourself be proud of me—and of your own accomplishments."

He stepped away. "I'll be proud when you're married to King Apophis."

"But Ra sent a messenger."

"Ra will change his mind. You can never be happy with a Hyksos." He grabbed my arm and hauled me along the sandstone-tiled street.

"You're hurting me," I cried out, but he ignored my plea. Anxiety rose with every step closer to our destination. Potabi shoved me to the right side of the uphill street to avoid the central drain that carried waste from the homes of the wealthy to the lowest of Memphis society. Our temple guards weaved through the crowd, following at a distance. Captain Nuru alone maintained our pace.

Potabi stopped his incessant march when we reached the city's golden beacon atop the hill. "The temple of Ptah," Potabi announced, sweat dripping down his face. The patron god of craftsmen had empowered its builders to construct the most elaborate temple I'd ever seen. As tall as twenty men and the length of three barques, Ptah's temple—though impressive—sparked no memories for me.

"I know Memphis is the center of Ptah worship, but I don't remember seeing this—"

Potabi pointed to a second structure a hundred paces to the east. "That's Ra's temple." Similar in style to every temple, it welcomed worshipers with an Avenue of Sphinxes and likely a priests' courtyard beyond. However, the entire complex was overgrown with weeds. I fought a wave of nausea.

Across the street a little boy kicked a ball of rags past a three-story dilapidated mudbrick building. A memory came so powerfully that I gasped. "That's it."

"Yes." Potabi stared at the building as if it were an akh come back to haunt him.

"Potabi, did I play with a cloth shabti—shaped like a baby and stuffed with lamb's wool?"

"Your ommi made it for you. It was your favorite toy."

It was my only toy—because I was too busy with lessons after we fled to On to be a child at play.

The sound of approaching horses startled me, and Jendayi leapt from my shoulder into the street. "Jendayi, no!" I lunged to save her from the same fate my sisters' nursemaids had suffered.

Joseph stepped off his chariot, caught Jendayi with one hand, and hurried toward me. "I was delayed. I'm sorry."

I kept close to his side and let Jendayi stroke my hair. "Will you come with me?"

"Of course. I'm here now, and I'll stay with you."

I linked my arm with his and walked toward the entrance of the mudbrick building. The whole structure was dark. Hami whistled, and a Medjay brought a torch from the chariot, lighting it with flint stones.

Potabi stood alone and sullen. "Will you carry the torch?" I asked. "Show me. Tell me about our life here."

He took the torch from Hami and led us toward the entryway of a three-level structure. Each level had two one-room dwellings— one on the right and one on the left of a central stairway. With our first step over the threshold, I stopped. "Potabi, we lived here, on the left, didn't we?"

He shined the torch toward a tattered curtain in the doorway. "Yes."

"And Zahra and Hotep lived somewhere upstairs?"

"Mm-hmm." His eyes took on a faraway look. "Zahra and Hotep lived on the right side with their nursemaids. Tenants on the right were unwanted family members of powerful people."

"When we spoke in Bubastis, they had no memory of their parents."

"To my knowledge, they were both given to nursemaids at birth to be raised for temple service."

I faced the street, and memories flashed. Soldiers shouting. Swords waving. Chariots racing. My friends screaming. Their maids running. "Why did Zahra and Hotep's nurses leave them with you, Potabi?"

"They didn't," he whispered. "They simply left."

"And you saved them." I wanted to embrace him, but he was handing Hami the torch.

"It was long ago," he said and marched toward the street, abandoning me to those memories.

Joseph offered his arm. I was grateful for the support to climb out of that experience and into the next. Jendayi perched on his shoulder, seeming content, while I crossed the street to explore the seedbed of my discontent.

If the beauty of Egypt's temples were meant to depict the gods' work of creation, Ra's temple was the image of creation gone wrong. Peeling paint, weeds, and shattered statues shouted neglect. The gates hung crooked and unbolted. Potabi paused inside the courtyard. "Ra's temple rivaled Ptah's in splendor. Now the sacred sea is dry." He scanned the public area and shook his head. "Even the palm trees are dead. No life at all."

No life at all. I mulled the grim words and followed. Joseph's Medjays provided rear guard. Potabi's captain pushed open the next gate, leading us deeper into the creation story. Floors slanted upward toward the pillared hall, where surroundings were more surreal. In any temple, prophets mingled amid the pillars like akh in the heavens. Their ethereal priestly services—reading sheep's livers or stars—earned significant silver.

"No one is here." I tilted my head back and turned in a circle like I remembered doing as a little girl. I'd watched the cloudless sky and imagined myself as a bird. Now I imagined the empty hall filled with people, the silence sweetened with Ommi's voice. Dizzy, I stopped twirling and closed my eyes, leaning against Joseph.

I began a chant to Ra—Ommi's favorite.

> *Awake, oh god.*
> *Wake peace and beauty.*
> *Bring creation to life*
> *With your winged disk shining!*
> *Split the heavens and*
> *Break through the night sky.*
> *Come from the east and*
> *Spread gold through the—*

"Katesch?" a raspy voice cried out.

Hami and his guards converged around Joseph and me, separating us from Potabi and his guards.

"Fadil?" Potabi said. "Fadil, is that you?" I struggled through the Medjays and saw an old man walking toward us from the dark chambers beyond the pillars.

"Don't stop singing, Katesch," he begged. "I've waited so long—" He stopped when his rheumy eyes focused on me. "Who are you? The temple is closed."

"Fadil, it's me. Potiphera." Potabi approached him slowly. "I've brought Katesch's daughter to visit you." He motioned me closer. "Sing for Ra's high priest, Asenath."

I began again, shakily, and searched for anything familiar about the old man. What should have been a priestly shaved head with a skullcap was covered with wild white hair. His priestly garments were soiled, and when I took another step toward him, he fled into the sacred court like an owl shunning daylight.

"Keep singing." Potabi grasped my hand and dashed after him. Joseph followed, Hami and Nuru close behind. We came to the doors of the priests' court and entered the room dimly lit by oil lamps.

Recognition extinguished my song. I froze. "This is where it happened."

The priest stood at the other end of a center aisle and turned slowly to face us. "You look so much like her. I thought she'd returned to escort me to the underworld." He scoffed. "You probably have questions Potiphera wouldn't answer. Come, girl. I'll tell you the *truth*."

I started down the aisle, but Potabi grabbed my wrist. "Wait."

Hami broke his grasp. "You don't touch the vizier's wife without permission."

"Enough, Hami!" Memories bombarded me. He was suddenly like a Hyksos soldier with a curved sword. I took Potabi's hand and led him toward Fadil, my memory filled with images of priests lying on the tiles in crimson-stained white linen in a room no larger than my tower's audience chamber. It had seemed so much bigger from a four-year-old's perspective. I shook my head to return to the moment and saw it. The altar. I stopped abruptly.

Potabi followed my gaze. "We can leave, Asenath, if seeing the altar is too much."

Was it too much? Was I pushing too hard? Demanding too many answers? I turned away, ready to retreat, and ran headlong into my husband's chest. His hands rested on my waist, steadying me. "We can go to the palace and come back tomorrow."

"Will it be any easier tomorrow?" I stared into his golden-green eyes.

"You're so brave." He pulled me to him, and I inhaled the scent of cloves and mint while Jendayi patted my head.

Me? Brave? Joseph was the brave one, the Hebrew vizier who faced hostile noblemen at every port. If we were to heal Egypt together, I must first allow Ra to heal me. I left the safety of his arms and said, "I'll be all right, but I need you close."

"I won't leave you."

With a sustaining breath, I turned to face what was both my tomb and womb, where Nathy died and a priestess was born. A few more paces, and we stood beside my darkest memory. "Show me, Fadil."

He hesitated, his bushy brows arched, then said, "Would you like to show her, Potiphera? You're the one who hid with three little girls while Katesch protected you."

Potabi tried to glare at him, but his head seemed weighted with shame.

"You wicked man. You know nothing about us." I shoved Fadil aside and approached the burnished-bronze altar. Its elaborate tapestry skirt was now tattered and faded. That covering had saved our lives. I knelt beside the overlap where it met in the middle. Hand trembling, I peered under the fabric into darkness. I let the cover fall back into place. Joseph helped me stand, then placed his hand at the small of my back. The gentle, protective gesture infused me with courage. I noticed the old priest and Potabi arguing, hissing insults at each other.

"Why are you whispering?" I said. "Are the gods unable to hear hateful whispers?"

Fadil cackled. "You have your ommi's fire *and* her chanting voice." He folded his arms across his chest. "The *gods* can't hear anything, girl. Ra is the one real god. The others are bedtime stories meant to frighten bad children and lull the good ones into sweet dreams. Mighty Ra is the only god with the power to save. You, Potiphera, and I are his witnesses."

Ra, the one real god? My heart thudded against my ribs. What other priest in Egypt believed that? None that I knew. Had Ra brought me to Memphis to confirm that his messenger spoke the truth to me?

"I'm not interested in your and Potabi's personal quarrels, Fadil. I want the truth about the night of the attack." Were my memories true or imagined? "Was there a soldier who took away Ommi's body?"

He sobered, deepening the craggy lines on his face. "Have you asked Potiphera?" He turned an accusing glare at Potabi.

"And where were you, Fadil," Potabi shouted, "when your priests and chantress gave their lives for Ra? Where were you hiding?"

The old man shuffled toward the altar, reached for a gold-leafed wreath—much like the one Joseph wore—and placed it on my head.

Potabi stared at the wreath. "The crown Pharaoh Monthhotep gave Katesch. I'd forgotten she wore it to convince the soldiers—"

"Your abi has forgotten much about that night." Fadil then took a pinch of cold ashes and tossed them over my right shoulder. "I bless you with your ommi's chantress crown, girl, and the truth you've long deserved. First, I confess that I'm no better than your cowardly abi. I hid in the birthing room with Ra's most holy image while your ommi and my prophets used every skill they possessed to bargain for our lives."

I spat at his feet. "How can you denigrate Potabi for saving three little girls when you saved yourself alone?"

"I've paid a high price for my cowardice. This temple's decay is my punishment. The people of Memphis have mocked and disregarded Ra's temple for years. True Egyptians fled to Thebes and now call their sun god Amun, not Ra." He turned a seething gaze at Potabi. "But I didn't stay hidden while enemy soldiers tortured and killed my wife."

"I had no choice!" Potabi shouted. "They would have killed the children if I'd shown myself!"

"That's a lie," Fadil sneered. "Tau said they killed no Memphis children but sent them to Avaris."

My blood ran cold. "Potabi, is this the same Tau who serves at On's temple?"

Head lowered, he refused to answer. Had Tau been the priest who sold Ommi's body to the soldier? I remembered the soldier's face in my nightmares, but nothing about the priest. Had Tau and Potabi escaped Memphis under the guise of transporting children to Avaris? "Potabi, look at me!"

He fell to his knees, sobbing, face buried in his hands.

Fury overwhelmed fear. "Fadil, did this priest—Tau—mention a soldier who took Ommi's body?"

Fadil shook his head. "No. I'm sorry. He said that he was leaving Memphis to take Potiphera and you three girls to a safer temple."

Tau must have been the priest! I nodded. "Thank you. At least I know part of the truth."

"I've told you nothing but truth!" Potabi shouted. "I simply didn't tell you what it cost us to save Zahra and Hotep." Our eyes locked.

Did I want to know if he'd traded Ommi's life for my sisters'? "Tell me, Abi."

With a barely perceptible nod, he began. "After their nursemaids were trampled, I carried all three of you to the temple. Katesch was hiding beneath the altar. She helped me hide you girls there instead. When we heard soldiers crashing through the pillared hall, Katesch insisted I hide with you. She was certain they wouldn't harm her. There was no time to argue. If I'd known . . ." Tears streamed down his cheeks.

How could I have forgotten so much yet remember other details so vividly? "Tell me about the soldier, Potabi."

"I don't know! There were many soldiers. Any of them could have killed her."

"I'm not asking about the soldier who killed her. I'm interested in the one who came back to barter with Tau for her body."

He shook his head. "That never happened. Tau cleared the temple of bodies, helped us out of hiding, and then took us to On."

"No, Potabi. Look." I pointed to a spot beside the altar. "Ommi lay there. I saw her. The soldiers left, and Tau started stacking bodies while her life drained away."

"Stop it." Potabi squeezed his eyes closed.

"Ommi spoke her last words, and then there was a soldier. He came alone. He gave Tau some silver and took Ommi's body away." The memory was so vivid. "I've seen his face a hundred times in my nightmares. Why did he take her? What did he do to her body?" The words came out in a desperate sob.

Joseph stepped between us and placed Jendayi in my arms. "We'll find him," he whispered. "That's enough for today."

"There was no soldier," Potabi said. "I would remember."

"You didn't remember this!" I snatched Ommi's wreath from my head and shoved it at him. "What if that Hyksos desecrated her body? What if Ommi has been a wandering akh all these years?"

Potabi's face went ashen, and I regretted the words.

"We'll do all we can to find him." Joseph's soothing tone felt like balm to my soul.

"You'll do nothing." Potabi glared at him, then turned to me. "If a soldier took Katesch's body, perhaps it was out of respect. Your ommi was beloved by so many."

"But I still need to know—"

"We'll discover the truth together, Nathy," Potabi said as he braced my shoulders. "With the intelligence your ommi passed down to you and my influence on Pharaoh's council, we'll sort through the chaos in Memphis that night. If this soldier paid Tau with silver and secured the skiff that took us to On, he must have been influential in General Salitis's army. We'll look for someone who might still hold a powerful position in Egypt's military." He released me. "Fadil, my daughter's courage has inspired me. Could it stir you to action?"

The old man's wiry brows drew together. "What do you mean?"

"With Asenath's voice, we could revive this temple and make it profitable again."

"We're here to build granaries, not a temple." Joseph spoke with the calm and authority of Pharaoh.

I swallowed my tangled emotions and tested our growing bond. "I need you to be my husband, not just Egypt's vizier." I placed Jendayi in his arms. "Perhaps you could take Jendayi to meet the governor and elders. She could win the allegiance of any grumpy nobleman."

EIGHTEEN

The realm of the dead below is all astir
  to meet you at your coming;
it rouses the spirits of the departed to greet you.
  ISAIAH 14:9

Potiphera

He'd started the day fearing his daughter's forgotten memories. Now Potiphera stood on the very tiles where his beloved died, his absent past equally terrifying. How could he have forgotten a soldier had taken Katesch's body? Or the gold-leafed crown she'd treasured—that now bobbed on their daughter's head while she and Paneah argued in heated whispers?

Asenath wanted to remain with Potiphera to help rebuild Ra's temple. Though relieved she wanted to spend time with him, panic rose at what else he might have forgotten of that night's terror. Potiphera reluctantly examined the skirting again, forcing memories to come.

That night, he'd turned his back to the mayhem and pulled the girls close like a hen shields her chicks. He'd been busy quieting them and hiding their eyes. When could he have peered behind himself through the skirting?

No. Fadil was right. Those were excuses.

You can lie to Asenath but not to yourself—coward!

He'd wept, his back turned to the slaughter, unable to cover his ears while the sounds of death roared outside the altar skirting. After all the bodies were removed from the room, Tau had dragged him from his hiding place. But how had they gotten to the docks that night? His memory failed him.

"Highness?" Paneah stood before him. "Did you hear what I said?" Paneah's impatience softened when Potiphera startled. "You're weary from travel. We should proceed to the palace."

"Yes, of course." Still dazed with emotion, Potiphera walked beside the vizier. Asenath walked ahead of them with Fadil and the guards. Was the old priest telling her more that Potiphera didn't remember?

"Asenath insists on helping rebuild . . ." Paneah's words faded into Potiphera's tortured thought.

Faces of Apophis's high-ranking officers flashed through Potiphera's mind. "What if I know the man but don't remember him?" he whispered to Paneah. "If I'd remembered sooner that a soldier took Katesch's body—if I'd turned and looked—I might have saved Asenath years of anguish."

"You saved three little girls, Potiphera. Sometimes courage means hiding when you're weak and fighting when you're strong. You're strong now. So, find the man and give yourself and Asenath peace." Continuing out the door, he held up his hand bearing the king's signet ring. "And if you need help, simply ask me. I'll do anything within the power Pharaoh gave me."

So Asenath will love you more than me? "You're too generous, Lord Paneah, but I alone will seek out the man who stole my wife's body."

"Why must every decision be a competition between us, Potiphera?"

"I don't believe you're capable of grasping the scope and depth of emotion this moment stirred in my daughter and me, Lord Vizier." Nor would he expect compassion from a stinking Hyksos. "However, I had hoped for a measure of respect."

The Hebrew's strides measured with his while the repugnant

monkey perched on the man's shoulder. "Forgive me, Potiphera, if I seem insensitive. I understand more than you realize. Today, you and Asenath lanced a fifteen-year boil. Your wounded memories will require time to heal. However, I remain Egypt's vizier and must obey Pharaoh's command to manage our whole nation that faces fourteen years of upheaval."

"It's all on you, Paneah." Potiphera scoffed. "Not my daughter or me. You're responsible for everyone and everything."

"So it would seem!" Paneah halted, his voice echoing in the pillared hall and capturing the attention of those waiting at the Avenue of Sphinxes. Lowering his voice, he said, "You were supposed to be my escort."

"I need not be your escort to be your ambassador." Potiphera glimpsed Asenath's concerned features and felt his ma'at restored. "Mine and Asenath's efforts in rebuilding Ra's temple and its priesthood will be more effective than my presence at your side, Lord Vizier."

Paneah fell silent, thoughts whirring behind his sharp eyes. "And if our time in Memphis proves your influence and presence unnecessary on our tour?" His tone held challenge. "I will suggest to Pharaoh Yanassi that you return to On. Asenath and I would then finish the tour without your interference."

He was a clever one. "Interference?" Potiphera feigned offense. "I'm the anchor that holds my daughter steady."

"You're the anchor that keeps her from sailing."

Potiphera sneered. "Asenath and I will never be parted, Paneah. The sooner you're reconciled to that, the easier your life will become." Without awaiting a reply, Potiphera strode toward the Avenue of Sphinxes, where his daughter waited with Fadil and both contingents of guards.

"Potabi, I must speak with you before I agree to help rebuild the temple." Asenath glanced at Paneah—a defiant, willful look. Potiphera's hope soared. "Because Fadil believes Ra has proven himself the one true god, the new prophets must take an oath and renounce the other gods of Egypt."

Potiphera felt as if she'd jabbed him with the blunt end of a spear. He considered Nuru's real spear to swipe off Fadil's sanctimonious expression.

Paneah stood beside Asenath. "Your abi couldn't renounce Egypt's other gods," he said. "If he rejected Pharaoh Yanassi's patron god, Seth, Potiphera might lose his seat on the royal council."

The Hebrew was shrewder than Potiphera realized. "Paneah and I disagree about many things, but I'm beginning to suspect there may be only one *real* god. Upper Egypt calls him Amun. We call him Ra, and Paneah calls him Elohim."

"Elohim is neither Ra nor Amun."

"*Paneah.*" Asenath's disapproving stare silenced him. "At least Potabi is willing to consider it. Don't you see what courage that requires?" She left Paneah's side and stood beside Potiphera. "I'm staying with Fadil and Potabi to help them rebuild Ra's temple in Memphis. Potabi will introduce you to the city's elders and the nome governor. When you travel to surrounding villages, it will be as it was in Bubastis. Your Medjays will keep you safe, and Jendayi will help you win the people's favor."

Her words drained Paneah's arrogance like a wineskin poked with a stick. His shoulders sagged, and, without a word, he turned and walked alone down the Avenue of Sphinxes.

"Jo—Paneah!" Asenath took a step to follow, but Potiphera caught her arm. "Your husband has his captain and guards to salve his wounds, Daughter. Let him pout. We have much to plan with barely a month to rebuild."

She broke from his grasp and addressed Fadil. "Potabi and I will return before dawn tomorrow for the Lighting of the Fire. Be sure you've completed your purification rituals before we arrive so we can guide Ra's barque safely into a new day."

"You are not the high priest!" Potiphera said. "Your purpose is to sing and—"

"I know my destiny." Asenath swallowed hard, a nervous attempt to calm herself. "Fadil is the high priest of Ra in Memphis, Potabi, and we believe that Ra alone is god. He and I will move forward with his plan for this temple and would greatly appreciate your help. The most important request I make of you, however . . ." Her words drowned in emotion, and she lowered her head.

His anger cooled. She'd been through much today. "Nathy, forgive me. I'll do whatever you ask."

She looked up, appearing more like his little girl. "You must find the soldier who stole Ommi's body. When I am healed, then I can bring healing to others."

He pressed his hand against her cheek. "Your chanting calls people to the temple and brings them healing. Fadil and his new priests will provide a House of Ra where people come for medical care, protection from evil, and to render offerings for answered prayers. Let that be healing to you while I use my resources and connections to find the soldier who tortures your dreams." He leaned in to kiss her forehead. "I will find the man. I vow it." He nodded to his captain. "Nuru, escort us to the palace."

Asenath looped her arm with Potiphera's, and they started toward the tallest building in the city.

"Daughter, you know I could never reject all gods except Ra. It would separate the family of gods."

Asenath pretended not to hear him.

"Must I remind you that Paneah is a Hebrew?" he whispered. "A Hyksos."

"How can you fight Paneah when Ra sent you a dream proving he should be my husband?" She pulled her arm from his, furious now. "I'm rebuilding this temple for the one god, Ra, but my husband says his god, Elohim—who gave Pharaoh his dreams—is the only god. You've predicted the future through Ra's omens, but Joseph says Elohim enabled him to interpret Pharaoh's dreams. Which is the real god: Ra or Elohim?"

Potiphera drew a breath to answer, but she shouted, "No! I must decide for myself if Ra and Elohim are one and the same. Either way, I can love both you and Joseph. Now, leave it alone, Potabi. I need to rest."

She resumed a resolute march—and Potiphera allowed it. Had

they been in On, he would have punished her. He hurried to walk alongside her. "Remember, you are still Isis Incarnate. Without Isis to create the serpent that sunk its teeth into Ra, she would never have become Egypt's great healer. The family of gods is too intricately entwined to separate—like you and me. Without Ra giving Lady Hathor too much beer, how could we explain the end of summer and beer's soothing properties? Every god has its purpose—as do you, Asenath."

She remained silent, eyes forward. They continued toward the palace without another word. It was fine. The Memphis songbird would be reborn in Ra's temple while Potiphera discovered the mysterious soldier and Paneah planned his silly granaries.

Fadil was right about one thing, Katesch. Our daughter certainly inherited not only your lovely voice, but also your fire. I promise you, my beloved, within the next thirty days, I will make many more sacrifices to Ra and win the favor of King Apophis. Then our girl will be well on her way to becoming the next queen of Egypt.

NINETEEN

Who cuts a channel for the torrents of rain,
and a path for the thunderstorm,
to water a land where no one lives,
an uninhabited desert,
to satisfy a desolate wasteland
and make it sprout with grass?

JOB 38:25–27

ONE MONTH LATER

Joseph

Jendayi sat on the barque's deck beside Joseph, snacking on fruit and vegetables from the palace cook. Joseph looked toward the sleeping city. Memphis had been a testing ground on which Elohim had given him resounding victories. Asenath had been right about trusting his Medjays' protection, and little Jendayi had brought laughter and warmth to each city and village they'd visited. She'd disarmed everyone from the palace cook, who prepared her a basket of fresh treats each morning, to the stodgiest old noblemen, leaving them malleable to Elohim's plan to save Egypt.

Joseph offered his new best friend a grape. "The one who holds the food holds the power and wins the favor." Zahra's advice was certainly true, but Asenath had also been right. "The one who holds

Jendayi holds the power and wins the favor." He scratched her beneath her chin and peered over his shoulder at the eastern horizon. Dread grew as the dawn brightened to morning.

Hami stood behind him. "We'll sail as soon as Mistress Asenath and Highness Potiphera arrive."

Joseph nodded. Asenath had sent a messenger this morning, informing him that they would assist Fadil one last time with Lighting of the Fire and Drawing of the Bolt before boarding. "Explain it to me," Joseph said. "Why would anyone worship a sun god who couldn't find his way out of the underworld each morning unless humans lit a fire in a brazier and unbolted the door to his sacred chamber?"

Hami didn't answer, which was fine. Joseph hadn't expected one.

Jendayi suddenly screeched and climbed onto Joseph's shoulder, then circumnavigated his neck. Searching the shore for what might have agitated her, he saw Potiphera approaching the docks— Asenath at his side. Joseph stood and sighed. He hadn't offered his wife more than a passing greeting since she'd chosen to help her abi rebuild the temple instead of accompanying him to meet the people of Egypt. He'd been hurt and angry, but now he realized Elohim had used the past thirty days to prove He was Joseph's most important escort. Joseph had met the nome governor and Memphis's city elders, traveled to nearby villages, and even sailed to the larger cities—Saqqara, Giza, and Dahshur—to see the pyramids and assess the damage from overabundant floods.

No matter where they went, Jendayi was his willing companion— one that didn't question his decisions or try to sabotage Elohim's plan. She drew friendly banter like blossoms lured bees. Easy conversation begat freedom to share new ideas and raise concerns. Elohim had opened doors for Joseph's gentle authority to implement Pharaoh's commands, proving Potiphera and Asenath were no longer necessary to the success of his tour. He started toward mid-deck to inform them.

Hami's large hand landed on his shoulder, halting him. "The answer to your question, Lord Vizier, is this: Egypt's sun god needs a fire to light his way because the gods demand ceremony, and their priests—like everyone—need purpose. Your god, though unseen, has proven very different—and far more powerful. As his emissary, you're effective because you, too, are different. You prove most powerful through understated authority." He removed his hand from Joseph's shoulder and motioned toward the plank where Asenath was about to board.

They had a full day of sailing ahead and would reach Meydum at dusk or later. Was it wise to confront her and Potiphera now, then spend the rest of the day in misery?

Joseph clapped Hami's shoulder. "Wise advice, my friend." Joseph would wait until they reached the Gurob Palace to send a request to Pharaoh Yanassi for Potiphera and Asenath to be relieved from the tour. By then, Asenath would likely be weary of traveling, and Joseph would have more proof of Potiphera's obstinance.

Joseph returned to the bow and sat beside Jendayi. Asenath and her abi would no doubt spend the day on their covered couches at the stern. She'd sent a message that they'd be late this morning—instead of walking down the hallway to tell him face-to-face. If his wife wished to speak with him during the sail, she could walk the fifty paces from stern to bow. He offered Jendayi a piece of cucumber. "I suspect if your ommi comes this direction, she'll wish to see you, not me."

"May Ra's favor shine." Potiphera's general greeting forecast a rough sail no matter how calm the water. Joseph looked over his shoulder and found the priest, as suspected, moving toward the stern.

"Jendayi, come," Asenath shouted. But the monkey climbed into Joseph's lap, ignoring her.

In the awkward silence that followed, sailors gathered hemp ropes, casting accusing glances at Joseph. He felt a sudden rush of guilt and whispered to the little creature, "You must return to your ommi."

"Have I lost you both then?" Asenath's voice was very near.

"Oars up!" the helmsman shouted.

"Mistress, you really should sit down." Hami guided her to Joseph's side. "The water level has decreased, so we must pull the boat from shore with ropes."

The boat lurched, and Joseph reached for his wife's arm to steady her. She shot him a surprised look, and he released her immediately. "Forgive me, I—" He untied the belt he wore containing Jendayi's food and tossed it into her lap. "Take this. The palace servants filled it every morning like Hotep used to do." Thankfully, the monkey followed the food.

Joseph turned away, pretending interest in the Nile's empty western shore. The barque lurched several more times, and then the helmsman began his rhythmic chant. "Pull . . . pull . . . pull!" A gentle breeze moved Joseph's curls. He dared look straight ahead and captured barely a glimpse of his lovely wife in the periphery. She stroked Jendayi's chest and stomach in silence. Then she sniffed and wiped her cheeks—and his heart shattered. How could he take Jendayi on the tour of Egypt without taking Asenath?

"I'm sorry, Joseph."

Startled by his wife's apology, he found that muddled thoughts tied his tongue.

She looked up, kohl dripping down her cheeks. "I'm sorry my choice to rebuild the temple with Fadil and Potabi hurt you. I'm sorry I placed finding the soldier's identity above our shared destiny of healing Egypt." She bowed her head, and Jendayi stroked her hair. "I hope to prove I can be a better wife during the rest of our tour."

Joseph's arms ached to comfort her, but he refused to give her false hope. Everything she'd regretted were valid reasons to send her back to Avaris. She could thrive there with Queen Tani's friendship, and Potiphera would adjust to his life at On's temple with two chantresses. "Asenath, I understand the need to reconcile with your past. During my first few years in Egypt, I was more a slave to my brothers' betrayal than to Captain Potiphar."

She looked up with a tentative smile. "Thank you, Joseph. I knew you'd understand."

"Did Potiphera discover the soldier's identity?"

"No, but he promised to continue his search."

She could personally oversee the search from Avaris. "I can send a message to Pharaoh—"

"I can't keep searching, Joseph." She placed a hand on his arm. "It's too consuming. I've told Potabi not to tell me any more about his progress—or failures. I can't remain focused on the past. I sent a message to Zahra and Hotep, telling them I would take the advice they gave me in Bubastis. I need to focus on the future, with you."

Joseph would rather the barque capsize than tell her, but . . . "Asenath, I've made a decision." Color drained from her cheeks. "I'd planned to wait until we reached Gurob to tell you, but I don't need an escort, so—"

"Don't say it, Joseph!" She pressed her hand against his mouth. "Please. Let me explain what happened in Memphis first."

Asenath's hand fell from his lips, and he was startled again by her fire and beauty. He withdrew a cloth from his belt and wiped her face, using her tears as the moisture to remove her cosmetics.

"Zaphenath-Paneah!" people shouted from shore. "Zaphenath-Paneah! The gods speak; we live!"

His wife took in the crowds. "Well, Lord Vizier, it would seem you didn't miss Potabi's presence or mine in the least." The hint of pride in her tone both surprised and pleased him.

"After Potiphera introduced me to the nome governor and Memphis city elders," Joseph began, "Jendayi softened their hearts, and Elohim gave me words to win their favor. I met a few engineers and builders whose families live in outlying villages, so they became my advocates in the surrounding fields and farmers' huts."

"Perhaps you and Jendayi should greet your people." She transferred Jendayi to his shoulder. They approached the rail together, waving at common villagers who lived south of Memphis.

After the crowds thinned, Joseph conveyed to his wife the more sobering aspects of his month. "When we arrived, Memphis was ready to follow history's example and kill any pharaoh or his official because the god-on-the-throne had allowed the Nile to destroy their lives—in this case by the overabundant Inundation. Livestock, huts, and even children were swept away. The people blamed Pharaohs Yanassi and Apophis, the sons of Seth and Ra, for failing to protect them. Once I realized their dire situation, I ordered engineers and builders to shift focus from building bigger granaries to constructing stronger dikes and rebuilding huts."

She covered his hand on the railing, sending warmth up his arm. "It sounds like you've done more than win favor. You've rebuilt lives."

He slipped his hand away, scratching Jendayi's chin as a diversion. "Well, you were right about Jendayi," he said. "She turned out to be a much better escort than Potiphera."

Asenath chuckled, looking toward the couches to be sure her abi was out of hearing range. "I'm a little jealous that I, too, can be so easily replaced." She grew pensive. "But because of our time in Memphis, my destiny is no longer filled with nameless, faceless images or abstract stories about my god. I, too, was awakened to the hardships both feast and famine can bring. Though Memphis itself didn't see the devastation you describe in the smaller villages, the pilgrims who came to Ra's temple were starving for more than legends and songs." She gripped the railing so tightly, her knuckles turned white.

Joseph was pleased she finally understood the urgency of their mission but didn't want her to feel frightened by it. "Though even old men and women never witnessed floods so high they split the dunes, there's no need to fear." He pointed at a deep channel where receding floodwaters had left white crystals glistening on the dune's contours. "Elohim proves His control as Master Artist and Creator by highlighting the edges with salt."

He heard her slight gasp and watched to measure her reaction to the full picture. "Over the next six years, even large cities like Memphis might need to fight abundant floods. So far the pyramid cities of Giza, Saqqara, and Dahshur have no flood damage. Hami and I took a contingent of Medjays and helped them begin new dikes so the monuments would remain protected. But smaller villages all over Egypt will need help rebuilding every year the river floods."

"For six more Inundations? If people must rebuild their huts every year, when—and where—will they build granaries?"

Joseph had asked Elohim the same question a hundred times. A child on shore ran parallel to the barque. Would *that* child be swept away by next year's Inundation? His chest constricted as the sailors rowed steadily against the gentler tide. *Elohim, help me protect these people to prove You are the one true and living God.*

"Potabi will never believe Ra is the only god," Asenath said.

"What makes you say that?"

"He says the family of gods is too intricately woven together to ever be unbound. I believe it's Potabi's ambition, too intricately woven with pride, that holds truth captive."

Joseph was stunned that she'd seen through Potiphera's deception. Using every sinew of restraint, he waited while she formed her next words. "Turning my back on Egypt's gods comes at great cost to me. It would require that I relinquish my status as high priestess of Isis and forego what I've seen as my life's purpose since Ommi's last breath."

He moved closer to whisper, "Are you saying you believe Elohim is the one true God, but you can't yet say it to your abi or publicly?"

She moved so close, they were nearly touching. "I'm saying that Potabi's argument is very convincing. Ra *is* too intricately woven together with the other gods of Egypt. So, if Ra cannot stand alone, then who but Elohim could be the *one god* that sent His messenger to me?" Her lovely brown eyes looked up at Joseph, searching and sincere.

Jendayi blew bubbles against his cheek, startling him into levity. Asenath forced a smile. "I seem to have lost my baby."

"I will never take Jendayi from you." He could say that now with absolute confidence—and new hope. *Thank You, Elohim. Perhaps Asenath and I can someday be united in purpose* and *faith.* Maybe even love.

TWENTY

*Do not arouse or awaken love
until it so desires.*

SONG OF SONGS 2:7

Asenath

Two days ago, at dusk, our barque had approached the small village of Meydum. A hundred paces from shore stood six mud huts atop mounds of sand. "Where are the buildings? I don't see any people." My observation had echoed loud on the water.

Joseph shushed me and said, "Look beyond the huts."

I examined the village again and noticed a lopsided pyramid. "If they can't even build a pyramid properly," I whispered, "how will they build granaries? Perhaps the people of Meydum should disperse to other villages."

He leaned closer. "Where do Meydum's hundred villagers *live,* Asenath?"

I finally scanned beyond the shoreline and past the imperfect buildings to the flood-ravaged plain. "Oh, Joseph . . ." I couldn't speak past my growing concern. Willow-branched lean-tos littered the muddy land, while naked children and excited strangers ran to greet us. Sniffing back emotion, I whispered to my husband, "How do we heal *this?*" I'd asked him something similar before, but now I ventured no easy answers.

"Tomorrow, I'll send a messenger to Memphis, requesting a team of engineers and builders to come and help build granaries for this year's harvest and dikes to protect them from next year's Inundation. We'll help rebuild huts and compile a list of people's other needs. We alone can't heal Egypt no matter how hard we try, but Elohim can help us protect it from its current and future wounds."

For the next two days, I worked alongside my husband and witnessed the truth of his convictions. Even Potabi showed he cared deeply for the people of Meydum, teaching the children about Ra and his barque sailing across the sky. The village women taught me to weave and make bread. I reveled in the children's laughter and cuddled them when they skinned their knees. Joseph picked splinters from my palms after we'd used wooden shovels to dig a ditch. My nails remained caked with Egypt's black earth, and I stank like a pig farmer. My hair stood on end like a lion's mane, and I wore no cosmetics. Still, Joseph called me beautiful.

As I lay now in my reed hut alone, the morning lark's song brought tears to my eyes. I'd watched the courses of the moon through my single window, dreading impending goodbyes.

"Are you awake?" Joseph's voice made me smile.

"Yes."

"Good, because I need your help." His smooth tone sent waves of pleasure through me.

"Help with what?"

Jendayi skittered around my tapestry door before I pushed it aside to see dawn's amethyst glow.

Joseph moved closer, his eyes holding mine though he didn't touch me. "I need your help to heal Egypt."

My stomach felt as if a thousand butterflies took flight. The feeling stole my breath, as it had many times since we'd arrived in Meydum. Was this love? Potabi would blame the village food. Captivated and tongue-tied, I stared at the most handsome man in Egypt.

"Many of the villagers have already come to say goodbye." He moved aside, and I saw them coming from their lean-tos and nearby fires.

My chest tightened, recognizing each face. "I hate goodbyes. Tell me again why we can't stay longer?" I'd already begged him twice before.

"Asenath." He looked at me from beneath a hooded brow.

"All right, then. Tell me again why we must travel on donkeys to Gurob Palace?"

His chastising look remained. "We'll save a full day's travel and arrive at Gurob Palace in two days instead of three."

"That means we must camp in the Faiyum, and Potabi says—" I hugged my waist, trying to still the intensified flutter.

"Don't let your abi's stories about the Faiyum frighten you. You're safe with me, Wife." Joseph slid his hands up my arms.

My breath caught.

He, too, seemed affected and dropped his hands. "Let's say our goodbyes." His smile suddenly tight and awkward, he wouldn't meet my eyes.

"Joseph." I caught his arm, stopping him before we joined the growing crowd. "Were you thinking of her just now?" *Ahira.* I knew her name but didn't wish to speak it.

He winced as if I'd slapped him. "Why would you ask me—"

"Because sometimes I see guilt shadow your features when you show any sort of . . . when you . . . when we . . ."

"Asenath, I'm trying. I do feel—"

"Come, oh great Ra," Potabi shouted, "from your victorious underworld journey!" He carried a brazier with the new day's fire toward the gathering and offered his blessing on the village. Joseph and I left our intimate moment to join them, sharing a tearful farewell and the hope that next month's sowing, the coming harvest, and future Inundations would be better managed.

Hami escorted Joseph and me toward the pack animals and the guides he'd hired from Meydum who would lead us into the Faiyum. The experts had pared down our supplies to fit into baskets secured on twelve donkeys. Joseph had requisitioned two more for Potabi and me to ride.

"You may walk with me until you grow tired." Joseph looked at me with those mesmerizing golden-green eyes. "Or would you prefer to ride—"

"My daughter will ride." Potabi mounted his donkey. "Neither you nor Asenath have experienced the Faiyum. I have. Danger lurks behind every sand dune, outcropping, and—"

Joseph whirled on him. "Asenath will decide for herself."

Temple guards tensed, and Potabi's face flushed. "I've protected my daughter for nearly twenty Inundations."

"You protected her from danger in a tower that separated her from the world." Joseph inhaled, then exhaled slowly, calmer. "I will protect Asenath while we experience the world together."

Potabi ignored Joseph and his well-phrased argument. "You're an intelligent woman who I taught about the dangers of the Faiyum. Will you ride the donkey or walk?" He'd done it again—changed a simple choice into a test of my allegiance.

"I . . ." Stammering, my thoughts shifted from one poor consequence to another. "Frankly, neither choice is appealing."

Joseph's hand slipped into mine. "Asenath." I looked up and saw sadness on his features. "You're frightened. Ride the donkey. I'll walk beside you. You need not choose between your abi and me again." He tugged gently on my fingers, leading me to the first donkey, and I gladly followed.

* * *

Could I ever walk again? Potabi and I had ridden our donkeys since dawn, stopping twice to refresh both humans and beasts. My backside had lost all feeling, and my legs felt like dangling palm trees. Yet the Faiyum's natural beauty had captivated me. How could Potabi's graphic warnings have excluded a thousand bright-colored birds on marshlands? Or the way sand dunes became rocky terrain within a single day's walk? But his fear-filled portrayals became perfect depictions when dusk descended and animals prowled.

"Joseph, how much farther to camp?" I asked for the third time. "Not far."

"I don't like you walking in that tall grass. There could be any number of—"

Another animal howled. "Joseph, we must stop! Please!" Fear stained all the beauty, reducing me to tears.

"Shh, Asenath." He pulled me off the donkey and held me. "We're almost to the camp. Hami sent a group of men ahead of us. It's not much farther."

"Could I camp in your arms?" I chuckled awkwardly but meant it—then pulled away. We'd avoided finishing our discussion about Ahira. I focused on the grass around our feet.

"Do you want to walk with me?" he asked.

I glanced ahead of us. The Medjays in front were tramping down a wide swath of grass. "All right," I said, "but hold my hand." Not only did he grasp my hand, but he kissed it before we started walking. Jendayi climbed over to my shoulder, perhaps sensing I needed her comfort.

I stole glances at my handsome husband as the day's last rays broke over his angular features. He'd worn kohl around his eyes to ward off gnats. Frankincense had replaced his familiar scents of mint and clove but still shielded the musky smell of a long day in Egypt's sun. "Tomorrow will be a shorter day of hiking." He grinned down at me. "Would you prefer to walk with me or ride the donkey again?"

"I'll walk with you—if you can provide a shield from my toes to my chin. Ew!" I swatted a beetle off my leg and shuddered. He laughed, so I swatted him, too. "You see? It's not merely howling things I'm afraid of. It's crawling, slithering, biting things, too!"

"I'm afraid there are no such shields, Wife, but perhaps applying vinegar or frankincense would be a deterrent for the crawling, biting things." He pointed toward the camp ahead. "Look! You made it. Very brave. You wait here with the donkey while I speak with

Hami." He placed the reins in my hands and left me before I could protest.

Potabi stopped his donkey beside me. "He's not worthy of you." Perched atop the beast, he watched Joseph while he poured out his venom. "What will you do when I find this soldier who took your ommi's body? Paneah won't even protect you from wild animals. Do you think he'll punish the man who stole Katesch from us?"

"Joseph will do what's right, Potabi, because he's a good man." I refused to be baited. "You should be pleased with the work we've done in Memphis and Meydum. I'm fulfilling my destiny and healing Egypt."

"I'd call it bedding a Hyksos."

I glared at him. "He is my husband, Potabi, and his god's plan will heal our nation."

He leaned close, teeth clenched. "A true healer would prevent the mighty Hapi from flooding every village for the next six years." He kicked his donkey's sides and trotted away.

Potabi was surly because he felt threatened. He was as afraid of being alone as I'd always feared losing him. "But by trying to pry Joseph and me apart," I whispered, "you're pushing me away."

Potabi met Joseph, and they exchanged a quiet conversation, seeming civil. Then my husband continued toward me. "You're pale," he said. "What did he say to upset you?"

"It's what we didn't say." I ignored Potabi's censure and gathered my courage. "I'd feel safer if you slept in my tent tonight."

He looked as if I'd thrust a dagger into his belly. "Asenath, I—"

"Never mind." Mortified, I shoved the reins at his chest and hurried past him.

He caught my arm. "You asked if I ever think of Ahira and feel guilty when I'm with you." I couldn't look at him. "Yes, to both—because I'm starting to have feelings for you. I don't trust myself to sleep in your tent unless you believe Elohim is the one true God." He paused, waiting for an answer I couldn't give. "Can you look at me and say you believe it?"

I considered lying, but this man was too valuable to risk deception. So, I looked up with a million regrets and said, "Not yet."

He swallowed hard and then wrapped his arms around me.
"Then I will sleep at the doorway of your tent."

"Joseph, no! It's too dangerous to sleep outside."

He grinned. "Remember, I was a shepherd and a Bedouin. I slept
in open fields or tents until I became a slave. I'm at home in land
such as the Faiyum."

He was a wonder, this Canaanite. "Will you tell me more about
your family? I doubt I'll sleep much anyway."

With my donkey's reins in one hand, he reached for my hand
with the other, and we started toward camp. "I'm not sure revealing
my family's secrets is wise now that you've started to like me."

I giggled like a besotted maiden, no longer fearing the howling,
creeping, or biting things, and concentrated fully on his hand
around mine.

TWENTY-ONE

This is what God the LORD says—
the Creator of the heavens, who stretches them out,
  who spreads out the earth with all that springs from it,
  who gives breath to its people,
  and life to those who walk on it.

ISAIAH 42:5

NEXT DAY
Asenath

Jendayi rode peacefully on Joseph's shoulder during our second day of Faiyum hiking. I accepted Joseph's hand to help me conquer a miniature mountain—actually a tall outcropping of jagged rocks, but a mountain to one who had lived most of life in a tower. We spoke very little after a night filled with stories of his family. Content with silence and needing all my breath for climbing, I splashed through a waterfall and tromped through tall grass, pondering a god who called one family his own.

From atop lofty dunes and towering rocks, we glimpsed a pyramid in the distance and continued toward it. As dusk approached, the howl of jackals frayed my nerves and sent Jendayi to my shoulder, her arms gripping my neck. I grabbed Joseph's hand and hurried our pace to catch up with the caravan. Medjays had surrounded us at a distance throughout the day, allowing us the illusion of roaming free.

I released Joseph's hand and caught up with Potabi, whose temple guards encircled him. Jendayi grew nervous as we approached, climbing beneath my hair at the back of my neck. I broke through his retinue and saw that Potabi had cushioned his ride with four woolen blankets. "Potabi, you could have enjoyed a walk with me."

He scowled. Then his donkey stumbled, and he cursed the poor beast.

Suddenly, Jendayi went berserk. Jumping and screeching, she lunged, and Joseph barely caught her.

"Hold her, Joseph!" I shouted. But she wriggled against his grasp. "Why is she trying to run away?"

I reached for her, and she nipped at me. "Jendayi, no! What's wrong with you?" She'd never bit me before!

"The monkey sees her own kind." Potabi pointed at a group of five monkeys—each twice Jendayi's size—near a copse of palm trees.

"Come here, baby." I took her from Joseph and cradled her against my chest. She whimpered while I stroked her.

"Guenon monkeys are everywhere in the Faiyum," Potabi explained. "I'm surprised we haven't seen more. They travel in families. Terrible pests—especially at the Gurob Palace." Jendayi perked her ears when the guenons made a strange sound.

"They're whistling at you." Joseph tickled her belly.

"It's a *chirp*." Potabi's biting tone silenced my husband.

"It sounds like a whistle." I glared at him. "You taught my sisters and me that monkeys have communicated this way since before the pharaohs ruled Egypt."

He nodded. "A pet monkey is a sign of elegance among Egyptian nobility, far more impressive than herding dogs or house cats." He sniffed with an air of superiority. "Perhaps Asenath's little friend could find a male and bear a child so Paneah could get his own pet."

Joseph's cheeks flushed, but I pressed my elbow into his belly before he could respond. Now was the time to tell Potabi what

Joseph and I had decided last night. "You've given us a wonderful idea, Potabi. Paneah and I plan to travel around the Faiyum in the same way he visited other villages while you and I rebuilt Memphis's temple. Perhaps we'll find a monkey for Paneah during our travels. While we're away, you'll have time to continue the search for the soldier who took Ommi's body."

Potabi's mouth opened but uttered no words. Then, somberly, "If that's what you wish, Daughter."

"It is." I saw his pain, but Joseph and I needed time together without his interference. "When Paneah and I return, you can continue with—"

"Your husband will make sure I'm gone by the time you return." He locked eyes with Joseph. "Isn't that right, Lord Vizier?"

Joseph's expression was like etched granite. "Your spies have served you well, Highness."

"What are you saying?" Neither of them had told me anything about this.

Joseph looked at me, softening. "I'll leave the choice to your abi, Asenath." He faced Potabi. "You may remain at Gurob Palace until your daughter and I return from our tour of Faiyum temples and villages. If, upon our return, you can prove yourself essential to healing Egypt's wounds, you may sail with us when we leave Gurob. If not, your temple guards will escort you back to On."

"No, Jo— Paneah, please. You don't understand."

"I understand more than you know." His look nearly swallowed me. "Potiphera must bow the knee or face the consequences. You know it's true." He searched my eyes, waiting, but I couldn't speak. To agree would betray the abi who saved my life. To contradict would betray my heart. "We need to keep walking." Joseph continued toward the pyramid with Hami.

Potabi gave a cynical snort. "Your husband had no time for you in Memphis, and now you're willing to go with him into the Faiyum? You're a fool." He scoffed and kicked his donkey's sides, trotting away. His guards jogged beside him, and I felt suddenly alone.

I tried to cuddle Jendayi, but she resisted, still fascinated with the guenons nearby. Even my monkey had found others like her. Potabi had his temple guards, and Joseph had Hami. Who did I have? Oh, how I missed Zahra and Hotep.

Another howl sent me scurrying to catch up with Joseph and Hami. "Was that a jackal or hyena?"

"Does it matter? Both attack after dusk," Potabi said, riding alongside me. Our whole procession now moved in tight formation. "It would be a shame to die this close to the palace."

I held my tongue.

As we crested the final dune, a flock of ibis flew over Gurob's palace complex. The pharaoh's historic sporting destination was civilization and culture within the Faiyum's feral beauty. Potabi had been right when he'd said the Faiyum was unlike anywhere else in Egypt.

I examined the mound of sand beneath my feet. "Joseph, we've seen no deep gashes in the sand dunes anywhere in the Faiyum." When I looked up, he seemed as startled as I. "Do you remember any part of our two-day hike that bore water scars like you saw elsewhere?"

He pointed toward the majestic palace. "Gurob shows no sign of flood damage either."

"You finally noticed?" Potabi watched us with a condescending smirk.

"How has the whole Faiyum been protected from flooding?"

"I told you. Ptah created no other place like it."

Joseph examined our surroundings in every direction. "God had help. He created natural wadis to connect the Nile to Faiyum marshlands, and then the twelfth-dynasty pharaohs used Amu slaves to turn the wadis into a canal that controlled the river's flow." He looked at Potabi. "This is an opportunity for you to prove yourself essential, Potiphera. Tell me all you know of this canal."

Potabi's lip curled, reluctantly acknowledging my husband's request. "Nearly two hundred Inundations past, Amenemhat-Nimaatra—most worthy son of Ra—partnered with Ptah, creator of the natural wadis. Ptah gave Pharaoh Amenemhat wisdom to form Magic Lake. His slaves dug the canal—building dikes and sluices along the way—that diverted floodwaters toward a rocky gorge Ptah prepared at the beginning of time. The project controlled the river's flooding, transformed a marshy floodplain into tillable soil, expanded Egypt's inhabitable land, and created a lake to pleasure the gods."

"But it's no longer a canal." I reexamined the narrow wadi we'd splashed across before climbing the dune. "Why has it been left unkempt?"

"The Faiyum is the gods' greatest masterpiece, and Amenemhat's effort was mediocre at best." Potabi swung his leg off the donkey, stumbled, but pushed away all offers of help. "We all heard the jackals howl when we crossed Amenemhat's canal because it was a warning, reminding us that men's efforts always fade into overgrown, underwhelming imitations. Giza and Saqqara—Egypt's greatest pyramids—are men's best attempts to duplicate the sun god's radiance." He scoffed. "Ra can't be reproduced by human hands any better than a canal can control the Nile."

My husband motioned toward a stagnant, algae-filled pond beside the palace complex. "Slaves built what King Amenemhat commanded, Potiphera. They didn't duplicate Elohim's creation. They simply used the wisdom and skill God gave them to make their lives better." His eyes sparkled with hope. "And restoring these dikes and sluices could keep Egypt from becoming a graveyard."

"Are the gods speaking to you again, Paneah?"

Joseph braced Potabi's shoulders. "Yes, He is! You said the canal leads to Magic Lake, but where does the canal begin?"

Potabi was already shaking his head. "It never carried the full flow of the river. The records at Gurob say—"

"Records, Potiphera? If you know there are records, you know where it connects."

"It won't work, Paneah."

"But the canal reaches the Nile, doesn't it?"

Potabi looked away. Joseph scanned the land in every direction. "It reaches to the Nile." His voice was filled with awe. "Elohim, my

God and mighty Creator, You've given us wisdom for a path of relief from the next six years of flooding. Ha ha, thank You, Elohim!" Without warning, he whirled and kissed Potabi's bald forehead. "And thank you, Potiphera. You restored a temple in Memphis, and now you'll restore a canal in the Faiyum. You're becoming essential!"

I giggled, and even Potabi couldn't hide a grin. "You're insane, Lord Vizier. It will never work."

"It *will* work. And you will oversee the project while Asenath and I travel through the Faiyum and assess the need for granaries. You know this canal and its history better than anyone in my caravan."

"Paneah, we don't even know if the canal still connects to the river."

"Then we find out." Joseph nodded toward Nuru and Hami. "You and I leave with our captains at dawn tomorrow to see where the canal connects."

"Wait!" I gripped Joseph's arm. "Both you and Potabi will leave?"

The excitement on his features drained like an overturned goblet of wine. "Forgive me. I wasn't thinking. We can . . ." He grew quiet, his words seeming to dissolve.

"Asenath," Potabi said, "your husband undoubtedly noted that the canal is barely wide enough for a skiff, and each skiff carries two men." He turned his attention to Paneah. "Nuru and I will be ready at dawn, Lord Vizier. The journey will require at least a week."

Joseph turned his back on Potabi, whispering, "Tell me now if you need me to stay with you." His eyes searched mine.

Could I be strong? Was I brave enough? "Go. Make Potabi essential so he can travel with us for the rest of our tour."

He smiled and offered his hand.

"It's all right," I said. "I'll finish our walk with Potabi." He nodded, then winked. My cheeks warmed as he and Hami hurried down the dune with the Medjays and pack animals.

Potabi and I lagged, his guards following. "Promise me you'll become essential." I linked my arm with his.

He scoffed as another jackal howled.

"You said a true healer would prevent the flooding," I reminded him. "You could become that healer by clearing the canal. If there's even a chance it could work, Potabi, shouldn't you try?"

"He's a Hyksos," he whispered. "Never forget that."

"And you should never forget that Zaphenath-Paneah is both my husband and second in power to the pharaohs. Respect him—and me."

I didn't dare look at him when his arm tensed around mine. Reminding myself of his sacrifices for me, we entered Gurob's palace complex in silence.

TWENTY-TWO

Arise, come, my darling;
my beautiful one, come with me.

SONG OF SONGS 2:13

Joseph

With the Gurob Palace in sight, Joseph and Hami pulled hard at the oars of their skiff. Every day, Asenath had been Joseph's first thought in the morning and his last thought at night. Images of the wraith he'd found in the tower of On tortured him. She'd been alone eight days then—and again eight days alone. Yet she'd grown stronger after the messenger's visit and now had Jendayi for company. She also seemed committed to their future together. *Elohim, protect her with Your promise.*

"Almost there, Lord Vizier." Sweat ran in rivers down Hami's back in the midday sun.

Though they rowed with the river's flow, sowing season's declining water levels meant a weaker current. It was easier rowing south for five days while they followed and inspected the canal from its source to its Nile connection. Elohim had confirmed His remedy for the destructive aspect of Egypt's abundance, and they'd immediately turned their skiffs around and started back toward Gurob.

When they navigated around the final bend in the canal, Joseph saw a crowd gathered outside the palace complex. "What's going on?" Joseph shouted.

Hami looked over his shoulder and shrugged.

The muscles in Joseph's arms and back burned with every pull. He wondered how long before the second skiff would reach them. Asenath would worry, but he'd reassure her that Potiphera had rowed at a slower pace during their entire journey. Nuru, though mighty, couldn't keep pace with Hami and Joseph's fervor. Rowing slowly wasn't Potiphera's lone protest. By the second day, he and Joseph had limited their conversations to necessary facts about the canal's restoration and avoided all comments about the woman they fiercely protected.

Sounds of celebration welcomed them as Hami guided the skiff onto a sandy shore. Joseph hopped out of the boat and was met by his Medjays racing toward him.

"What sort of festival is this?" he asked, realizing many in the crowd held monkeys.

"Mistress Asenath says it's education, not a festival," one of the Medjays said. "She invited people from Gurob and Lahun to learn from our Faiyum guides about the proper care of pet monkeys and from the Meydum engineers the necessity of building efficient granaries." He pointed toward the musicians and dancers. "She knew the people would stay longer if entertained."

Joseph released eight days of fear with a belly laugh. "Has her instruction been successful?"

The same guard inclined his head respectfully. "For that answer, Lord Vizier, you must speak with your wife."

"You're a smart man, my friend." Joseph strode through the crowd to find his wife.

"Paneah!" Her voice was like healing balm.

Both Asenath and Jendayi rushed toward him. The little monkey leapt into Joseph's arms moments before his wife reached him. "I would hug you if you weren't so sweaty, Lord Vizier." Asenath's precocious grin added to her natural beauty. With nothing but kohl around her eyes and her hair in tightly braided rows, she was stunning.

"I must hurry and bathe so I can claim my hug." He held her gaze, pleased when she grinned in response.

"I've worked with the Medjays, Faiyum guides, and palace servants to prepare for our journey, Husband. Simply give the command to load the feluccas, and we can be on our way." She looked beyond him, sudden fear rising with her frantic searching. "Where is Potabi? Why isn't he—"

"Potiphera is well." Joseph caught her arm. "Our journey was productive, and he'll arrive soon. However, he will remain here while we tour the Faiyum." He tried to keep his tone light. Jendayi patted Joseph's cheeks, giving him a timely distraction.

"Potabi wasn't helpful, was he?"

Joseph looked into her lovely dark eyes. "He wasn't a hindrance. If he can remember that he loves Egypt more than he hates me, he'll restore the canal while we're gone."

"And if he doesn't?"

Joseph shook his head. She knew the answer. Needing to change the subject, he turned his attention to the incredible achievement around them. "I see you've been healing Egypt while we've been away." He motioned toward the crowd.

The diversion worked, and she began chattering like the monkeys around them. The Faiyum guides had shown the city dwellers how to interact safely with both their pets and wild monkeys. "I knew guenons traveled in families," Asenath said, "but I didn't know a family group accepts only one or two males. You may be the one male Jendayi ever accepts."

"Unless she finds a male she likes while we're in the Faiyum." Joseph wiggled his eyebrows, which earned a swat from his wife.

"The guides said it would be wise to let her roam while we're moving between villages." She grimaced. "I don't know if I can let her do that. I'm afraid she'll get hurt."

"We can decide as we go," Joseph said, scratching Jendayi's belly. Asenath's attention wandered again toward the canal. Her face lit up. "Potabi!" She gathered her robe and ran to greet Potiphera with the same gusto she'd greeted Joseph. Would she always long to be near him? Joseph exchanged a concerned glance with Hami. Together they waited for his wife to return with the grumpy high priest. *Elohim, prepare her heart if I need to send Potiphera back to On.*

"Every part of me aches." The high priest groaned as Joseph and Asenath joined them. "By the gods, I need a hot bath and a frankincense rub."

"You've earned some relaxation," Joseph said, "but be sure you bid farewell to Asenath before you retreat to your chamber."

"Farewell to Asenath?"

"She and I will sail for Hawara as soon as I get a fresh robe and eat a midday meal. You're welcome to join us for the meal."

His cheeks flushed. "I left my daughter for eight days to assess your ridiculous canal project. Is it too much to ask—"

"We couldn't have created this workable plan without your input, Potiphera." Joseph offered his hand with respect. "I'm in your debt." The priest hesitated but gripped his wrist and quickly released it— then marched toward the palace complex.

Asenath offered Joseph an apologetic glance. "I want to go urge him to join us for the meal." She hurried after him.

Joseph watched them go, and Hami whispered, "He could do great harm to the canal while we're touring the Faiyum."

The thought had plagued Joseph since he'd rashly made Potiphera overseer of the project. "If Potiphera ruins the canal, I'll have indisputable proof for Pharaoh, the queen mother, and Asenath that he's a detriment to Elohim's good plan for Egypt. Then I'll oversee the rebuilding of the canal with the plan he helped us prepare."

"That would slow our journey considerably."

"For now, we keep moving forward and leave the hearts of men to the One who created them. Frankly, I'm looking forward to a month in the Faiyum with my wife, our Medjays, and guides who know the temples, villages, and people we're trying to save." He grinned at his captain. "I'm very proud of my wife, who prepared for our journey while she was alone. She's surprised me more than once."

Hami's right brow lifted slightly. "I can promise you, Lord Vizier, your wife will surprise you again."

TWENTY-THREE

They will eat the fruit of their ways
and be filled with the fruit of their schemes.
PROVERBS 1:31

Potiphera

Potiphera ignored his daughter's pleas for conversation and declined her request to join her and Paneah for a midday meal. Aside from his open loathing of her arrogant husband, guilt and separation seemed the only punishment to which she responded.

Nuru and his temple guards escorted Potiphera to his chamber. Once inside, Potiphera inhaled deeply the aromas of frankincense and lotus oil, then flopped onto the cushioned couch.

"By all the gods, I hope to never pick up an oar again." He closed his eyes, listening to the hum of Asenath's ambition outside his courtyard wall. Why had she tried so hard to impress the vizier? Perhaps he'd mention her ingenious celebration in his next correspondence with Apophis. It had been more than six weeks since he'd sent Ra's priests with a vow of loyalty and a mere two weeks since he'd sent the second message with the carefully phrased question: *In your victory over the Memphis dynasty, Great and Mighty Son of Ra, did you per chance take for yourself the body of the Great Chantress of*

Ra? He needed to know the answer before he could continue to pursue Apophis as Egypt's true and only pharaoh. Surely, he'd responded by now.

"Nuru!" Potiphera shouted.

"Yes, Highness." His captain slipped through the door.

"Has there been any word from King Apophis?"

He removed a scroll tucked in his belt. "One of our men said this arrived yesterday."

Potiphera sat up, his pulse quickening at the sight of the co-regent's seal. He broke it and unrolled the short missive.

I took Memphis, not a chantress. Bring Asenath to Edfu. Leave the vizier to me.

No introductions or blather. King Apophis was clear. He was not the soldier who stole Katesch's body from the temple, but he was a man who took what he wanted. Potiphera hurried to his washbasin. "Get me a fresh robe. I must bid my daughter and the Hebrew farewell."

"Of course, Highness." He began sorting through the few robes they'd brought from Memphis. "Does your improved humor indicate good news from King Apophis, Highness?"

"Indeed. I can concentrate on regaining my daughter's affection and trust Apophis to deal with the Hebrew since he's committed to marrying my daughter." He patted his face dry. The whole matter would have been easier if Asenath weren't smitten by the handsome vizier. *But I can be the comfort she needs when Apophis forces his will.* As long as the Hebrew didn't put a child in her belly before then. A child would complicate a divorce. "Tell me at least one of Paneah's Medjays agreed to spy for us while my daughter is alone with him in the Faiyum."

Nuru's solemn features forecast the disastrous answer. "I'm sorry, Highness, but no. Every Medjay on the vizier's detail has been loyal to Captain Hami and the Hebrew for many years."

"Then offer more incentive." Potiphera spoke through clenched teeth. "My daughter is about to leave with a Hyksos vizier who has stolen her heart and the gods' favor from me. If Asenath carries a Hebrew child in her belly, Apophis could refuse the marriage. Get *someone* on that Medjay contingent to work on our behalf, Nuru."

"We dare not press the Medjay, Highness." Nuru hesitated. "But my men made it clear that our incentives are available to any Medjay who sends valuable information during the Faiyum tour."

Potiphera studied his captain's expression. He was a good soldier. Loyal. "You've done well, Nuru." How far into this deception would this man follow his high priest? "Make sure I have plenty of papyrus, reeds, and pigment. I'll need to communicate with both pharaohs regularly about our canal project if I'm to keep myself out of prison." He chuckled. "It's one thing to poke a Hebrew lion but another entirely to betray the son of Khyan."

Nuru didn't flinch. "You'll have everything you need, Highness." A slow grin brightened his countenance. "And perhaps all you *want* as well."

Potiphera clapped his shoulder and sent him out the door. Need and want were too often intermingled. His needs were food, water, and shelter, but he *wanted* peace—and power. He'd held both before the boy pharaoh gave Asenath to a Hebrew.

Paneah was like every other Hyksos. He wielded power like the weapons the Amu brought to Egypt generations ago—the dog-leg sword, the complex bow, and the horse-drawn chariot. They all made Egypt fiercer than their enemies in battle, but at what cost? Zaphenath-Paneah—the gods spoke, and Egypt would live—but, again, at what cost? He had blinded both Asenath and the gods, but Potiphera refused to sell his soul to a descendant of the Bedouin prince who caused Egypt's defilement.

He pondered Apophis's words. *Leave the vizier to me.*

Did he plan to kill Paneah? He could only hope.

Whispers of regret niggled at Potiphera's conscience. Asenath had suffered many losses in her life. The loss of her husband—even this Hyksos—would cause some pain, but marrying a king was her destiny. Potiphera checked his reflection in the bronze mirror. "If I wait until we arrive in Edfu at harvest, Apophis may no longer wish to deal with the Hebrew." He must find a way to destroy Paneah and the canal project, for the idea to restore it was truly brilliant. Why did the gods still favor him?

Great and Mighty Ra, give me wisdom and sway the other gods to honor my plans against the arrogant Hebrew.

TWENTY-FOUR

Wounds from a friend can be trusted,
but an enemy multiplies kisses.
PROVERBS 27:6

Asenath

"Wait!" Potabi shouted from the palace portico behind us. "Lord Vizier! I said wait!" He and Nuru hurried to catch up.

I gently tugged on my husband's arm, and he met Potabi's pleas with a sour expression. "What is it, Potiphera? We must get underway to Hawara."

"You would leave without allowing me to say goodbye to my daughter?"

Joseph scoffed. "You refused our meal invitations."

Potabi waved him off. "Nathy, you must do exactly as the Faiyum guides instruct you."

"I will, Potabi."

"Take no chances." He glared at Joseph. "I will hold you personally responsible if my daughter is harmed. Faiyum crocodiles are more aggressive than river crocs. Make sure you're off the water and away from the shore by dusk."

"I'll protect my wife, Highness. You have enough to occupy your mind with the canal project while we're gone. It's no longer simply a good idea—it's essential to Egypt's flood survival. If I return to Gurob and find you haven't implemented our plans, I'll consider your inaction treason." Joseph leaned close. "And I won't send you back to On. You'll go to Avaris and explain to Pharaoh Yanassi and the queen mother why you refused to save thousands of lives."

Joseph strode toward our waiting feluccas, leaving me terrified and Potabi overly calm. "What did you do to make him so angry?" I asked.

Potabi pretended to kiss my cheek but whispered, "Keep your distance from the Hebrew. When we reach Edfu at harvest, your destiny will finally be fulfilled." He released me and stepped back. "Goodbye, Daughter. Remember your training and make me proud."

"Asenath!" Joseph called from the dune. "Hurry!"

"Potabi, what have you done?" My panic rose as his smile widened.

"What any loving abi would do. Now go. I'll make sure the canal is restored by the time you return."

"Asenath!" Joseph shouted again.

"I'm coming!" I dashed away. My side cramped and thighs burned as I struggled on legs as weak as wet papyrus to climb the dune. When I reached Joseph, he took my hand, and we started toward the canal. Jendayi seemed content on his shoulder. I continued to roll Potabi's words around in my mind. Why must I keep my distance from Joseph? We wouldn't arrive in Edfu for months. What foolishness had Potabi secretly arranged?

"What did Potiphera say to upset you again?" My husband's jaw muscle twitched.

What should I tell him? I knew nothing but Potabi's foreboding promise. "The guides said we could only pack enough food and water for today's travel," I said, offering an alternate concern. "What if someone gets hurt and we must camp overnight? Isn't it better to take too much than not enough?" It was nervous chatter, but the Faiyum still frightened me. "Perhaps I should have a Medjay request another felucca for our supplies—"

He stopped and faced me. "We trust our guides, Asenath, and you must trust my decisions about Potiphera."

I searched his eyes for the tenderness he'd shown me this morning, but it was gone—replaced by the stern determination of Egypt's second-in-command. He turned and continued his frenzied pace. No warmth. No compassion. And not a shred of gratitude that I alone had prepared for our journey.

Lengthening my strides, I ignored the hurt inside and out. Upon reaching the Faiyum guides, Joseph became the gracious vizier. Smiling, patting shoulders, and locking wrists, he then offered his hand to help me into the lead felucca. I stomped past him toward the second boat, in need of time away from both powerful men in my life to ponder the war they'd waged on my heart.

The guards helped me into the boat. Jendayi remained on Joseph's shoulder—the little traitor. I sat facing the stern, leaning against a basket of fruit, furious that I had to face sailing into the Faiyum alone. Why had I tried so hard to please a husband who disregarded my efforts? And how could I circumvent whatever plan Potabi had set into motion?

"Thank you for making preparations for our journey." Joseph's voice startled me. Standing beside my felucca, he placed Jendayi in my lap. "We'll have more time to talk later, but we must get to Hawara before dusk—as your abi said." He offered a conciliatory smile and walked away. Perhaps it was best.

I cuddled Jendayi and let our afternoon sail soothe the chaos within. Though breathtakingly beautiful, our surroundings provided indisputable evidence that Joseph was right. We must trust our Faiyum guides. A lion lounged in the shade of a tamarisk tree. Antelope with spiral horns fled their watering sites as we sailed past. Later in the afternoon, a family of hippopotami blocked the canal. Our seasoned guides lured the long-toothed beasts ashore while Jendayi and I cowered in our felucca. Soon all our boats continued safely toward Hawara.

Rodents, wildcats, and lizards scurried along the banks, not nearly as fearsome viewed from a felucca as they'd seemed when I hiked among them. Joseph laughed at Jendayi each time she whooped and squealed at guenon families. I felt guilty that he was a boat-length away, robbed of her hugs and cheek pats. The guides encouraged her antics, mimicking the wild monkeys' chirping. Our little girl stared at the guides, then the guenons, and back at me, seeming more confused the farther we sailed.

I pulled her closer at the first sight of Hawara's pyramid. Long before our shadows lengthened, its looming presence haunted me. I'd soon face the priests of Sobek. Whispers of secret rituals demanded by the crocodile god had kept Zahra, Hotep, and me awake at night. This evening, I would face them without Potabi beside me, and if asked, I must confess I'd rejected all of Egypt's gods, save Ra. Rejecting a lifetime of belief had seemed the right thing to do when a glowing messenger had stood before me with a dripping honeycomb—but now? Even our guides fell silent as the sun neared the western horizon and our pleasurable felucca journey drew to its end.

"Asenath?" Joseph called to me, concern wrinkling his brow. "Stay in your felucca until Hami helps you debark."

I nodded, fascinated by the pyramid. I'd anticipated seeing Amenemhat's second great creation since I'd missed Joseph's excursions to Giza, Saqqara, and Dahshur. But after seeing the Faiyum's natural splendor, the mammoth stone structure looked more like a scar on a lovely face.

The silhouette of a bald priest on shore was equally jarring. "Welcome, Lord Vizier!" he shouted. "Please row your feluccas up the causeway to the temple quay. We've prepared the king's villa for you and your escort." He motioned toward the right, guiding us into the narrower waterway.

My husband nodded, silent and sober. Our merriment suddenly shrouded. With the setting sun at our backs, darkness settled over my ka, lifeless as a mummy in the labyrinth of tombs. I'd never felt such heaviness—such a weight of fear—without an external threat. Had Joseph felt the same strange darkness when he'd visited Amenemhat-Nimaatra's first pyramid in Dahshur? After engineers found structural concerns in Amenemhat's wife's Dahshur tomb, he conscripted Hyksos slaves to build a more spectacular burial solution for himself—the Labyrinth. Should his heart weigh heavy on Anubis's scales when he reached the underworld, he'd planned to hide from Ammut, the heart eater, in the Labyrinth's temple and many chambers. Did his akh still roam? If Ra was the one god, what happened to a ka in the underworld?

Jendayi buried her face against me. Unanswered questions stirred the darkness as though our feluccas floated toward death itself. I'd promised Joseph I would reject other gods, but who could deny the powerful force radiating from these tombs?

The stir of oars in the water and Jendayi's soft whimper echoed in the silence. Our boats slid onto the sandy quay across from the pyramid and temple. Jendayi wriggled from my arms. "Wait!" I dashed out of the boat after her.

"Welcome, priestess." Sobek's high priest, Shu, towered over me, the sight of his crocodile headdress stealing my words. Why had he traveled to Hawara from Sobek's temple in Shedet? How did he know we were coming?

"My wife and I are very tired." Joseph cradled my elbow. "You may show us to our chambers, Highness, and bring a small meal."

"But, my lord vizier, we've prepared—" His words slammed into Joseph's hard stare. "Of course, my lord. Your guards may stay in the barracks with the wab priests, and—"

"Thank you, Highness," Hami interrupted, "but my Medjays station themselves in precautionary positions around our vizier and his wife. I suggest neither you nor your priests attempt to approach them unannounced."

The priest's eyes widened. "Of course, yes. Well, follow me." He stomped through the sandy, grassy shore toward a gated courtyard.

Without a word, Joseph motioned me in the priest's direction. He walked behind me, Hami beside me. Was Joseph angry because I didn't wait on Hami before getting out of the boat? "I needed to save Jendayi," I whispered to my husband.

"Hami could have—" He pursed his lips. "Later."

We continued following the priest. I felt chastised and wounded.

Sobek's high priest led us into a small gated complex, waved away six bald prophets, then continued through a manicured courtyard. The awkward silence was oppressive. Surely, Joseph was as curious as I about the high priest's appearance in Hawara. Why did men never ask questions?

We entered a modest home, and I broke the silence. "This villa is lovely."

"It's not the palace at Gurob," the priest said and pointed to a bowl of dried fruit and nuts. "Potiphera sent word from Meydum that you would stay in Gurob one night and immediately sail to Hawara. We had a finer meal prepared days ago." His disapproving frown demanded an answer.

"Yes, my husband and—"

"We were detained." Joseph interrupted.

I looked at him, curious. Why conceal their eight-day canal inspection?

"No matter." Sobek's high priest continued through a small audience chamber and down a narrow hallway and motioned toward an open chamber. "Pharaoh Khyan and Queen Tani stayed here on many occasions. I hope you find the accommodations adequate."

"We require two chambers." Joseph said, his tone definitive.

The priest's brows rose. "We have a single chamber for visitors. Our wab priests occupy all other accommodations."

"One chamber will do nicely, Highness." I shouldered my way past Joseph into the chamber, waiting for the door to close behind me. Jendayi peeked over my shoulder. I heard the quiet click of the latch falling into place but refused to face my husband. "Why were you so rude to the high priest? Why is he in Hawara? Why—" But my throat closed around more words after a long day of too much upheaval and too little rest.

"I'm your husband, Asenath, but I'm also Egypt's vizier. There will always be things I can't tell you, and you must trust that the secrets I keep are meant to protect you."

"Protect me?" I whirled on him. "Like Potabi's secrets?" The moment the words escaped, I saw the damage they'd done. "Joseph, forgive me, I—"

"Sharing all my thoughts or suspicions with you would be unproductive and even cruel." He held my gaze. "But I will never deceive you."

I swallowed hard. Should I confess Potabi's vague threat? Turning away, I spotted a cushioned couch in the private courtyard. "I'm tired. I'll sleep on the couch."

Jendayi wriggled from my arms as I made my escape. She scampered toward Joseph, and I heard him whispering to her while I entered the courtyard alone. Joseph said it was unproductive—even cruel—to share all thoughts or suspicions with me, so why should I fuel his hatred of Potabi by relaying a vague whisper about destiny? I plopped down on the couch and stared up at a moon growing brighter as the sky darkened.

"You will sleep inside." Joseph rested his hands beside my hips. "You need a soft bed. I don't."

I turned away, unable to face his kindness. "Leave me alone."

He sighed. "Good night, Wife."

I heard shuffling behind me—the sound of his retreating. I was so confused. Lonely. Frustrated. "Oooh!" I beat a lump out of the cushion and let my tears soften the linen—and remembered nothing else until the birds woke me with dawn's first light.

Bolting upright, I surveyed my surroundings, forgetting where I was for a moment.

Hami sat in the doorway between the courtyard and inner chamber, long legs outstretched and crossed. His eyes opened slowly. He nodded a silent morning greeting, then pressed a finger to his lips, pointing to my husband, who lay on a reed mat barely inside the doorway.

I released a soft huff. Why hadn't he slept in the soft bed he'd offered me?

Hami shrugged a shoulder and rolled his eyes—a torrent of communication from the stoic Medjay. I covered a giggle. At least Hami seemed in good humor this morning.

Jendayi sat on my chest, rousing from her sleep as well. She shook her head, ruffling the tufts of hair on her cheeks, forehead, and ears. Her yawn was the most ferocious thing about her—showing teeth sharper than a Medjay's blade. I smoothed her furry face and whispered, "Let's see if Joseph is a lamb or a lion this morning."

I left Jendayi on the couch with a plate of fruit someone had placed beside it and found Hami already gone. Entering the small villa, I approached my sleeping husband and knelt silently beside him. He lay on his side, head resting on a bent arm. The other hand was tucked under his cheek, revealing a boy beneath the man weighed down by Egypt's demands. His hair was wavy and brown, not black and silky like Egyptian boys before their sidelock was shorn. His eyebrows were perfectly shaped even without the kohl-shaped Eye of Horus. My chest ached. I loved this man—yes, this Hebrew. He had never harmed me. Always fought for me. I could trust him—even if I didn't like or understand his decisions.

We needed to talk about what happened between him and Potabi before we left Gurob. About how he treated Sobek's high priest last night. And I needed to tell him exactly what Potabi whispered to me.

I reached out slowly, brushing his cheek. "Joseph—" The lion roared, and I was instantly on my back with a cold, sharp blade at my neck. "Joseph! It's me!"

Wild eyes cleared, and he dropped the small dagger. "Asenath." Falling back against the doorframe, he cradled his head, panting. "I'm sorry. I thought—I didn't—"

I ran into the courtyard. Jendayi, too, had skittered away. I coaxed her from her hiding place beneath the couch and held her close, both of us trembling. I felt my husband's presence behind me. Jendayi hid her face against my chest.

"Asenath, please. Look at me."

Slowly, I turned. Tears came.

He held us tenderly. "I'm so sorry."

"I didn't even know . . ." I sniffed. "Why do you carry a dagger?"

"Hami taught me long ago that a man should always carry a weapon." He wiped away my tears. "If we're to share a chamber, you'll need to learn some important things. Men know to never approach while another man sleeps."

His grin was sweeter than honey, and I needed a little taste of his lips. I released Jendayi, circled his neck, and pulled him into a gentle first kiss. He was tentative, as was I, but then his hands found my waist, pulling me so close our bodies melded together, lying as one on the couch.

"Lord Vizier—forgive me!" Hami's unexpected entry launched my husband to his feet.

"Hami, you must knock!"

"Where would I knock in a courtyard?"

I sat up, giggling, and reached for my husband's hand. "We're married, remember?"

"Forgive the intrusion." Hami turned away.

"No, my friend, come in." Joseph finally laughed, too. "I've already delayed our departure by sleeping later. We should visit the villages as soon as possible."

"We're leaving?" I blurted. "Without a tour of the pyramid or Labyrinth?"

All humor fled, and my husband exchanged a concerned glance with his captain.

Last night's frustration resurfaced. "Joseph! What is it you're not telling me?"

He sighed and knelt beside my couch. "We know that Potiphera sent messages to high priests other than Sobek's at temples of various gods."

"High priests often communicate with each other," I said, omitting that they usually corresponded about nationwide festivals. "He likely sent other messages to discover who took Ommi's body from the Memphis temple."

"Mistress." Hami's tone gave nothing away but demanded my attention. "He also sent two messages to King Apophis at Edfu Fortress." The words dropped like a boulder in my belly.

When we reach Edfu at harvest, your destiny will finally be fulfilled.
Potabi's parting words were now more terrifying. Surely, he didn't
hold out hope I'd marry Apophis—not when the true god had confirmed Joseph as my husband through a messenger and dreams.

"Asenath?" Joseph's brows drew together. "If you know something, tell me now so I can stop your abi before anyone gets hurt."

No! You'll send him to Avaris to be judged for treason! "Perhaps
King Apophis needs regular consultations with Ra's high priest since
Apophis chose the throne name Nebkhepeshre, Ra is Lord of
Strength. Potabi is, after all, the true god's mouthpiece on earth."

"Don't do this." Joseph's stare turned as hard as flint. "Your abi
still hopes to make you Apophis's bride."

I tried to pull my hand away, but he gripped it tighter.

"Did you know?" His whisper felt like a hammer against my
chest.

I shook my head violently, holding back tears and words. Search-
ing my husband's face, I wished we could hide from the world.
Were it simply Joseph and I, how happy we could be. As stern as
Joseph was, his gaze was that of a reasonable, compassionate man.
"I didn't know about any recent messages to Apophis," I confessed.
"But right before we left Gurob, Potabi said something about my
destiny being fulfilled when we arrived in Edfu." I slid to the court-
yard tiles and knelt beside him, pressing my forehead to his hand.
"Please, I beg you, don't send him to Avaris to be condemned for
treason."

He pressed his lips against my hair. "I'm giving him the chance
to redeem himself by restoring the canal. If he shows he cares more
about healing Egypt than harming us, I'll confront him about his
messages and work with him to repair the relationship—for your
sake."

Reluctantly, I agreed, knowing the man commissioned to restore
the canal in Gurob wasn't as reasonable or compassionate. "I trust
you, Husband, to do all you can to save Potabi from himself." Then
I said to Hami, "Potabi isn't a bad man. Please don't harm him—if
you can avoid it."

His eyes held mine. Then he nodded. An agreement of sorts. He started toward the courtyard gate.

Joseph called after him, "Check the feluccas to be sure they're ready for today's sail and knock at the gate when you return."

"I won't be long, Lord Vizier. We have many villages to visit on our way to Shedet."

Joseph stood and offered me his hand. "I'm sure Sobek's high priest has already left to prepare for our visit."

"Why go to Shedet when you know Potabi corresponded with Sobek's high priest? Why sail into a crocodile's jaws?"

Joseph called Jendayi while I impatiently waited for his answer. She jumped into his arms and skittered onto his shoulder.

"Joseph, I fear we're in danger!"

"Shh, Wife." He slid his hands down my back.

I was sure he'd kiss me again.

But he suddenly stepped away. "We *are* in danger—two different types. The first is King Apophis's anger, which I hope to assuage with Elohim's wisdom, but the second is what almost happened between us before Hami entered this courtyard. We must never be alone again, not until you believe Elohim is the only God."

He left me standing in the courtyard, aching with desire. In that moment, I would have vowed anything to be in danger with Joseph.

TWENTY-FIVE

I have come into my garden, my sister, my bride;
I have gathered my myrrh with my spice.
I have eaten my honeycomb and my honey;
I have drunk my wine and my milk.

SONG OF SONGS 5:1

Joseph

Joseph knelt in the stern of the lead felucca, rowing with all his might. He'd spent all day trying to divert his attention from the lovely form of his wife, who sat less than an arm's length away. She'd worn the same sort of sheer linen since the day they'd met, but since that kiss in Hawara, his eyes refused their bridle, and his patience was lost. The sooner they arrived at Shedet, the sooner he could distance himself from the temptation before him.

Hami knelt in the bow. "Pull harder!" Joseph shouted. "You row like an old woman."

The insult garnered an over-the-shoulder glare from his captain. "Perhaps your pent-up frustration has given you the strength of a god."

Heat crawled up Joseph's neck as Hami returned his gaze forward. *Pent-up frustration?* What a gentle phrase to describe three days of anguish. At each village they'd visited, the elders graciously provided fine lodging—always a single chamber or hut that he and Asenath shared. Hami had remained in the room with them, but Joseph's desire for his wife had mounted with each glimpse of her perfect form. After using every shred of restraint all night long, he had no tact or diplomacy for his wife or Medjays during the day. Even now, he ached to hold her. She was within reach, yet untouchable. His wife, yet not one flesh. *Elohim, how can it be Your will that a husband and wife remain apart?*

A growl escaped, and Asenath looked at him, startled. "What pent-up frustration does Hami know of that you won't tell me? Are there more secrets, or do you hold Potabi's scheming against me? You might as well send me back—" She turned away, crying.

"He didn't mean—"

When Asenath wiped her tears, Jendayi wriggled free, bounced to a side-strapped basket, and scampered ashore.

"Jendayi, no!" Joseph jumped from the boat to follow her. "Hami, help!"

The Medjay was already beside him, then past him. His friend's long strides made Joseph appear to be strolling. Jendayi raced toward a family of guenons gathered under a terebinth tree. The dominant male saw Hami's approach and charged him. Head bobbing, tail raised, teeth bared, and screaming, the guenon was daunting. Even Jendayi fled, racing right into Joseph's arms. Hami, spear drawn, protected their retreat to the boats.

Joseph waded into the canal and buried his face in Jendayi's fur. "You must stay with us, little girl." Then he placed her in Asenath's lap.

"It's my fault, Joseph. I should never have taken my hand off her."

He climbed into the felucca and nodded his gratitude to Hami. "Everyone is fine," he whispered to Asenath. "Jendayi saw the guenons and wanted to play, like she's done with monkeys in the villages. She doesn't know we're approaching Crocodile City."

"Little Jendayi can be contained for a time," Hami said, holding Joseph's gaze, "but no one can restrain natural desires indefinitely."

The procession of boats resumed their frenzied pace, foregoing the midday break to reach the City of Crocodiles before dusk. Shedet needed no pyramid. Evidence of Sobek's temple lined both sides of the canal's banks.

The Faiyum guides pointed to the reeds. "Look for two rounded eyes and jagged scales poking above the water's surface."

The guide in the second felucca pointed to Joseph's left. "Look there—a big one!" At his announcement, the beast rolled into a dive, revealing its full, terrifying mass—twice the size of a felucca.

A horrendous tussle erupted barely a barque's length ahead when two monsters grappled, locking teeth and claws. "Reverse oars!" Hami shouted.

"Reverse oars!" repeated the guides.

The battle was short-lived, but floating remains and bloody waters provoked more crocodiles to voracious feeding. Every man in the twelve boats held a spear or an oar, guarding the three supply boats roped in the middle.

Asenath sat at Joseph's feet, clutching Jendayi. "The same darkness that's in Hawara lives here."

He felt it, too, but she needed comfort, not fuel for her fear. "Elohim is greater than imaginary gods or created things. Trust His power, Asenath."

A crocodile slipped off the bank and swam toward them. Joseph lifted his oar out of the water as a jagged tail propelled two eyes toward them. Hami rose to his knees, spear poised, as did every other Medjay and guide. A lump formed in Joseph's throat—but the creature veered off, bumping their baskets with a whip of his tail as he swam away.

Asenath whimpered her relief, hiding her face in Jendayi's fur. Joseph released a sigh and found Hami with the biggest smile he'd ever seen. "That was exciting!" The Medjay released a war cry and set aside his spear to begin rowing again.

With celebration still ringing in the air, a guide behind them shouted, "No!"

Joseph glimpsed something in the water shooting toward them like an arrow from a bow. The monster charged their boat, churning the water at a staggering pace. Joseph had time for a few words. "Elohim, stop it by Your hand!"

For no apparent reason, the giant whipped its body around and opened its mouth wide, as though confronting an unseen attacker, then vanished into the dark waters. Only the canal's gentle trickle invaded the silent awe of heaven and earth. In the distance, a lion roared. A hippo groaned. Every man picked up an oar and rowed as rounded eyes continued watching from the reeds.

Joseph's heart hadn't yet slowed when he heard, "Welcome, Lord Vizier! Did Sobek greet you personally?" The crocodile-headed high priest stood atop a mudbrick wall on the southern bank. "My priests will receive you at the reed-free banks of Shedet's quay."

They rowed past the jubilant priest and the mudbrick wall and found a section of canal where priests waited to help unload their supplies. The felucca slid onto the sandy shore, and Joseph pressed a kiss against his wife's head. They were both shaking. The arrival itself seemed like a victory.

"Welcome." The high priest appeared on the bank, arms open like an old friend. "Congratulations! You survived your first journey down Crocodile Causeway."

Joseph felt like throwing sand in his eyes but took the diplomatic approach instead. "Indeed, Highness, the journey was unlike any-thing we've yet experienced." He offered his hand. "Nor do I wish to meet your Sobek again."

The priest locked wrists with seeming sincerity. "You'll be amazed at how docile Sobek becomes when you sail toward Magic Lake, Lord Vizier. All the gods push travelers to the one place on earth where they gather as stars."

"I've heard it's quite spectacular." Joseph released the man's wrist and drew Asenath into the conversation. "You remember my lovely wife."

"Of course, welcome." After a quick nod, he said, "I hope you aren't too weary from travel to honor Sobek in his inner sanctum before joining me for the evening meal."

Asenath's shoulders tensed.

"Of course, Highness." He glanced at his wife. "Would you like to refresh yourself before we honor Sobek?"

She looked up at Joseph, eyes wide and cheeks pale.

"It's settled then." The high priest started toward another mud-brick wall—this one as tall as two men. "Our accommodations in the Faiyum aren't as lavish as the pharaohs' palaces in Memphis or Avaris. I enjoyed the hospitality of the Memphis pharaohs many times but have only visited the new capital once."

Joseph glanced at Hami. *The* new *capital?* Avaris had been Egypt's capital since Memphis was destroyed fifteen years ago. Why hadn't Sobek's high priest journeyed to Avaris for the annual akhet festivals, as most high priests did to honor the kings who appointed them?

"I'm sure the accommodations will be satisfactory, Highness," Joseph said. "Tell me, were both you and Potiphera appointed by King Apophis?"

"Yes." The high priest said no more until they halted at the gated compound. Then he turned, his feigned smile revealing teeth sharpened into points like those in his headdress. "Potiphera and I share similar political views. It was he who recommended me to King Apophis."

If Sobek's high priest still called Avaris the *new* capital, he was almost certainly one of the Egyptian rebels Joseph had heard still dwelt in the Faiyum. By reputation, these rebels weren't simply malcontents. They were zealots—seeking Pharaoh Yanassi's death. Could Potiphera be included among them? How could he have hidden his affiliation so completely that he'd infiltrated Pharaoh Yanassi's own royal council?

Wouldn't King Apophis, who had rooted out Abydos's nest of zealots, wish to know if Potiphera might be involved? A staggering thought flashed through Joseph's mind. What if Apophis already knew—and was complicit? He swallowed the awful possibility. No. Apophis was ruthless and ambitious, but he loved his nephew. Which love was greater? Apophis's love for Yanassi or his desire for the throne?

Apophis was a full-blooded Egyptian, a military leader from noble blood—the kind of king zealots would choose to unite Egypt. He'd marched most of Lower Egypt's army to Edfu Fortress and remained there for over a year. A mere one-day sail from Upper Egypt's capital in Thebes, Apophis could easily mount an attack against Pharaoh Sobekhotep and his smaller army.

Joseph's blood ran cold. If King Apophis and Potiphera conspired against young Pharaoh Yanassi, the boy would lose his kingdom and his life.

"Welcome to our humble temple." Sobek's high priest pushed open the compound gate.

Asenath gasped and Joseph halted midstride. "It's stunning, Highness." Joseph reminded himself to breathe while he took in one of the strangest sights in Egypt. Crocodiles no larger than a man's arm roamed an expansive compound and played in a large square pond. A narrow channel supplied water from the canal through a small opening in the wall. Sobek's priests fed the crocodiles with meat and fish from their own hands.

Asenath hugged Jendayi closer. "Are your priests ever injured?"

"Occasionally, an oversize image of our god will make its way through the portal, into our sanctuary, and cause harm. However, most injuries occur when our priests are careless. Follow me."

Their host continued toward a sprawling villa where baby crocodiles roamed the courtyard. "I remembered your request for separate chambers at Hawara," the priest said. "I was sure the priestess would want the room closest to the gods, so we've prepared the chamber adjoining the courtyard—"

"No!" Asenath said. "The vizier and I will share a chamber." Her eyes glistened. "Joseph, please."

His inner battle raged. "One chamber."

"Splendid. You may choose the chamber adjoining the lovely courtyard or the loft chamber overlooking the whole complex."

Neither Joseph nor Asenath cared to be near crocodiles. "We'll take the loft. Thank you, Highness."

"After you've refreshed yourself, I'll escort you to Sobek's temple." He bowed.

Before he straightened, Asenath had fled toward the stairs. Joseph hurried after her. He'd barely closed the door when she whirled on him. "We can't 'honor Sobek in his inner sanctum.'"

He reclined on a cushioned couch, needing a moment's rest. Jendayi perched on his belly. "I will not 'honor Sobek,' Asenath. I'll watch a man feed his pet crocodile." He'd witnessed many temple rituals, all of them meaningless because their gods were a lie.

Asenath wedged herself into the narrow space beside him, pressing her hip against his to make room. He groaned inwardly. *Elohim, how can I resist her for a whole night in this chamber?* She was saying something, but he couldn't hear anything over his screaming thoughts. He bolted upright and faced her. "I need Hami to stay with us at all times."

She appeared shocked. "It won't matter. To honor Sobek in his sanctum means whoever the high priest allows to enter must *nourish* the god and make him stronger."

He stifled a grin. *She has no idea why I need Hami in this chamber right now.* He moved toward the door. "We'll simply feed a crocodile and then I must speak with you and Hami—"

"No, Joseph. It's Sobek's *inner sanctum.*" She came close, her voice low. "Potabi once told me the sacred crocodile can grow larger than a hippopotamus. They feed it every day with meat, wine, and honeyed milk; each year the priests cast a spell over it, then cover it with jewels and gold. When it dies, they embalm it and place it in the Labyrinth with the pharaohs. By feeding it, we would be *worshipping* Sobek. I realize now that I can't."

Joseph grinned at her. "It sounds like stories of the Leviathan my cousin Job used to tell."

"This isn't funny." She was trembling. "Please, Joseph, if you trust Elohim, don't do this."

"If I—" He tilted up her chin and lost himself in her eyes. He swallowed all he wanted to say, grasping at control. *Elohim, I've fallen in love with this woman. Help me protect her from my own selfish desires.*

"Lord Vizier!" the high priest called from the courtyard below. "Are you ready to present yourself to Sobek?

Asenath brushed his cheek. "Joseph, I believe in Elohim—only."

Why was she saying this now? Had she sensed his desire or—"If you're afraid, just tell me."

"Yes, I was afraid, at Hawara and again here in Shedet. Something about Egypt's gods brings with them a darkness I can't define."

"Asenath, there is one God."

"Yes, but I'm telling you, there is another force, something beyond human reason or power. I refuse to walk into the crocodile temple and offer myself to any being other than your God." She held him with her gaze, sacredly stubborn and gloriously sure.

"Wait. Are you saying . . . When did . . . How—"

"Lord Vizier?" The priest shouted again.

Joseph crossed the chamber, opened the door, and stood at the railing on the landing. He looked down at the crocodile-headed priest, who stood beside Hami. "I'm sorry, Highness, but my wife isn't feeling well. I must honor her needs before Sobek's. My captain will visit the inner sanctum in my stead."

"But, Lord Vizier, it's important—"

Hami's hand shot up. "The vizier's word is law, Highness. Surely, Sobek won't mind. I was Pharaoh Khyan's vizier until his untimely death."

The priest's eyes widened. "I didn't realize. Yes, please, Captain. Our great god, Sobek, would be honored to receive you."

Hami glanced up at Joseph. "Should I send another Medjay to your chamber, Lord Vizier? Or will exterior guards be sufficient?"

Palms sweaty, Joseph looked over his shoulder and saw his wife's sheer robe piled on the floor beside the couch. "Nothing separates us now," came Asenath's coarse whisper.

"No guards necessary, Hami. Go to the temple." He hurried into the chamber and closed the door.

Jendayi lay sleeping on Asenath's robe, and his wife waited in the shadowy corner wearing nothing but a coy smile. "Let me tell you why Elohim is my God."

"I love you already. You need not do this to win my approval." He remained by the door, his breathing ragged.

"You love me?" She took a step closer.

"Don't." He pressed his back against the door. "Not until you explain."

She halted, smiling sweetly. "I have believed in one Creator since the messenger's visit. When Potabi explained Egypt's family of gods, those hundreds of bickering beings, I realized there were flaws in every nation's legends. Their greatest god couldn't be Elohim by another name. Do you know why?" She stepped closer, within a handbreadth.

"Tell me why." Joseph felt like his heart would leap from his chest.

"Because those gods don't love, Joseph. Elohim *loves*." Moisture gathered in her eyes, but her features brightened. "I was so frightened when the crocodile charged our felucca today. I felt the same evil force here that I'd felt when we approached Hawara, but it fled when you spoke of Elohim's power. That crocodile didn't simply swim away. Elohim was a wall between us and danger. He displayed His love and protection for me personally. Not just today. Also at Hawara." Her breath caught. "Has Elohim been with me *all* my life?"

"He's always been the only God, but now He's—"

"He's mine!" she cried.

The sheer joy of her declaration crumbled the remaining walls around his heart. Joseph lifted her into his arms and carried her to the rear chamber. Hungry kisses hurried them toward the soft mattress.

When he placed Asenath gently on the elevated bed and lay beside her, she pressed a hand against his chest. "Are you thinking of Ahira?"

Shocked by the question, he stuttered incomprehensible sounds and watched the passion drain from his wife's features. "No! I *wasn't* thinking of her." Joseph waited, letting the truth settle into joy for them both. "You are the center of my thoughts, love, the only object of my desire. Ahira will always hold a sacred place because during the darkest days of our lives, we were alone in our trust of Elohim. Now you, Asenath, are my heart. We are bound in body, soul, and spirit—one flesh as Elohim intended—man and woman, husband and wife." He kissed the tip of her nose, her forehead, her cheeks, and then brushed her lips. "And no one will ever take you from me."

TWENTY-SIX

When I consider your heavens,
the work of your fingers,
the moon and the stars,
which you have set in place,
what is mankind that you are mindful of them,
human beings that you care for them?

PSALM 8:3-4

MAGIC LAKE, THE FAIYUM
THREE DAYS LATER
Asenath

I lay on a reed mat beside Magic Lake under a tapestry of stars.
Between the sky and its reflection off the clear, smooth water, I felt
cradled in a dream—until my husband approached. I turned on my
side, holding Jendayi close. He curved his body around mine and
then slipped his arm over me. I melted into him. After a day of such
joy and sorrow, words would tarnish the moment.

We'd left our feluccas at the canal last night at dusk, then hiked
the mountains of sand dunes toward Magic Lake. When we arrived,
we were too exhausted to appreciate the beauty around us and fell
into a deep sleep. Thankfully, the guides woke us for the Creator's
spectacular dawn display. The sun's emerging radiance reflected

against earth and sky, casting vivid colors in ever-widening angles, like a flower in bloom. Invigorated by the wonder, Joseph declared a day of leisure to celebrate Elohim's artistry.

Our day began with one of the Medjays climbing a sand dune and then racing down it seated on a felucca oar. The newfound activity turned into a contest. Even Hami joined the fun. "You should never attempt to defeat your captain," he'd said and eventually bested every guard. It was the first time I'd heard Medjays laugh. Afterward, everyone frolicked in the cool lake—guides, Medjays, the vizier, and his wife. Strict lines of social class blurred at least for a day.

My throat constricted with the memory of a Medjay missing from our evening meal. I noticed when he arrived late and whispered something to Hami. Betrayal registered on the captain's features. He looked at me first—not Joseph—and I knew. Potabi had done something awful. Again.

Joseph's arm tightened around me, bringing me back to the moment. "Are you angry with me for having you escorted away from camp?" He whispered against my ear. "I needed to be with Hami while he questioned the two spies and meted out Medjay justice."

Medjay justice. I'd heard every blow, heard the guilty cry for mercy.

"I'm not angry, Joseph. I'm grateful I didn't have to watch, but you've known those men for years. I spent the day laughing with them and found them delightful. How could they betray—" The thought of Hami having to beat his faithful guards made me nauseous.

"Anyone can betray if they're pushed into the cleft of a rock. The two Medjays needed silver to help their families. Potiphera's temple guards approached them before we left Gurob with an offer to buy information about our Faiyum tour. They had sent reports from Hawara and Shedet. Hami's lieutenant found another message—hidden but ready to send—in the traitors' tent."

"Perhaps they were simply reporting our travel so Potabi will complete the canal on time."

"Do you really believe that?" The sadness in his voice reflected mine.

"I want to believe he can change, but he's always been convinced I would become Isis Incarnate if I married a pure-blooded Egyptian king." I didn't dare confess his seething hatred of all Hyksos or that he'd once planned to harm Pharaoh Yanassi. Surely, he'd given up by now. "I want nothing more than to be your wife and heal Egypt—whatever comes, feast or famine. I now see my destiny was always part of Elohim's much greater plan through Abraham's covenant. Like the messenger promised, our children will bless *all* nations." I sat up to emphasize my next words. "I mourn Potabi's stubborn hatred, and I wish I knew what would change his heart."

"We can't change him. Only Elohim can change a heart, love, and He never forces His will over ours. During our nome tour, He gave Potiphera the same dream I had, proving you and I were to be married. I chose to believe the dream, obeying Elohim's will. Your abi chose to fight Elohim—at least, so far."

So far. At least Joseph held out some hope that Potabi could change. "What will you do to him when we return to Gurob?"

He paused in excruciating silence for several moments. "We'll continue to pray that Elohim works in him, but it's ultimately his decision to obey or rebel."

Rebel was such an ugly word, but so were Potabi's actions. The consequences for the Medjays' betrayal would likely be as dreadful. "What will happen to the spies?"

"We're sending them back to Gurob tomorrow with ten faithful Medjays and all fifteen feluccas. We'll continue our tour inland on foot and with donkeys."

"But what about . . ." A hundred questions raced in my mind. I released Jendayi to play between us, sorted my thoughts, and voiced a single question. "Will we be safe hiking in the more remote areas of the Faiyum?"

"We'll be safer, actually, since we'll be too far inland for communication with Gurob. If other Medjays were tempted by Potiphera's offer, they'll have no opportunity to succumb. Changing our itinerary to visit the eighteen remotest villages also gives us a chance to meet people untarnished by Egypt's politics. By tomorrow morning, we'll have five donkeys—four to carry supplies and one to carry you whenever you tire of walking. We'll see what the villagers need, estimate harvests during years of abundance, and arrange for engineers and builders to return and help build adequate granaries."

I tried to hide my anxiety with levity. "I'm glad I sent Zahra and Hotep a message before we left Gurob." My chuckle came out like a squeak.

Joseph offered a knowing grin. "You've become quite the traveler. You're more adept at spotting vipers than I, and you're getting better at using a sling and stones. The frankincense has kept the buzzing, biting things away, hasn't it?"

"Yes, but—"

"Jendayi will enjoy hiking better, too. Did you see how she interacted with the guenon family today?" A few days ago the guides had pointed out the guenon family following us. "They seemed to accept her as one of their own."

"I'm not sure I like wild monkeys accepting my baby."

A shooting star crossed the sky, and both Joseph and I gasped. A startling realization came with it. "The same God who sent that star racing through the darkness sent His messenger of light to my tower."

"And the same God promised Abraham his descendants would outnumber those stars. We will have children. Our children will have children. Their children will have children, and all will bear the covenant to bless all nations."

I shifted my thoughts to the here and now. "You've known generations of family, Joseph, but I know nothing about grandparents, children, or covenants. My life has been Potabi and two sister-maids in a tower. I'm all Potabi has. He loves me so much he'd rather defy his gods than give me up."

"That's not love, Asenath. Elohim calls us to a love grounded in obedience to Him. That's the one love that fully satisfies. We remain empty when driven by other motives."

His words were uncomfortable and true. "When did you become an expert on love?"

Humor fell flat on his serious brow. "I've known generations of family, and most of them had hollow hearts. Only one lived the godly example of obedience that glimmered like gold."

"Your abba Jacob?"

He chuckled without mirth. "No. Abba Jacob was like Potiphera in that aspect. His love for my ima and me was so fierce that it damaged others in the family and still left him wanting. Saba Isaac was the same. He favored Abba's twin brother, Esau, and fought against Elohim's will to make Abba Jacob the covenant bearer. Abba stole the covenant blessing from Saba through deceit, but Elohim allowed it."

"Joseph, I had no idea—"

"Elohim is perfect," he said with a faraway stare. "His covenant bearers aren't."

I brushed his cheek, calling his attention back to me. "Who in your family lived in obedience?"

"Great-Saba Abraham," he said with a sweet smile. "He wasn't perfect either, but when God spoke, he obeyed. And Elohim declared his faith a stronger tether than the failures that tugged him away."

"I want that kind of faith." I blurted out the words before I realized their depth. Now spoken, I tried to clarify. "What kind of obedience tethered Abraham to Elohim?"

He held my gaze, and I witnessed the silent battle raging behind his eyes. What sort of actions could make my husband hesitate to even speak them?

"Elohim asked Great-Saba Abraham to sacrifice his only son on an altar atop Mount Moriah." Once begun, the words tumbled out quickly.

Surely, I hadn't heard correctly. "A human sacrifice? Like the Phoenicians and Canaanites?"

"Saba Isaac was sixteen years old when he and Great-Saba climbed that mountain alone. Saba Isaac climbed onto the altar, knowing what Great-Saba intended to do."

"So Isaac showed great faith, too."

Joseph nodded. "In that moment, he did. Great-Saba had told their servants, who waited at the foot of the mountain, that both he and his son would return after the sacrifice. Both he and Saba Isaac believed the covenant promises and reasoned if Elohim commanded the sacrifice, He could also raise the dead. So when Great-Saba raised his knife to kill his son, Elohim sent a messenger—"

"Like the messenger He sent to me?"

Joseph smiled. "Yes, my love. And the messenger showed Great-Saba a ram trapped in the thicket nearby that became the sacrifice instead of Saba Isaac."

"Oh . . ." I sighed as if I'd lived through the ordeal myself. "I can't imagine killing your only son—even if you believed Elohim would give him back."

The distant chirping of wild guenons intruded on the moment. Jendayi's ears perked, and I caught her hind legs before she dashed away. She squawked and chirped, as if answering their call, then buried her head against my chest and whimpered.

Heartbroken, I asked Joseph, "Would she rather be with the guenons?"

"I don't know, love." He reached over to stroke her furry cheeks. "She certainly enjoyed roaming with them freely today."

"But I . . ." My throat closed around more words. How could I release her into the Faiyum, this wild and dangerous place?

"Why not let her roam tonight?" Joseph whispered. "We know guenons are nocturnal, and we've got Medjays on guard through the night who love her like we do. I'll have Hami assign Jendayi her very own Medjay to follow her if she leaves camp."

I thought of those Joseph described as empty inside because of a fierce love that clutched too tightly. Isaac, Jacob, and Potabi—they'd damaged those they loved and others, leaving themselves hollow in the process. A tear dripped onto Jendayi's head. Could I entrust the one 'child' I'd ever known to the God I'd so recently met? *Elohim, if I trust You with Jendayi, will You keep Your promise to fill my womb with Joseph's children?*

I tied my tether to the One who sent a messenger to save me and kissed Jendayi's furry head. "Be careful, little girl, and return to us immediately if you sense danger." I opened my arms, hoping she'd curl up on my lap. She didn't.

Our little girl skittered away, chirping merrily toward the jubilant sounds of her waiting Faiyum family.

TWENTY-SEVEN

I swear by myself, declares the LORD, that
because you have done this and have not
withheld your son, your only son, I will
surely bless you and make your descendants
as numerous as the stars in the sky and as
the sand on the seashore.

GENESIS 22:16–17

Asenath

I was so tired, my lips could barely form the words. "I love you, Joseph." We'd affirmed it hundreds of times since the first time we'd said it in Crocodile City. Tonight, I needed to say it again—needed to hear it again.

He propped himself on one elbow next to me in our reed hut. "Jendayi will come back. She always does." Moonlight flooded his handsome face. "Hami said his men may have spotted her family—"

"*We're* her family," I snapped.

My petulance silenced him.

I stared through the small window of our hut. The village of

Tebtunis sat amid a sea of sand, yet it bloomed on the Faiyum through well-watered irrigation, the result of more of Amenemhat's genius. It was the eighteenth and final village on our thirty-five-day tour and our last night before tomorrow's hike to Gurob. We'd left Magic Lake four weeks ago and hiked through the Faiyum's variegated terrain with our supplies and five donkeys. We'd met hundreds of grateful Egyptians and planned for each village's seven bountiful harvests. We were returning to Gurob feeling satisfied with all we'd accomplished—and anxious at what we'd find when we arrived. I'd never been so weary in my life. "Forgive my short temper, Husband." With great effort, I lifted my hand to comb his wavy hair. "I miss Jendayi, and I fear what Potabi has done in our absence."

"I know, love." He wrapped me in his arms.

I rested my head on his chest. "Repeat for me again Elohim's promise to our descendants." Although he'd recited Great-Saba Abraham's blessing to me on both the day after our wedding and during our visit to Magic Lake, I needed to hear it now. The midwife at Tebtunis had given me a knowing wink when I confided that my monthly courses were late this month.

"The Almighty One said to Abraham"—Joseph began in the familiar sing-song tone he used when reciting his family history—"I swear by Myself that because you have done this and have not withheld your son, your only son, I will surely bless you and make your descendants as numerous as the stars in the sky and as the sand on the seashore."

"Or perhaps as numerous as the sand of the Faiyum?" I asked.

"Great-Saba came to Egypt once, but I don't think he ever visited the Faiyum."

He nuzzled my neck. Yet even his nearness couldn't soothe me. "I know Abraham was willing to sacrifice his son," I whispered. "But he knew Isaac would be returned to him somehow. Would Elohim ask me to give up Jendayi with no promise of her return?"

He pulled me closer, rubbing circles on my back while he spoke. "Abba Jacob told me Great-Saba's faith increased with each recognition of Elohim's faithfulness. El Shaddai—the Almighty One—had already proven His power to bring a healthy baby from Great-Savta Sarah's barren ninety-year-old womb. First, Elohim proved faithful; then he asked Great-Saba Abraham to obey a command he didn't fully understand." He squeezed me tighter. "Elohim has proven Himself to us in many ways, I know, but are we tethered to Him enough to trust Him if Jendayi doesn't return by the time we leave Tebtunis tomorrow?"

His answer was personal. Intimate. He ached with confusion, as I did. "Shouldn't this be easier, Joseph? Elohim freed you from prison and made you vizier of Egypt. He sent a messenger to me, healed me with honeycomb, and calmed my fears at Shedet. Why is trusting Him still so hard?"

"Trusting Elohim is always a choice between doubt that sends us spiraling or faith that reveals an awe-inspiring aspect of God's character. I would never have known His power to save had I not been unjustly imprisoned."

I both loved and hated my husband's wisdom. I didn't want to give up Jendayi, but Elohim had given me hope of a child in my womb before asking me to give up my precious monkey. "I love you, Joseph." It was all I could whisper from my constricted throat. I turned away but snuggled backward into the bend of his body.

He laid his arm over me, and I laced my fingers with his across my belly. I didn't dare tell him my suspicions yet. The midwife had inserted a small onion inside me with the instruction that if its taste traveled to my mouth by the evening meal, I was almost certainly with child. I'd barely eaten anything tonight. Even the dates had the faint flavor of onion. I squeezed my eyes shut, contemplating Hotep's warning from a few months earlier. If Jendayi came back, how would she adapt to a new baby? Had Elohim provided a new home for my first 'child' to make room for Joseph's child growing inside me?

Oh, how I missed Zahra and Hotep. Five weeks of traveling with men had proven how much I'd depended on my friends. The village women had been welcoming when we'd visited, but it was different than *belonging* to my sisters. They wouldn't have known the midwife's trick to determine if I was with child, but they would have sensed my unspoken needs.

"Talk to me, love," Joseph whispered in the stillness.

"I miss Zahra and Hotep." It was true but not the whole truth. A question had burrowed deeper into worry with each passing day. "Has Elohim left me? I haven't felt His presence since we left Shedet."

"Elohim doesn't leave, Asenath. Our Creator is everywhere all the time, but He *chooses* when to reveal His nearness just as each of us chooses to either draw near to Him or push Him away. Maybe Elohim waits for us to come near like we're waiting for Jendayi to come home. He can hear your thoughts. Talk to Him anytime you wish."

"I will. Goodnight, my love." *Elohim, are You there?* I fell asleep waiting for His answer in the comfort of my husband's arms.

* * *

I awakened at dawn to the sound of twenty-five men chirping like guenon monkeys. I darted from the hut and joined Joseph, searching the horizon for Jendayi. He raised his fist in the air, stilling the guard's calls. I scanned the rugged terrain in the dim glow of a new day and listened to its waking. Birds squawked, insects trilled, and an owl gave us a farewell hoot. But no little guenon scampered across the dunes. My empty arms ached.

Keeping my eyes on the horizon, I spoke in a whisper. "I'll get our supplies loaded."

Joseph turned me to face him. "I already packed everything from the hut." Concern creased his brow. "You slept through it, love. Are you feeling all right?"

"Just tired. Could we wait a little longer before—"

"Here she comes!" Hami shouted. He had started running

toward Jendayi, but the large male guenon charged him. The Medjay drew his spear, stopping abruptly, while wild monkeys and humans devolved into panicked chaos.

"Hami, move back!" I shouted, easing my way toward Jendayi.

Joseph caught my arm, but I shrugged off his grasp. "She was coming back before Hami started running to her." I began a very slow, measured pace toward my precious girl, who cowered halfway between the Medjay and the fierce-looking male guenon. "Come here, little girl. Are you all right?" I hadn't held her for almost a week. She and the wild guenons had remained near our camp and had been most active at night when we were sleeping. The guides had assured me she was safe and suspected she'd come back to us with a baby in her womb.

With five paces between us, she skittered across the sand and leapt into my arms, climbing to the back of my neck, her favorite hiding place, beneath my hair. Relief washed over me. "You little scamp! How I've missed you." She wrapped her arms around my neck, pressed her lips against my cheek, and blew bubbles. I giggled, enraptured, and didn't notice Joseph's approach.

Jendayi leapt to his shoulder, giving him a greeting like mine. His deep chuckle proved he was as delighted to see her as I. "She'll always be our first baby."

Our Medjays and guides formed a line of defense between us and the family of guenons. I noticed the male nervously pacing on the other side, watching Jendayi closely.

Dread rose with the sun as our departure settled into reality. "Joseph," I whispered, "I don't think that male will let us take her without a fight." I pointed. "Look."

He lifted Jendayi from his shoulder to my waiting arms and stepped up to Hami and our lead guide. "What will we do if he charges?"

Before he could answer, Jendayi lunged out of my arms and scampered away. "Joseph, grab her!" But Joseph and Hami knocked heads when they both bent to grab her, and she escaped between them. Hami started to follow, but the male guenon raised his tail, bared his teeth, and screeched a deafening threat.

"Don't Hami." I paused. A moment passed. "Let her go." The words tasted bitter, but I was the only one who could say them, the only one who could truly release her to a new family. Jendayi ran toward her protector and sheltered beneath the big male's arms, his fury no longer a threat but now her shield.

I felt all eyes on me. Squaring my shoulders, I walked toward the donkeys. "We should say our goodbyes if we hope to reach Gurob before dusk."

I let the tears come—grieving, yes, but not wrenching. I placed my hand on my belly, somehow knowing I carried Joseph's child. Elohim had given me an indescribable peace amid the sadness. *Thank You, Elohim, You do hear my thoughts.*

Joseph and I said goodbye to our new friends. The old midwife promised she'd watch for Jendayi and tend to any of her babies. Joseph thanked her, oblivious to the woman's wink and our shared glance.

Joseph and I walked hand in hand most of the morning, slowing the whole company to match my pace. No one seemed to mind. None of us were overly eager to return to the demands of luxury. A few antelope scattered ahead of us. We saw a dozen hyraxes scurry into their holes as we plodded northeast. But there was no sign of guenons ahead or behind us. My Jendayi was truly gone.

When we stopped to graze the donkeys, I sat beneath a terebinth, feeling as if I might never move again. Joseph handed me a waterskin. "We can still turn back," he said. "The guards say we're exactly halfway, and the next half is desert hiking, much harder."

I tried to hide my tears. If Potabi knew how much I'd cried on this journey, he'd be ashamed of me. Would I be ashamed of him? Had he finished the canal project, or would Joseph be forced to charge him with treason?

I inhaled sharply, refusing more emotion but feeling even weaker. "I'll be fine for the hike. I must accept that Jendayi will be happy . . ."

Small gray spots covered my husband's face. A terrible roar erupted, and the ground rose to meet me.

In my next conscious moment, I was held aloft in Joseph's arms.

His face hovered over me, eyes boring into mine. "Asenath, say something!"

"What should I say?"

"You fainted! What happened? Are you ill? Do you fear seeing Potiphera again? Is it grief over Jendayi? Tell me. I can't bear—"

"Joseph, I'm fine, really."

"You're *not* fine!" Fear glistened in his eyes. "I love Jendayi, and I'll miss her, but I *need* you, my love. You must tell me what might help. Should we go back to Tebtunis and get Jendayi? We can do it. If we must stop for the night, we'll stop. We can ration water, and the guards will hunt for meals. We'll do whatever is necessary. Just tell me." He pulled me into a ferocious hug. "Please, I can't lose you now."

"Lose me?" Why was my calm and capable husband in such a panic? "I think I overheated, Joseph. I'm exhausted. I need a soft mattress, a hot bath, and scented oils." I nudged him away and peered into his worried features. This was definitely not the time to mention I might be with child.

"You're sure you can continue to Gurob?" He examined me as if I were a fig in the market. "We don't know what we'll face with Potiphera when we arrive."

Dread of seeing Potabi nearly made me turn back to Tebtunis, but we had to face him sometime. "Put me on a donkey for the rest of our journey. If I'm quiet, it's because my mind is whirring and I'm tired, but I think it's best for everyone if we get to Gurob tonight." I leaned forward and kissed him, distracting us both with a taste of passion. His features were much more relaxed when we parted.

The guards padded the donkey's back with extra reed mats and a woolen blanket before Joseph placed me gently on my perch. "I feel like Queen Tani." My husband kissed my hand, while twenty-four other men placed fists over their hearts and bowed to me. "Thank you," I said, fighting tears. "You have protected, served, laughed, and shared life with us. I'm so grateful for all of you." When they straightened, I scanned the dear faces. It was one of the most clarifying moments of my life. *This* was healing Egypt, trusting the God who united us, regardless of tribe or status, rather than the ancient legends of Egypt that divided and demeaned.

Our company continued toward Gurob, and my husband walked beside my donkey like an overprotective ommi. I offered my hand and most reassuring smile. "I am yours, Joseph ben Jacob, and no matter what awaits us in Gurob, we are Elohim's."

TWENTY-EIGHT

I will save you from the hands of the wicked
and deliver you from the grasp of the cruel.
JEREMIAH 15:21

Joseph

Asenath wilted like grass in summer's heat during the last half of their journey to Gurob. She was keeping something from him, something that was sapping the life from her, but she was as stubborn as the donkey she rode. The little beast attempted to graze on every patch of green it passed, slowing their pace even further. Dusk descended when the tip of Lahun's pyramid was in sight. The guides unpacked torches and surrounded the company as they continued through the darkness. Animal eyes glowed beyond the ring of safety and kept Medjays on alert with spears in hand. Nearby howls made Asenath cringe, so Joseph joined her on the donkey, his arms wrapped around her for the rest of the way. Truth be told, he needed to have her close as much as she needed him. "We're almost there, my love."

As they neared the torchlit glow of Gurob in the distance, the sound of rushing water greeted them. "Shh! Listen!" Joseph said, sliding off the donkey. Every man and beast stilled. "The canal! It must be working!"

The men cheered and rushed up the last dune toward Gurob's palace gates, hoping to get a better look in the brightening moonlight. Joseph led Asenath's donkey up the dune, and his wife simply wept. She'd been so emotional lately. He hardly knew whether she was happy or sad.

"Help me down," she said. "I want to join the celebration." She wiped her cheeks and forced a bright smile. Relief and confusion warred within, but Joseph granted her request, and together they celebrated with the others. Good-natured banter ushered them toward a well-deserved rest.

Trumpets blared, startling the whole company to silence.

Gurob's complex gates flung open. Two columns of soldiers ran toward them in battle formation. Shields in hand, swords at the ready.

Hami whirled to face his men. "Defense positions!" Every man—including their Faiyum guides—drew weapons and surrounded Joseph and Asenath. "Protect!" Hami shouted.

An army of Medjays surrounded them as trumpets continued blaring, announcing a pharaoh was in residence. Joseph shouted at Hami, "Are these King Apophis's men?" Though they were outnumbered five to one, if Apophis had come to steal Asenath, Joseph's men would make an impressive stand. After spending five weeks with his enchanting wife, every guard would give his life to defend her.

"These are Pharaoh Yanassi's Medjays." Hami held his ground, scanning the surrounding faces. "I don't know why the young pharaoh has become angry during our absence, but I believe he'll tell us very soon."

Hodari stood halfway between Joseph's caravan and the complex gates. "Welcome back, Zaphenath-Paneah. Pharaoh Yanassi and the queen mother will question you in the throne room."

"My wife is exhausted," Joseph said. "Let me escort her to her chamber and then—"

"Pharaoh and the queen require Mistress Asenath's presence as well."

Silent fury rose as Joseph circled Asenath's waist and began their march toward the gates. Hami, their Medjays, and even the guides remained a faithful circle of protection into Gurob's palace complex. Once they reached the palace, however, Hodari refused entrance to all except Joseph, Asenath, and Hami. A single Medjay opened the throne room door. The queen mother and Pharaoh Yanassi each sat on gold thrones, positioned on a dais barely large enough for the modestly sized chairs. Two men stood on the floor before them, shoulders back and chins held high. Gurob's palace steward appeared as arrogant today as the day Joseph demoted him to Overseer of Stables. The second man was a stranger but equally aloof.

Joseph halted at the base of the dais. He and Asenath bowed to the royals. His wife wobbled as she straightened and leaned against him to steady herself.

Tani studied Asenath, then exchanged a concerned glance with Pharaoh Yanassi. After what seemed a reluctant pause, the queen handed him a scroll.

The young pharaoh turned to Joseph. "Zaphenath-Paneah, you will answer my questions with a simple yes or no. Is that understood?"

"I understand, my king."

"Did you order Potiphera to restore the canal built by Amenemhat?"

"Yes, my king." Joseph cast a suspicious glance at the steward. Where was Potiphera?

"Did you threaten to send Potiphera back to Avaris if he didn't make himself essential to *your* purposes?"

The steward now wore a smug grin. Joseph looked at Yanassi. "Yes, but—"

Pharaoh lifted his hand. "You'll be given time to explain." He unfurled the scroll, scanned it, then looked again at Joseph. "Did you instruct Potiphera to name the restored canal Bahr Yussef— River of Joseph—to honor yourself above your pharaoh?"

"What?" The question stung like the bite of a blade.

Pharaoh pursed his lips, eyes glistening. Queen Tani glimpsed his struggle and leaned forward. "Must my son repeat such a painful question, Vizier Paneah?" The venom in her tone was like vinegar in the wound.

Asenath hugged Joseph's waist, trembling now. "Potabi," she whispered, recognizing—as he did—the stench of Potiphera's betrayal in the accusations.

"No," Joseph answered the queen. "I neither need the question repeated nor did I instruct Potiphera to name the restored canal with my Hebrew name." Though longing to scream the truth, Joseph fell silent, obedient to Pharaoh's guideline of refraining from explanations.

Pharaoh Yanassi nodded to the palace steward. The man offered an abbreviated nod to the king and said, "Vizier Paneah arrived with the most honorable Highness Potiphera more than a month ago and commanded his Highness to restore the canal to greatness. The vizier forced Mistress Asenath to accompany him on a perilous tour through the Faiyum in order to steal the loyalty of Pharaoh's people and stir dissention among the zealots who remain in the wild. Among the detailed instructions he left for Highness Potiphera, he also threatened to accuse Highness of treason and return him to Avaris if he didn't include the title on the canal's commemorative stele: Bahr Yussef." The man bowed low. "Only Mighty Pharaoh should be honored in such a way."

Yanassi nodded to the second man. "What do you have to add?"

His eyes darted from Joseph to the king. "I'm the construction foreman who worked side by side with Highness Potiphera. He took instruction from the vizier's commands—including etching *Bahr Yussef* on the stele. He was anxious to leave Gurob before the vizier returned because he feared for his life."

"Potabi wants to discredit you," Asenath whispered, "so we'll be forced to divorce."

"Silence!" Yanassi addressed Joseph again. "Though your authority is second only to mine, you will die a traitor if you have attempted to steal my glory or my kingdom." The silence crackled with tension. Finally, Pharaoh Yanassi shook the scroll in his hand. "I received this message from Potiphera two weeks ago urging me to come to Gurob before you and Mistress Asenath returned from the Faiyum. He said you'd commanded him to restore the canal—which you confirmed. He said you'd threatened him with treason—also confirmed. And he said you insisted on your wife's company in the Faiyum to win the favor of Egyptian zealots who might otherwise resist your charm."

"There are shades of truth to all of those things," Joseph said, "but Potiphera skews the truth with deception in his favor."

"Well, the 'shades of truth' come with two corroborating witnesses and Potiphera's written testimony." He shook the scroll again. "He's the most respected high priest at the largest temple of Ra in Egypt. And while he was overseeing the canal's reconstruction, he was also working with my uncle Apophis to set up a meeting with six key merchants from surrounding nations. They'll soon open trade on the Nile from Edfu to the Great Sea—for the first time since Abi Khyan died." He left his throne and stood over them. "When Hami was my vizier, he taught me to heed my counselors. Potiphera is a valuable member of my council."

"He's also—" Asenath began.

"Please," Joseph whispered, "let me speak for us."

"But I . . ." She searched his eyes, and he realized she needed a voice.

"I'll ask permission for you to speak after I've testified." A tentative smile bloomed as she nodded her approval.

Joseph looked to the young pharaoh. "I understand your dilemma, my king. May I now explain my dilemma and then give Asenath an opportunity?"

"You may explain, Vizier."

Joseph laid out the truth, beginning with his first conversation with Potiphera upon arrival at Gurob, the priest's uncooperative scouting of the unkempt canal, and the couple's quick departure for the Faiyum on the day they'd returned. "Although my wife showed her valued partnership at each village, Potiphera proved a hindrance at every port and with every attempt at rebuilding. So, I told him he must prove himself essential by rebuilding the canal at Gurob or I'd send him back to Avaris to explain why he'd failed to obey your command and help the people of Egypt."

"Even if all that's true, Paneah, how do you explain the canal's name?" Yanassi sounded more sad than angry. "Everyone knows Potiphera has no respect for the Hebrew clan. He would never, of his own choice, have honored you by naming the canal Bahr Yussef."

"The name didn't honor me, did it? It's placed me under suspicion." Joseph added. "The beginning of Potiphera's message bears shades of truth, but if he said I ordered him to name the canal Bahr Yussef, that's a lie."

Yanassi cast a suspicious glance at the two witnesses and back at Joseph. "The steward and foreman told us you ordered Potiphera to name the canal. Yet there's nothing written in Potiphera's hand—"

"But Highness told us—"

"Take them to the prison," Yanassi said to Hodari. "Have your Medjays discover the truth." The captain signaled to four of his men, who escorted the protesting witnesses out of the throne room.

When Yanassi returned his attention to Joseph, the king asked, "What evidence can you provide for your defense, Vizier?"

"I have several witnesses who can attest to the truth of my testimony, my king." He motioned toward Hami. "The man Pharaoh Khyan, Queen Tani, and you trusted as your vizier before me has been my constant advisor since my appointment as vizier. You may wish to question him." Joseph shrugged. "But if I've lost your trust, my king, I implore you to choose another vizier to lead Egypt through the coming feast and famine. Your people have suffered great losses from the floods. The canal will help control future damage, but there is still much work to be done before granaries can be built and lives restored to normal. If a change is to be made, please, my king, make it quickly."

Joseph started to remove the king's signet ring, but Asenath stilled his hand. He lifted his eyes to the royals. "May my wife have permission to speak?"

"Of course," the queen answered.

Asenath shifted from foot to foot. "Do you remember the wisdom you gave me on my wedding day, my queen?"

"We said many things while I prepared you to wed Vizier Paneah."

"Do you remember who you told me to trust above all others?"

Queen Tani's eyes narrowed, and she remained silent.

"You told me to trust my husband above all others," Asenath said, "even above my own abi. At the time I didn't believe you, but I'm telling you now, Queen Tani, that your advice was sound. Potabi is lying. You and Pharaoh Yanassi should trust Paneah."

Queen Tani lifted a single brow, then bent to whisper something to her son. While they spoke privately, one of the Medjays who had escorted the witnesses from the throne room returned. When Pharaoh Yanassi saw him whisper something to Hodari, the king asked, "What is this about?"

Hodari gave permission for his guard to speak. "While the witnesses were escorted to the dungeon, I searched their chambers and found this behind a loosened stone in the wall." He handed a tattered papyrus to Yanassi. "I suspect in Highness Potiphera's rush to leave Gurob, he left the message, which the steward likely kept in order to extort Potiphera."

Queen Tani moved close enough to read the message. Their expressions clouded. Yanassi crumpled the missive, then glared at his ommi. "Did you know both Potiphera and Apophis held ill will against Paneah?"

"No, my son!"

"Paneah, are you aware my uncle plans to take your wife?"

"I'm aware of Potiphera's disdain for me and his personal correspondence with your uncle. Potiphera also has political ties with Shedet's high priest—a known zealot—and King Apophis appointed them both as high priests."

"Be very careful, Vizier." Queen Tani held Joseph's gaze. "You may question Potiphera, but don't ever accuse the Son of Ra who sits on Egypt's throne."

"I make no accusation, my queen. I hope to clarify what we know to protect Pharaoh Yanassi."

"Continue, Zaphenath-Paneah." Yanassi remained standing, arms folded.

"Potiphera is as clever as he is ambitious. I believe he's cultivating a friendship with King Apophis so he can make Asenath a queen and secure more political power. My fear is that he'll use that power against you, my king."

"Why? I've never wronged Potiphera."

"Nor have I. But our Amu heritage is an affront to his pure Egyptian blood and fertilizes the soil in which his grudge has grown strong against those who destroyed Memphis."

"It's true, my king." Asenath was shaking now. "I beg for mercy as I tell you the whole truth. Potabi has hated the Amu since the night my ommi was killed in Ra's Memphis temple. He arranged for me to marry King Webenre before King Apophis killed him. I'd hoped Potabi would change his bias when Elohim sent Potabi a dream to confirm my marriage to Paneah. It didn't work. He still hoped to somehow discredit Paneah, force us to divorce, and marry me to King Apophis. I fear Bahr Yussef was his attempt to implicate my husband."

Queen Tani and the young pharaoh had a whispered conversation. The queen nodded as if in agreement, then addressed the vizier. "I gave Asenath more advice at her wedding—that Potiphera would say or do anything to control her. What if the message he sent us was an elaborate scheme to control us *all*?" She looked at Asenath. "I suppose I should listen better to my own advice."

The young pharaoh locked eyes with Joseph. "I have Potiphera's scroll, two witnesses, and an engraved stele that testify against you. Yet you can provide equally convincing witnesses and have demonstrated months of faithfulness in preparation for Egypt's greatest famine." Yanassi stared into the distance, thoughts whirring behind his sharp eyes. Finally, he said, "I believe what you say about Potiphera is true. It all makes sense. Unfortunately, we have no proof that he has committed a crime. He has proven himself a sly fox. Ommi and I fell prey to his manipulation. He's likely done the same to my uncle. They may be waiting in Edfu to do you harm."

"I believe you're correct," Joseph said. "Potiphera whispered a cryptic message to Asenath about her destiny being fulfilled when she arrived in Edfu."

The king nodded. "If Potiphera has convinced Apophis you named the canal, what real evidence do we have of his deceit? We'll hope the Medjays get more details from the steward and foreman, but my guess is that Potiphera never showed them any written proof. Why wouldn't they take him at his word? And I dare not accuse Potiphera publicly—or to my uncle—without proof of his wrongdoing."

"At least change the name of the canal," Joseph begged. "It should become *Bahr Yanassi* to commemorate your leadership—"

Pharaoh Yanassi lifted his hand for silence. "A good king admits when he has wronged a friend, Paneah. Ommi and I should have thought it through. An Amu vizier couldn't raise a rebellion in the Faiyum where rebels are still active." The young pharaoh had grown in both stature and wisdom in the three months since Joseph and Asenath had married. "I will send a message to my uncle, declaring Bahr Yussef as the name of the reconstructed canal. It will be up to you, Lord Paneah, to reveal Potiphera's treachery."

"May I speak?" Joseph asked. *Elohim, give me wisdom and favor.*

Yanassi nodded.

"Potiphera's deception raises many questions, but my main concern as your vizier must be the continued preparation of the Two Lands for the coming feast and famine. We must use what we know to our advantage. King Apophis wishes to marry Asenath, and Potiphera has gone to Edfu to ingratiate himself to the co-regent. He'll likely accuse me of treason in hopes of taking my position as vizier—which is what he's wanted from the beginning." Joseph broached the other possibility carefully. "Or he may simply mediate the trade agreement to strengthen Apophis's reign."

"To weaken mine?" Yanassi said.

"Apophis wouldn't betray you," Queen Tani said. "Paneah, you must go to Edfu immediately."

"Forgive me, my queen, but that would be unwise."

"Why?"

"If Potiphera convinced you and Pharaoh Yanassi I'd committed treason, though you believe in my integrity and loyalty, imagine how he's twisted the opinion of a king who already had a poor opinion of me. I'm sure when King Apophis is told I named the canal Bahr Yussef, he'll be eager to execute me for treason."

"Potiphera is quite clever, isn't he?" Queen Tani released a huff.

"But your wisdom today—recognizing the deception and sending a message to exonerate me—will disarm him. Allow Asenath and I to continue our tour of cities on the way to Thebes. In Thebes, I'll meet with Pharaoh Sobekhotep and explain that each nome will store their own grain, and I'll emphasize Pharaoh Yanassi's wise decision to distribute the grain from one location—Avaris. He may feel threatened since King Apophis has been camped with his troops in Edfu for months. I'll reassure him about the upcoming trade meeting at Edfu and hope it calms him."

Queen Tani rubbed her forehead. "Apophis said he was staying in Edfu to improve trade, but now he seems more like the bully from our childhood."

"I'll gain Sobekhotep's loyalty," Joseph promised, "and with it the protection of Upper Egypt's army for myself and Asenath. Then I'll invite King Apophis to meet me in Thebes and confront Potiphera's deception face-to-face."

Queen Tani shook her head, and Joseph thought she meant to squelch his plan. "You are a gift from the gods and a tool in their hands, Zaphenath-Paneah."

"Stay alive, Paneah." The young pharaoh looked at Joseph with wide, dark eyes. "I don't believe my uncle intends me harm, but if he aims to have your wife, you're in grave danger."

"We'll pray for my God's wisdom and protection." Joseph and

Asenath bowed and backed out of the royals' presence. Hami escorted them to their chamber in silence. Asenath retreated directly to the adjoining courtyard.

Hami paused at the threshold and nodded her direction. "Comfort her, my friend. She lost Jendayi today and will likely lose Potiphera in the days to come. We'll leave at dawn for the journey south." He closed the door behind himself, leaving Joseph with a jumble of his own emotions to untangle.

TWENTY-NINE

Blessed is the one
who does not walk in step with the wicked
or stand in the way that sinners take
or sit in the company of mockers.

PSALM 1:1

Potiphera

Representatives from six nations—Persia, Tyre, Canaan, Syria, Crete, and Cush—reclined around King Apophis's table, enjoying a midday meal Potiphera had planned with the king's opinionated cook. He'd arrived at Edfu Fortress yesterday after fleeing from Gurob. He was exhausted but determined to make today's negotiations flawless. He'd insisted on choosing the menu himself and immediately recognized King Apophis's cook and her assistant from the dream he'd had that matched Paneah's. Pushpa and Ahira were as unwelcome in Edfu as they'd been in his dream.

"Have another helping of lamb." Potiphera moved the platter of meat closer to the Persian trader. "Ra's resources are as endless as his power."

"Yet our patience has limits." The Tyrian merchant shoved his meal aside and spoke to King Apophis. "You promised a treaty with unencumbered trade from Cush to the Great Sea, but my felucca was detained at Thebes for three days. I used considerable silver to persuade Sobekhotep's men to let us continue to Edfu. I won't risk shipping valuable goods this far south without Sobekhotep's signature. Why isn't he here to sign the treaty?"

King Apophis reached for a silver pitcher of honeyed wine, smiled kindly, and filled the man's goblet. "Speak to me again with such disrespect, my friend, and you'll ship your goods from the underworld." He slammed the pitcher onto the table, casting a pall over the room.

Potiphera shot a concerned glance at King Rehor, the only man there who matched his cunning. "My Tyrian friend's frustration is justified," Rehor said to King Apophis, "though his manners need improvement." The Minoan king brought calm to any gathering and had negotiated a similar treaty during Pharaoh Khyan's reign years earlier. Trade had gone smoothly between Nubians in the deep south, Thebes in Upper Egypt's middle nomes, and Lower Egypt's northern delta until Pharaoh Khyan's untimely death.

"King Apophis, my friend." Rehor leaned forward, tone as smooth as butter. "It's not your diplomacy we doubt but Pharaoh Sobekhotep's integrity. When Memphis fell and Egypt divided, the pharaohs who established their rule in Thebes—"

"You mean the cowardly royals and nobles who fled to Thebes and ignored their soldiers stationed in the Edfu Fortress?" The Cushite trader had been one of those soldiers cut off from family and northern support fifteen years ago and nursed his wounds with a lucrative trading business. "Pharaoh Djehuty set up his army and throne in Thebes and abandoned us. My compatriots and I celebrated when Sobekhotep assassinated him, but the old pharaoh has been as heartless as the other Memphis kings." He scoffed at the Minoan. "We don't doubt Sobekhotep's integrity. We know he has none. So, whether he signs the treaty or not, the traders and soldiers of Cush follow King Apophis—a soldier-king who's loyal to all Egyptians."

"The trade agreement reaches beyond Egypt's internal conflict," Potiphera said. "If you would all listen to King Apophis, I believe you'll realize his plan prepares us for imminent disaster and could also line our pockets with silver." Potiphera inclined his head toward the regal figure on his left. "Now, my king, may Ra, the almighty creator, give you—his perfect son—great wisdom for this moment." He tossed a pinch of ashes over the king's shoulder.

Apophis scanned the seven faces around his table, pausing to meet each man's gaze before moving to the next. The simple exercise established his authority and quieted rebellion in a way shouting never would have. "Through the dreams the gods gave my young nephew, Pharaoh Yanassi, we know Egypt will experience seven years of abundance and seven years of the severest famine ever recorded. When the famine comes, it will ruin your nations, too. Egypt will be the only nation that can fill your bellies."

The merchants exchanged glances, some concerned, others suspicious.

Apophis continued, "You six merchants represent the finest trade goods on the King's Highway: spices, pottery, cloth, dye, and more." A slow grin curved his lips. "You've dabbled in trade with Egypt before, but I suggest you make us your best customer during the abundance—because when the famine begins, we'll be your *sole* source of grain." He lifted his goblet and motioned toward the door. "You may leave now if you wish, or you may remain at the table with the only pharaoh in Egypt who has a plan to save the world."

No one moved while he took a long draw of wine and refilled his goblet.

Potiphera wished he could shout to the gods! *Praise Ra, Katesch! Apophis has proven he is without a doubt the one for our girl!*

Every man in the room awaited the king of king's next word.

Suddenly, the kitchen door swung open, and Pushpa barged in with more roast meat. "Roebuck, fresh off the spit, my lords." Ahira followed with a platter of fruit and cheese.

"Get out!" Potiphera shouted, scurrying to his feet. "Get out, both of you!" He shooed them back toward the kitchen, but Apophis's bodyguard stepped into his path.

"You'll speak to my ommi with respect or deal with me, Priest," said Potiphar, who was intimidating even when not growling a threat.

"I didn't know she was your ommi. Forgive me." Potiphera offered a silent apology to the old woman and resumed his seat beside the king.

Apophis nodded toward the two women as they disappeared into the kitchen. "My captain is protective of them, especially after our new vizier sent a message saying he planned to marry your daughter instead of keeping his promise to marry Ahira."

Paneah's lost love was a kitchen maid? How could Paneah have begged Queen Tani to marry a *maid* rather than Asenath? Potiphera's loathing for Paneah shifted to rage at the gods. Why had they tainted his dreams with lies that matched Paneah's? *Show Ahira our love is secure enough to welcome her home.* The words Asenath spoke in the dream assaulted Potiphera. How could his well-trained daughter fall in love with a Hyksos? *Gods forbid!*

Apophis resumed his explanation, drawing Potiphera back to the moment. "My nephew appointed a new vizier, Zaphenath-Paneah, to tour Egypt and assess the needs of each village, city, and nome. He's clever and even reopened Amenemhat's canal in the Faiyum to drain off the excess flooding. However, he overstepped his authority when he renamed it Bahr Yussef."

"He gave it a Hebrew name?" The Canaanite merchant cackled. "I'd say he's poking Egypt in the eye."

Apophis's dead stare sobered the man. "When I execute Zaphenath-Paneah for treason, I'll marry his wife—Potiphera's daughter, Isis's high priestess—and I'll unify the Two Lands. I've already eradicated the pretender, Webenre, who tried to become a king in Abydos. I have no doubt Pharaoh Sobekhotep will sign this trade agreement as a first step to bring Egypt under a centralized government. During the famine, all nations will come to Avaris for nourishment, where I will dispense Egypt's plentiful grain."

"I see how easily you could erase Upper Egypt's throne, King Apophis." The Persian trader twirled his curled beard. "But what about your nephew? Can you so easily kill your beloved sister's son?"

"I would never harm Yanassi! I'll continue as Lower Egypt's military king and purveyor of power until my nephew comes of age. By that time, I will have unified the Two Lands and Yanassi will be old enough to assume the full responsibility of a long and peaceful reign."

Potiphera maintained a smile through Apophis's recitation, although Potiphera's long-term plan differed greatly about who would reign during the final years of peace. In his plan, the young pharaoh would meet a tragic end while King Apophis and Queen Asenath were young enough to give Potiphera a lasting legacy.

"Any more questions?" King Apophis slammed his goblet on the table and shot to his feet. "Or are we ready to sign the trade agreement?"

King Rehor spoke. "Since overthrowing thrones takes time, Great King, will your long-term plan secure Pharaoh Sobekhotep's signature on our agreement? If each of our ships could carry a treaty with Sobekhotep's signature, we'd all enjoy safe passage along the Nile."

"I'll do more than *attempt* to gain Sobekhotep's signature, Rehor. I intend to visit Thebes as soon as word of the vizier's arrival reaches me. I'm quite anxious to meet my new bride."

THIRTY

The LORD sustains them on their sickbed
and restores them from their bed of illness.

PSALM 41:3

EIGHT DAYS LATER

Asenath

Sailing as the Nile's water levels decreased meant slower travel and a more arduous journey for us all. Rowing grew more difficult in the shallows, so the sailors set aside their oars for giant hemp ropes as thick as my leg. Divided into two teams, they attached one end of each rope to the bow; the other extended to opposite shores in order for the men to tug our heavily loaded barque through shallows and across emerging shoals. Medjays stood watch for crocodiles while the brave sailors pulled us against the very natural and necessarily dwindling river. Only when the Nile receded could farmers plant their crops. And only when the Nile was a slender stream could we harvest its life-giving fruit in three months.

My body had also struggled against natural and necessary changes. Like the dwindling Nile, I had barely enough energy to navigate my own life while creating another inside me. After days of vomiting, I hadn't even the strength to hold up my head.

"We've arrived, love." Joseph lifted me gently, as if I were an injured lamb and he my shepherd. "Get us to a chamber and bring a midwife—now!"

"Joseph?" The effort to speak made me gag again, but the well was dry. The repetitive sway-and-whoosh of our sailors' rowing and tugging had created a cesspool in my belly. Had it been days or a week since I'd eaten? My singular reprieve came when we docked at night. Early in our sail, I met a few village women as usual while Joseph promised the Faiyum's restored canal would protect them from next year's abundant flood. But now our sail had gone from days to weeks, and I couldn't remember the last time I'd left the barque. "Jos—" I gagged again.

"Shh, love. The midwife will come."

Panic rose. "Is . . ." I tried to swallow but couldn't. "Is my baby . . ."

"So far, the baby seems fine, but sometimes the first months of pregnancy make a woman quite ill." He'd learned much from his ima Rachel, a midwife. "You haven't kept down water for several days."

He called for help again, pulled me closer to his chest, and hurried his pace. I groaned at the jostling, regret almost as miserable as the illness. Why hadn't I told him about his child when we could have celebrated together? Instead, my weakness had trumpeted my announcement. In a panic, he'd sent Hami for a physician when we ported at Thinis, thinking I'd contracted some terrible disease from the Faiyum. I'd stopped Hami at the threshold with my announcement.

"Pregnant?" Joseph's eyes instantly misted. Hami disappeared, giving Joseph and me much of that day to bask together in solitude and joy. The next day resumed the repetitive sway-and-whoosh, and I remembered little else. Had my illness stopped Joseph from visiting many villages? Had he gone ashore without me? *Elohim, please. Save me. Save Joseph. Save our baby . . .*

Two Days Later

"There you are." A woman's voice. Gentle. Distant. "Can you open your eyes, Asenath?"

Was I dreaming? My body felt like it was floating. My eyes fluttered open. I saw a white haze. No, not haze. It was linen. Draped over a canopied bed, as sheer as butterflies' wings.

"I'm glad you've come back to us."

I turned and stared into the face of a monster. Trying to scream, I could only gasp. My dry lips cracked. The taste of blood made my stomach lurch.

Someone held me. "Asenath, look at me."

"Jo—"

"Yes, love. It's me." He pressed a wet cloth against my stinging lips.

I had no tears. Couldn't swallow. Tongue swollen, I felt dried like a raisin.

"Queen Sitmut has been with us since we arrived in Thebes." He laid me back on the bed and pressed a fresh wet cloth on my lips. "Her scars prove a painful life, Asenath, but she's a gifted healer. A caring and gentle woman."

He moved aside and the monster came into view. "I'm sorry I frightened you," she said. "My face can be disconcerting." Her smile lit the still-lovely side of her face. The other side was missing an eye and bore the webbed scarring of a burn. "The palace midwife told us to give you water with the wet cloth. She said if you woke within three days, you and your baby had a good chance of survival."

How long had I been sleeping? I shot a terrified glance at my husband. I wanted to scream my questions but could merely pant. Panic stole all dignity.

My husband leaned over me, his tears dripping onto my cheeks. "You're going to live—our child, too, if Elohim wills it." The queen passed him a freshened wet cloth. "I'm with you. I won't leave you." He pressed his forehead against mine, forcing strength into me.

"All right, Lord Paneah, out of the way. Let's feed her broth while she's awake."

Joseph shifted so he could lift my head. The queen held a spoon to my lips and ladled broth into my mouth. "It was your husband's dedication to you that won my Sobekhotep's respect. Had Paneah arrived like any other strutting vizier, your whole company would have been sent right back to Lower Egypt. My brother and I come from a long line of viziers. They're all liars."

Was Pharaoh Sobekhotep her brother or husband? I glanced at Joseph, thinking my foggy brain had misinterpreted what she'd said.

Sitmut ladled another spoonful of broth and said, "My husband-brother, Sobekhotep, was an overseer in Memphis when the vizier— Queen Tani's abi—betrayed Pharaoh. The Amu general, Salitis, destroyed the city and became the first Amu king in Avaris." She waved the empty spoon. "Forgive me. I'm sure you know that, but the part you've likely never been told is that Sobekhotep's first wife and daughter were killed in the Memphis attack. He came to Thebes to join me, his only remaining relative, and discovered that my husband, Pharaoh Djehuty, was mistreating me. The Theban nobles and priests knew of Djehuty's abuse but did nothing to stop it, so my brother killed him, brought justice to Thebes, and married me. We now have a handsome son, Neferhotep."

Joseph chuckled. "When you regain your strength, my love, Neferhotep will no doubt challenge you to a game of senet—and likely beat you."

Sitmut nodded. "Our son is a jewel in our crowns, as your child will be." She ladled in another spoonful of the delicious broth, and my thoughts began to clear. This woman had endured an abusive first husband and her brother's violent rescue, yet she fairly glowed when she spoke of their son.

She grinned as I studied her. "You need not fear for your safety or Paneah's. Sobekhotep is protective of his family and his welcome guests."

I turned to Joseph. Were we truly safe in Thebes?

Joseph kissed my forehead. "I've explained Pharaoh Yanassi's dreams to Pharaoh Sobekhotep and about the years to come. He understands the importance of having a single distribution center during the famine and has agreed to Avaris as the location. Yesterday, he invited Apophis to come to Thebes for a treaty negotiation."

I stared into those golden-flecked green eyes, too tired and weak to ponder the conflict ahead of us, my body still too parched to produce tears.

The queen set aside the bowl while Joseph arranged my pillows, enabling me to sit up and face them both. "I can see you're upset," the queen said. "Paneah explained your Potabi's deception and the danger Apophis poses to your marriage. Know this, dear girl. My Sobekhotep is an impeccable judge of character. He'll know immediately upon meeting King Apophis if he's to be trusted—or ousted from our shores."

I glimpsed tension hardening Joseph's features. Queen Sitmut mustn't think we hoped they'd turn Apophis away. Joseph needed the two pharaohs to cooperate during the feast and famine for Egypt to survive.

"I know how important the trade agreement is." The queen leaned close but whispered loudly enough for Joseph to hear. "Paneah was very wise to win *my* favor with his devotion to you and then let me convince Sobekhotep it was vital that Apophis come to Thebes. Your husband has a silver tongue," she said, giving him a sidelong grin, "but I think it's attached to a heart of gold. I never thought Sobekhotep would agree to meet with King Apophis, but Paneah convinced us this trade agreement may be Egypt's only chance at survival."

I felt both relief and terror. When Apophis arrived, would he somehow claim me for his own? My body tensed, then trembled. I tried to stop, but with the effort came whimpers.

Joseph held me, rocking me like a child. "Shh, love. You're safe. *We're* safe. Pharaoh Sobekhotep's whole army will meet Apophis when he arrives next week. You'll be stronger by then. We'll be fine." He hummed the shepherd's tune I first heard at Magic Lake.

My eyelids grew heavy. "No, Apophis," I pleaded and let sleep take me away.

THIRTY-ONE

This is what the LORD says—
  he who made a way through the sea,
  a path through the mighty waters,
  who drew out the chariots and horses,
  the army and reinforcements together,
  and they lay there, never to rise again,
  extinguished, snuffed out like a wick:
  "Forget the former things;
  do not dwell on the past."

ISAIAH 43:16–18

Joseph

The young prince reached for his crocodile-shaped game piece, and Joseph lifted a brow. Neferhotep's hand stilled on the cone. "You think this move unwise, Vizier Paneah?"

"I think a different move would be wiser, Your Majesty."

Asenath swatted Joseph's arm. "You're not allowed to advise your wife's opponent."

"I haven't won a senet game since yesterday morning, Mistress Asenath," the ten-year-old prince groused. "Your skill has improved with your health and lessened my chances of victory. The great and mighty Pharaoh Sobekhotep says a wise king finds a way to win, Mistress." He studied the senet board more closely and moved a different cone three spaces to exit the board at the *House of Happiness*. He sat back with a satisfied smile. "You may proceed."

Asenath growled, feigning offense, and the prince's features fairly glowed. He'd been enamored with her since their first introduction, begging to see her each day. They began playing senet together as soon as she was strong enough to sit. The boy had shown the same compassion for others that seemed to pour naturally from his parents. He'd also proven as meticulous in learning how to reign and would likely be as ruthless as Sobekhotep toward Thebes's enemies when the aging pharaoh died.

The sound of trumpets startled Asenath, skewing the game board and the pieces on it. "Forgive me, Your Majesty." She nervously attempted to restore the pieces to their right places, but Joseph stilled her hands and met her gaze. They both knew what the trumpet meant. King Apophis had arrived—earlier than expected.

"The prince and I must go," Joseph said. "I'll send the midwife so you won't be alone."

"My ommi will stay with you," Neferhotep offered. "She doesn't like meeting new people either." He scooted off the bed and flashed a playful grin. "I'll come back tomorrow and beat you, Mistress Asenath." He strode toward the door, regal restraint quelling boyish excitement.

"I'll look forward to it." Asenath's wobbly voice betrayed her nervousness.

Joseph kissed her before joining the prince. "I'll come before the banquet to say good night."

"Be careful." She forced a smile.

"Elohim has brought us this far. He'll give us wisdom to travel whatever path lies ahead." He pressed those words like a seal on his memory and left the chamber. They'd sailed on the Nile's flood and shallows and hiked through sand, marsh, and rocky hills. Elohim had provided guides and supplies for every impossible obstacle. *People seem to be the most difficult obstacle of all, Elohim.*

Hami was waiting when Joseph and the prince emerged from the palace's guest hallway. "The watchmen report a contingent of thirty men on two small barques," he said, then added, "Two women accompany the king."

The prince ran ahead with his own palace guards, but Joseph was shocked to a halt. "Ahira?"

"Likely Pushpa *and* Ahira."

They strode toward the quay, Joseph silently chiding himself for overlooking the possibility that the woman he almost married might accompany Potiphar to this meeting. He'd considered the awkward reunion with Potiphar, the man who'd been both kind master and unfair jailer, but he'd been too worried about Asenath and their unborn child to consider that Ahira and Pushpa would likely join Potiphar on the journey. *Dear Pushpa.* The thought of the woman who'd been like an Egyptian ommi soothed some of his anxiety.

As he neared the quay, the sight of three distinct groups on Thebes's shore heightened Joseph's tension. Separated by heavily armed guards, Pharaoh Sobekhotep stood with Prince Neferhotep and five counselors closest to the dock. Pharaoh motioned for Joseph to join them. He passed the second group, Amun's priests, dressed in gold and white raiment that gleamed in the midday sun. Sobekhotep hated all priests—even those who served him—and seldom let them stand closer than twenty paces to his dishonored left side. The third group was massive and covered every footprint of land like a well-armed tapestry between the quay and Pharaoh's palace. Upper Egypt's military was an impressive sight but frayed Joseph's nerves.

The first barque slid onto the sand as Joseph reached Pharaoh Sobekhotep's side. The king made no move to welcome the ship full of guards but leaned toward Joseph. "How is your dear wife today, Vizier? Still beating my son at senet?" Though a friendly question, his stare remained soberly fixed on Apophis's guards, who debarked in preparation for their king.

"When the trumpets called us to the quay, Your Majesty, Prince

Neferhotep had made a strategic decision that might have won him the game. He's challenged Asenath to another game tomorrow with high hopes of a victory."

He patted his son's shoulder. "Well done."

All banter ceased when the second barque's bow slid ashore. King Apophis stood at the prow, Master Potiphar at his side.

He's no longer my master. Nor was Apophis Lower Egypt's "annoying general," as Potiphar had often described him while Joseph was a slave. Though he knew Apophis wished to steal his wife and perhaps kill him, he had no idea what to expect at his first confrontation with Potiphar. Though honorable in many ways, the captain of Apophis's guard had unjustly imprisoned Joseph and then left him to rot despite the certainty of his innocence. Stubborn fears rose as Apophis leaned over to speak with his captain. What were they plotting?

I'm Zaphenath-Paneah, he reminded himself, sorting logic from emotion as each fought for control. *Pharaoh Yanassi and Pharaoh Sobekhotep support me. King Apophis wouldn't dare attack me while Upper Egypt's army stands on Thebes's shore.*

When Apophis looked up, the two pharaohs locked eyes in their own silent battle. Each king had suffered on opposing sides of political schemes. Deep wrinkles and weather-worn faces attested to similar heartaches. Neither would easily compromise. *Elohim, only Your presence can lead us to peace with so many obstacles in the path.*

"Joseph!" Startled by his Hebrew name and a woman's voice, he saw Pushpa standing on the bow, waving. Potiphar, who stood at King Apophis's right shoulder, leaned down and whispered emphatically to his ommi. Her eyes widened, and she waved again. "I mean, Lord Paneah!"

"A friend of yours?" Sobekhotep asked wryly.

"As dear as my own ommi."

His smile died when he saw Ahira standing between Pushpa and Potiphar. She was dressed like a queen in pure white linen. Her hair was braided atop her head, and she wore a gold chain around her neck. Potiphar placed his hand at the small of her back. Possessive. Too familiar. He whispered something to her and then met Joseph's gaze.

"Lord Vizier, your face shows concern." Sobekhotep's coarse whisper was urgent. "If you discern danger, tell me so I may protect my son." He watched Apophis intently.

"Neferhotep is not in danger, Your Majesty." Joseph swallowed hard. But what about Ahira? Had Potiphar forced her into his bed when she was no longer promised to Joseph? Or, worse, had Joseph's marriage to Asenath left Ahira with no choice but to become Potiphar's concubine? Blind fury drove him toward the dock.

"Paneah!"

He ignored Sobekhotep's shout.

Hami appeared at his side, keeping pace. "Do not confront Potiphar publicly, Lord Vizier. You must know *facts* before you accuse." He blocked Joseph's path. "*Think*, Vizier. You appear to be advancing against King Apophis."

The startling truth halted Joseph. Medjays surrounded the visiting king, with Potiphar leading his royal guards, hand on his dagger's hilt. Joseph's fists clenched. "If Potiphar forced her—"

"Would Pushpa allow him to do that?" Hami's logic restored Joseph's wits.

"Never." He released the answer and shook out the tension in his arms. Hami moved aside, and Joseph forced his expression to geniality. "Welcome, King Apophis!"

The visiting king showed no fear, pushed past his Medjays, and met Joseph face-to-face. Hami stood between them, while Potiphar lagged three paces behind his king, scanning the quay for threats. Knowing Joseph wasn't a threat, Potiphar had found a convenient way to avoid their first greeting. A short, stocky man slipped from behind King Apophis—Potiphera, slithering from the shadows like a viper.

"So, you're the Hebrew slave who stole my wife," Apophis said for Joseph's hearing alone. A long scar ran from the king's left temple onto his cheek, making him even more intimidating.

"I am the man God chose to save Egypt and the vizier Pharaoh Yanassi chose to marry Asenath."

"What of my choice?" Potiphera said, teeth clenched.

Joseph ignored him. "King Apophis, you and I should speak about Potiphera's treason after we've negotiated the trade agreement." He paused. "That is, if you've come from Edfu to save Egypt and not simply to bemoan your broken heart." Joseph stepped back, hoping an attempt at diplomacy would outweigh his insult. "I would be honored to introduce you to a king whose love of family and commitment to the Two Lands equals what I've witnessed in Lower Egypt. Pharaoh Sobekhotep is as committed to saving this nation as you are, King Apophis."

"At least you're a man and not a mouse. Make your introductions, Vizier." He gestured toward Sobekhotep. Joseph's legs felt like water, but he led the visitors toward the waiting king.

As they approached Sobekhotep, Potiphera rushed ahead and stood between the two kings, opening his arms wide as if receiving old friends. "How gracious of you to welcome us to Thebes, Pharaoh Sobekhotep. Never has Egypt seen such a historic encounter between two pharaohs—the epitome of cooperation in these trying times—who are truly committed to unity."

Sobekhotep sneered. "Away from me, you vile insect."

Apophis's belly laugh brought a smile to Sobekhotep's face, which softened his first words to the visiting king. "If you don't mind, King Apophis, I would prefer all priests—including yours—were banished to the Temple of Amun during our negotiations. I've discovered priests are no more than vipers in sheep's clothing who usually strike at the most inopportune times."

Apophis waved his annoying high priest toward the scowling priests of Amun. "Go, Potiphera, and take your temple guards with you." Nuru emerged from the troops that had sailed from Edfu to accompany Potiphera.

"I believe we may get along better than I'd anticipated," Sobekhotep said to Apophis, and the two began exchanging pleasantries.

Joseph felt someone's stealthy approach behind him and spun to defend himself. Pushpa yelped and swatted his shoulder. "I came to ask Egypt's vizier for a hug!"

He embraced her, closing his eyes to block out all else. "Oh, how I've missed you, dear Pushpa."

"Did you miss Ahira and me, *Lord Vizier?*" Potiphar's gravelly whisper startled Joseph's eyes open. Ahira stood behind him, head bowed. "Perhaps you've been too busy to think of old friends, but I've thought of you often," he said. "I'm confident Elohim will favor Egypt under your care as He once favored my estate."

Was he taunting Joseph or seeking reconciliation? "We have much to discuss, Captain Potiphar."

"Indeed—"

"Paneah!" Pharaoh Sobekhotep drew his attention.

Both kings and the prince focused on him. "Yes, my lords?"

King Apophis appeared flushed. "Asenath carries your child?" His tone was taut, words clipped.

"She does." He glanced at the visitors' varied responses. "She's been quite ill, but she's feeling better—"

"Did you know?" Apophis snapped at Potiphera, who fell to his knees.

"No, my king. I would never have—"

"A child changes everything." Apophis turned his fiery stare to Joseph. "I won't raise a—"

Subspecies of non-Egyptian urchins. Joseph grinned at the memory of Asenath's angry prophecy of their children, spoken before the angel promised they'd bless all nations.

"Why are you smiling, Vizier?" Apophis's eyes narrowed. "I came here to execute you for treason."

Sobekhotep lifted his hand, and a hundred of Upper Egypt's soldiers gathered around them, swords drawn. The Theban pharaoh sheltered Prince Neferhotep in front of him, the boy's eyes wide with fear.

Joseph spoke calmly. "Prince Neferhotep, what should we do when both kings seem so angry?"

"I don't know. I'm only a child."

The deep ridges on both kings' faces softened. Although Sobek-hotep wore the gray pallor of failing health, he valued his son's needed training. "Remember, Neferhotep. The gods spoke through the dreams of a boy near your age to save the Two Lands."

Joseph added, "And because Pharaoh Yanassi listened to my God, we now have seven years of abundance during which we can prepare for seven years of famine. Though you don't yet sit on your abi's throne, my prince, you may yet influence the decisions made today during negotiations that could set Egypt's course for generations." Joseph returned his attention to the pharaohs. "With your combined wisdom, skill, and experience, Egypt won't merely survive. She can thrive. Train the prince, my kings. Prepare the Two Lands. Don't let personal vendettas stand in the way of saving Egypt."

Sobekhotep remained stone-faced, but Apophis smiled. Then a low chuckle rumbled in his chest. "Your tongue spins golden thread, Vizier. I see why Potiphera fears you." He glanced at Prince Nefer-hotep. "My nephew likes to play senet. Dare I challenge you to a game?"

The prince looked at his abi, a silent plea for permission.

Sobekhotep hinted at a smile. "I warn you, King Apophis, my son beats me regularly."

"Asenath is also a master at senet." Potiphera spoke from his exile among the priests. "At least meet her, King Apophis."

"My *wife* isn't ready for visit—"

"Yes! They must meet her," the prince said, grasping his abi's hand. "May I see Mistress Asenath, too?"

A simple glance from Sobekhotep quieted the prince into regal bearing.

"No, my son, but we'll make time for your senet game with King Apophis before negotiations begin." He turned to his guests. "My son is right, King Apophis. Paneah's wife is too delightful to keep hidden, but she's under my protection—as is the vizier. I suggest we congregate in the throne room to sign the treaty. Perhaps you can visit Mistress Asenath tomorrow after she's had another day of rest."

"My daughter is not ill," Potiphera protested. "She is with child.

We could wait for months before she feels better." At Sobekhotep's hardened stare, he softened his demeanor. "Mighty Pharaoh, I'm grateful for the tender care you've shown Asenath; however, she is a citizen of Avaris and under the authority of King Apophis. If he demands to see her, it is within his rights to do so."

The Theban king remained silent, eyes locked with Apophis. Joseph felt muzzled, not daring to argue with two kings already engaged in silent battle.

"I will see Mistress Asenath but vow not to overtire her with my introduction." Apophis's concession got a nod from Sobekhotep.

The kings and their escorts started toward the palace—Pushpa and Ahira with them. Joseph wouldn't have time to warn his wife. Just the mention of Apophis's name when she'd first regained consciousness had terrified her. Forcing himself to move, he hurried to the front of the escort, passing the two women and taking his place behind the pharaohs.

Potiphera shouldered his way through the guards and other officials to walk alongside Joseph. He leaned close and whispered, "Captain Potiphar's wife is quite beautiful, isn't she?"

"His wi—" Joseph's head whipped around to stare at Ahira. She looked as startled as he felt. Facing her now, he had to say something. "You look lovely, Ahira." He turned away and hurried ahead of the procession like a nervous adolescent, arriving at the palace entrance before anyone else.

Hami kept pace beside him. "Better a wife than a concubine." His quiet consolation did little to cool Joseph's rising temper.

"It's been less than five months since I sent word of my arranged marriage, Hami. Ahira couldn't have been too heartbroken if she so quickly gave herself to Potiphar."

When the processional reached the palace, Pharaoh Sobekhotep placed a hand on the prince's shoulder. "We'll reconvene in the throne room after you've met Mistress Asenath." They walked away, and Joseph led the others into the guest chamber hallway. "If you'd be so kind," he said, halting outside Asenath's chamber, "please wait here until I've prepared her to meet so many new faces."

Potiphera started to follow him inside. "I'm not a new face."

Joseph pressed a hand on Potiphera's chest, leaning close to whisper, "Asenath is no longer your daughter, Potiphera. She's *my* wife. And the sail from Gurob nearly cost her life." He shoved him back into the hall, knowing Hami would ensure no one else entered.

"Joseph?" Asenath was propped against pillows in her bed. The midwife removed a tray of dishes. "I didn't expect to see you so soon."

"I'm glad to see you've eaten."

"Sitmut approved more than broth for me today." She held a faience cup in her hand. "This is mint tea with frankincense. The queen said it would soothe my stomach."

Joseph sat on the bed, took the cup from her, and handed it to the midwife. "Your abi is waiting outside, love."

Her features clouded. "Now?" Dawning came with the fear he'd expected. "With Apophis?" Her breaths came in ragged, quick succession. "No, Joseph. I don't want to—"

"Apophis knows you carry my child," he said, taking her into his arms. "Sobekhotep will protect us, and Neferhotep has charmed the man completely." Would she believe what he was about to say? "King Apophis poses no more threat to us. We're safe now."

He rocked her in the silence until she looked up at him. "He *is* our king, so I suppose I must meet him eventually." Her trembling continued. "Will Hami be here to protect me?"

"Hami will be right beside us." He eased her back against the pillows.

"I'm honored to be your wife, Joseph."

He pressed a kiss to her lips. "And I love you, Wife. Potiphar is also here. He'll likely come in with his king and—" He hesitated. Dare he even mention Pushpa and Ahira?

"What?" she asked, suddenly flushed. "I hope he finally gets the punishment he deserves for your false imprisonment."

"He's married now. He brought his wife and Pushpa with him— his ommi, the woman who treated me so kindly while I was a slave."

Pale and trembly, she hesitated. "Joseph, what aren't you telling me?"

"Lord Vizier," Potiphera shouted from the hallway. "You mustn't keep King Apophis waiting any longer."

Asenath squared her shoulders. "Bring them in."

Joseph remained seated beside his wife and nodded to the midwife. "You may open the door."

Potiphera rushed in, darting toward Asenath like an arrow released from a bow. "Daughter, you look well," he said before truly getting a glimpse of her. At her bedside, he sobered. "Move aside, Paneah, so Apophis can get a good look at her."

"You have no authority here." Joseph towered over him. "If you disrespect Asenath or me again, I'll remove you from the chamber."

"You see why I never married?" Apophis stood beside Asenath's bed with a mocking smile. "A wife can be troublesome, but her family is unbearable." He reached for Asenath's hand. "I'm honored to finally meet you, Priestess. I've waited too long for this moment." He lifted her hand to his lips.

Asenath whimpered, snapping Joseph's last thread of control. He lunged toward Apophis, but Hami and Potiphar became a wall between them.

"Joseph, it's him!" Asenath's screams pierced Joseph's fury. "It's him, Joseph!" Shrieking, she pressed her back against her headboard to escape.

Her terror silenced them all, and only Joseph moved toward his terrified wife. "Shh, Asenath. Of course it's him. It's King Apo—"

"That soldier, Joseph!" With a trembling hand, she pointed at Potiphar. "He's the one who took Ommi's body from the Memphis temple."

THIRTY-TWO

But as for me, my prayer is to You, O LORD, at an acceptable time;
O God, in the greatness of Your lovingkindness,
Answer me with Your saving truth.

PSALM 69:13, NASB

Asenath

Joseph sat on the bed between me and the soldier from my night-mares. Though the man was more wrinkled and scarred after nearly sixteen years, he was undeniably the soldier who had stolen Ommi's eternal peace. "Make him pay for what he did, Joseph," I hissed.

"Are you sure Potiphar is the one who took your ommi from the temple?" Joseph asked.

"My captain answers to me, Vizier, not to your wife." Apophis's rancor turned on Potabi. "Did you know your daughter was mad? Perhaps it's you, not the vizier, who committed treason by convincing me she should be my wife."

"May I speak, King Apophis?" The soldier—Captain Potiphar—spoke quietly. His deep voice rattled my chest, stirring more memo-ries. *I'll give you gold, not silver,* he'd said to the priest while standing over Ommi's body that night. *You will give me her body and say nothing to anyone.* He'd pressed a hand against the priest's chest, forcing his will—the same posture Apophis used now with his captain.

"You need no defense against this woman's hysteria."

The soldier looked at me, features softening. "It's not a defense, my king. I've done nothing wrong. May I speak to her?" Apophis stepped out of the captain's path and let him approach my bed.

I cried out and tried to scoot closer to my husband, but my strength was gone. *Please protect me, Elohim. I've feared this man as long as I can remember.*

"That's far enough, Captain." Joseph's warning stopped him three paces from the bed. My husband coaxed me into his embrace. "You're all right, love. Potiphar wouldn't dare harm you."

I peered out from my fortress, and the nightmare bowed to one knee. "Mistress Asenath, the Chantress of Ra was also *my* ommi."

"You lie!" Potabi shouted.

Potiphar continued as if he hadn't heard. "Though everyone knew her as the Great Chantress, few people knew her name— Katesch—and even fewer knew her whole story."

"That's enough." Potabi rushed forward.

King Apophis halted him with an iron grip and a warning glare. "We will hear the truth, Priest. I'm beginning to wonder if you know the meaning of the word." He glanced at his captain. "Continue, Potiphar."

"I was born when our ommi was barely fourteen," Potiphar said to me. "My abi was a violent man, given to gambling and too much drink. Ommi found her escape from him when Pharaoh Month-hotep chose her as his personal chantress."

"His *personal* chantress?" I asked.

Potiphar glanced at Joseph, the awkwardness bringing with it my whispered realization. "She was his concubine."

The captain nodded. "As a young man I hated her for abandoning me and considered her a harlot. After our troops liberated Memphis from that cruel lineage of kings, I heard talk of a courageous chantress who chose death rather than selling herself to our soldiers' perversion. I was proud of our ommi's courage but not yet willing to divulge her identity, so I gave her a secret but proper burial." Potiphar's lips quivered, eyes misting. "I had no idea my ommi had married again or borne another child, but I'm relieved she found happiness in her final years."

Hope restored my strength. "You gave her a proper burial?"

"She's embalmed and wrapped in a tomb with other priests and chantresses of Ra in Memphis."

I covered a sob, relief washing away years of pain and grief.

"Thank you, Potiphar." Joseph's tone bore a strange tension. "I know you're a private man and sharing your past is costly to you."

"That may have been true before." Potiphar turned and motioned the two women who stood near the door to come closer. The older woman came willingly; the younger was hesitant. With Potiphar's insistence, both were sheltered, one on each side, beneath his massive arms. "I share my past more freely now because my future is brighter, Lord Vizier." He inclined his head toward the woman on his right. "Mistress Asenath, this is Pushpa, the ommi of my heart and the woman who raised me. She's a spring of compassion and served as an ommi to many, including Pharaoh Khyan and your husband." The woman on his left kept her eyes averted, but he pulled her into a sideways embrace and kissed her temple. "This is Ahira, my wife."

Joseph's arm tensed around me.

So, this is the woman he was pledged to marry . . .

"Ahira is Elohim's gift to me." Potiphar held my gaze.

Elohim's gift? Joseph had never mentioned his long-ago master had embraced the Hebrew God.

"Mistress Asenath," he continued, "I hope my explanation will relieve some of your painful memories. I'm sure with the next Inundation, we'll likely return to Avaris. I hope you might become friends with Pushpa and Ahira—since we're family."

I was speechless. Potiphar wasn't the monster in my nightmares, but I wasn't yet ready to call him *brother.*

"Well, your daughter isn't mad, Potiphera," King Apophis said, breaking the uncomfortable silence. "But neither will I marry my captain's sister who carries the vizier's child." Apophis started toward the door. "I'm ready for that game of senet with the prince."

Ahira hurried to leave as well, but Pushpa lunged to catch her elbow. "Potiphar is right, Joseph. Ahira and I should get to know your wife. May we stay while you men negotiate your treaty?"

Joseph searched my face while he answered for me. "Asenath's first months of pregnancy have been difficult. She's still quite weak." Was he offering me an escape with a valid reason to deny them?

Pushpa's kind smile, sparkling eyes, and rounded pink cheeks warmed me. Ahira looked as pale as my linen sheets. "I'd like it if you and Ahira stayed," I said.

Joseph squeezed my hand. "Asenath, you need rest." Evidently, he'd meant for me to deny her request.

"I can rest later, while everyone else attends the banquet." Leaning forward, still a little shaky, I whispered against his cheek, "I want to discover more about the women who once held your heart."

He straightened. "I'll return to say good night before the banquet." Then he kissed my forehead and hurried from the chamber like he was being chased.

Beautiful Ahira watched him go. Her cheeks pinked when she caught me watching.

"Choose a cushion from the couch and join me." I patted the spaces beside me on the large mattress. "Make yourselves comfortable. There's plenty of room." With a feigned smile, Ahira followed Pushpa. She chose an understated light blue pillow, and Pushpa chose an intricately embroidered one. I rang my tinkling bronze bell to call the chambermaid and order a pitcher of honeyed water. Weariness suddenly descended on me like a load of bricks. "Whew! I'm afraid Joseph might have been right about me needing to rest. Perhaps I'll feel more energetic after hearing your stories."

Ahira looked like a doe in a hunter's bow sight. "You go first." She patted Pushpa's arm, voice quavering. We were both uncomfortable, of course, but our marriages were secure—weren't they?

"I'm a simple woman, really," Potiphar's second ommi began.

But her story was anything but simple. She spoke of her noble parents, the husband she loved enough to relinquish her title, and the life they'd built together in Avaris. She laughed while recounting Potiphar's adolescent pranks and wept when reliving her husband's death.

"I'm so sorry." I cradled her wrinkled hand, feeling the depth of her grief as I relived my own losses. "Grief is a ruthless taskmaster, relentlessly causing us to relive the most painful memories." I thought of my goodbyes to Zahra and Hotep and the difficult parting with Jendayi. My chest ached, and I wondered if my friends were safe. Were they happy? I pressed my hand over my belly, praying Joseph's child would fill the void left by the absence of my friends.

"We should go." Ahira set her goblet on the tray. "I can see you're tired, Mistress Asenath." She scooted off the bed.

"Please, wait." When I reached for her arm, she lurched away.

Pushpa glared at her, as if scolding a child.

Embarrassed and confused, I asked, "Have I offended you somehow, Ahira?"

She lifted her head, eyes swimming in unshed tears. "I know you're a priestess, Mistress Asenath, and the vizier's wife—but I know Joseph ben Jacob." She stared at my belly. "Perhaps giving him a child convinced him Egypt's gods had power, but he'll break without Elohim. He's as weak as any man without Elohim's favor. If you compromise Joseph's faith in Elohim, you've compromised the core of—"

"I haven't compromised his faith! I've adopted it as my own."

"But Potiphera said you were Isis Incarn—"

"Will you believe Potabi's lies or Elohim's promise that my children will inherit Abraham's covenant?"

Ahira sprang off the bed. "Pushpa, come. We've overtaxed the priestess."

A wave of nausea swept over me. "I'm no longer a priestess." I reached for the pitcher, but my belly rejected the honeyed water.

Pushpa held my hair back, whispering softly. "Ahira is protective of Joseph. They have been friends since childhood. Yes, they loved each other deeply, but try not to worry, Asenath. I saw love in his eyes for you, too." Pushpa called for my maid as she scooted off the bed.

"Wait!" I tried to call out, but the rest of my stomach contents hurled into the pitcher. The maid came in as Pushpa hurried out the door and my stomach continued to heave.

I saw love in his eyes for you, too. For me, *too?* Had I been too distracted by my own pain to see that my husband still loved Ahira? I was too weak to wail and too weary to weep.

Elohim, You saved me from Apophis. Please keep Joseph's heart securely tied to mine.

THIRTY-THREE

*In each city he put the food grown in the fields
surrounding it.*

GENESIS 41:48

Joseph

Pharaoh Sobekhotep watched the senet game from his throne a few
paces away, while Prince Neferhotep and King Apophis battled to
see who would first complete the journey of ka with every game
piece through all thirty squares. The competition had eased the tension on both pharaohs' features, but Joseph's insides rattled every
time either royal tossed the four painted sticks across the low marble
table.

Potiphera cast silent daggers at Joseph from across the throne
room while he huddled in whispered conversation with Amun's
high priest. Amun was originally Egypt's god of the air but morphed
into a sun god when Memphis royalty escaped to Thebes. Politics
seemed a humanly pretentious reason to redefine a god. Joseph
hadn't yet met the mediator of Upper Egypt's sun god, but Sobekhotep's description—a slithering viper in sheep's clothing—seemed
fitting. Potiphera had discarded his disguise and borne full-fanged
treason by plotting Joseph's death. But without King Apophis's
backing, Joseph had little protection—until today. Apophis had

seen Sobekhotep's favor, and Asenath's pregnancy disqualified her to become his queen. Though King Apophis had clearly recanted his decision to take Joseph's wife, for some reason he'd still insisted on Potiphera's presence during the treaty negotiations. What bound him so closely with Ra's high priest?

"We're even now, young prince." Apophis sat back on his heels with a satisfied smirk. Only one game piece each remained on the senet board.

"Not for long." Neferhotep reached for the throwing sticks and tossed them, and all four landed with unpainted sides up. "Aha!" Apophis groaned as the boy moved his crocodile-headed piece four spaces, and the fifth took him off the board. "I win!"

Nuru, captain of Potiphera's temple guards, continually scanned the expansive courtroom, as did other skilled guardians. Protectors stood like pillars between two kings, a prince, and a nervous Hebrew vizier. Unfamiliar Medjays had strategically spaced themselves around the perimeter to prevent violence—or did they plan to start it?

When Apophis and his men had arrived, they'd seemed ready for a fight, but did the king's relaxed laughter signal his changed agenda? "You are tenacious, Prince Neferhotep." Apophis pushed to his feet and offered the boy his hand. "And a fine strategist."

The prince stood and locked wrists with the king who towered over him. "You are a worthy opponent. I offer you a rematch tomorrow."

Apophis tugged playfully on the prince's sidelock. "I accept tomorrow's challenge. That is, if your abi and I reach an agreement today."

Sobekhotep struggled to stand, refusing help from his captain. Neferhotep raced to the dais, providing his shoulder as Sobekhotep's support. The proud abi smiled at his son and looked again at Apophis. "More than a senet game hinges on today's agreement. All of the Black Land depends on our willingness to set aside petty squabbles and consider the lives of our people equally important to our own families."

"Ha!" Apophis exchanged a glance with Potiphar. "I didn't believe you, but you were right about him."

Sobekhotep's gracious manner evaporated like morning mist. "What did your captain say about me that so amused you?"

Apophis sobered. "He assured me that you, Pharaoh Sobekhotep, are unlike the cruel Egyptian kings. You care about people more than wealth. You love your family more than power. And you are worthy of my trust." He reached for his weapons belt, and every Medjay in the room tensed. But Pharaoh Apophis untied it, letting his dagger and sword clatter to the floor. "We *will* reach a peaceful decision today because we are two kings who love the Two Lands."

Joseph wanted to shout his praise to Elohim. Only One could have brought such strong-willed kings to this moment. Instead, he signaled the waiting scribe to bring the documents he'd prepared and started toward the dais. "God will bless this step toward unity, my kings."

Potiphera, joined by Amun's high priest, also approached the dais but was stopped by a wall of Medjays. "King Apophis, we have yet another step of unity to offer," Potiphera pleaded. "Amun's high priest and I have come to an agreement that will unify the Two Lands in worship."

Apophis stood beside Joseph and exchanged a sidelong glance. "After meeting both you and Asenath," he said quietly, "I must admit, I'm glad I didn't kill you and take your wife. I couldn't have tolerated her abi."

Joseph had no time to express his relief before Apophis nudged him aside. "Priest, we're here to agree on trade. Food. Water. *Survival*," he shouted. "Let the Two Lands worship whichever gods they please."

Both high priests bowed. Potiphera dared speak. "When people become frightened, my king, they turn to the gods and, more precisely, the incarnate god on the throne. If you and Pharaoh Sobekhotep aren't united in your worship, the people will doubt your deity and choose a king who they believe *is* born of the sun." He straightened, meeting Apophis's hard stare. "You know it's true. The ancient scrolls tell of pharaohs sacrificed during famines because people become desperate when frightened. Unity in worship calms their fears."

"And priests control kings by inciting fear in our people, King Apophis." Sobekhotep sighed and sat on his cushioned throne. "Tell us your scheming, Priest, so we can proceed with the important work of the gods."

Amun's high priest scowled at his king, but Potiphera's feigned pleasantry never dimmed. "Thank you for hearing the will of the gods, Great Sobekhotep. In the short time we've spent together, Amun's high priest and I realized we've previously witnessed miracles from the gods—omens and signals in the stars—that have brought us to this moment. The gods have confirmed *one* sun god that we call by two names: Ra in the north and Amun here in Thebes. In an effort to comfort the people, protect both pharaohs' deity, and unite the Two Lands, every temple that sacrifices to the sun god will now worship him as *Amun-Ra.*"

Sobekhotep scoffed. "Neferhotep, let this be your first lesson on priests. While Egypt's kings seek to protect our people and save them from impending doom, Egypt's priests find ways to swindle them. The priests of Amun and Ra will no longer *compete* for offerings, my son. As servants of one god, Amun-Ra, they'll control all access to the sun and charge more for every priestly service." He sneered at both priests. "Tell my son if I've misrepresented the truth in any way."

"We do not swindle the people!" Amun's priest shouted. Potiphera placed a calming hand on his arm. Still seething, Amun's priest fell silent but openly glared at his king.

Sobekhotep returned his stare and, with the flick of two fingers, motioned his captain closer for a whispered conversation.

The priest's countenance instantly softened. Sobekhotep's captain straightened. He then nodded toward two Medjays, who descended on Amun's high priest. "No!" the man shouted. "I'm protected by Amun!"

"You may think you're protected by Amun," Sobekhotep replied, "but you were *appointed* by me, and I'll happily choose your replacement."

The priest howled as they dragged him from the room. Potiphera watched with disdain until the throne room fell silent. Then he stepped forward. "Pharaoh Sobekhotep, may I humbly offer myself as the high priest of Egypt's single god, Amun-Ra. I'm a descendant of the family of priests Ra birthed on the Creation Mound. My life is yours, Great Sobekhotep, and I will serve Egypt well in her time of need." He bowed, and Joseph could remain silent no longer.

"I'm sorry, Pharaoh Sobekhotep, but Potiphera will be unavailable to serve as high priest of Amun-Ra." He knelt before the throne.

"Unavailable?" He paused, but Joseph kept his head lowered. "Stand, Paneah."

He obeyed, finding Apophis beside Neferhotep, equally interested. "I'm sending Potiphera back to Avaris," Joseph explained. "He's committed treason against me twice. He will answer for those crimes."

"I see." Sobekhotep nodded slowly. "You told me he'd named Amenemhat's canal Bahr Yussef to stir the young pharaoh's suspicion against you, but what was the second act?"

"Potiphera won't be returning to Avaris." King Apophis's tone was as sharp as a razor. He held Joseph's gaze, his threat implied, understood, and unassailable. "There was no second act of treason," he said to Sobekhotep, "only a miscommunication between the vizier and me about who holds greater power. Now that I've seen how the gods favor Paneah in his vital new role, I'll honor Zaphenath-Paneah's name: *the god speaks—he lives.* For as long as the gods speak through him, he will live."

"Don't you dare threaten Paneah." Sobekhotep's hand slammed onto the arm of his throne. "I care nothing about your secrets with Potiphera as long as they don't impact my kingdom. But Paneah impacts *all* of Egypt, and his god favors Egypt because he favors Paneah. If your scheming threatens Paneah, it jeopardizes Egypt— and that I won't allow."

"Allow?" Apophis sneered. "I would never jeopardize Egypt."

"My kings," Joseph pleaded. "Potiphera jeopardizes us all. I beg you, don't trust him."

"Trust him?" Apophis laughed. "I don't trust anyone, Paneah. Why do you think I'm still alive?" He returned his attention to Sobekhotep. "I'm simply saying Potiphera is the wise choice for the first high priest of Amun-Ra. Your removal of Amun's high priest will surprise the other prophets in Amun's temple, but I know Potiphera. He's a king cobra among vipers. He'll find a way to turn that little hiccup to his advantage among the faithful Amun followers who remain."

"No!" Joseph's outburst drew both kings' attention. "I will *not* allow Potiphera to continue his deceptions." He expected anger. At least surprise. But Sobekhotep merely nodded, considering.

Apophis gave him a lopsided grin. "You are as tenacious as the young prince here." He winked at Neferhotep, relieving a measure of tension.

Joseph glanced over Apophis's shoulder at Potiphar. Eyes intense, he offered Joseph a nod, his lips curved in a barely perceptible smile. That was the friend Joseph remembered. Though they'd been master and slave, Potiphar had respected him and even trusted him for advice. But Potiphar had married Ahira. Joseph didn't know *this* man.

"Paneah!" King Apophis snagged his attention. "Are you amenable to the arrangement?"

"The arrangement?" Joseph chided himself for contemplating Potiphar's friendship and missing the plan for his future.

"Paneah." Pharaoh Sobekhotep's tone was softer. "When Asenath is stronger, you'll travel to Edfu Fortress with Apophis and train our villages to build granaries as you've done in Lower and Middle Egypt."

Fear struck like lightning. "How many troops will you send to protect me?"

"Potiphera is your protection." Apophis clamped a hand on Joseph's shoulder. "Pharaoh Sobekhotep, the old crocodile, made

Potiphera high priest of Amun-Ra here in Thebes. He's promised not to send him back to Avaris—for as long as you stay alive." His forced smile looked more like a jackal's snarl.

Joseph looked to Hami, his trusted protector, for guidance. An extended blink gave approval.

"All right," Joseph said to the kings. "After my wife regains her strength, I'll entrust her to Queen Sitmut's care and go to Edfu." He pinned Sobekhotep with a stare. "You must protect her from Potiphera while I'm away. He'll try to turn her against me."

"Your wife will be under my queen's personal care, Paneah. She's as safe as a lioness's cub."

"And I'll play senet with her every day," Neferhotep said. His unbridled joy lightened the solemn mood.

Joseph bowed to his young friend. "I'm counting on you to let her get an occasional victory, my prince. She grows testy if she loses hope."

"As do we all," he said, moving to his abi's side. Joseph saw the boy's deeper meaning as he placed a hand on Sobekhotep's shoulder. He knew his abi was dying, and there were some things even a son of Egypt's gods couldn't change.

Joseph motioned toward the scribe and papyruses waiting at a waist-high table. "Let's talk about increasing trade on the Nile from Cush to the Great Sea. Our years of abundance must be stockpiled, but our first harvest begins next month. Projections show we'll have seven times our normal harvest of grain, enough to fill granaries *and* trade with the six nations proposed in the treaty." One sticking point—distributing all grain from Avaris only—caused more conflict between the kings, but both yielded to Joseph's reasoning and finally signed the agreement.

"Your priests have one request." Potiphera pulled a scroll from his belt. "Since we are representatives of the gods—and Pharaoh is the son of Amun-Ra on earth—all temples in Egypt should be exempt from the one-fifth taxation during the years of abundance." He unfurled his scroll on the table. "I've already sent messages to the priests in every temple assuring them the vizier would never rob from gods' houses to pay the gods on Egypt's thrones. To tax Egypt's temples or priests would be an afront to her gods."

Apophis grinned at Sobekhotep. "I'm glad he's staying in Thebes with you." He shoved Potiphera aside and signed the priests' exemption.

Sobekhotep dipped the reed in the black pigment, tapped it against the clay jar, and paused, glaring at Amun-Ra's new high priest. "You cross swords with me, and your heart will be in a canopic jar."

Potiphera didn't flinch. "I'll never cross swords, my king, but I hope I've proven my wits can be a valuable tool in your hands." He took his papyrus and backed out of both pharaohs' presence.

"Please, Pharaoh Sobekhotep," Joseph said, "don't get entangled with him."

"I'm tired." The old king started toward the door at the back of the dais, Neferhotep providing support. "I'll see you at tonight's banquet."

Apophis marched toward the exit, Potiphar at his side, but Joseph wasn't finished. "King Apophis, I'd like to speak with your captain— alone."

Apophis glanced at Potiphar, who nodded, so Apophis waved him away. "Return my captain in one piece, Paneah. We didn't like each other at first, but I've grown rather fond of this decrepit old soldier." He laughed at his wit as more than half of the Medjays exited with him.

Joseph noticed Hami was smiling—fully *smiling*—at Potiphar. "Decrepit old soldier?"

Potiphar scowled. "Apophis is insufferable." He scanned the Medjays who remained in the throne room and spoke quietly. "Might we speak somewhere more private, Lord Vizier?"

Again, Joseph looked to Hami. Was this a trick to get Joseph alone and harm him? "Potiphar won't betray you, Lord Vizier."

Jaw clenched, Joseph whispered, "How can you say that?" But he strode past Potiphar toward the exit, trusting Hami's word. "We'll meet in my chamber." *Elohim, I trust You above all.*

They filed through palace hallways to the chamber beside Asenath's. Joseph marched past the guard at the door. Potiphar and Hami followed him into the chamber and closed the door.

Ahira bolted off the couch. Pushpa remained seated with a smug smile. "I'm so glad we're all here," she said. "We can finally get to the truth."

Joseph couldn't speak. Mouth dry, he stared at the woman walking toward him. But Ahira veered to his left, directly into Potiphar's arms. She hid her face in the bend of his neck and whispered something only he could hear. In a world all their own, they shared too many secrets, and Joseph would abide it no longer.

"Enough!" he shouted. Potiphar turned, placing Ahira behind him as if Joseph were the threat.

Pushpa stood between the two men she'd called her own. "Look at me, Joseph. Look at me!" She raised her voice, snaring his attention. "You're a powerful man, but you're still the man of integrity I knew in Avaris. Don't let your emotions turn your power into a careless weapon."

"I made that mistake, Joseph." Potiphar used his familiar name with tenderness and stepped around Pushpa. "I wronged you because I feared losing Khyan's friendship and the power that came with it. Though I knew you were innocent when Zully accused you, I not only imprisoned you, but I left you there even after I freed her." He lowered himself to one knee, bowing his head. "I offer no excuses. I sinned against Elohim and against you, my friend. I deserve whatever punishment you give me—Lord Paneah."

I sinned against Elohim. It was the second time Master Potiphar had spoken the name of Joseph's God since he'd arrived in Thebes. Was it a ruse? More games from an Egyptian nobleman who had been master *and* friend? Joseph stared at three strangers from his past. So much life had been smashed into their years of separation. So many questions remained unanswered. How could he suddenly accept these people's new lives? How could they accept him—no longer Joseph, the Hebrew slave; now Zaphenath-Paneah, Egypt's vizier?

"Stand, Captain Potiphar." Throat tight with emotion, Joseph looked into the eyes of the master he'd prepared each morning, the one who'd guarded Pharaoh Khyan. Something had changed this fierce captain—deeply. "Why admit your wrongs? With Elohim's favor and Sobekhotep's influence, I could ask Apophis to strip you of your position and ruin your reputation by revealing that your first wife is still alive and in Crete. I could take away everything you live for."

"Now I live for Elohim's favor." A slow smile curved his lips. "No matter what you choose to do to me, you can't take that away."

Joseph glanced at Ahira. "Is he—"

"That's why Pushpa and I came," she said. "We knew you wouldn't believe Potiphar. He rejected Egypt's gods when he signed my emancipation paper three years ago, Joseph."

Incredulous, Joseph looked at Potiphar. This had been the man who sent monthly offerings to four temples—not for the gods, but to gain priests' favor.

"It's true, and I asked Elohim to soften Ahira's heart toward me so she'd agree to become my wife." He extended his hand to her. She accepted and nestled into his side. "She didn't agree to the marriage until after she discovered you married Potiphera's daughter. I love her, Joseph, and she respects me. Perhaps someday she'll look at me the way you're looking at her now . . ."

Joseph's eyes darted to meet Potiphar's. "I love Asenath."

"Good. Remember that when you come to Edfu and must look at my wife every day." Potiphar's gaze held warning. "You should know, Lord Vizier, that your wife may not feel the same about you. Potiphera made it clear she was anxious to marry King Apophis and become Isis Incarnate."

Joseph felt as if the floor shifted beneath him. "I don't believe—"

"Pushpa and I no longer believe it either," Ahira said. "We confronted her, Joseph, and she was adamant that she now serves Elohim. But we should have listened to you. I fear we overtaxed her."

Panic struck him. "What happened?"

"The midwife is with her," Pushpa reassured him. "Queen Sitmut sent word that Asenath is doing well."

Ahira's cheeks flushed, making her even more beautiful. "Are you angry?"

"I'm not angry, but I am weary," he said, clamping a hand on Potiphar's shoulder. "Might we start our new friendship at this evening's banquet?" He needed time to process today's surprises.

"I would be honored." Potiphar bowed and offered his arm to Ahira, who left without a farewell. Pushpa kissed Joseph's cheek, and the door clicked shut behind her.

Hami stood like a boulder in the middle of the room, impossible to ignore in the silence. "What?" Joseph's frustration erupted.

"You were unjustly accused of pursuing Potiphar's first wife, but you'll need your god's help not to pursue his second." He strode from the chamber without awaiting a reply.

What was there to say? *Elohim, You've turned my heart toward Asenath. Keep it there.*

THIRTY-FOUR

Where then does wisdom come from?
Where does understanding dwell?
It is hidden from the eyes of every living thing,
concealed even from the birds in the sky.
Destruction and Death say,
"Only a rumor of it has reached our ears."

JOB 28:20–22

THEBES PALACE

NEARLY SEVEN MONTHS LATER

Asenath

"Mistress, wake up!" My maid approached my bed, but I was already awake.

"What is it, Esi?" I struggled to sit up, and she offered a hand to pull me upright.

"Queen Sitmut summons you, Mistress." Her eyes glistened in the lamplight. "Pharaoh Sobekhotep . . ." She bit her bottom lip.

"Help me up!" My overlarge belly made every movement a chore and bending over a distant memory. My ankles, hands, and face were swollen, and I felt as if my eyes might pop if my child wasn't born soon. *But, please, Elohim, not before Joseph returns from Edfu.*

Like towing a barque, Esi pulled me out of bed. "Tell me what you know," I said as Esi slipped a fresh linen robe over my head.

"Only that the queen sent for Amun-Ra's high priest."

I rushed ahead of her, hoping she hadn't seen me wince. Though partly a reaction to the cramping across my belly, it was more so the thought of seeing Potabi that pained me. "Stay with me, Esi. I need someone trustworthy beside me when I face Highness."

"Of course, Mistress." She linked her arm with mine. "But don't you trust Queen Sitmut?"

"Yes, but if her husband is as ill as you say, she won't be able to help deflect Potabi's hatefulness." I waddled down the guest hall to its end, where one of the king's guards ushered us into a royal chamber I'd never entered before. Pharaoh Sobekhotep lay in a wide bed, his eyes closed.

Queen Sitmut sat at the king's left and Prince Neferhotep on the right, cradling his abi's hand. The prince looked up when we entered, seeming even more childlike without his cosmetics. "Hurry, Asenath. Anubis is circling."

Sitmut whimpered, and I hurried to her side of the bed. Esi helped me sit on the wool-stuffed mattress beside my friend. She turned into my embrace. "I woke to the sound of him gurgling. He's barely breathing."

I held her as she wept and then noticed a bevy of priests looming in the shadows. Potabi emerged into the circle of lamplight near the bed. "Dire circumstance brought us together tonight, Asenath, but Isis has always known Ra's secret name was *Amun*-Ra."

"I don't understand."

The heka priest joined Potabi. The sem and kherep priests also moved into the light.

I gasped. *The death priests.* "Do you plan to embalm our king before Anubis even greets him?"

Potabi's cool demeanor chilled me. "King Sobekhotep's ka is anxious to leave, but Isis has brought powerful protection this night. On the night Neferhotep is born as Ra's son, you will become Isis Incarnate."

"I thought marrying a king made me Isis Incarnate." Panicked, I turned to the queen. "Don't let him persuade you with false stories."

"It isn't false, Asenath." Sitmut shook her head. "You came to Thebes with a child in your womb for this moment. Neferhotep will hold his abi's hand when Anubis comes, and *Isis*—the Great Ommi of Egypt—will protect my son through you."

"Sitmut, Elohim is my God, not—"

"Isis is privileged to protect our new king," Potabi interrupted. "Her powers will be even stronger since her body carries a child in the moment of your son's incarnation."

"No!" I said.

"Though we weep at Pharaoh Sobekhotep's passing"—he spoke loudly and with a glare to silence me—"we rejoice that the gods have provided such a strong birth moment for Prince Neferhotep."

I returned the high priest's glare, but the queen seemed comforted. "Yes, Potiphera. I hadn't realized the powerful connection." Sitmut turned her weepy eyes toward me. "Thank you, Isis. I've known you as a dear friend, and now I'll know you as the Great Ommi who carries my son and Thebes through our crucial transition."

"Sitmut, I—" A sharp cramp stole my argument.

The king's chesty rattle was a disconcerting sound—and then his final exhale.

My cramp eased. I looked up.

"Abi?" Prince Neferhotep shook the king's shoulder. "Abi, don't leave me!"

"He's gone, my son." The queen squared her shoulders. "Look at me, Neferhotep."

He buried his head against Sobekhotep's shoulder. "I'm not ready, Abi. I need you."

"Neferhotep!" Sitmut's tone startled him from his grief. She pointed at his hand—the one still grasping Sobekhotep's. "The divine spirit of Amun-Ra has entered you, and you are now Sekhemre Khutawy—*He Who Protects the Two Lands*—the living son of a god. You *are* ready. You have no other choice." She sniffed back emotions. "You will dry your tears, Neferhotep. The divine son of Amun-Ra never cries."

The new pharaoh released the dead king's hand and slid off the bed. Though trembling from head to toe, Neferhotep straightened his shoulders and spoke to the priests. "You may take his body to the temple for embalming and chant the proper incantations. And when the time comes for Lady Isis to deliver Lord Paneah's child, she is to be taken to Amun-Ra's birth house—"

"Not the *mammisi!*" I tried to scoot off the bed, but the sudden effort caused another cramp.

I cried out, and Neferhotep rushed to my side. "Mistress Asenath, Amun-Ra's high priest swears you are Isis Incarnate. Your purpose is to protect me, but I must also protect you. I cannot—I *will not*—lose someone else I regard with affection." His voice broke. He cleared his throat. "I am your king, Lady Isis, and you will birth a healthy child under the care of priests and physicians in the mammisi." Without awaiting my reply, he fled the room.

Another cramp gripped me, and I fell to my knees. "Joseph," I whispered. Why hadn't he returned to Thebes today as his message had promised? I'd told him last month the midwife predicted our child would come today, the tenth day of akhet.

"Come, Daughter." Potabi helped me to my feet. "Your maid will call your midwife to the mammisi if it will make you more comfortable."

I nodded, too despairing to speak.

"Potiphera, stop." Queen Sitmut strode toward us. "I've known men like you all my life. Don't imagine that because your daughter is favored by my son that you've gained my approval as well. Though you've done an admirable job of uniting the Two Lands in worship, I've intentionally shielded your daughter from your lies and will continue to do so. My husband's journey to the underworld does *not* give you free access to Asenath."

Potabi's hand tightened on my arm, but he bowed in submission. "Of course, Queen Sitmut. I am, as always, obedient to the wishes of my king *and queen*." When he straightened, I saw no anger. He seemed utterly forlorn. "I'm sure you've noticed, my queen, that Asenath wears no amulet of the most powerful childbirth gods, Bes and Taweret. I fear continuing to shun them may endanger both Isis and our new king."

"You serve Amun-Ra, Potiphera." Sitmut's eyes narrowed. "What are you scheming?"

"I'm not scheming!" His tone held genuine fear. "Every evil eye will be upon Asenath and her child because she's become Isis Incarnate on the same night Neferhotep was born into divinity. Many gods will see her emerging power as a threat."

"I'm *not* Isis Incarnate!" I shouted. "I serve only Elohim."

"They're all the same," Potabi said. "Remember?" His patience was more startling than the anger I expected. He returned his attention to the queen. "I hope to speak with Paneah about his god—if he ever returns from Edfu Fortress—and suggest we unite the Amu's greatest god with Egypt's sun gods. All of Egypt would then worship one god, Amun-Ra-*El*."

"No!" Another pain stole my breath and further protest.

"Take her to the mammisi *now!*" Sitmut commanded.

"Please," I gritted out between clenched teeth.

"You may accompany her, Potiphera. Your daughter will wear the amulets of Bes and Taweret from this day forward and deliver her child under the care the king has commanded. If Isis's child comes on the same day that my son's reign begins, the gods have given him an exceptionally strong endorsement indeed."

Nuru swept me into his arms to carry me. "Wait!" I shouted over his shoulder.

"Don't fight me," Nuru whispered, tightening his grasp.

As the pain in my body ebbed, the torture of my soul surged. My resistance was futile, and the journey to a life I'd rejected seemed inescapable.

Joseph, why haven't you come home to me? He'd left nearly seven months ago. I'd begged him to stay longer—until I was healthy enough to travel with him to Edfu—but the declining river levels and increasing demands called him away. He'd written to me several times during the first few months. Less often as the abundant harvest exceeded all expectations and historical records. I hadn't received a message from Egypt's busy vizier in weeks.

"Don't cry, Nathy," Potabi whispered, walking at Nuru's right side.

"Please, don't force me to betray my God and Paneah's trust."

He patted my head. "I'm protecting you and my grandchild by adding the Canaanite god's name to our worship. Don't you see? Even your stubborn husband must admit that I'm trying to unify our family. I need to be part of my grandchild's life." His last words were choked on a sob.

"Abi, I . . . I don't believe . . ." How could I tell him the Canaanite god El was different than Elohim? Another pain tightened my belly.

Potabi sighed. "Daughter, I *need* to be in my grandchild's life—for the child's sake. For your sake."

It was the second time he'd emphasized *needing* to be in my baby's life. "If there's something you wish to say, Potabi, say it." But did I want to know?

The temple guard and Potabi exchanged a glance.

"What are you keeping from me?" Had Joseph been injured in Edfu? Or murdered by Apophis's men and the crime hidden?

As we entered the temple precinct in predawn darkness, Potabi said, "Concentrate on Paneah's good work, Asenath. His granaries have ensured Egypt's most profitable harvest, and Bahr Yussef will avert this akhet's higher-than-normal floodwaters."

Why is he defending Joseph to me?

Another pain pulled my knees to my belly. "Tell me what you know!" I couldn't endure both pain and uncertainty. Nuru halted at the mammisi's door—the threshold of my reunion with the gods.

Potabi turned my chin to face him. "Your husband has abandoned you for another, Asenath. You'll *need* me to help raise my grandchild."

THIRTY-FIVE

The LORD inflicted serious diseases on Pharaoh
and his household because of Abram's wife Sarai.
So Pharaoh summoned Abram. "What have you
done to me?" he said. "Why didn't you tell me
she was your wife? Why did you say, 'She is my
sister'?"

GENESIS 12:17–19

SEVENTY-ONE DAYS LATER

Joseph

"Please, Lord Vizier," Hami said, "come away from the bow." He'd been hovering next to Joseph like a nervous ommi.

"Will she ever forgive me?" Joseph's chest ached. He'd missed his child's birth. "Tell me she'll understand."

"Mistress Asenath is a reasonable woman." Hami stared at the Theban quay, his tone unconvincing. "But in my limited observations, a woman who gives birth may require years to recover her ability to place reason over emotion."

"True, but surely, Asenath will see the repair on Apophis's barque and understand this was beyond our control." When the second year of the Nile's raging flood tossed their ship aground, word of

Pharaoh Sobekhotep's death had kept them—and every other ship—moored for seventy days of mandatory mourning.

"We must brace, my lord."

The oarsmen battled the raging northern tide. Too sharp a turn, and the cumbersome ship would capsize. Too soft, and they'd overshoot the docks entirely and delay Joseph and Asenath's reunion further.

He and Hami strapped themselves to the rail as the captain shouted his prayer over the tempest. "Oh great god Hapi, safely deliver our honorable vizier."

The bow hit straight on, sliding nearly half the ship ashore, but it didn't overturn. Hami and Joseph stumbled, fell, and hung by their hemp ropes. While oarsmen cheered at the safe landing, Joseph fumbled with nervous fingers at the knot around his waist. "Untie me, Hami! I must see my wife and child!"

In moments, both he and his captain were racing toward the palace. The streets of Thebes teemed with the post-mourning celebration and the beginning of Neferhotep's reign. Hami, a head taller than most and more frightening than any, cut through the crowd like a plow through a field. Joseph followed, grateful they were recognized and not detained when they entered the rear palace entrance.

"This way, Lord Vizier," one of Neferhotep's Medjays said. "Your wife is in the throne room with Pharaoh Neferhotep and the queen."

Joseph exchanged a concerned glance with Hami as they fell in step behind the guard. Neither Asenath nor Queen Sitmut enjoyed crowds. He'd hoped to find his wife in her private chamber, certain she would already have fulfilled her duty to appear at Sobekhotep's burial procession. Their last words had been angry, their parting contentious. For nine months he'd tried to silence regrets and replace them with hope for a new beginning. The love he'd once felt for Ahira had shifted to a comfortable friendship. When her feelings for Potiphar had proven to be loving and deep, Joseph had been happy for her and encouraged that two such different people could overcome any obstacle.

As they approached the public entrance, the mass of noise and chaos grew louder. The guards sliced through the public corridor amid jeers and protest. Two Medjays at the courtroom doors stepped aside, allowing Joseph and Hami to enter.

The sight before him stole Joseph's words. He had no breath. Three people sat on thrones. The boy king sat in the middle, Queen Sitmut on his right—both covered with seeping sores. Joseph's wife sat on a throne at the king's left, holding their newborn—both seeming in perfect health. Potiphera stood at Asenath's left shoulder, bearing sores like the king and queen mother. A quick glance around the room revealed every guard and council member suffered the same affliction. Only Joseph's wife and child had been spared.

Elohim, what's happening?

"Your arrival is woefully late, Lord Vizier." Neferhotep spoke quietly but with a sharp tone. "Too late to honor Pharaoh Sobekhotep's journey into the underworld and too late to welcome your son into this world."

A son?

Shoulders back, Joseph proceeded toward the dais, watching Asenath, though she avoided his gaze. Both she and the baby were dressed in fine linen. Asenath wore heavy cosmetics, and tight braids formed a crown around her head. Joseph's steps faltered when he saw her necklace—a priestess's golden collar—bearing the amulets of Egypt's gods.

"Lord Vizier," Hami whispered, "remain calm. I beg you."

Elohim, what do I do? His hand rested on the hilt of his dagger. He'd never killed a man, but with the rage surging through him now, he could slit Potiphera's throat. Egypt would be better for it. Asenath would be safer. And his child . . .

"What have they done to my wife and son?" he whispered.

"Speak up, Lord Vizier," Pharaoh Neferhotep said. "I'm sure Lady Isis is also interested in your explanation."

Lady Isis. Joseph glared at his wife, but she focused on their son.

Upon reaching the carpet's edge, Joseph inhaled a shuddering breath and met the young king's anger with the truth. "We left Edfu seventy-two days ago, Pharaoh Neferhotep, but the early flood drove us against the shore at Nekhen on our first day's sail. While in port for repairs, we received word of Sobekhotep's death. Out of respect and obedience, our captain and oarsmen refused to sail during the seventy days of mourning."

Asenath's head shot up, misty eyes meeting Joseph's before she looked away. Her shoulders shook. In that moment, Joseph realized how alone she must have felt in his absence.

Swallowing his regret, he looked beyond the king's anger to consider his pain. "Have your physicians determined the cause of your strange ailment, my king?" There had been no sign of it outside the palace.

"The magicians say the gods are displeased but haven't yet revealed the reason." His chin quivered. "I've given Highness Potiphera until midnight to determine the cause."

"And we will discover it," Potiphera added.

"Trust Amun-Ra, my son." Queen Sitmut reached for the boy's arm but stopped in midair, wincing in pain. "Lord Vizier, give us good news from Edfu," she said. "Something that will salve the wounds of missing Neferhotep's coronation celebration."

Now Joseph understood why Pharaoh had been conspicuously absent from the festivities. The divine son of Amun-Ra could never appear ill or weakened before his people—especially at his coronation. "Forgive me, Pharaoh Neferhotep," Joseph offered, inclining his head. "I waited to begin our return from Edfu because I desired to provide you with completed reports of granary construction, bountiful harvests, and grain's safe storage."

"I see." The king's features softened. "Well done, Paneah. Show me the reports."

Hami passed his shoulder bag to the king's bodyguard.

"A copy was kept in Edfu," Joseph explained, "and another sent to Avaris. We'll keep records of granary totals in every nome to ensure all three pharaohs have an accounting of Egypt's bounty." Wishing Pharaoh Sobekhotep were here to witness the fruit of their first harvest, he said, "Queen Sitmut, I'm sorry for your loss. I know you and King Sobekhotep loved each other very much."

"Thank you, Paneah." She glanced at Potiphera and back at Joseph. "What's important is that you've returned to the wife and son you love."

Joseph bowed to hide his confusion. "Might I steal them away to speak with my wife privately?" He ignored Potiphera's hostile glare. "As you can imagine, I'm anxious to meet my new son."

Neferhotep's brows drew together as if he might refuse. Sitmut leaned close and whispered something. The king sighed. "You may have my Lady Isis until I summon her for the senet game we play before each evening meal."

Neferhotep's begrudging tone sparked Joseph's anger, but he forced a smile. "I'll return my wife for the battle before anyone takes nourishment." Joseph waited for the king's grin, but none came. Asenath remained seated, still watching their son.

"Go ahead, Priestess. My guards will protect me in your absence."

She nodded, cast a quick glance at Joseph, then marched toward the door at the back of the dais. Joseph raced up the steps and across the platform after her, Hami in pursuit. Joseph heard the king make a comment about chasing a goddess as he slipped into the private hallway behind the dais.

He glimpsed his wife rounding a corner at the far end of the hall. "Asenath, wait!" The sound of his son's cries led him and his captain to a chamber with a double cedar door and four Medjay guards.

"Egypt's vizier bids you open that door," Hami said. The guards hesitated, but only for a moment.

Joseph entered the luxurious chamber alone. Asenath stood in the middle of three rooms, tiled floors covered with rugs of crimson, purple, and blue. She held their screaming son and could have sat down on any of the four cushioned couches. Instead, she stood like one of her pagan idols, ignoring their son's cries and glaring at Joseph.

"You lie like Potabi!" she shouted. "You cleverly distract a boy king with excuses of harvest reports, but I know it was your lover who kept you in Edfu. How is Ahira? Do you share her with Potiphar, or did you simply command him to—"

"No! Asenath! That's a lie!" He went to her, bracing her shoulders. "Potiphar and Ahira are happily married." Joseph's hands fell to his sides with the first glimpse of his son's squinched face. "He has your mouth."

"Because he's screaming?"

Joseph looked at her again and understood she was covered with sores too—but hers were lodged *inside* her heart. "No, Asenath, because his lips are shaped like yours." He wiped the smeared kohl from her cheeks.

"Don't." She stepped back. "I loved you, but you chose Ahira."

"I don't want Ahira. I choose you, Asenath. Ahira is my friend. *Only* my friend. But you are my love and the wife I adore."

"But Potabi said—"

"And you *believed* him?" Catching a glimpse of the amulets she now wore, he tried hard to control his tone. "It is you, Wife, who has repeatedly chosen another."

"No!" she said, now swaying their son. "You left me, Joseph. You sent no messages and let duty come before family. Now you must accept the consequences."

"*I* must accept the consequences? I'm second in command to Pharaoh, Asenath. *You* will accept the consequences when Potiphera is punished for treason."

"Potabi married Queen Sitmut today."

The revelation hit Joseph like a slap. "What?"

"Potabi locked us all in a tower the night Sobekhotep died, and neither you nor Elohim's messenger came to my rescue."

"I'm here now," Joseph said, his spirit plummeting. "Tell me what happened."

She paused, measuring him, then began. "Potabi used Neferhotep's fear of becoming king to trap us all. Labor pains stole my wits so I couldn't reason my way out of it. I almost died bringing our son into the world, Joseph. I had to rely on Bes and Taweret to save me because you and your god abandoned me."

"I didn't abandon you. *We* didn't. Elohim is always with you, even when I can't be." Joseph hung his head. The words sounded hollow in the face of all she'd suffered. *Elohim, what can I do to make this right?*

"Potabi preyed on Sitmut's grief with feigned kindness and lofty promises. He gave her the title God's Wife of Amun and power to match it. He brought her estranged firstborn—Mentuhotepi, son of Djehuty—back to Thebes and made him lector priest." She shook her head, tears pooling. "Don't you see, Joseph? Every nobleman and priest in Neferhotep's throne room bears Potabi's mark."

Potabi's mark—the sores! "When did the sores first appear?"

"The sores?" Her brows drew together. "Early this morning—before the wedding contract signing."

Joseph looked down at his son. "Don't you think it strange that you and our son are the only ones without sores?"

"Potabi said it was because Isis is the great healer," she whispered.

He opened his arms. "May I hold him?"

She hesitated. "Do you know how to hold a newborn?"

"I practically raised my baby brother, Benjamin, after Ima died in childbirth. Please, Asenath." She placed him in Joseph's arms. He was barely the weight of a pitcher of beer. "What did you name him?"

The baby squirmed, his little face shading an alarming crimson.

"Is he hungry or—" Joseph felt an eruption on his forearm.

"He's better now." Asenath chuckled.

Joseph laughed too. "Such a big noise from a small package!"

When Asenath reached for the baby, Joseph waved her away. "I'll do it. Where are the fresh cloths?"

Her momentary surprise pleased him. "In my bedchamber." He followed her to where a stack of clean napkins lay folded between a small rocking cradle and her elevated mattress.

Joseph placed a leather mat on the floor and then started a chore he hadn't done since Ben was a baby fifteen years ago. "A child's name defines him. Ima Rachel named my brother Ben-oni—son of my trouble—with her dying breath, but Abba renamed him Benjamin—son of my strength. I'm sure you gave our boy an honorable name."

His wife handed him a wet cloth but didn't speak.

Her silence drew his attention. "Asenath?"

She swallowed audibly. "Potabi named him Masa-harota to honor an ancient high priest of Amun."

Joseph returned his focus to their son's soiled napkin and considered the soiled name. "Why would you allow Potiphera to honor the priest of a false god with our son's name?" His voice shook with barely contained rage.

"It's part of what I need to tell you. Please don't judge until I tell you everything."

He continued his task in silence, grateful for the distraction.

"Potabi has promised to incorporate Elohim as part of the great god so every temple in Egypt will worship Amun-Ra-El."

Joseph's eyes met hers. "No."

"Please, Joseph. I asked that you listen to everything."

He quieted, bracing for the rest.

"Though I know El represents the strongest Canaanite god, not Elohim, incorporating El could draw Amus and Egyptians into unified worship. I could worship Elohim while still playing the part of Isis—healer and protector—that young Neferhotep so desperately needs. He's terrified, Joseph, and because my labor began the night of his abi's death, he's convinced I'm the Mother Goddess."

"You can't protect him with a lie."

"I can protect him by staying, Joseph." Her features hardened. "You broke your promise and left me alone. At least Potabi, Sitmut, and Neferhotep were with me when our son was born. They cleared a path through my darkest days. Now, you must either walk the path with Masa-harota and me or release us to walk it without you." She turned her head, hiding from him when he most needed to read her expressions.

Joseph's hands trembled, but he finished tying the fresh napkin around his son's waist. Without a word, he stood, spotted a clean linen swaddling cloth, and laid it on Asenath's bed. Wrapping the boy like a tightly closed lotus blossom, he stood over the babe, watching his eyelids grow heavy. He was a content little one. Peaceful when his needs were met.

As is his ommi. Memories of their days at Magic Lake raked across his heart's raw wounds. Joseph scanned his wife's bedchamber. Filled with the finest linen, Minoan paintings, and pottery. Nearly every piece of furniture was made of ebony and ivory. Every floor tile was perfectly arranged in a stunning mosaic. During their month traveling across the Faiyum, his wife had proven she didn't require riches to be content. She needed only Joseph—and Elohim—and only Joseph had failed her.

Turning to face the woman he loved, he found her standing in a ray of sunlight, staring at the child they'd created together. "When I left you here," he said, "I truly believed Sitmut would keep you safe from your abi. She hated him almost as much as I did—or so I thought. I didn't think I'd left you alone or without protection, but I see now that I shouldn't have left you at all. Will you forgive me?"

She pursed her lips, nodding.

"Your abi has tricked you, love. You aren't now, nor have you ever been, Isis Incarnate."

"I know, but—"

He lifted his hand but quickly dropped it, realizing his mistake. "Sorry. Habit."

She offered a tentative smile. "I should allow you to finish speaking before I protest." She lifted one beautiful brow.

Hope peeked from beneath its shroud. "Elohim can never be placed among other gods. He is the *only* God. He is One. You're correct that El is the Canaanites' main deity. In our efforts to explain Elohim, my family has used this term in conjunction with aspects of Elohim's nature: El Shaddai, El Roi, El Elyon, and El Olam. Elohim is almighty. He sees all. He is Creator of heaven and earth. He is everlasting. He won't be contained in temples or manipulated by Potiphera's lies."

Joseph scooped up their son and carried him to his wife, cradling the babe between them. "Our child will not bear the testimony of a false god. He will be called Manasseh because he will help us *forget* our past. You'll find that being his ommi is more important than pretending to be a goddess that secures more political power for your abi."

She tensed when he mentioned Potiphera. "Because Potabi chose the name, he'll be angry—"

"Have I ever told you about how Great-Saba Abram gained his wealth?"

She answered with a puzzled look, so Joseph began, "When he and Great-Savta Sarai first came to Canaan, there was a terrible drought, so they drove their small flock toward Egypt to survive. Because Great-Savta bore the ethereal beauty of Eve, Great-Saba told her to say she was his sister rather than his wife."

"He told her to lie?"

"It was partly true," Joseph clarified. "She was his half sister, the daughter of his abba but from a different ima. Great-Saba Abram's suspicions proved true when Pharaoh took Great-Savta into his harem. Before he slept with her, however, Elohim afflicted Pharaoh's whole household with serious diseases. When the king realized Great-Savta was Abram's wife and his household affliction was likely the judgment of a god, he asked Great-Saba to pray for healing and showered Great-Saba Abram with wealth, livestock, and servants."

Asenath's features brightened. "You think Potabi's sores are Elohim's way of protecting *us?*"

"I do." Manasseh wrapped his tiny hand around Joseph's finger. "Manasseh will be a daily reminder of Elohim's miraculous power and, at the same time, help me forget the troubles I endured while with my family in Canaan."

"Joseph, how can you be sure the sores will—"

"When Pharaoh Neferhotep agrees to release you, we will leave Thebes, and Elohim will heal them."

Doubt lingered. "Neferhotep's grief over a missing senet partner won't cause the greatest upheaval at court. It's Potabi who will wreak holy havoc if I leave him, so Sitmut will try to force me to stay simply to protect herself and her sons from his wrath."

Joseph searched the lovely face he'd memorized in Faiyum moonlight. Was she making excuses, or did she truly feel trapped? Though Elohim had powerfully proven Himself to her, she was still young—only twenty-one Inundations—and Potiphera had masterfully manipulated her whole life. Her clear brown eyes screamed desperation, not stubborn denials. Her red lips were slightly parted, not pursed in defiance. *They need to be kissed.*

Giving himself an inner shake, he transferred their sleeping son to her arms. Manasseh was who mattered most. Asenath must choose—and Joseph must choose his next words carefully. *Elohim, give me wisdom.*

When he lifted his gaze, tears coursed down his wife's cheeks as she said, "If Elohim proves He's for us, I'll leave Thebes with you."

Thank You, Elohim. "He is for us, Asenath, but you must also prove faithful. When we leave Thebes, we must travel through all of Egypt to record the granary figures of each nome. It will be difficult, but we'll be together."

"I understand." She smiled. "I'm ready."

He took a deep breath to address the greater obstacle that stood between them. "When I entered this chamber, you accused me of taking Ahira as my mistress and asked if I shared her with Potiphar or forced him to relinquish her. Only Potiphera could have convinced you I was capable of those things. Your abi continues to undermine me and our relationship with deception," Joseph continued. "You said yourself that you need to be rescued, my love. I will rescue you from him, but you must refuse any future attempts he makes to contact you or our son. Can you agree to that?"

The horror on her features was answer enough. "How could you ask me to—"

"I'm not asking, Asenath." His pulse pounded in his ears. *Elohim, give me strength.* "Manasseh and I are leaving Thebes, and I desperately want you to come with us." He leaned over to kiss their son's forehead. "You have until the evening meal to decide if you'll stay with your abi or leave Thebes with your son and me." Joseph hurried toward the door before his courage failed.

"Joseph, wait!"

"There's no time to wait." He paused, his hand on the door latch. "Rising floodwaters make lingering dangerous, but it would be far more costly to leave my son near Potiphera."

He strode into the hall, where Hami stood guard. "When Asenath agrees to discontinue all contact with Potiphera, we'll inform Pharaoh Neferhotep that my wife is neither Lady Isis nor the best senet player in his kingdom—and she's leaving Thebes with me."

The Medjay's brows rose. "And if Mistress Asenath doesn't agree to abandon contact with her abi and leave Thebes?"

Joseph motioned him to follow. "Then I take my son with a wet nurse, and we continue to serve Egypt as the pharaohs have commanded."

THIRTY-SIX

Turn from evil and do good;
seek peace and pursue it.

PSALM 34:14

Asenath

I left my son in my maid, Esi's, care to visit Queen Sitmut in her chamber. The God's Wife of Amun groaned in pain as three priests and a midwife huddled around her bed, each attempting to heal her sores.

"Mother Goddess, Isis, great healer," she moaned as I approached. "I beg you to petition the gods. Heal my sons first. I'll take their pain if you'll spare both Neferhotep and Mentuhotepi this torture."

Her pleas tortured me, now understanding an ommi's emotions. *Elohim, if You still hear me, let Sitmut look with favor on my demands.* I donned my fraudulent authority and addressed others in the room. "Leave us. The God's Wife of Amun and I will speak alone."

Priests and servants bowed and backed away. Only the midwife hesitated. "Please, Great Goddess, I beg to remain at my queen's side, now and in the next life."

Sitmut's condition was more serious than I realized.

"Go." I didn't dare meet her eyes, fearing my own tears would fall.

I waited until the door clicked shut. Silence drew me closer to the bedside of Sitmut, the woman who had been my advocate. The queen. The protector. My friend. I no longer noticed her scars, but her fear was undeniable.

"I'm dying," she whispered.

"You don't have to die." I sat on the bed beside her, and she winced at the slight movement. I reached for the jar of honey. After coating bandages with the sticky balm, I lay them across her exposed sores. "Joseph knows the cause of the sores. His God revealed it— my God, Sitmut."

"Your god did this?" Her tone, though weak, was razor sharp.

"Stubbornness and deception did this." I laid a bandage across her arm. "I told both you and Potabi that I'm not Isis Incarnate, yet you forced me into the mammisi to deliver my son. I share the blame—because I allowed myself to be bullied. Potabi bullied you, too. You warned him that bringing your firstborn to Thebes would place Neferhotep's throne in danger, but he convinced you that by making Mentuhotepi his lector priest and you the god's wife, Neferhotep's throne would be secure."

"Potiphera promised—"

"He'll betray you like he's betrayed me and others many times."

"Why are you frightening me when I'm dying?"

"Let me leave Thebes, and Elohim will heal everyone's wounds."

"No. If Paneah takes you, Potiphera's rage will consume us all."

"If I don't leave, you and your sons may die."

"Why are you doing this?" Her eyes met mine. "After all I've done for you and Masa-harota?"

"Listen to me carefully. I'm about to give you the only possible escape from this and future calamity." I swallowed my warring emotions and whispered, "When I leave Thebes with Joseph and our son, I'll have no further contact with Potabi—ever. If you wish to protect Pharaoh Neferhotep, yourself, and Upper Egypt, Neferhotep must exile Potabi and Mentuhotepi with the support of his general."

The shock I expected was merely resignation. "Neferhotep is too young to recognize traitors so close to his throne." She lifted her hand to my cheek, tears forming on her lashes. "If your departure allows you to escape Potiphera and gives me more time with Neferhotep, then go."

THIRTY-SEVEN

Surely the righteous will never be shaken;
they will be remembered forever.
They will have no fear of bad news;
their hearts are steadfast, trusting in the LORD.

PSALM 112:6–7

Three months ago, we'd returned to the Edfu Fortress, where my husband finalized his reports of Egypt's second miraculous harvest. Manasseh and I traveled with Joseph while Elohim proved His faithfulness with even greater crop yields than in the first year. Now, at the beginning of our third abundant akhet, floodwaters were rising higher than the first two. Soon Nasseh and I would accompany Joseph on another nine-month journey. He would work long days and late nights, continuing to record Egypt's stockpiles and strengthening diplomatic relations.

My work was most hectic before our tour began. Packing to ensure our family had everything needed to serve and celebrate with Egypt's Two Lands required help from my dearest friends.

"Take the blue faience necklace to wear at the akhet festival in Thebes." Pushpa offered her suggestions from a nearby couch, where she massaged Ahira's swollen feet. Her daughter-in-law was due to give birth any day and was as uncomfortable as I'd been last year.

"What about this one?" I held up the gold chain Neferhotep had given me the morning we'd said goodbye at the docks. It bore one of his senet game pieces as a pendant.

"You must wear that tomorrow when you arrive in Thebes," Ahira said. "He should see how much you treasure it."

"Potabi was so angry when I left." I handed the chain to Esi and moved my hair aside so she could latch it. She'd come with us from Thebes, continuing as Nasseh's maid and mine. "Pharaoh Neferhotep was upset, too, but at least grateful for Elohim's miraculous healing. I'm nervous about how I'll be received or if I'll be welcomed at all."

"You said Sitmut is a reasonable woman," Pushpa said. "Surely gratitude and time have helped her realize you need to be with your husband, not pretending to be something you're not."

"I hope you're right." But Pushpa hadn't seen the betrayed faces of those watching me sail away.

"Ooommiiii . . ." Nasseh tugged at my robe, holding his chubby finger in the air. "Owwey!"

"He touched a bee!" Pushpa bolted off the couch. "Come, Nasseh. Let Gidety Pushpa put some honey on it."

A bright smile bloomed on his face, pain forgotten. Gidety Pushpa swept him into her arms and blew bubbles on his tummy, making the horrendous noise he loved.

Giggles consumed him as they left my disheveled chamber, Esi trailing behind them. "If he were truly stung by a bee," I said, "he wouldn't have been so easily comforted." I grinned at Ahira. "I wish I had Pushpa's confidence that everything will be fine in Thebes."

"I can't imagine all you endured alone there." My friend shifted, wincing as she pressed hard against her belly. "Then you set sail on floodwaters with a two-month-old. And now? To willingly endure nine months on a ship with a one-year-old?" She chuckled. "You're either courageous or suffering hysteria." Then she sobered. "What if you get pregnant on the journey? You were so sick with Nasseh."

"I was. But if I get pregnant, there are a dozen women friends along the way who would feed me broth.

"But what if—"

"Ahira, there are too many what ifs to consider in a day. If we feared every what if, we'd have a life of if onlys." I folded a robe and placed it in a basket. "A yearly tour gives us a chance to revisit the friends we've made in every nome. The midwife in Tebtunis said last year she'd seen Jendayi with a new baby. And I'll see Zahra and Hotep again."

"It sounds wonderful." Ahira's tone softened. "I wish I made friends easily. Pushpa is the one woman I've ever really trusted."

I paused my packing. "Many women in Edfu consider you a friend."

"Yes, but I'm describing the special connection Elohim knits together. You're another sister-friend to me, Asenath."

I was stunned and honored by her vulnerability. "You've been one of Elohim's greatest blessings to me as well—and perhaps one of His biggest surprises." We both laughed.

"We didn't begin well, did we?"

"But we have a lifetime of friendship ahead."

I helped her to her feet and was pierced by the tears falling down her cheeks. "I wish you could stay until after I gave birth."

"As do I, my friend, but we are bound as sisters—whether I'm here to greet the newborn or meet the babe at the next harvest."

Her features fell. "By the time you return, Nasseh will be able to introduce himself to my little one."

"Someday, they'll make mud cakes together by the river."

"Or catch lizards—if I have a boy."

"Or get married—if it's a girl." We giggled at the thought.

"Ahira." Potiphar appeared at the doorway with Joseph. "Come. We should give the vizier and his wife some privacy."

"Where's Nasseh?" Panic sent me racing toward the door.

Joseph caught my shoulders. "Nasseh is safe." The door closed, and he released a sigh. "Neferhotep has been murdered."

I stumbled back. "How? Who?"

"King Apophis received a message saying God's Wife of Amun placed her true son on the throne after helping depose the usurper."

"No!" I shouted. "Sitmut would never—"

He pulled me into a ferocious hug. "We know who's responsible."

My legs felt like water. "It's my fault. I knew when Potabi made Sitmut's firstborn his lector priest, Neferhotep would be in danger."

"When Potiphera made Sitmut his wife and Mentuhotepi his lector priest, he ensured Pharaoh Neferhotep could never casually replace him as he'd seen Sobekhotep do to the preceding high priest. We warned Neferhotep that Potiphera would betray him, but he was determined to have his family whole again—and trustworthy. Sitmut couldn't have changed Neferhotep's decision to bring his brother back to Thebes because Potiphera had convinced him it was Amun's wish to heal his family."

"King Apophis knows Sitmut is innocent. He must protect her."

"And we will protect her." Joseph braced my shoulders. "We leave for Thebes at dawn with most of our troops. If Mentuhotepi punishes those responsible, he'll sign the treaty in Neferhotep's place. If he openly acknowledges his part in the assassination, it means war."

"But you know he did it!"

"We can only punish what we can prove, Asenath. If Mentuhotepi honors the treaties Sobekhotep and Neferhotep signed, we must honor his throne."

I glared at him, refusing to acknowledge such reasoning.

"King Apophis has ordered a Cushite auxiliary force to remain in Edfu," he said. "You and Nasseh will be safer here with Pushpa and Ahira."

"I must go with you and help prove Sitmut's innocence."

"Apophis will protect her, but I can't concentrate on my duties if

I'm worried about Nasseh's safety and yours." He spoke calmly, but his grip on my arms felt like a vise.

"I know you're concerned for us, but if Potabi had a hand in Neferhotep's murder—" My throat closed around the words. How could I explain the awful compulsion? "I know I promised to have no more contact with him, but if Potabi is to be executed, I *must* say goodbye."

He was shaking his head before I finished. "You said goodbye when we sailed away from Thebes. If Potiphera is responsible for this coup, accept your last parting as the best you could hope for."

"He spat at my feet and cursed me!"

"And we've lived in peace since." His jaw muscle flexed, and I knew he wouldn't be swayed.

But I was desperate. "Perhaps you can forget your abi, Joseph, but I won't forget mine."

Shock and pain registered on his features.

My fiery words had hit their target, and I regretted them immediately. "Joseph, I'm sorry—"

"Don't ever compare Jacob ben Isaac, Elohim's covenant bearer, to the scheming viper called Potiphera. If you're determined to watch Apophis kill your abi, I'll order a special detail of Medjays to protect you and Nasseh."

His tension melted as he examined the pendant around my neck. He took the crocodile-headed game piece between two fingers. Our foreheads met, and we wept together for the boy we had both loved.

THIRTY-EIGHT

Know therefore that the LORD *your God is God;*
he is the faithful God, keeping his covenant of
love to a thousand generations of those who love
him and keep his commandments.

DEUTERONOMY 7:9

THEBES, UPPER EGYPT

NEXT DAY

Asenath

Riding the raging abundance of Egypt's third-year flood had been
even more traumatic knowing my stubborn insistence to see Sitmut
could place Esi and Nasseh in danger. While the sailors wrangled
the vizier's barque toward Thebe's shore, I wrestled unruly emotions. Joseph had barely spoken to me since I'd made the reprehen-
sible comment about forgetting his abi. He said he'd forgiven me
and was simply busy with preparations for the duties that faced
him, but I suspected we'd have much more to say when we sailed
away from Thebes again.

When the barque was moored, a full detail of Medjays remained
with Esi, Nasseh, and me on the boat. Potiphar and Hami accompanied King Apophis and my husband with two contingents of
royal guards to meet Pharoah Mentuhotepi, who stood on Thebes's

quay. When I'd been forced to serve as Isis after Nasseh's birth, I remembered Mentuhotepi as a simple lector priest but always present at Potabi's right hand—a place of honor. Now Potabi stood at his right hand, no doubt the dishonorable man who helped Mentuhotepi steal Neferhotep's throne.

"I don't see Queen Sitmut," Esi whispered. "Do you think they've arrested her?"

I shook my head, unwilling to voice what ifs. When I'd boldly declared to Ahira I wouldn't let my life become an if only, it had sounded so brave. Now all I could think about was Sitmut in a dark cell—or worse. "Joseph promised he'd take us ashore when it was safe." Nasseh squirmed, pushing against my chest, determined to set his feet on the deck.

"Shh, my love. Not yet. You must stay in Ommi's arms." Of course, the Medjays could form a human play yard for him—as they'd done for a good portion of today's turbulent sail—but I needed him close. The thought of Sitmut losing Neferhotep, never seeing or hugging her son again, was too tragic to bear.

"Mistress, I don't hear any shouting." Perhaps Esi was unfamiliar with the deadly stealth of Egyptian politics.

"A dagger makes no sound, Esi." I peered around our tall and broad-shouldered guards, catching only glimpses of Pharaoh Mentuhotepi, Potabi, and a bevy of white-robed, bald-headed priests. Laughter erupted from the royal huddle, and my stomach churned. "He's done it again," I whispered to no one, certain Potabi had found a way to win Apophis's favor. *Elohim, I don't wish for Potabi's death, but please stop the destruction he incites.*

Another burst of laughter, and Joseph started toward the ship with purposeful strides, Hami following him. I instinctively bounced Nasseh on my hip. "I believe we're about to go ashore."

My husband's anger was like the tide rolling in. He stood over me, eyes searching mine. "Apophis agreed to let Potiphera see you, but he's not to touch you or Nasseh. Is that clear?"

"We'll be fine." I tried to reassure him and looked past his shoulder to Hami. "You'll be right there with us, won't you?"

"I'll stand close to you and the priest, Mistress. There will be no contact or trickery."

"You see?" I said. "Hami will protect us." But my legs trembled as I linked my arm with Joseph's, and the full contingent of Medjays followed our family off the barque.

Potabi's face brightened when Nasseh returned his wave. "What a bright little boy!" He started toward us, causing Joseph and Hami to draw their daggers. Two armies unsheathed their swords—a horrendous rasping of metal against leather—and Esi screamed. Nasseh wailed. And I saw nothing but the backs of five Medjays, holding a defensive stance around my maid, my son, and me.

"I simply wished to see my grandson more closely," Potabi shouted.

"You will not approach my son," Joseph said without condition. "If not for King Apophis's intervention, you would not see him or my wife at all."

"What lovely sentiment," Mentuhotepi intruded with a sarcastic edge. "If someone had protected me so fiercely, we might have avoided last week's harsh decisions. Come, friends. Put away your blades, and we'll pick up reeds and pigment instead. Better days are ahead!" I heard two sharp claps and sensed our Medjays relax, then break formation. Pharaoh Mentuhotepi and his guard retreated toward the palace.

I raced to Joseph. He took Nasseh from me, then cradled us both. "I'm sorry, love. Are you all right?"

"I'm fine. Just a little shaken." I looked to Esi. "Are you all right?" She nodded. "Joseph, where is Sitmut?"

"Potiphera said she didn't wish to be disturbed. I'll press more when we get inside."

We followed King Apophis's contingent. Upper Egypt's soldiers lined the path toward the city and its streets. Market booths were closed, and citizens peeked from curtained doorways and windows as we passed. "Are they afraid of us or their new pharaoh?" I asked.

"I don't know," he said, "but it's not the same Thebes of Sobekhotep's or Neferhotep's rule."

As we approached the pink granite palace, I nearly wept. The series of shadufs Sitmut had engineered for irrigation were gone; her gardens were withered and brown. The grand Avenue of Sphinxes was deserted. "Fear brings death," I whispered to Joseph.

He kissed Nasseh's forehead, holding him closer. "Love conquers fear."

We entered the palace complex, leaving Egypt's regular army outside the gates, and hurried across the mosaic-tiled courtyard. Our three contingents of Medjays far outnumbered Mentuhotepi's guards. I let myself hope Sitmut would be waiting for us in the courtroom—but she wasn't. A few guards and a single gold throne awaited our arrival. Joseph transferred our son to my arms and joined King Apophis at the head of the procession.

"I've prepared a new document," Mentuhotepi explained as he ascended the dais steps and sat on his throne. "Similar to your agreement with the little usurper."

Without speaking, King Apophis mounted the dais steps and towered menacingly over the arrogant pharaoh.

Blades unsheathed again. Our Medjays' huddled protection blinded me to what happened next, but I heard Apophis demand, "Where is Queen Sitmut?"

"Please, King Apophis," Potabi spoke haltingly. "She doesn't wish to be disturbed. Surely, you understa—"

"*You* should understand, Priest. I will not sign anything until I see Queen Sitmut alive."

"I hope you'll reconsider," Potabi said, strained and weepy. "My wife took her own life this morning."

"Liar!" I shouted through my Medjays. "Tell the truth, Potabi. At least once, speak truth."

"She hung herself from her balcony with a linen sheet, wearing Sobekhotep's robe and a necklace of Neferhotep's game pieces. Is that enough truth, Asenath?" My name came out on a sob.

"As Potiphera explained," Mentuhotepi said with eerie calm, "my ommi chose death in the underworld with the husband and son she loved—usurpers of my abi's throne—rather than life with me on Thebes's throne."

Silence reigned. Something was desperately wrong. The Potabi I knew would have been orchestrating an arrangement to his benefit, not wordless and weeping while a lunatic stole Egypt's throne.

"Was it you or Potiphera who planned Neferhotep's murder?" Apophis asked the king.

No answer. I tried to peer around my Medjays but could see only guards huddled on the dais around powerful men and a throne.

"My ships will continue to Avaris and raise an army against you, Mentuhotepi." Apophis ground out the words. "You'll be squeezed between Lower Egypt's forces and our allies in Edfu and Cush."

I heard a sudden roar, then clanging metal—a scuffle and groaning ended in silence.

"Let me through!" I pushed the wall of muscle and armor in front of me, crying for release. "Please, I need to know what's happening." Two Medjays moved enough that I could see Potabi's new captain holding a dagger at Apophis's throat. Potiphar's blade was poised at Mentuhotepi's neck, and the mad king's bodyguard held Joseph with his blade threatening.

"All of Egypt suffers if both kings die today," Mentuhotepi said.

"I think it rather convenient." Apophis grinned. "My nephew would rule it all."

"Tell them, Great Mentuhotepi," Potabi begged, his voice trembly. "You have every right to Thebes's throne."

Mentuhotepi sighed and looked at Potiphar. "If you'll put down your blade, Potiphera's guard will release your king."

"Release Apophis!" Potabi shouted, and his captain obeyed. Apophis motioned for Potiphar to lower his blade, as did Mentuhotepi to his captain.

"Joseph!" The Medjays parted, but my husband's subtle wave bid me remain with our son.

Mentuhotepi concentrated solely on Apophis. "Potiphera helped me take this throne because I'm the rightful heir. From the moment he summoned me to Thebes, I intended to murder my half brother. My abi, Pharaoh Djehuty, was a strong leader who expected Ommi, his great wife, to be equally tenacious. He trained with pain—as I do. Uncle Sobekhotep was too weak to protect his family in Memphis, so he came uninvited to Thebes, killed my abi, and took Ommi as his wife. He would have killed me, as a boy of sixteen, had Ommi not sent me away to serve as a priest in the temple of Ra at Herakleopolis. Shedet's high priest knew my lineage and told Potiphera my whereabouts, and the gods helped me retake the throne stolen from me."

"What have you done with their bodies?" My voice seemed to startle the men on the dais. I met the mad king's eyes. "Please. I couldn't honor my own ommi with a proper burial. Let me honor Sitmut and Neferhotep."

"They'll both be honored with a sacred burial since Ommi was God's Wife of Amun and Neferhotep was her son. I have at least twenty priests in mind who will accompany them to the underworld and serve them for eternity."

"No, my king." Potabi knelt before him. "We need not send so many priests to their deaths."

Mentuhotepi ignored him. "Mistress Asenath, would you like to see their bodies?"

Prickly flesh crawled up my arms. I glanced at Joseph. He was poised to refuse for me, but would a refusal jeopardize the treaty? "I can wait to see them until both kings sign the agreement."

Mentuhotepi turned a lazy smile toward Apophis and motioned toward the waiting papyrus. "Shall we?" With minimal conversation, the two kings signed multiple documents, and then Mentuhotepi said to Potabi, "Take them to the mammisi." He left through the private door at the back of the dais.

Potabi waited until he was gone before gesturing to Apophis. "Follow me." He descended the dais steps. King Apophis and Joseph followed. I was one step behind, Esi holding Nasseh next to me. Our Medjays surrounded us like the flooding Nile, a torrent of protection through the palace halls and under the portico that connected the temple complex. Memories of Manasseh's birth came rushing back. I reached for Nasseh's tiny hand, overwhelmed at Elohim's forgiveness and for the healing of my marriage.

We arrived at the freestanding building where I'd given birth to our son. "What is this place?" Joseph asked.

I barely heard Potabi's explanation, dread rising inside me. Was the sem priest embalming the bodies inside the birth house? "It's for Asenath's protection." Potabi's voice broke through my dread.

"That's the excuse you always used to hold me captive."

"This time he's telling the truth, love." Joseph leaned down to whisper, "We dare not stay for the mourning period."

I looked at Potabi again and noticed his hands shaking, chin quivering. "Everything I've done is for you, Nathy."

"That's a lie," Joseph said. "Repeat what you told King Apophis." My husband placed his arm around my waist, my true protector.

Potabi's eyes narrowed, his hatred for my husband evident still. When he looked at me, however, his features softened. "When I brought Mentuhotepi to Thebes and married Sitmut, I promised to protect them and meant it." He glanced around us and lowered his voice. "I realized too late that Mentuhotepi would promise me anything to help him arrange Neferhotep's murder. He's not the king I hoped he'd be."

"I feel no sympathy for you."

"He's going to kill twenty innocent priests!" His coarse whisper drew attention, so he lowered his voice. "He says it's to attend Sitmut and Neferhotep in the underworld, but it's to intimidate every priest in the temple and force their allegiance."

How many times had I felt the fear I saw in his eyes? "It's terrible to feel trapped, isn't it, Potabi? You deserve to be punished for the way you've tortured others."

His eyes glistened. "I loved Sitmut, and I love you, Nathy."

"You know nothing of love."

"I tried to do the right thing, but—"

Apophis gathered Potabi's collar in his fist. "You want to do the right thing?"

Potabi nodded.

"Help me kill Mentuhotepi, and you may live."

"I won't listen to this!" I said to Joseph. "Get us out of Thebes."

THIRTY-NINE

When the sentence for a crime is not quickly
carried out, people's hearts are filled with
schemes to do wrong.
ECCLESIASTES 8:11

THEBES, UPPER EGYPT
ONE YEAR LATER (1688),
FOURTH YEAR OF PLENTY
Potiphera

Potiphera stood at Mentuhotepi's right hand—chief advisor to Upper Egypt's Great Hope turned viper. They watched King Apophis's expert sailors battle the swollen Nile and wrestle his barque safely onto shore. Today would be the last time Potiphera played Amun-Ra's mediator for Thebes's despicable pharaoh.

"Twelve ships?" Mentuhotepi murmured. "Tell me, Potiphera, why does a king come with twelve ships full of soldiers to renegotiate a peace treaty?"

"Apophis has always enjoyed pomp, Great Son of Amun-Ra." Potiphera soothed the prey. "He wouldn't dare attack with a mere twelve ships when General Nebiriraw and Upper Egypt's whole army stand behind you." The arrogant king seemed appeased.

Potiphera searched the visiting king's ship for a specific audience—

and found them missing. Neither Asenath nor her arrogant husband had come to witness the retribution for Sitmut and Neferhotep's deaths.

Mentuhotepi shaded his eyes. "It would appear King Apophis left Zaphenath-Paneah in Edfu this year." He laughed and elbowed Potiphera. "Perhaps the Hebrew couldn't stomach the entertainment I described in my invitation." Having quashed Potiphera's suggestion to incorporate El in the name of the god Amun-Ra, Mentuhotepi thought a public sacrifice—a Canaanite tradition—during the akhet celebration would make Paneah feel more "at home."

"The priests will be relieved we need not kill a goat on the Avenue of Sphinxes, my king."

"Greetings!" King Apophis lifted his hand as he marched toward Mentuhotepi, then glanced at Upper Egypt's General Nebiriraw, who stood at his king's left. Apophis sliced his hand down as if swinging an axe.

"What—" Mentuhotepi couldn't finish his question because of the dagger in his belly.

General Nebiriraw faced him, one hand on the king's shoulder, the other on the dagger. "May Anubis repay you for the innocent blood you've shed."

Staring wide-eyed at his betrayer, Mentuhotepi crumpled to his knees. His bodyguards descended on him like bees on a hive, slashing him in a violent frenzy.

Potiphera watched with morbid fascination. *For you, Sitmut.* Though he hadn't loved her as he had Katesch, he'd admired and respected the regal queen. He'd only agreed to help kill her younger son, Neferhotep, because Mentuhotepi was a better manipulator than Potiphera realized. Sitmut's firstborn had pretended to love her, pretended to be broken and needy when, in fact, he had lied about everything except his hatred for Sobekhotep. At least the boy, Neferhotep, gave up his throne with honor. He didn't cower or wail after Nuru's dagger met his throat. His eyes darted toward Potiphera, stunned betrayal frozen on the child's face as his life drained away. How long had he suspected Potiphera's duplicity?

That day, Neferhotep's guards had immediately killed Nuru. Potiphera had comforted his grieving wife, assuring her that Mentuhotepi would rule well. Before the day ended, however, Potiphera realized the gravity of his error. At his first council meeting, Mentuhotepi laughed like a hyena and openly thanked Potiphera for helping him murder the little *usurper*. The betrayal on Sitmut's face still haunted Potiphera's dreams. Today, the true usurper would meet the heart eater at Anubis's scales.

"You're smiling." King Apophis dropped a small bag of silver into Potiphera's hand. "Is it because I'm paying you well or because you enjoy watching the bloodshed?"

Potiphera bowed as Thebes's general approached. "I smile because I'm pleased General Nebiriraw is my new king."

Apophis clamped the general's shoulder. "Well done, *Pharaoh* Nebiriraw. You'll restore dignity to Upper Egypt's throne."

"And I will serve you with all my heart," Potiphera said.

Nebiriraw's lips curled with disdain. "I will kill you if you remain in Thebes."

"But I . . . I helped you coordinate the coup," he said, then turned to Apophis. "And I kept you apprised of everything that happened in Thebes."

Apophis shrugged. "Which is why Pharaoh Nebiriraw could never trust you."

"But I've been loyal!" Potiphera shouted, glancing at one king, then the other.

"Loyal to yourself." Apophis's dangerous smile sent Potiphera to his knees.

"You're right. I'm loyal to myself. What honest man would deny it? But I'm also loyal to those I admire and respect. Have I not always served *you* above all others?" He reached for Apophis's dagger hand, hoping to avoid unexpected punishment. "Have I ever betrayed you? You, Great Apophis—Ra's divine spark. Please, my king, I could still be useful to you. I'm still Amun-Ra's instrument on earth with many connections and much wisdom to—"

"Rise, Potiphera."

He scrambled to his feet.

Before he could gush his gratitude, Apophis said, "You'll return to On's temple."

Potiphera sighed his relief. "My king, you are too kind—"

"You'll serve as a *wab* priest."

"B-b-but," Potiphera sputtered. "A wab priest is the least of all temple servants."

Apophis chuckled, low and menacing. "You'll scrub floors. Empty waste pots. Chop vegetables."

"But why—"

"Because as the lowliest, most invisible priest, the when and how of your death would go unnoticed." He leaned close and sniffed. "At the first whiff of betrayal, Potiphera, I will kill you, and every memory of you will be stricken from priestly records."

Potiphera gulped. "I would never betray you. All I've done—all I'll *ever* do—is serve Ra and you, his true son. Let me prove my loyalty to you, Great and Mighty Pharaoh."

Apophis turned a slow grin on Nebiriraw. "Are you married, General?"

Nebiriraw seemed surprised. "I am. In fact, I plan to marry two more wives now that I'm pharaoh and have a legitimate reason for more women." He chuckled, but Apophis's stern gaze sobered him.

"I view marriage as a sacred thing, and my life has never been settled long enough to properly care for a family. With you on Thebes's throne, my friend, I can send word to Edfu of your *peaceful* succession and lend my full support from Avaris. Zaphenath-Paneah will begin his annual granary tour in a few days and spread the good news of our stable alliance and safer trade routes between Cush and the Great Sea."

He returned his attention to Potiphera. "Prove your loyalty to me by sending the two chantresses of On to Avaris—the ones you kept in the tower with Asenath. I'm convinced a wife can make my life complete—as Tani has said many times—and my deep commitment to Ra will surely find its match in one of your chantresses. Paneah took one songbird. The other two are equally desirable.

Send both women to me, and I'll determine which one Ra has chosen for my bride." Both kings walked away without awaiting a response, leaving Potiphera to ponder his untenable future.

Returning to On's temple as a wab priest would be humiliating, but he'd saved enough silver through the years to pay others to perform the mundane duties. Potiphera tossed the small bag of silver into the air and caught it. On, situated on the heaviest trade route, would bring him merchant's gossip from every corner of the world. He'd soon remind Apophis of his worth and regain the power and position he'd lost.

A grim thought darkened his mood. If he used all his wealth to pay others to do his lowly wab tasks, what treasure would he have left to bury in his tomb for the afterlife? Most people had descendants—generations upon generations—to offer annual sacrifices at the Sed Festival for dead relatives. Without Asenath, he would have no one. *Katesch, I must regain Asenath's trust and influence our grandson's future.* Otherwise, he and Asenath's ommi might live a pauper's life in the underworld—which would be far worse than returning to On as a wab priest.

As descendants of the ancient priest born on the Mound of Creation, both Potiphera and his grandson, Masa-harota, deserved a life of ease—in this life *and* the next. Potiphera would never allow Masa to grow up with a Hebrew name that meant "forgotten." *And I will never forget you, Masa-harota.*

With his vow came the clarity of a new purpose and plan. Yes, becoming a wab priest might give him *more* freedom to finally accomplish the passion that had burned since he'd heard Katesch's dying breath.

"I'll return to On and show other wab priests how true humility has changed me." He spoke the lie aloud, tasting it, growing accustomed to the bitterness. He would never voice the exciting truth blooming anew, not even with a whisper when alone. He would kill Pharaoh Yanassi to wipe the throne clean of filthy Amu blood. But he must plan this assassination very carefully—so Zaphenath-Paneah would be executed for the crime.

FORTY

Joseph stored up huge quantities of grain, like the
sand of the sea; it was so much that he stopped
keeping records because it was beyond measure.

GENESIS 41:49

Joseph

Pharaoh Yanassi, now a gangly fourteen-year-old with blemishes and his own opinions, measured the rushing river, and King Apophis shouted the result: "Amun-Ra has blessed this year's akhet beyond any in Egypt's history!" The akhet festival crowd roared in response, hundreds dispersing across the palace complex to enjoy the festivities planned for them despite the sweltering heat.

Joseph and Asenath strolled behind their son and his maid. "Manasseh should meet at least one of his gidys." Asenath would be pleased if their son could meet either Prince Jacob or Potabi.

"Nasseh has all the family he needs right here." Joseph gestured toward Ahira's children, Bomani and Salama. Blood relatives through a painful past, they were now bound by love in a protective family who cared more about people than power.

King Apophis had become "Uncle Poppy" since he'd taken Hotep as his bride. He'd proven utterly smitten when he placed a gold throne at his left side—Pharaoh Yanassi on his right—and often bent his head to hear Hotep's wise advice before he and his nephew rendered final judgments. And now that Hotep was with child, the mighty King Apophis had become a doting abi-to-be, fulfilling his wife's every desire. Zahra served as her maid and favorite auntie to Ahira's and Asenath's children. Tani and Pushpa were honorary gidetys, irrevocably spoiling each little one.

"I need to know Potabi is well," Asenath whispered. Though Hotep and Zahra brought Asenath a measure of security, they also carried with them the constant reminder of Potiphera.

"He's well!" Joseph noticed he'd garnered unwanted attention and lowered his voice. "Hotep and Zahra told you he's become content as a wab priest." The deep lines between her brows proved sympathy had spiraled to longing. Well, Joseph had longings of his own—to keep Asenath and Nasseh safe from Potiphera . . . and to add more children to this loving family. *Elohim, Asenath and I have more love to give. Why haven't You blessed us with another child?*

While the children played and the royals laughed at their antics, Asenath searched the windows of his soul. "Something troubles you. While everyone else wears a smile, Egypt's vizier looks as if he's lost his last friend."

"That's certainly not true. My best friend is right here." He looked away before she read anything else on his features. She'd become too intuitive for him to hide the slightest care.

Slipping his arm around Asenath's shoulders, he slowed their pace and they provided rear guard for the royal company. Nasseh's nursemaid, Esi, joined Nasseh and Bomani in battle, clacking wooden swords a few paces ahead. Little Salama toddled between Pushpa and Queen Tani, jabbering instructions like Egypt's newest general while melting hearts as the lone princess in the palace.

"Will you tell me what's really bothering you? Must we tour the nomes again? I can leave Hotep if it's necessary."

"No, travel isn't necessary," he said. "Though I'll confess to you alone that Elohim's abundance of grain has exceeded our ability to measure it. We won't leave Avaris until the famine is over. God has provided for all our needs, and everyone we love is safe here."

"Not everyone." She held his gaze. "If we could bring Potabi to Avaris, too—"

"No!" Joseph's shout drew stares and brought color to Asenath's cheeks. He offered a forced smile to nosy spectators and whispered, "Let Potiphera prove faithful in On. Then someday I *might* allow him to see our son again."

Barely controlled anger simmered beneath her lovely features. "And what of *your* abi, Joseph?"

"What of him?"

"Will we remain fat and happy in Egypt and ignore your family completely? Will Prince Jacob's camp starve with the rest of Canaan?"

"Asenath . . ." He released a slow sigh, combing both hands through his hair. "Elohim will care for my family—"

"What if Elohim chose you to care for them? You said the famine will reach Canaan. They will be affected. Even if you're still angry with your brothers, how can you turn your back on the abi who adored—"

"You know nothing!" His shout garnered more stares, and he again feigned a smile. "I'm not merely angry with my brothers," he whispered, lagging farther behind the royals. "I love my abi, but he'll never see our son. Manasseh helps me forget my life before Egypt, yet he's also a constant reminder that everything but your womb has been abundantly fertile during the past five years."

Asenath halted, choking on tears and unspoken pain.

"Forgive me. I didn't mean—"

She fled toward their villa.

"Asenath!"

"Ommi!" Nasseh dashed after her, but Esi caught his arm.

"Stay with Nasseh," Joseph shouted. "Asenath isn't feeling well."

Following his wife through the crowd, Joseph crossed the courtyard and climbed the stairway to the vizier's opulent villa. Inside, he caught a glimpse of his wife disappearing into the residence hallway.

"Asenath, wait!" But he knew where he'd find her. The rooftop was her favorite respite from him, Nasseh, or the world. He'd placed a canopy on the southeast corner to protect her from the sun.

Maahir greeted him in the hallway. "Good morning, my lord!" His pink gums glistened with a toothless smile. "Did I forget something during your preparations?"

His personal steward had made the switch from Joseph's favorite old shepherd to his daily companion. "No, I'm looking for Asenath. I said something I shouldn't have and need to explain."

"That's the song every wise man sings before and after he marries." The old man laughed at his own wit.

Joseph proceeded toward the rooftop stairs. The scent of lotus oil lingered, his wife's aroma as intoxicating now as it had been when their love bloomed that night in Shedet. He raced up the steps and reached the roof breathless. "My love. Forgive. Me."

Asenath stood near the knee-high mudbrick wall, facing the city. "I've prayed for more children, too, Joseph."

"I know, love. It was thoughtless of me—"

"I even asked for the midwife's help." She turned to him, intense but not angry. "She gave me teas, herbs, lotions, and balms, but nothing made my womb fertile. There seems to be nothing wrong, yet I'm barren. You've taught Manasseh about the barren women in your family—Sarai, Rebekah, and your ima, Rachel. I remember one husband reacted differently."

Though Joseph could repeat the memorized stories without error, they'd become rote recitations. "I don't remember which husband—"

"*Isaac prayed for Rebekah because she was childless,*" she recited, closing the distance between them. "*Elohim heard Isaac's prayer, and Rebekah conceived.*" She held his gaze. "Have you prayed for me to conceive?"

"Of course. I pray for you every day."

Her eyes drilled past the easy answer. "Have you prayed specifically that I would conceive another child?"

Swallowing hard, he winnowed every memory and found no kernel of such a prayer. Would she blame him for her barrenness? "Forgive me. I . . . I'll begin right now. I . . ."

"I know you will. It's settled. I know Elohim will bless us with
another child when He deems us ready."

The kohl was still smeared from her earlier tears, but she was
calm. No tears now. Was she hiding her turmoil for his benefit?
"You seem too easily soothed."

"Would you rather I rant or complain?" She wrapped her arms
around her waist.

"I'd rather you be honest."

A soft huff escaped. "I spent most of my life in a tower, Joseph,
believing gods in an eternal world knew better than humans on
earth. When Elohim sent an angel to tell me that you were the man
I should marry, I believed He knew better than anyone on earth
what I should do. Perhaps fully trusting in gods—even false
ones—as a child made it easier to fully trust Elohim. Maybe easier
than a childhood in which you watched your abba wrestle with
God. It seems that a humble prayer, asking for His perfect timing,
would be more beneficial than demanding He give me a child when
I don't know the future He has planned for me."

Joseph stared at her, awed by such unassuming faith. He'd come
to Egypt twenty years ago, and every master had put him in charge
of something. Potiphar made him chamberlain. Ubaid promoted
him to assistant prison warden. Then Pharaoh placed all of Egypt in
his care. In every role, Joseph had often tried to carry responsibilities on his own shoulders instead of relying on Elohim to bear the
burden. "Thank you for reminding me that only Elohim is truly in
charge."

Asenath slipped her arms around his waist. "Will you invite your
family to Egypt—"

"No! I've forgotten—"

"But you haven't forgotten." She pulled him close. "Even in

these few moments, you have changed from soft and malleable to hard and closed. The hatred you carry for your brothers—and for Potabi—will destroy you."

He bit back anger, choosing words strong enough to leave a mark but not wound. "My brothers and Potiphera are cut from the same cloth. They're beyond redemption, and I won't allow them to poison our son. They went to great lengths to expel me from their lives. I've simply made that desire permanent. Never speak of them again. Is that clear?"

Her serenity condemned him. "You only raise your voice when your heart is breaking, my love. Have you considered how our descendants will be added to the records of Abraham's covenant if they're never reconciled with Prince Jacob's household? You tell Nasseh stories of your abba, his abba, and his abba before him. How will our children survive as a lonely branch of Abraham's seed, cut off from the vine that gives it life and meaning?" Without awaiting his reply, she led him to the canopy and began untying his belt.

"What are you—"

She lifted a single brow and stared into his surprise. "You're going to pray for me as Isaac prayed for Rebekah, Lord Vizier, and we're going to enjoy our unplanned privacy." She slipped off his belt, but her brave words dissolved into tears. She let her hands fall and lowered her head. "I feel as if I'm forcing everything. Demanding your prayers. Requiring you to lie with me. This doesn't seem pleasing to Elohim."

Covering his face, Joseph dropped to his knees and wept. Broken before his wife's transparency, he lost all sense of time. At some point they moved to the comfort of her canopy and comforted each other with the tenderness of one-flesh lovers. Why hadn't he prayed for her earlier? *Elohim, You are in charge.*

FORTY-ONE

*The seven years of abundance in Egypt came to
an end, and the seven years of famine began, just
as Joseph had said. There was famine in all the
other lands, but in the whole land of Egypt there
was food.*

GENESIS 41:53–54

TEMPLE OF ON, LOWER EGYPT
TWENTY-ONE MONTHS LATER (1684),
FIRST HARVEST SEASON OF FAMINE

Asenath

The city of On had swelled with visitors and esteemed guests from
every corner of the world for today's historic meeting. I was seated
among the other royal women on the Avenue of Sphinxes in front
of Amun-Ra's temple, Queen Hotep at my left, Zahra behind us. I
glanced up at the tower where we'd spent most of our childhood
locked away and then whispered to my fellow freed captives, "Could
we ever have imagined we'd one day be seated with kings?"

"I never thought I'd marry," Hotep said, brushing the black curls
off her daughter's forehead. "Let alone receive my beautiful girl as a
gift from the great god." She was too focused on her baby to see
Zahra roll her eyes.

My sisters' arrival in Avaris had been bittersweet. Zahra had willingly become Hotep's maid but had grown increasingly resentful of her humble duties. Hotep dared not complain to Apophis lest he beat Zahra—or worse. Whenever I attempted to mediate with talk of Elohim, both friends resisted with the argument that Elohim was merely Amun-Ra, the same deity by a different name. I ached at their delusion and growing divide.

"Herit, come to Auntie." Zahra reached for Hotep's little princess and whispered to me, "We owe Potiphera our lives. Why won't Paneah let him see his grandsons? Highness hasn't seen Nasseh since he was Ephraim's age."

I held our second son a little tighter and remembered the awful goodbye I exchanged with Potabi in Thebes. "You may think Joseph spiteful," I whispered, "but you don't know the despicable acts Potabi has committed." And I would never tell her or Hotep Thebes's ugly details. I hoped Potabi had truly changed, as Zahra kept telling me, but when we'd arrived in On, his request for a private audience with *only* me and our sons suggested otherwise. Joseph had declined with my support. Neither he nor I would risk another deception now that Elohim had given us two sons to protect.

"Shush." Hotep glowed with pride. "My husband is about to speak."

"It is my pleasure to welcome Pharaoh Nebiriraw," Apophis shouted over the gathering, "mighty of Birth, Healer of Thebes, and adored by all gods, on his first and unprecedented visit to Lower Egypt's fertile delta."

With great pomp, he and Yanassi strode side by side down the Avenue of Sphinxes to the center of the wide alleyway where my husband waited with Nebiriraw. Potiphar had suggested the ceremony after quashing an assassination attempt on King Apophis. The other captains agreed, eager to stave off Egypt's ancient practice of killing the divine god on the throne when prayers to him didn't end the drought.

Joseph held two sacks of grain, each the size of an amphora of wine. He hoisted the bags onto his shoulders as the kings approached.

"Elohim's predicted famine has arrived," he shouted, "and we have made ready. All nations on earth will come to Egypt and buy grain from the great abundance we've stored. Let every citizen rest assured in their pharaohs' good care." Zaphenath-Paneah placed a bag of grain in Nebiriraw's hands. Apophis and Yanassi balanced the second bag between them.

Three pharaohs raised the bags of grain overhead, and a deafening cheer rose from the gathered throng. Our royal children, startled by the sound, joined the screeching. I covered Ephraim's ears, and Esi held six-year-old Nasseh close. His big brown eyes never left his abi. He was bright and intuitive. With the coming of akhet in two months, we'd celebrate his seventh year of life. How much could he understand of family, faith, and forgiveness?

While the noblemen made more speeches, I glanced through the temple gates and into the complex I once called home. Had the drought affected the fruit trees in the high priests' courtyard?

I whispered to Queen Hotep, "Did you have time to tour the temple grounds?"

"It was so sad, Asenath. The pond was completely dry, and every tree was withered to dry branches. I can't imagine what Egypt will be like after six more years like this."

Her words were like arrows to my heart. We'd noticed some changes in Avaris—a few withered palm trees—but the fronds were still green near the trunk. The river had become a narrow ribbon of water. Reed beds had decreased.

Musicians played a lively march as six men joined Joseph and the pharaohs at the center of the avenue. Pharaoh Nebiriraw began the introductions. I knew the Cushite and Minoan from Edfu Fortress. Their reputations for cunning surpassed their integrity. "Adonibaal trades his Tyrian purple dye," Nebiriraw continued, "and Navid brings Persia's finest pottery. Albib trades Syria's most expensive damask cloth. Yabil, from Canaan, offers Prince Jacob's speckled and spotted wool, pistachios, honey, and the balm of Gilead."

My breath caught. *Yabil knew Prince Jacob.* Had Joseph spoken to him about his family's welfare?

King Apophis stepped forward. "These six merchants have culti-vated healthy trade in the years of plenty and now turn to Ommi Egypt, who will be milk and bread to their nations." He lifted his arms, calling for applause.

The Canaanite trader began shouting, "Canaan must have lower prices! With no latter rains, where will Prince Jacob pasture his flocks when both his Hebron and Shechem camps are cracked earth?"

"Egypt is my concern now," Joseph shouted back, visibly shaken.

"You're quite cavalier about your own family, Vizier." Albib from Syria joined the inquest. "Will you care if Damascus becomes as parched as Prince Jacob's land?"

Uneasy whispers rolled like a wave through the audience. "*If*, did you say, Albib?" Joseph's hands rested on his hips. "There is no *if* about this famine. The whole world *will* suffer. However, Elohim will use Egypt's abundance to feed all those in need." Softening his stance, he donned his practiced smile. "Egypt has plenty of grain to sell, my friend—including to Prince Jacob's family—at a fair price." Silence met the declaration. My husband strode back to the area reserved for Pharaoh's council, leaving three pharaohs and the mer-chants to entertain the frightened crowd.

Zahra leaned forward and kept her voice low. "You should go to Potiphera now, Asenath, while Paneah is distracted. I'll make an excuse for you and help Esi with Nasseh. Your abi needs to see you. It could be your last chance."

I turned to her, panicked. *Last chance?*

Expressionless, she nodded.

I glanced over my shoulder. Potabi stood at the tower's window where we'd sung our morning chants. The sight of him as a simple wab priest crushed me. How could I still care for an abi who had hurt me so deeply? After all he'd done to Joseph? To Neferhotep and Sitmut?

I nuzzled Ephraim, inhaled his scent, and returned my focus to Joseph, the faithful husband who never betrayed. "If Potabi has truly changed, he would beg for my husband's forgiveness before requesting an audience with me."

Ephraim started to fuss, no doubt sensing my tension. "Shh, lovey. The ceremony will be over soon."

"He knew you wouldn't come," Zahra whispered, then shoved a folded papyrus into my beaded belt. "Read it when you're alone and before you leave On. Perhaps you'll change your mind."

"Ba-ba-bah." Ephraim reached for Zahra's beaded wig, and she kissed his hand.

The secret message in my belt felt like a trumpet blaring—calling me to read it, condemning me for betraying my husband without even knowing its contents. When the ceremony finally ended, I told Esi, "I'll take Ephraim back to our chamber while you let Nasseh play with the others. Send Joseph to see me right away."

I fled before anyone could ask why, hoping they'd assume I'd gone to nurse my son. Hotep had employed a wet nurse, but both she and Ahira understood my need to be Ephraim's source of life. *You are Isis Incarnate, the Great Ommi of Egypt.* Potabi's oft-repeated lies came back like a flood. Would I ever forget the false purpose I'd lived with for so long?

Our chamber guards opened the door, and I rushed inside as the first sob escaped. Ten-month-old Ephraim patted my cheek. "Mi-mi-mi?" Concern wrinkled his little brow; he was already displaying Joseph's tenderness.

"Ommi is all right, lovey." I settled onto a couch and untied one shoulder of my robe. We both relaxed into the quiet stillness of Elohim's gift for ommi and child. I laid my head back and closed my eyes, resisting the call of Potabi's deception tucked inside my belt.

"Asenath?" Joseph knelt beside me. "Are you ill? Esi said—"

"No, I . . ." Tears came unbidden. I laid Ephraim beside me on the couch and fell into my husband's arms. "Potabi sent a message through Zahra, and I didn't want to read it until you were here with me."

His whole body stiffened as he lifted me from the couch and stood facing me. "Let's see it." He held out his hand.

"Please, Joseph. I need my kind and gentle husband, not Egypt's decisive vizier."

"We've already made the decisions, Asenath. You only waver when Potiphera finds a way to divide us. I'm not sure why we must have this conversation."

"Is this a conversation?" My angst turned to anger. "A conversation means we talk and listen. Zahra said this could be the last time I see Potabi. What if he's sick? What if—"

"He's deceiving you again!" His shout woke Ephraim.

I glared at him, then went to settle our son. Quietly fuming, I whispered, "You may return to your politics and pretending, Lord Paneah. I'll read Potabi's message alone and make my own decision since you seem incapable of compassion for your abi or mine."

Lips pursed into a taut, thin line, he glared at me. "Yabil was using his ties to my family to get a better price on grain. That's all. Abba's camp at Shechem will be the last ground in Canaan to go dry."

Was he really so blind? Ephraim had fallen asleep again, so I faced my husband, hoping to reason with the man beneath the anger. "You are compassionate, wise, and equitable in every circumstance— except when it comes to your family and Potabi." He started to interrupt, but I silenced him with my hand. "It's my turn to talk." I lowered my hand. "I agree Potabi is trying to deceive me with this message, but we should read it to understand his tactics. Just as Elohim gave us seven years to prepare for this famine, so we should faithfully prepare for Potabi's schemes. You built granaries and pre- pared reports to prepare for the disaster. We didn't wait and simply rage against the dry ground. If this message can help us prepare, perhaps we can avoid any harm Potabi is planning."

"I should listen more often." His low chuckle was like water to my soul.

I handed him the papyrus. He paused—and gave it back to me. "Read it and tell me what you think."

His trust felt like a victory. I unfurled the short missive and read:

Potiphera, your humble abi and wab servant of Amun-Ra.

To Asenath, my beloved daughter, may our great god shine on you, and may your ommi's spoken destiny ring forever in your heart.

With a contrite spirit I beg your forgiveness and mercy, hoping one day you and Paneah will allow me to enter my grandsons' lives.

In order to prove how Ra has transformed me, I offer information from my contact in Canaan. Prince Jacob has gathered his whole family to Hebron due to waning food supplies and dry wells in other regions. Should you ever need my help to reunite Paneah with his family, I am—as always—devoted to you, Nathy.

I swallowed the bile rising in my throat. Clearly, I'd shared too freely with Zahra about Joseph's reticence to reconcile with his family, and she'd passed the information along to Potabi. I handed the papyrus to my husband. "It's as we suspected. Potabi has stirred my sympathy for your family in hopes that the tension between us will drive me back to him."

Joseph read the message, then gave it back to me. "Do we need to have another conversation?"

My cheeks warmed. I'd been a fool to read the message. "No."

"You were right about preparing, my love. Now we're certain Potiphera will try to use my family to separate us."

FORTY-TWO

When all Egypt began to feel the famine, the people cried to Pharaoh for food. Then Pharaoh told all the Egyptians, "Go to Joseph and do what he tells you."

When the famine had spread over the whole country, Joseph opened all the storehouses and sold grain to the Egyptians, for the famine was severe throughout Egypt. And all the world came to Egypt to buy grain from Joseph, because the famine was severe everywhere.

GENESIS 41:55–57

Joseph

Joseph stood on the highest step of his villa's grand staircase at dawn and scanned the empty palace complex below. "Our second akhet without a festival," he said to Hami.

"And five more to come with entitled noblemen crowding the southeast gate." The Medjay nodded toward the nobility who bribed guards for first place in line but were indignant when Joseph wouldn't give them unrestricted grain vouchers based on their bloodlines.

Egyptian commoners waiting at two public gates were equally offended that they weren't given preferential treatment over foreigners. Yesterday, one man had been arrested and held in Joseph's villa prison overnight for his violent protest of the distribution process. "Has the man from Shedet calmed down enough to give him his grain vouchers and send him home to the Faiyum?"

Hami lifted an eyebrow and gave Joseph a wry grin. "One night in prison won't settle a zealot, my lord. This morning he was still ranting about the injustices of traveling all the way to Avaris and paying for a grain voucher to simply return home to redeem his own grain from granaries he built. I'm afraid he ignored your eloquent explanation and may have stirred more prisoners to his cause."

Joseph had run out of patience with troublemakers. "I'm sorry the man had to trade his wife's faience earrings for grain, but I wish we could all stay focused on Elohim's faithfulness. How can I kindly remind Egyptians that they have less inconvenience and pay lower prices for grain than foreign travelers?"

"No amount of words will salve a husband selling his wife's earrings, my lord."

Joseph sighed as the morning trumpeters greeted the dawn. The palace gates opened, and a stampede of people raced toward the booth at the base of his villa's staircase.

Maahir joined them at the top of the steps. "They're like frightened sheep running from a predator they can't see." He saw the whole world through the eyes of a shepherd since he'd spent his first sixty years herding flocks.

Joseph started down the steps. "Yes, but these sheep run because fear rules them. Canceling today's akhet festival for a second year in a row feels like we're shepherds who stepped aside to let wolves attack. People need hope—or at least distraction." They reached the grain booth, where Hami joined two contingents of Medjays and another troop of Egypt's army to maintain order amid panicked chaos. Maahir arranged the papyrus, reeds, and pigment on a table to record the grain sales, while Joseph scanned the faces of those who were first through the gates. Many had waited all night. Why couldn't they trust there was enough?

His breath caught at a familiar face. Then another. And another. Stumbling back, he steadied his breathing and blinked to be sure he wasn't dreaming. Could his ten older brothers really be waiting to buy grain from him?

"My lord?" Maahir jostled his arm. "Are you ready to begin?" Brows drawn together in concern, he motioned toward the high-backed chair on the elevated platform where Joseph sat each day.

A throne. He'd never considered it such until now, but the thought of sitting above the brothers felt ostentatious.

"My lord?" Maahir said again.

"Yes, yes. I'll hear the first petition," Joseph said in perfect Egyptian. How many years had it been since he'd spoken Hebrew? Now he spoke, thought, even dreamed in the Egyptian tongue. He sat on the high-backed chair and faced the long line of supplicants, while Maahir sat cross-legged at the low table among other scribes on Joseph's left.

Hami drew close. "Who are the men that have captured your attention, Lord Vizier?"

Joseph ignored him. "First case!" A nervous young man stepped forward, respectfully dropping to one knee.

"You may speak."

The man launched into a tedious story about his wife, their difficult first year of marriage, and a newborn child. Joseph lifted a hand for silence. "How much grain will feed your household for six months?"

"We can make one heqat last six months, Lord Vizier. I know the whole world needs grain. We must all work together to—"

Joseph lifted his hand again. "I'll give you one and a half heqats for the same price, my friend. May the Great God bless your family."

The man's exuberant gratitude was as verbose as the request. One of Pharaoh's soldiers nudged him toward Maahir, who would ensure the overseer of grain sales dispensed the appropriate papyrus vouchers.

"Next supplicant," Joseph shouted.

"Good morning, Lord Vizier." His stomach drew into a knot when Judah led his brothers to the dais. *Do they not recognize me?* Paralyzed by the moment, Joseph remembered the hemp rope around his wrists and ankles, his desperate cries from a dry cistern. His brothers had laughed, coldly contemplated his fate until slave traders made their betrayal profitable.

He turned to his interpreter and spoke in Egyptian, "These men don't know I speak Hebrew. You will interpret what they clearly intend for me to hear as though I don't understand anything they say. Do you understand?"

The interpreter appeared puzzled but nodded. "As you wish, my lord."

Hami whispered, "Wouldn't any Hebrew come from your family's own camp? Why wouldn't you—"

Joseph silenced him with a lifted hand while glaring at each brother, waiting for the first dawning of recognition. He would relish their fear with deep satisfaction. He watched Reuben first. Then the murderers: Simeon and Levi. Still no recognition. Surely, Judah would—but no. Each one lowered his eyes. None held any spark of knowing.

Joseph shot off his throne. "Bow!" All ten dropped to their knees. Faces pressed to the ground. No interpretation needed.

Joseph swallowed the lump in his throat. How could they not recognize him? Granted, the last time they'd seen him, he was a boy of seventeen with a scraggly beard and long, wavy hair. Now he stood before them a clean-shaven Egyptian wearing a wig and cosmetics. Simmering anger rose to a boil. How dare they ask him for grain when they wouldn't even give him a sip of water in that dark hole. "Where do you come from?" he growled, the interpreter translating.

"From Canaan," two or three answered together.

Reuben raised his head. "To buy food."

In that moment, past and present collided, and the dream Elohim had given him as Abba Jacob's favored son came rushing back. He'd glibly told his brothers, *We were binding sheaves of grain when suddenly my sheaf stood upright. All your sheaves gathered around mine and bowed down to it.* No wonder they'd hated him. How many times had Joseph himself doubted the dream came from God? Asenath had offered an alternative interpretation—perhaps the bowing sheaves were the people of Egypt bowing to their vizier. Yet here were his brothers, the sheaves Elohim had shown him in the dream, bowing to him—sheaves asking for grain!

The translator fell silent, Rueben's plea hung in the air, and a sudden—even uglier—thought pierced his soul. *Potiphera.* Had Asenath's abi sent them as torment? Potiphera would gladly conspire with Joseph's brothers, but the men bowing before him showed no sign of recognition. They were genuinely frightened of the Egyptian vizier. A simple test would reveal if their conniving hearts remained unchanged.

"You're spies—all of you!" Joseph shouted. "You've come to see where our land is unprotected." A grain conspiracy—the surest path to the vizier's prison without raising suspicion at the palace.

Their shocked faces turned to horror at the interpreter's translation. "No, my lord! No!" they all protested at once.

"No, my lord," Reuben said. "We are your servants. The sons of one man. Honest men—all of us—not spies."

Honest men, ha! "No!" Joseph repeated. "You're lying. You've come to get vouchers and roam our land."

"Please, Lord Vizier, believe me." Reuben stood. "We are twelve brothers, the sons of one man. The youngest is with our abba in Canaan, and the other brother—"

"Reuben!" Simeon gave him a threatening stare. The brothers exchanged worried glances. Joseph recognized that even after twenty years, Simeon still bullied them to follow his lead.

"What happened to your other brother?" Joseph dared them to prove they weren't the same conniving vipers they'd always been.

While the translator interpreted Joseph's question, Reuben's eyes never left Joseph's. "Our other brother—he is no more."

He hadn't lied, but he hadn't told the whole truth. Joseph leaned back in his chair, pondering his next words carefully. They'd told him the wonderful news that Abba and his younger brother, Benjamin, were still alive. Had Abba blatantly favored Ima Rachel's other son with the same possessiveness he'd shown Joseph?

A sudden fear for Benjamin's safety rose up like a desert storm. "I say you are spies, and you will not leave this place unless your youngest brother comes to Egypt. One of you will return to Canaan and bring your brother to me. The rest of you will be kept in prison so your story may be tested."

"But, Lord Vizier—"

"Arrest them!" Joseph shouted. "You'll sit in Pharaoh's prison until you learn to hold your tongues!" He watched without flinching as the Medjays bound them with shackles. Finally, the great wrong done to him was being righted.

He watched his ten brothers being led away and waited for the satisfaction of revenge. But it didn't come. Where was the peace he was sure this moment would bring? He rubbed the back of his neck, clearing his thoughts.

"My instincts tell me you know those men, my friend." Hami's whisper startled him. "You owe me no explanation, Lord Vizier, but if those men are truly spies, shouldn't we alert Pharaoh?"

If the pharaohs knew what his brothers had done to him, Egypt's kings would execute them without hesitation. "I recognized the men from Abba's camp, but I don't believe they'll harm Egypt. They are dangerous men, however, and could harm my family in Canaan if I allow them to return." He met his friend's gaze and held it. "Trust me to deal with them my way."

"I trust no one more, Lord Vizier."

Four Days Later

For three days, Joseph had continued his daily routine, eaten a quick evening meal, and then rushed down the prison stairs to hide in the darkened hall while watching his brothers in their barracks cell. Larger than the dark cubicle where he'd been imprisoned, their cell still cramped ten burly shepherds. They'd bickered. Shouted. Wrestled. Fought. The same loutish brutes who had sold him twenty-one years ago.

This morning he'd decided to send nine of them back to Canaan, keeping only the wickedest in custody. If Simeon remained in Egypt, Benjamin would be safer. Reuben had begged for Simeon's life, so Joseph offered the terms of his release—the same terms that applied to their future purchases of Egypt's grain. *Bring your youngest brother to Egypt if you hope to buy more grain or want your brother released from my prison.*

Tonight, Joseph had hidden in shadows again, watching Simeon alone. The prisoner wept in the corner and refused to eat or drink. He tore at his beard, beat the stone wall till his knuckles bled, and shrieked curses at the air. Rage. It was Simeon's singular talent.

Joseph marched up the prison stairs for the fourth night in a row. What was this unhealthy compulsion to watch his brothers from the shadows? *Perhaps if I tell someone Simeon is my brother.* But who? If he told Asenath, she'd want to meet him and expect Joseph to forgive the brute. He wasn't ready for that. He was embarrassed to tell Hami those cowards were the brothers who sold him into slavery. And Potiphar? Potiphar would kill Simeon if he knew that the man who tried to make Ahira his concubine—and sold her as a slave when she refused—was in Joseph's prison.

Ahira. Could he tell her? *Should* he tell her? Would knowing that Simeon would likely rot in Pharaoh's prison for the rest of his days give her a sense of closure? A feeling that Elohim's justice had been served? The righteous thought propelled him to the villa's courtroom, where he found a reed, pigments, and a clean piece of papyrus. His hand fairly flew, creating the hieroglyphs to communicate the short message: *Your tormentor from Hebron now in my prison. Be at peace, my friend.* He rolled the papyrus, poured a dollop of wax on the seam, and pressed his seal into the warm liquid to ensure privacy.

He found a courier to send the message and then retired to his private chamber. Asenath hadn't returned yet for the night. She must have remained with the boys. Joseph's conscience niggled at him. He hadn't spent much time with them since his brothers arrived. Asenath had asked more than once about his dark mood and why he suddenly chose work over family. He'd invented a ridiculous excuse about skewed grain totals on reports and immediately recognized suspicion on her lovely features. Why did he try to lie? She knew him too well. He must tell her about Simeon eventually, but he needed more time to work it out in his own mind before he could defend his actions to another.

Maahir emerged from his adjoining chamber. "Ready for evening preparations, my lord?" His pink-gummed smile glistened in the torchlit chamber.

"I am." Joseph started toward the couch, sighed, and lay back, ready for the most relaxing part of his day. "Let's do this in silence tonight, Maahir. I have a lot on my mind."

Maahir honored his request—for a while. Having finished removing Joseph's cosmetics, the steward's hands stilled. "You seem tense, my lord."

"My responsibilities weigh heavily on me."

"If I may be so bold, it seems you've had a lot more on your mind since you arrested those *spies* from Canaan." He emphasized *spies*, but Joseph tried to ignore it.

Joseph left his couch to remove his jewelry and change his robe. The old man followed. "Did you recognize the men?"

War raged between Joseph's heart and mind in the silence. He'd never lied to Maahir, not since the first day he'd worked for him in Potiphar's fields. "Yes. I know them."

"You seemed quite bothered by their arrival. I wondered . . . were they from your family's camp?"

Joseph sighed. How long could he keep their identity secret? When he was a slave in Potiphar's household, he told both Maahir and Hami of his brothers' betrayal.

Maahir's hand rested on his shoulder. "Are they your brothers, my lord? The ones who sold you into slavery?"

"You can't tell anyone, Maahir," Joseph said. "Not even Asenath. Not yet."

The old man nodded. "It's not my secret to tell."

A knock on the door startled them both. "Come!" Joseph shouted.

Hami escorted the messenger Joseph had sent to Ahira. "He says he has an urgent message for you but won't tell me from whom."

Joseph took the message from the courier's trembling hand, broke the seal, and read the words in Ahira's writing: *I need to see him—now.*

FORTY-THREE

Joseph gave orders to fill their bags with grain,
to put each man's silver back in his sack, and to
give them provisions for their journey. After this
was done for them, they loaded their grain on
their donkeys and left.

GENESIS 42:25–26

Asenath

Esi and I lay on her mattress in the boys' chamber, watching my
sons sleep between us. It was our favorite way to end a tiring day.
"We should move them to their own beds." I sighed, wishing Joseph
were here to enjoy the moment with me.

"It's unusual for Lord Paneah to work so late four nights in a
row." Esi twirled a lock of Ephraim's curly brown hair. "The boys
were ill-tempered today. I think they miss their abi."

"We all miss him." For four days the cares of Egypt had become
Joseph's mistress and I the nagging wife. He'd closed the grain booth
at dusk but then sent Maahir with apologies for missing evening
meals. For the past three nights, he'd tiptoed into our chamber well
after darkness fell. Each time I confronted him, he offered a weak
explanation. The last one, about skewed numbers on grain reports,
was too detailed to be true. Why had Joseph lied to me? *Elohim,*

what's happening inside my husband? Joseph had always given our family the firstfruits of his time, then allotted Egypt its share. But since the voucher distributions on the first day of akhet—

A knock on the door interrupted my brooding. I signaled Esi to remain on the bed and answered the door myself. "Zahra?"

"Asenath, you must come." Panicked, she reached for my hand.

"Wait!" I pulled away. "Joseph isn't home yet. I don't want to leave the boys—"

"It's Hotep. She may be miscarrying."

"Call for the midwife!"

"We did." Zahra met my eyes. "But you're the only one who can calm her. She won't listen to me."

It was true. The tension between them had grown unbearable. "All right, let me tell Esi." I kissed the boys and told their maid my palace visit would likely keep me out late, then followed Zahra into the hallway.

As we approached the villa's courtroom, I saw Hodari and Potiphar waiting and felt a niggling dread. I pulled my hand from Zahra's grasp. "Is Hotep's baby in danger or not?"

Potiphar glowered at the queen's maid, then turned to me. "Hodari and Zahra are lovers, Asenath, who bear you and I ill will. They've brought us together in hopes of ruining our marriages with some secret they've discovered Joseph and Ahira are keeping from us."

I turned to Zahra. "What is he talking about, *ill will?*"

"I thought the three of us were sister-friends, but you and Hotep moved ahead with perfect lives while I'm left alone and trapped. Tonight, you'll realize that Paneah and Ahira have secrets that could ruin you all. Vizier Paneah sent a secret message to Ahira. She returned an immediate reply and received an invitation from him to meet in the prison below this villa." She released a hateful huff. "Perhaps Lord Zaphenath-Paneah isn't as righteous as he seems."

"Lord Paneah and my wife are friends," Potiphar said. "There's a logical reason—"

"Surely, you have a kernel of doubt, Captain"—Hodari lifted a brow in challenge—"or you wouldn't have followed me to the vizier's villa. If you wish to know the truth, follow us to the prison and descend the stairs silently so we can all learn the truth behind their clandestine meeting." Without awaiting an answer, he placed a possessive hand at the small of Zahra's back and they marched down a darkened hall.

Something inside me screamed a warning, but when Potiphar followed, so did I. We lagged behind to whisper privately. "When did Hodari become so close to the queen's maid?" I asked.

"I'm not sure when their relationship began," Potiphar said, "but several months ago, Hodari requested permission from Pharaoh Yanassi to marry Zahra. As captain of the guard, Hodari isn't allowed to marry without Pharaoh's permission. The young pharaoh sought my counsel, asking if I thought Hodari could maintain both his first-and-foremost duty of protecting pharaoh plus a homelife. I told him the truth. Zahra was too much like my first wife and would be a distraction to Hodari's duties—thereby placing Pharaoh's life in danger. As a result, young Yanassi denied Hodari's request and shared that it had been my counsel—"

"Now Hodari blames you?"

He nodded, distracted by what lay ahead. "Have you ever visited the prison, Asenath?" We reached a door guarded by two Medjays. "Breathe through your mouth and cover your nose with your scarf if needed."

One of the guards opened the prison door, and the stench of human suffering rose like legends from the underworld. Zahra followed Hodari down the descending stairway, her hands placed gently on his shoulders. I followed the woman who'd once been my friend, and Potiphar closed the door behind us. Wall-holstered torches lit our way as the odor of waste and blood grew overpowering.

As we neared the bottom, the voice of a woman and man became more distinct. Both spoke in Hebrew. I recognized a few words Joseph had taught me. *Abba. Ima. Brother.* Then I heard Joseph speak in perfect Egyptian—and use an interpreter. I glanced at Potiphar. He shook his head and shrugged. There was far more going on here than Hodari and Zahra realized.

Zahra looked over her shoulder, cautioning me to silence with a finger against her lips. We halted on the last step, pressing our backs against opposite walls to listen. The woman speaking in Hebrew was clearly Ahira, but who was the gruff man who shouted what sounded like accusations?

I heard a sickening thud. Then Joseph told his interpreter to tell the prisoner, "You will speak with respect to the wife of Pharaoh's bodyguard."

A Hebrew prisoner?

The captive's low chuckle sent prickly flesh up my arms. He said something else I didn't understand. Ahira replied without giving the translator time to maintain Joseph's ruse. Her words were slow and calm, however, as if she spoke to a child. She ended with a name: *Simeon.* I covered a gasp. Were there many Hebrews named Simeon? Or was this Joseph's brother who had sold Ahira? While I was still considering, Potiphar charged down the stairs like a raging bull.

"Is this the Hebrew?" he shouted.

I raced after him into a room filled with bloodstained wooden tables, chains, and weapons. Hami and three more Medjays stood beside a well-muscled, shackled prisoner. Joseph wore the vizier's full regalia with a wig and heavy cosmetics—appearing dressed for a festival. He cradled the crook and flail Pharaoh had given him, symbols he normally saved for ceremonies to emphasize his authority. Ahira wore a simple linen robe and no paints at all. I was certain my shock matched Joseph's and Ahira's, but theirs quickly shifted to dread.

"Potiphar, don't." Ahira pressed her hands against his chest, then whispered something no one else could hear.

Joseph started toward me. "Asenath, I wanted to tell you, but—"

"Vizier Zaphenath-Paneah is questioning Simeon ben Jacob." Ahira spoke in loud, clear Egyptian. Her eyes locked with mine.

This is *Joseph's brother.* But she meant something more. She never used Joseph's full Egyptian name. Why had Joseph employed an interpreter as if he couldn't understand Hebrew? Realization dawned.

Simeon doesn't recognize Joseph! And Joseph wants to keep it that way.

"When Vizier Paneah and I served as slaves in Potiphar's household," Ahira was saying, "I told the vizier about the Hebrew man who had unjustly sold me. The vizier arrested this man a few days ago on unrelated charges. He sent a message to me, sharing the prisoner's name, and I insisted on facing the man who had wronged me." Ahira turned her attention to Hodari. "It would appear my chamber guards are more loyal to you than to me, Captain."

Potiphar laid a protective arm around his wife's shoulders. "Ahira's guards will be returned to Cush, dishonorably discharged from Medjay service."

Hodari scoffed. "They knew the risks."

"And you, Hodari?" Potiphar released Ahira and stepped toward his enemy. "You and Zahra risked much by revealing your hate, yet you've gained nothing except distrust from those at the highest level of Egypt's government."

"My guards tell me," Hodari said through clenched teeth, "that Vizier Paneah accused ten Hebrews of spying and put them in his prison, but he failed to notify either pharaoh. Why wouldn't he notify the pharaohs of spies in our land?"

"I don't know, but—"

"This morning"—Hodari cut off Potiphar's explanation—"Lord Paneah released nine of the prisoners, keeping this one." He pointed at Simeon. "Shouldn't we investigate further why our Hebrew vizier is passing secret messages to your Hebrew wife about Hebrew spies, *Captain*? Or has your second marriage made you as unfit for duty as your first?" Hodari's hands flexed as the two captains stood toe-to-toe. "King Apophis would be very interested to learn that Lord Paneah is conspiring with the Hebrews to take Egypt's land—as they did in Canaan."

Terror launched me toward them. "Wouldn't King Apophis also

be interested to know how rebellious his wife's maid, Zahra, has become? I can attest to many times she's refused to perform her duties or to obey her queen's direct commands."

Zahra's eyes filled with fear. "Apophis would kill me."

"Yes, but if the truth would save my husband, I'd tell both pharaohs everything that's happened." I blinked away tears.

"Save your husband?" She scoffed. "Surely, you know by now. Paneah will never be safe as long as Potiphera molds the truth to his liking." Zahra offered her hand to Hodari. "Let's return to the palace and leave these *high-level government* friends to explore their broken trust."

Hodari sneered at Potiphar and led Zahra upstairs. Simeon made a comment in Hebrew. I didn't understand his words, but the rancid tone was easy to decipher.

Ahira turned to the interpreter and said in perfect Egyptian, "Make sure you translate every word I speak so my husband and friends understand." Then she stepped to within three paces of her betrayer. Hami tightened Simeon's shackles as she began. "Whether or not you apologize to me is of little concern because I've forgiven you. It's a choice I must make repeatedly, every time I think of you. You wronged me, Simeon, and whether inside or out, we both bear the scars of your betrayal." She inhaled deeply and exhaled a noticeable serenity. "The difference between us is, my scars are nearly invisible because Elohim's healing balm covers them. I hope someday you'll allow the God of your abba to do the same to yours." She inclined her head with the elegance of a queen and walked away from the man who nearly destroyed her—and into the arms of the man who had given her a new life.

Joseph offered his hand, calling me to his side. I fell in step as we started toward the stairs, wincing as Simeon again started shouting. The awful thud of Hami's fist meeting flesh brought predictable silence. Leaning close to my husband, I whispered, "What was he shouting?"

"He said, 'Kill me now. My abba would never risk Benjamin's life for mine.'" Joseph released a soft huff. "I wouldn't give Simeon the mercy of a swift death. At least I've protected Benjamin by keeping the worst of my brothers from returning to Canaan."

The venom in his tone surprised me. How many more surprises would come when I asked the questions screaming in my mind?

FORTY-FOUR

Do not seek revenge or bear a grudge against anyone among your people, but love your neighbor as yourself. I am the LORD.

LEVITICUS 19:18

Joseph

Asenath, Ahira, Potiphar, and Hami had followed Joseph from the prison to his private chamber where Maahir waited in silence. The five people he trusted most now sat in a circle on cushions, waiting to hear why he'd hidden the truth from them for three days. Shame attached like a leech, draining Joseph's courage and challenging his faith.

Elohim, I've begged You to change my heart. Why can't I forgive my brothers?

"Simeon is one of the brothers who sold me." He began with the obvious; he tried to breathe deeply but couldn't. He turned to his wife. "I should have told you, but I was—I am—embarrassed. I still hate him, and when I saw Simeon intimidate Reuben to silence, I knew they hadn't changed. I fear they're doing the same things to my younger brother that they did to me—"

"Joseph!" Asenath said sharply, startling him. "You need not fear anything your brothers do. You're second in power to Pharaoh.

Arrest them or forgive them but be wise." Her voice broke. "Be the man of integrity Elohim chose to heal Egypt."

The disappointment in her eyes gutted him. "I can't forgive them, Asenath. I won't. And as much as I'd like to, I can't order Egypt's army to retrieve my abba and little brother from Hebron."

"Anger is a weak weapon, Joseph." Ahira's soft tone cut like a dagger. "Forgiveness is an archer's bow with unlimited arrows. They can pierce even the hardest heart."

"Pretty words but wasted on Simeon." Why had Joseph told Ahira his brother was in prison? He hadn't expected her to request an audience with her betrayer. "My brother will turn your forgiveness into dung," Joseph said.

"Good," she said, grinning a little.

"Good?" several asked in chorus.

While the others grinned, Joseph wasn't amused. "A shepherdess would think dung a good thing. As long as sheep graze and pass dung, the flock is healthy. My brother isn't grazing on your forgiveness, Ahira."

"What matters most is that I am wholly free of hate, and I can focus forward instead of behind." She paused. "Release Simeon from prison."

"No!" Hami and Potiphar protested together.

"I share the vizier's weak weapon of anger," Potiphar said. "Joseph's brother treated Ahira worse than his dog. He'll receive no mercy from me."

The slight twitch in his left cheek sealed Simeon's death sentence.

"I'm holding my brother prisoner to secure Benjamin's safety. I forbid you to harm him."

"You *forbid* me?" Potiphar's eyes narrowed.

"Remember, Captain," Hami said, "Zaphenath-Paneah is your vizier, no longer your slave."

"Most importantly, we're friends," Joseph reminded Potiphar. "Let me tell you the whole story."

Joseph offered Asenath his hand, but she kept hers clasped in her lap. She wasn't yet ready for the peace offering.

"My brothers came to buy grain four days ago," Joseph began. "Though I recognized them, they had no idea who I was. I spoke to them through my interpreter and accused them of being spies to test their character."

Potiphar glanced at Joseph. "Are they spies? Conspiracy and papyrus are the two things that grow in famine. If your brothers are spies—"

"They're not spies," Joseph assured him. "I accused them of spying out the land for grain, which technically falls under my jurisdiction, but I shouldn't have used such a volatile word publicly. Anyway, when I accused them, they tried to prove their honesty with facts about their younger brother and abba who remained in Canaan. When they were about to tell about my unfortunate end, they allowed Simeon to bully them into silence. Because they proved to be the same spineless men who sold me, I kept them in prison for three days. I released all but Simeon under the condition that if they want more grain, they must return with my younger brother. If they never return, Simeon will die in Egypt's prison and my brother Benjamin is safer in Canaan."

Potiphar tugged at his chin, thinking. "How much time did you give your brothers to return to Egypt?"

It was a logical question. Reasonable. Wise even. Unfortunately, Joseph hadn't given his brothers a deadline and felt rather foolish. "I gave no time limit."

"Then let me tell you plainly what I intend to do, Lord Vizier. If your brothers don't return by the end of next akhet season to redeem that vile creature, their indifference will testify against his very existence. I'll rid the earth of the man who discarded Ahira. If your brothers do return and decide to remain in Egypt—as spies or simply as descendants of the same Bedouins that drove the Amu into Egypt generations ago—then we have an even bigger problem."

"I hate Simeon as much as you do, but the breath of life is Elohim's to give or take. My brothers came to Egypt for grain, not to drive anyone off their land. I don't want them here either."

"The mere fact that you kept the meeting secret is damaging. If they return and Hodari tells the pharaohs that you've had secret meetings with your brothers, it could damage your credibility."

"His credibility is already damaged," Asenath said, "with me." Tense silence descended. "I wish to speak with my husband alone, please." She stood and extended her hand toward the door.

"I think Elohim will understand a maggot is only allowed to breathe until next year's akhet," Potiphar said to Joseph. "And though I trust you and my wife, don't ever summon her to another meeting without my knowledge."

Ahira was out the door before Potiphar finished. Hami followed the couple, quietly closing the door. Maahir disappeared into his adjacent chamber, leaving Joseph alone with his wife.

Asenath shook her head, eyes glistening. The disappointment on her lovely features cut between bone and marrow, creating an ache in him that reached into his soul. "I should have told you the day my brothers came. I was ashamed of my rage. How can I fix what's broken between us?"

"What if Elohim's plan for us to 'bless all nations' starts with healing your family? What if Potiphar's concerns prove true and they want to live in Egypt—even Simeon, the brother you most despise?"

"I won't allow it!" He snatched off his wig. Frustration roiled, unbridled and ugly. "Why won't Elohim take away my hate?" He fell to his knees with a growl, fists balled.

"How are you different than Simeon?"

Startled, he looked up. "What are you talking about? I am *nothing* like my brother."

Asenath cocked her head as if he should ignore his brothers' depravity.

"Simeon and Levi killed an entire city of innocent men," he said.

"You told me it was because their prince raped your sister."

Her calm certainty infuriated him.

"Simeon and Levi refused to forgive the offense. They were driven by hate, Joseph, and I imagine Simeon has never forgiven Ahira for refusing to become his concubine."

"That's different and you know it."

"Is it? You're a man of integrity, but for how long if you refuse to forgive? Already you've lied to me, kept secrets from your friends, and given anger priority over your family. How long before your justifications dissolve your character because you—like Simeon—refuse to forgive?"

Joseph looked away, unable to argue with the truth. A dark part of him had rejoiced when Potiphar threatened to kill Simeon. Had someone put a dagger in Joseph's hand tonight when Simeon shouted obscenities, he might have done it himself.

Asenath reached for his hand. "I want Manasseh and Ephraim to know their Hebrew family."

He pulled away. "You have no idea what you're saying. My family doesn't know how to love. They hurt people. They deceive."

"Yet Elohim chose them to be His covenant bearers. He chose me—an Egyptian priestess—to bear your sons and be included among them. Perhaps if we treated Simeon like family, he'd change."

"Like Potiphera has changed?"

She winced, and Joseph regretted the harshness—but not enough to rescind it. "Some people choose evil, Asenath. Every time. No matter how many chances they're given. They continue to choose bad over good, and their way over Elohim's way. People like Simeon and Potiphera will keep hurting us—and others—if we let them."

"But how do you know your brothers haven't changed? It's been over twenty years since you've seen Simeon."

"My sons will not meet that murderer!" he shouted.

She swayed slightly, like a palm tree in a storm. "May I go, Lord Vizier?"

Her defenses had risen; walls went up around her heart with the use of his title. "It's late," he said, gentler now. "Where are you going?"

"I'm moving to a guest chamber, my lord. The same way you chose a name-only marriage while I worshipped false gods, I likewise refuse to share myself with a man who chooses bad over good and his own way over Elohim's." Asenath turned on her heel, leaving Joseph gaping.

He choked on a mirthless laugh, then scanned his empty chamber and felt as dry inside as Egypt's earthen crust. *Elohim, where are You? I need the gentle rain of Your presence.* Even in prison, he hadn't felt this alone.

FORTY-FIVE

When Joseph saw Benjamin with them, he said
to the steward of his house, "Take these men to
my house, slaughter an animal and prepare a
meal; they are to eat with me at noon."
GENESIS 43:16

I held Ephraim to my breast for the morning's first feeding, giving life and nourishment to the son of Egypt's vizier, a man I loved more than my own life. But I'd become no more than a tenant in his villa after moving to the chamber across the hall from Esi and the boys. He was a benevolent landlord, making polite conversation at each evening's meal, humoring me with continued recitations of his covenant-family stories. Together we kissed our sons good night and then retreated to separate chambers.

Esi and I spent our mornings with the boys beneath a portico. Nasseh clacked his wooden sword against Esi's weapon—a brown palm frond. "Stay away from my ommi and little brother, bandit!" My rambunctious eight-year-old swung at Esi's head.

"Manasseh ben Joseph!" I shouted. Ephraim, two years old, bolted upright and wailed in my lap.

"We're playing, Ommi." Nasseh rolled his eyes. "Esi is a skilled swordsman and always blocks my attack." The maid giggled.

They'd both earned my sternest glare. "Regardless of Esi's skill, you must never harm those you love." The words struck me harder than Nasseh's sword. *Never harm those you love.*

I wished I'd heeded my own advice. I motioned for the warriors to resume their battle and remembered yesterday's disastrous encounter with Joseph. Maahir had given me weekly updates on Simeon's condition, so I'd presented Joseph with last week's report of his brother's good behavior and asked again if we could introduce him to Manasseh and Ephraim. The fury in Joseph's eyes had been frightening—but not as terrifying as his threat to take the boys from me if I mentioned Simeon's name again in his presence.

Elohim, I know only You can heal, but is there nothing I can do to help?

"Mistress Asenath?" A man's voice called from the chamber behind me, and Ephraim startled again—this time with a bright-eyed smile for Maahir.

Ephraim squirmed off my lap and toddled toward the old man, giving me time to close my robe. "It's good to see you, my friend." I met Maahir with a hug at the courtyard's threshold. "How have you been?"

He picked up Ephraim and kissed his cheek but was clearly troubled. "I'm well, Mistress, but I come with news."

"What's happened, Maahir?"

"The master's brothers have returned with his younger brother." His pause sent dread skittering down my spine. "The vizier invited them to join him for a midday banquet."

"A banquet? Did they recognize him?"

"No, Mistress, but Master Joseph appears more pleasant." Maahir held my gaze, speaking more with his eyes than his words. "His brothers are afraid. I believe your presence at the banquet would reassure them."

I looked down, fiddling with my hands. "Did Joseph ask me to do this?" I knew the answer.

"He did not. But he needs you, Mistress. His brothers need you."

"Bubba?" Ephraim pointed toward Nasseh. "Bubba."

I melted inside. "Yes, brothers need brothers, Ephi." I transferred him from Maahir to Esi's arms. "Prepare the boys to appear publicly today but keep them in our chambers until I send for them. Joseph and I will host a banquet at noon, but I'm not yet sure if we'll present the boys to our guests."

"Yes, Mistress."

Grateful Esi had already applied my cosmetics, I left the chamber with Maahir. "Will Joseph be angry that you've invited me?"

"Perhaps, and he'll be even more angry if you agree to my second request." He pulled me aside and kept his voice low in the empty hallway. "When the master sent his brothers home last year, he instructed me to hide the silver they'd paid for their grain inside their saddlebags so it wouldn't be discovered until after they arrived in Canaan."

"Why would Joseph—"

"I don't know, but . . . they came today with enough silver to repay what was returned, double the amount to purchase more grain, and many gifts from Canaan. They proved their honesty with the confession and seemed relieved by the vizier's friendly welcome—until his feast invitation."

"What is Joseph thinking?"

"I'm not sure, Mistress, but when I led his brothers to the stables and offered straw to tend their donkeys, they implored me to speak to my master on their behalf. That's when I said, 'Don't be afraid. It must have been Elohim that returned your silver last time because I received your payment.'"

I gasped. "You said it was *Elohim*?"

"They looked at me as if I'd sprouted another nose." An impish grin deepened the wrinkles in his cheeks. "I left them with the interpreter before they could ask questions. As I returned to the villa, I thought of the second thing you could do to help calm them before Master Joseph arrives."

"Anything, Maahir."

"I believe seeing their brother Simeon safe and well would significantly calm the brothers' fears. The warden wouldn't release a prisoner into my custody, but he might if you accompanied me."

I swallowed the sheer panic his words triggered. "I can't."

"The master gave his word," Maahir said gently. "His brothers returned to Egypt with their youngest brother, Benjamin. Joseph will release Simeon. We would simply do it earlier, at a time when the brothers could enjoy their reunion."

The logic was flawless but still felt dangerous. "Does anyone else know Joseph's brothers have returned?"

"Hami and I alone know, Mistress. I don't believe word has reached the palace—yet."

If we could free Simeon for the reunion this morning, Joseph could have his banquet at midday and send his brothers on their way before word of their presence reached Hodari or Potiphar in the palace.

Anxiety rising, I nodded. "Let's go."

Maahir led me through darkened hallways to the well-guarded prison door. Two Medjays examined us with suspicion as we approached, but I marched toward them with an authority borne of desperation. "You know who I am," I said without slowing my pace. "I've come to retrieve a prisoner for my husband's banquet. Open the door."

They exchanged a glance and obeyed. Maahir and I continued down the steep stone stairway, ignoring the stench. The warden met us in the audience chamber, befuddled at my presence. "Mistress Asenath? What . . . How may I—"

"We've come to free the Hebrew, Simeon. The conditions of his release were met." I stared at the man as if any challenge would be futile. He glanced at Maahir, and I preempted any questions. "The vizier's steward will accompany the Hebrew to a guest chamber and prepare him for presentation to Vizier Paneah at noon. Is there a problem?" I dared him to question me.

"No, Mistress. The Hebrew will cause no trouble." He strode into a torchlit hall. I exchanged a terrified glance with Maahir but donned my confident air before the warden returned.

Hair matted and his tattered robe wreaking of filth, the frightened Hebrew studied Maahir, then me. Joseph's brother said something, and I realized Maahir must find the translator if I hoped to communicate at all.

"Thank you, Warden," Maahir said, gently taking hold of Simeon's arm. "I'll escort the prisoner to a guest chamber."

The reality of the burly shepherd in a weak old man's custody weakened my confidence. "But he's—"

Maahir's sharp stare silenced me. "He's in need of a fresh robe, a good washing, and scented oils, Mistress. Then you may present him to the vizier's honored guests." Maahir's calm tone sent Simeon's confused gaze to meet my frightened indecision.

"Is everything all right, Mistress?" the warden asked.

Heal My people. The words came softly, and I submitted to Elohim's bridle of peace. "More than all right." I said to the warden. "Today, we celebrate the akhet festival despite a second full year of famine. For the third year in a row, the Nile's flood hasn't come, but God's healing has."

FORTY-SIX

When Joseph came home, [his brothers] pre-
sented to him the gifts they had brought into the
house, and they bowed down before him to the
ground. He asked them how they were, and then
he said, "How is your aged father you told me
about? Is he still living?"

GENESIS 43:26–27

Joseph

The sun rose toward midday slower than ever before. Joseph
drummed his fingers on the arm of his chair. Counted each grain
voucher written. He was anxious to close the booth, feast with his
brothers, and finally speak to Benjamin. Ben had been Ephraim's
age when Joseph last saw him. Today, the brothers stood like shields
around him, blocking Joseph's view.

At the banquet, Joseph planned to separate them from Benjamin. He would give the scheming brothers five years of grain and
exile them to Canaan. They'd have no need to return. Joseph would
then send a contingent of Medjays to retrieve Abba so he could live
in Avaris near Benjamin. Or was Elohim's promised land more
important to Jacob than Rachel's sons? Abraham's promise soaked
into Joseph like the dampness of a misty morning. *All the land that*

you see I will give to you and your offspring forever . . . walk through the length and breadth of it. Perhaps Joseph's inability to forgive was Elohim's way of ensuring the covenant bearers remained in Canaan. Then he scoffed at his poor justification.

"Is my family's hunger funny to you, my lord?" The supplicant appeared on the verge of panic.

"No! Of course not." Joseph regained focus. "You shall have a bag of grain per member of your family."

Hami announced to the crowd, "That's all for today. The vizier will reopen the booth for more grain sales tomorrow." The petitioners had grown increasingly aggressive as the famine worsened. Their groans turned to jeers and menacing threats. Four Medjays surrounded Joseph as Hami extended his hand toward the villa's grand staircase. "I believe your guests are waiting, Lord Vizier."

Joseph motioned for his interpreter to follow and turned to Hami, keeping his voice low. "Have you received word from Maahir? Is everything prepared *exactly* as I commanded?"

"No word. But I'm sure Maahir did as you asked. Though if you intend to remain anonymous, why seat your guests in order of birth and show preference to your youngest brother?"

"I'm sending subtle messages." Joseph took the steps two at a time to avoid further probing.

Hami caught Joseph's arm at the top of the stairway and motioned the interpreter to continue into the banquet. The young man bowed and left them alone.

Although they were alone, Hami still whispered, "The young one, Benjamin, looks like you and has your charm. Three women traded silver to get closer to him in the grain line."

Joseph laughed. "We'll find a nice Egyptian wife for him—like Asenath." They both sobered at the mention of her name.

"He would be fortunate to find such a woman. Did you invite her to the banquet?"

Joseph shook his head. "I don't want them to hurt her. I need you—and Asenath—to trust me."

He left his captain and strode toward the laughter and happy sounds in his banquet hall. When he reached the threshold, he felt like he'd hit a mudbrick wall. Instead of a small gathering of just his brothers, every attendant in his household was there—including Asenath. His wife and brothers sat on an elevated platform in front, Asenath alone and the Hebrews at a second table. The rest were seated in the large courtroom, reclining at tables placed in neat rows on opposite sides of a center aisle.

Maahir stood watch on the dais, continually scanning the room. His eyes met Joseph's, his countenance turning ashen, guilty as a child caught stealing. Asenath turned toward the old steward and followed his gaze. Rather than seeming surprised or guilty, she waved when she spotted Joseph. Perched on her favorite embroidered pillow, she patted Joseph's empty cushion beside her.

Turning slowly to his captain, he asked, "Were you aware Maahir and my wife had invited so many witnesses to this banquet?"

"Is that what they've done?" His brows lifted slightly. "I thought they invited your faithful attendants to feast with your honored guests—producers of the famed speckled and spotted wool from Canaan." With the subtle reminder to be cautious, he again extended his hand toward the feast.

With a deep breath, Joseph stepped into the room, knowing he need simply win Benjamin's favor and then he would send the others on their way at dawn—before anyone at the palace realized who they were.

The merriment around him faded. Every eye followed him up the center aisle. Trying to soothe the obvious tension, he affixed a smile and nodded to his scribes, secretaries, overseers, keepers, and heralds. He stole glances at his wife as he ascended the dais steps and paused between the two tables. He turned to his honored guests, speaking through his interpreter. "I see my steward has made you welcome—" He nearly choked at the sight of Simeon. Jaw clenched, he said, "Who released—"

"My lord, we bring gifts," one of them said.

"Many gifts," added another. All eleven scrambled to gather nearby baskets, bags, and pouches, then skidded to their knees at Joseph's feet.

"Balm. Honey. Spices. Myrrh. Pistachios. Almonds." They all spoke at once. The interpreter tried to keep up, but it was impossible to translate while they shoved their parcels at his feet and then prostrated themselves, faces on the bare tile.

Like spokes in a wheel, his brothers lay around him, the aroma of myrrh filling the room. Joseph's throat tightened. *The sheafs bow again. Oh, Elohim, I don't want this.* "Rise. Please." He waited as they tentatively rose to their knees. "Tell me, how is your aged abi? Does he still live?"

"Your servant, our abba, lives. He is well." Benjamin's voice was like hearing his own. Joseph met his gaze—and saw Ima Rachel looking back.

"Is this the youngest brother?" Without waiting for affirmation, Joseph cradled Ben's chin. "May God be gracious to you, my son."

The interpreter translated his words—*May El be gracious*—and Joseph gave him a sharp look. But he dared not correct him. El was the correct *Canaanite* god. Yet Joseph would never bless Benjamin in any name but Elohim's.

The dam inside him burst. "Out of my way!" He raced toward the nearby door to the residence hall. Gulping great gasps, he held back tears until he passed the guards at his private chamber. Then, falling to his knees, he rocked and released his turmoil in groans words couldn't define. His chest ached, heart shattering. Benjamin was clearly safe. They protected him. Treasured him. *But I want Ben with me, Elohim! They don't deserve him!*

A gentle hand rested on his shoulder. "I'm here, my love. I'm here." The aroma of lotus and honey surrounded him—Asenath. He leaned into her, sobbing. She guided his head onto her lap, slid his wig off, and twirled his short curls around her finger. "I love you, Joseph ben Jacob."

"I miss us," he whispered. He ached for the way their love used to be, but if the condition of her return to his chamber was his reconciling with his brothers, their love was lost.

Asenath could celebrate with them. She had been willing to read Potiphera's message at On. Ahira, too, was able to freely forgive. *How, Elohim? How do they find strength to forgive, but I can barely look at my brothers?*

The familiar anger roiled inside. He sat up but couldn't face his wife. "Now that Benjamin has arrived, I'll protect him here in Avaris and send for Abba to join us—as you've always wanted." Her silence screamed disapproval. He forced himself to look at her. "I can't let Benjamin return with them. I've missed his whole life. I wouldn't have known him if he'd come to buy grain alone."

"You would have known him. He has your eyes—and your charm. Your other brothers have changed, too. Reuben has four sons. Judah left the family but came back with a new wife and twin sons. Benjamin plans to marry, and Simeon—"

"Stop," he said, refusing her pleading. "They'll hurt us, Asenath. My brothers aren't safe."

"No one is safe. Remember?" A slight wrinkle formed on her brow. "Zahra said that to threaten us when she realized I could hurt her with truth more than Hodari could harm you with lies. But she was right, Joseph. No one is safe. Everyone wounds us somehow, someday. Zahra frantically seeks safety, but you and I rest in calm assurance that Elohim meets us in our pain."

Elohim meets us in our pain. Joseph considered how much more intimately he knew Elohim because of his brothers' betrayals. "If I hadn't been forced to rely on Elohim as a slave and a prisoner—and for wisdom to become a vizier—I wouldn't know Him as I do today."

"If Potabi hadn't been such a manipulator, I wouldn't have been locked in a tower and become the bride of Egypt's new vizier." She tried to smile, but the merriment died in her eyes.

"Did I mention how much I've missed you?"

Her sad smile broke his heart into smaller pieces. "Should we return to your banquet, Lord Vizier?"

"Only if you promise to return to my chamber tonight."

"Perhaps we should discuss it when we don't have a banquet room full of brothers and attendants." She reached for Joseph's hand. "I believe Elohim brought your brothers here to heal your family."

He lifted her hand to his lips. He remembered the emaciated woman he'd found in the tower after Elohim's messenger appeared to her, promising her offspring would share in Abraham's promise. Her faith had grown strong since then. She may not understand Joseph's plan, but she deserved to hear it. "I'm sending all my brothers back to Canaan at dawn with enough grain to sustain them for the last five years of famine. Benjamin will return today—willingly—then we'll send for Abba Jacob."

She removed her hand from his, a dubious look marring her lovely features. "I've spent all morning with your brothers, Joseph. They adore Benjamin, and he loves them deeply. I don't think he'll—"

"You know nothing about my brothers." His defenses rose. "They'll do whatever they must to save themselves."

She lifted a single brow in challenge. "I may have spent barely two ticks on the water clock with the eleven sons of Jacob, but it's more than you've been with them in twenty years. Perhaps after you've spent the afternoon talking with them—and they realize you're not the vicious vizier of Lower Egypt—you'll discover they're men who love their wives and children." She brushed his cheek. "As you love us."

FORTY-SEVEN

*As morning dawned, the men were sent on their
way with their donkeys. They had not gone far
from the city when Joseph said to his steward,
"Go after those men at once."*

GENESIS 44:3–4

NEXT MORNING

Asenath

I lay on my cosmetics couch, too distracted to chat and too nervous
to doze. "Hurry, Esi. I want to say goodbye to Joseph's guests before
they leave this morning." I'd spent another sleepless night in my
private chamber. Though yesterday's banquet seemed pleasant,
Joseph still wasn't willing to discuss his feelings, and I wasn't willing
to compromise mine. Though I understood the danger of revealing
his brothers' presence to those in the palace, why hadn't Joseph
revealed his own identity to his brothers?

All afternoon, my husband had been the consummate host, leading his guests in easy conversation. Attempts at quick wit were awkward through an interpreter, so he watched their banter with feigned
detachment. Had he discerned his brothers' camaraderie? Did he
realize Benjamin deeply loved his older brothers and would never
willingly stay in Egypt without them?

"All done." Esi sat back on her stool and offered me the bronze hand mirror.

"I'm sure I look fine." I darted toward the door while conveying the day's plan. "I've already fed Ephraim, so I'll return to help you prepare for laundry day after bidding farewell to our Canaanite guests. I shouldn't be too long." I flung open the door and found Maahir poised to knock.

"Good morning!" he said, wide-eyed. I chuckled, but his demeanor sobered me. "I must speak with you privately, Mistress."

I stepped into the hall and closed the door behind myself. We walked a short distance away from my guards. "What? Tell me."

"The master has already sent our guests away, but he's instructed me to retrieve them—immediately."

"He wants Ben to stay."

Maahir's brows drew together. "Of course. Before they left, Joseph told me to hide their payment in the grain sacks—"

"As you did last time."

He nodded. "But he also told me to hide his silver wine goblet in Benjamin's pack. Now he wants me to ride after them with a contingent of Medjays and accuse them of stealing the cup he uses for divination."

"Divination? Joseph has never—"

"Of course he hasn't, but he means to ensure they still believe the vizier to be thoroughly Egyptian." He sighed. "Please, Mistress, he's more himself when you're with him. Go to the banquet room and wait for the brothers' return."

"The banquet room? Joseph always sells grain at dawn."

"Not today. He's summoned all those who attended last night's banquet to meet in the villa's courtroom. They're reconciling last year's household records. Today, it's Joseph who wants witnesses."

We'd hoped inviting the villa's attendants to yesterday's banquet would forestall any harsh judgments against Joseph's brothers, but it seemed he'd saved his vengeance for their predawn departure.

"I'll go to the banquet room after I help Esi."

Maahir hurried down the hallway, and I returned to the boys' chamber. Nasseh was whining about his gruel, and Ephraim was fussy. I nursed my toddler again and helped soothe Nasseh with some honey in his gruel. Esi needed me to watch the boys while she gathered the dirty laundry and prepared a basket of snacks for their trip to the river. When I finally dashed out the door, I called over my shoulder, "When you return from the river, prepare the boys again to be presented publicly. Keep them here in the chamber until I send someone."

I raced toward the banquet hall and realized dozens of people were also rushing up the grand staircase and into our villa. Had those waiting for grain heard of the arrest—or simply heard Joseph's raised voice? "What were you thinking?" he shouted. "Don't you know a man like me can learn things through divination?"

I stopped abruptly at the threshold. The lovely banquet space had been transformed into the vizier's courtroom. Our household attendants sat at the same tables, but now they worked with scrolls, reeds, and pigments while the vizier's harsh plan unfolded. Joseph's brothers lay prostrate before a single platform where my husband sat enthroned on his high-backed chair. He was an intimidating figure—even to me.

"Word has reached King Apophis that the vizier hosted thieves last night." Potiphar's low voice jolted me. He stared at the men lying facedown on the floor. "Hebrew thieves. I count eleven, Asenath. Is there something you should tell me?"

"They came for Simeon before the year ended." I gulped audibly.

"Have they requested to stay in Egypt?"

"They still don't recognize Joseph."

"Interesting, but not an answer."

I had no answers to satisfy him.

His eyes felt like daggers making a thousand cuts. "We'd better find out before Apophis makes the wrong assumptions."

"Shouldn't we all be asking what *Elohim* wants?" I whispered, then strode up the center aisle, determined that Joseph would see me before rendering judgment.

My breath caught when one of the brothers struggled to his knees. *Judah.*

"What can we say, my lord?" He wept and tore his robe.

I ascended the dais, nodded at Hami, then leaned over to kiss Joseph's cheek. "Please don't do this," I whispered and stood at his right side.

Judah kept pleading, "Please, my lord. Elohim has uncovered our past misdeeds. We will all be your slaves. We'll serve alongside the one found with your cup."

Joseph's silence was excruciating but gave me time to pray. *Elohim, is my husband working with You or against You?*

"You think me an unjust master?" Joseph asked Judah through the interpreter. "I would never enslave innocent men. Only the one found with my goblet will become my slave. The rest of you will go back to your abi in peace."

The brothers released a mournful wail. Judah, Leah's fourth-born, ascended the first step of the dais. Hami moved to defend, but Joseph motioned him away, allowing Judah to proceed to his throne.

Judah knelt and kissed the vizier's jeweled sandals. "Though you are equal to Pharaoh himself and I have no right to speak in your presence, may I tell you our plight and beg for your mercy?"

Joseph gripped the arms of his chair. The knob in his throat bobbed up and down—once, twice, three times. He was struggling for control.

Judah must have interpreted his silence as consent. "When my lord asked his servants if we had an abba or a brother, we answered truthfully and even told you our youngest brother was the only one of his ima's sons left—and that our abba loved him. When you insisted we bring Benjamin to prove our honesty and free our brother Simeon, our abba couldn't bear it. He refused at first. But when we needed more grain, he commanded us to return to Egypt with gifts and extra silver. I vowed to be personally responsible for Benjamin's life."

Joseph's soft gasp registered his surprise before the Egyptian translation was complete.

Judah paused, searching the vizier's features. Had he felt a spark of recognition? He continued with a stronger voice, "Our abba reminded us—as he does every day—that his beloved wife bore him only two sons. He's never stopped grieving his favorite son, who was torn to pieces. So, if he loses Benjamin, his gray head will go to the grave in misery. Abba's life is so bound together with Benjamin's that he can't—he won't—live without the boy, my lord. I will personally bear the blame all my life. Please, Lord Vizier, please." Tears pooled in his eyes. "Please, let me remain as your servant in the boy's place so Benjamin can return to our abba. To see my abba's misery would be worse than slavery or death for me. My life for Benjamin's, my lord. Please." He covered his face, broken and sobbing.

"Out!" Joseph bolted to his feet. "Everyone, get out!" With his back to the crowd, he whispered desperately to me, "Make everyone leave except . . . the Hebrews."

Judah and his brothers had scurried to their feet. Medjays surrounded them.

"Leave the Canaanites," I said to Hami, "and take everyone else into the hallway—including your Medjays and the soldiers."

"I take orders from Lord Pancah—"

"They are Paneah's orders!"

After another glance at Joseph, Hami commanded his Medjays to clear the room. Potiphar remained at the doorway, his expression unreadable.

Two more observers lingered in the rear of the room long enough to meet my eyes—Zahra and the high priest of Shedet in his crocodile headdress. The priest held a baby monkey in his hands that looked exactly like Jendayi. Had he come for the akhet festival? But why this year when he'd proven himself a zealot years ago? He lifted the baby monkey as if making a toast with a wine goblet. Then he and Zahra followed the crowd out of the room, Zahra turning long enough to laugh at me.

I felt the blood drain from my face. Was Zahra connected somehow to the priest? To the zealots? What lies would they spin at the palace from the scene they'd just witnessed? Even if they didn't know our Canaanite guests were Joseph's brothers, they could fashion Egypt's fears into a lethal weapon against my husband.

Elohim, what do I do?

Heal Egypt. The words came as clear as if someone shouted them.

But what did they mean? I glanced at the eleven terrified men awaiting an uncertain fate and then whispered to my husband, "I'm leaving, too." He looked startled. "Elohim will give you words." I kissed his cheek and hurried down the center aisle.

Potiphar and Hami stood at the door of our empty courtroom. Hami asked as I rushed past, "Where are you going?"

"To find out why the high priest of Shedet brought a monkey to Avaris." I paused at the top of our grand stairway to scan the crowded palace complex below. The crocodile-headed priest was easy to spot, and Zahra had just caught up with him. They were hurrying in the direction of Hodari's villa.

FORTY-EIGHT

There was no one with Joseph when he made
himself known to his brothers. And he wept so
loudly that the Egyptians heard him, and
Pharaoh's household heard about it.

GENESIS 45:1–2

Joseph

Until everyone, including the interpreter, left the courtroom, Joseph kept his back turned to his brothers. The double cedar doors slammed shut, and he flinched. It was time. *Elohim, break them as You've broken me.* Overcome, he released a sob and reached for the cloth in his belt. He pressed his face against the fine linen, wailing. Tears soaked the cloth. He wiped away the kohl and malachite from his eyes, the crushed carmine from his cheeks. He grabbed the wig off his head and tossed it aside. Trying to quell a new wave of tears, he pressed the heels of his hands against both eyes. He gasped.

Then he whirled on the brothers, shouting in Hebrew, "I. Am. Joseph! Your brother!"

Eleven terrified men stepped back. Stricken with horror but no recognition.

He rushed at them. "Tell me truthfully—is Abba Jacob still living?" Trembling from head to toe, he waited for their answer.

None spoke, but one by one recognition dawned. A mosaic of emotion swept their faces. Sheer horror marred Reuben's features. Simeon, normally ready for battle, appeared shaken and unsure. Judah wept, his softened heart wrung out like a filthy rag. Behind them stood Ima Leah's other three sons: Levi, Issachar, Zebulun. And the slave wives' sons—Dan, Naphtali, Gad, and Asher— provided rear guard, always in their brothers' shadows. Benjamin stared at Joseph, awestruck, protected at the center. Their treasure.

As Joseph studied them, his weeping subsided. "Come close to me. Please," he said, feet planted. "I won't harm you."

His brothers exchanged glances. Silent pleas. *Are we doomed? Will Joseph hand us over to Pharaoh for what we did to him?* Joseph read it in their expressions, glimpsed it through the windows of their souls. They had no idea Maahir feared more for Joseph's safety than theirs. As Pharaoh's vizier, he'd need to quickly report his family's arrival and future plans before gossips spread irreparable lies.

Joseph knelt before the men who had betrayed him, capturing their attention immediately.

"Sit down," he commanded, and every one of them was quick to obey. "Don't be distressed or angry with yourselves about selling me to Egypt. Look what Elohim has done." He motioned toward the fine tapestries, the Persian pottery, and his high-backed chair and then refocused on the men who'd sold him like unwanted goods. "I came to Egypt as a slave and spent years in a prison, falsely accused. But Elohim delivered me so I could show His great power to Egypt. It wasn't you who sent me here, but God. He made me like an abba to pharaohs, rulers of all Egypt. It was to save lives that God sent me ahead of you. So, then, I want you to return to Hebron, gather your families, and bring Abba back to Egypt."

They couldn't have appeared more shocked if he'd asked them to dance naked before Pharaoh.

They leaned into a huddle, and Joseph heard coarse whispers but no clear words. Reuben was first to return his attention to Joseph, but he yielded spokesman duty to Judah. "You've made a kind and generous offer, Lord Vizier, but—"

"I'll provide for you," Joseph said, realizing they planned to refuse him. "Otherwise, you and your families will become destitute. There are five more years of famine to come! Do you understand?"

They bowed their heads. That's when he noticed their trembling hands and whole bodies shaking. They were still afraid of him.

Elohim, give them courage, and soften my heart. Only Benjamin met his eyes. Joseph offered a tentative smile and spoke to the group. "You can all see that I'm your brother, and Benjamin knows it's Ima Rachel's firstborn speaking to him." The young man met his smile with a nod. Encouraged, Joseph continued, "It will be difficult to return to camp and confess to Abba that I'm alive in Egypt—but you must. Tell him of the honor bestowed on me here and how Elohim has used this hardship to bring life to many. Then bring Abba with your children, your grandchildren, your flocks and herds—all that you have."

He'd barely finished when Benjamin rushed toward him, skidding to his knees in front of Joseph. "I couldn't remember what you looked like."

"We both look like Ima Rachel." Joseph threw his arms around his brother, and they wept.

FORTY-NINE

There are six things the LORD hates,
seven that are detestable to him:
  haughty eyes,
  a lying tongue,
  hands that shed innocent blood,
  a heart that devises wicked schemes,
  feet that are quick to rush into evil,
  a false witness who pours out lies
  and a person who stirs up conflict in the community.
PROVERBS 6:16–19

Asenath

I lingered behind a pillar at the top of our villa stairs, watching She-det's priest and Zahra weave through the teeming crowd in the palace complex, past the central fountain where children received free bags of grain in hopes of soothing their parents' second-year-of-famine concerns. When last year's akhet festival was canceled, the nation's morale plummeted. This year, the pharaohs agreed to celebrate an amended festival that focused on the plentiful grain stores rather than the waning Nile.

I hurried down the stairs, shouldered through the people, skirted the public pond, and raced after the bobbing crocodile headdress.

We knew the crocodile priest was a zealot—had Zahra joined his cause?

She seemed to be leading him toward the second grand villa in the complex. *Why would she take him to Hodari's home instead of to the celebration at the palace?* I scampered behind a withered acacia tree and peered around its slender trunk, watching as Zahra and the priest approached Hodari's villa entrance.

The priest handed the monkey to Zahra, who introduced the little guenon to the guards. She chatted casually—her previous inhibitions with men vanquished. After the brief exchange, the guards opened the door and let them enter.

So many questions roiled inside me. Uppermost was the burgeoning fear of conspiracy since Hodari and Zahra had threatened harm against Joseph in the past. With a fortifying breath, I marched toward the villa's guards.

"Mistress Asenath." Both Medjays bowed. Joseph's position ruined any hope of anonymity.

"I hadn't realized Highness contacted you yet," one man said.

Why would the high priest plan to contact me? I forced a smile. "I'm anxious to see Highness." But what I really wanted was to run back to my villa. "Which chamber is he in?"

The second man opened the door. "Go through the banquet room and down the residence hall. The guards will direct you from there."

"Thank you." Inside, my steps echoed across the empty banquet room. Faded wall reliefs spoke of its former grandeur. I silenced the gossip I'd heard about Potiphar's wife, the woman who had painted them, and moved aside a tattered tapestry to enter a long residence hallway.

Two guards stood twenty paces ahead beside ornately carved double cedar doors, likely belonging to the master of the villa. They looked my way.

"I'm looking for—"

"Last chamber on your right," one of them said.

I inclined my head and strode past them. The hall jogged left, becoming a long hallway with doors on both sides. Four guards waited beside the last two doors. My heart thudded so loudly I was certain they could hear it.

"Mistress Asenath, welcome," one guard announced when I was still five paces away. He tapped his spear head on the door. "Highness, your daughter has arrived."

Your daughter?

"Asenath?" The door flung open, and Potabi's arms opened just as wide.

I stood like a statue at the threshold, gaping.

"Come in, my girl! Amun-Ra brought you at exactly the right moment." He pulled me into the chamber and closed the door.

Zahra stood beside Shedet's priest, both wearing infuriating smirks. I ignored them and turned my ire on Potabi. "Why are you in Hodari's villa, and why were Zahra and the high priest in my villa this morning?"

His eyes widened, patronizing me. "My friend Shu brought you a gift." He motioned toward the monkey in Zahra's hands.

"No." Zahra clutched the monkey tighter and turned away. "She's already bonded with me."

Potabi shot Zahra an angry glare. "Today, you get a husband, and Asenath loses hers. Give her the monkey."

I staggered back. "What?"

Before Potabi could answer, Shu, the crocodile-headed priest, loomed over me. "Who were those Hebrews in your villa? Are they part of the vizier's Bedouin family? Is your Hyksos husband plotting to take land in Egypt as his ancestors did in Canaan? Has no one informed Apophis of Paneah's treason?"

"Is that why you've come to Avaris? Because you believed Potabi's lies? My husband is more loyal to Egypt than Potabi ever was."

I held my breath as the priest studied me, his face turning a deep crimson. After a few moments, instead of the intensifying inquest I expected, the priest turned his fury on Potabi. "Your daughter thinks your suspicions about her husband are unfounded, and I wonder if she's right."

Potabi looked as if he'd been stabbed. "What—"

"My spies tell me Pharaoh Nebiriraw refused to send troops to support today's coup."

"We must *do* something," Potabi gritted out between clenched teeth. "A *Hyksos* controls the lifeblood of the Two Lands. Paneah will continue to dictate grain distribution to pure-blooded Egyptians for the next five years unless we stop him! When we take the first step, Pharaoh Nebiriraw will join our triumph and unite the Two Lands from his throne in Thebes. We must—"

"There is no *we*, Potiphera!" Highness Shu scoffed. "I came to Avaris hoping you'd somehow coaxed Apophis to the zealot cause. Then I heard the vizier was entertaining Hebrews instead of celebrating at the palace, and I thought the gods might have smiled on us." With a disgusted sigh, he removed his headdress and tossed it on the nearest couch. "But you have no coup. No Nebiriraw. No Apophis. And after hearing your rant, it's clear. Your true goal isn't to unite Egypt but to gain revenge on your son-in-law—at any cost."

Potabi responded with silence, clenching and unclenching his fists, while his face flushed the color of ripe grapes.

I saw my chance to destroy this dangerous alliance. "Highness Shu, I haven't seen or corresponded with my abi in years, but you're right. His hatred for my husband has clouded his judgment."

"Asenath!" Potabi shouted.

Shu lifted his hand, silencing Potabi, a mere wab priest. "I also made the long trip to Avaris to visit you, Mistress Asenath." He lifted the monkey from Zahra's arms. "I arrived last week with this orphaned monkey as an excuse to win your favor. I'd planned to make it a gift to you at the akhet festival—whether Potiphera's coup had merit or not. Isn't this little guenon a benevolent beginning to a friendship with the vizier's wife? Together, you and I could expand my network of zealots in Avaris."

Did he think himself indestructible? I tamped down revulsion and whispered, "Leave Avaris. Now."

A slow grin curved his lips. "Gladly."

"No, wait!" Potabi lunged toward him as Shu reached for his headdress.

But the high priest shrugged him off and stared down at the shorter man. "You need never contact me again, Potiphera. Your so-called plans are fanciful delusions, no longer rooted in reality." He strode toward the chamber door and met Hodari on his way out. "Goodbye, Captain. Thank you for your hospitality."

"Highness Shu?" Hodari's brows crumpled. "I thought—"

Shedet's high priest continued down the hallway without pause or explanation, leaving Hodari's features scarred with confusion—then outright shock when he turned and saw me. He recovered almost immediately, assuming the cool captain-of-the-guard façade. He placed a full wineskin on the table near the door and turned to Potabi. "It was my understanding that we wouldn't involve Mistress Asenath until later today."

"Paneah's brothers have returned," Potabi told the captain—though I hadn't confirmed his assumptions. "And Asenath's premature arrival strengthens our plan. I was about to tell her how she would help us heal Egypt today." Looking to me, he produced a small pouch from his belt. "Hodari will use a small amount of the hemlock inside this bag. He'll put it in the wine you deliver to Pharaoh Yanassi on behalf of Paneah—a gift from his homeland in Canaan."

"No!" I bolted toward the door, but a large arm grabbed my waist. I landed hard on the tiles, shocked but unharmed.

Hodari stood over me, hand on his dagger hilt. "I told you she wouldn't do it."

"Soldiers use violence to encourage change." Potabi offered his hand to help me up. "But the priestess simply needs persuasion."

I slapped away his help and stood alone.

Potabi ambled toward Zahra, placed his arm around her shoulder, and led her toward the gathering area. "Let's sit down while I explain all the ways our lives will become better when I am obeyed." His tone was as chillingly familiar as his words.

Hodari moved in front of the door, blocking any chance of exit, so I followed Potabi and Zahra. I hated the memories his measured tone conjured—all the past conversations that started so calmly but ended with veiled threats and my compliance.

"Zahra will return to the vizier's villa," Potabi began, "with a written message from Asenath giving her permission to take my grandsons to the palace for a day of playtime with Queen Tani and Mistress Pushpa. Zahra will instead bring the boys to this chamber until you complete the simple tasks I ask of you, Daughter."

Zahra's breath caught. "You never mentioned involving Nasseh and Ephraim."

I scoffed. "Have you forgotten, Zahra? Potabi often omits details that might pique conscience. I've learned to expect the worst from him, and I'm never disappointed."

"Your sons will be safe in this chamber with Zahra as long as you obey me."

Obey me. It's what he'd required my whole life. Blind, unopposed compliance. But the familiar surrender now battled an ommi's protectiveness. If I confessed the truth about Joseph's brothers, would it distract Potabi? Maybe entice him to a new plan that would give me more time to alert help? Would he discover the truth anyway—and harm my sons?

I swallowed my emotions and began, "How can you threaten your own grandsons?"

"Are you referring to the boy named Masa-harota?" he asked with a sneer. "The one you renamed *forget me*? Or the other child, Ephraim, whom I've only glimpsed from a distance? I don't know them as my grandsons yet, but after today they'll be mine to raise as I please."

I ground out in desperation, "You can't have them."

"If you do exactly as I say, you may live to see them become priests of Amun-Ra." He leaned forward, piercing me with his stare. "By the end of this day, Paneah will be dead, and if you disobey me, I'll ensure the vicious Ammut greets you in the underworld, too."

His threats of monsters and nightmares no longer frightened me, but the thought of my sons worshipping his lies was terrifying.

"What must I do?"

"Tell me plainly. Are the Hebrews Joseph's brothers?"

"Yes."

His satisfied smile made me nauseous. "You will offer a cup of wine to both Pharaoh Yanassi and King Apophis as a gift from Vizier Paneah—wine from his family's vineyard in Canaan."

"Apophis, too?" I swallowed hard. "But I thought he—"

"In the beginning, I was loyal to Apophis. Now he deserves to suffer for making me a wab priest at On's temple. Pharaoh Nebiriraw is a warrior king. He'll unite the Two Lands and make my friend Shu the new high priest of Amun-Ra—though I'm not sure he deserves the honor after his disrespect. I'll receive amnesty from Nebiriraw and make the Faiyum my home, honored at Gurob Palace as Amun-Ra's most sacred servant on earth."

Shu was right. Potabi was deluded. Pharaoh Nebiriraw would never honor a man who had killed two pharaohs.

"That wasn't our plan," Hodari growled. "Taking the children was supposed to bring *both* Asenath and Paneah to the villa. How do we now connect the vizier to the poisoned wine?"

Potabi looked over his shoulder. "Leave the planning to me. I'm giving you Zahra and a way to be rid of Potiphar."

"Not Potiphar, please." I glanced from one evil man to the other. "He's done nothing—"

"He takes everything." Hodari spat the words. "He guards a true king, and I guard a spoiled Hyksos. He has a family yet denied me a wife." He turned to Zahra. "Come, I'll escort you to get the vizier's children."

Elohim, give me strength! "No, please! Don't force me to help you kill innocent men."

"Innocent?" Potabi choked on a laugh. "I will finally have revenge on the Hebrew who ruined my daughter's life."

"Joseph didn't ruin my life, Potabi. He *gave* me a life."

"He stole you from me! And that, my dear girl, ruined your life *and* your destiny."

His rage silenced me, as it had for years. He could never understand the fuller purpose I'd been given through Elohim's promise.

"By sunset, two pharaohs and one captain will be dead," he continued. "If you help me, you'll be exonerated as a pawn in Paneah's conspiracy. If you refuse me, both you and your husband will be executed as masterminds behind this elegant plot in which even his brothers are murdered."

"His brothers? Why would you harm them?"

"I will take everything Paneah holds dear. When his brothers hear of Paneah's arrest, I'll send tainted wine to the vizier's villa. We'll make sure Paneah knows they drowned their sorrows and joined the others in the grave before his execution. I'll testify to Paneah's longtime hatred of his kinsmen and the likelihood that he exacted his vengeance for their twenty-year-old betrayal. My unexpected arrival in Avaris will seem ordained by almighty Amun-Ra. I'll be the lowly wab priest who came for a spontaneous visit with my daughter and grandsons and—through Amun-Ra's providence and favor—protected you in Hodari's villa from Paneah's murderous rampage." He chuckled, pleased with himself. "And you, my daughter, will once again belong to me completely—as will your sons."

I was shocked. Horrified. He hadn't even bothered to veil his threats this time. "Why not let the brothers return to Canaan? They're no threat—"

"And reject Amun-Ra's gift?" he shouted. "The great god has made my revenge even sweeter by robbing Paneah of his brothers on the day they're reunited."

Stunned by the absolute evil before me, I let despair force the question from my lips. "How will you treat my sons, knowing Paneah's Hebrew blood flows through their veins?" Though terrified, I needed to know his answer.

"I would never harm my grandsons, Asenath." He lifted one brow. "Unless, of course, you or they force me to do so."

I covered a sob, barely maintaining control.

"I'm willing to train the Hebrew out of them," he continued. "If they refuse, I'd be forced to start fresh with new grandchildren, but I'm proficient at finding strong Egyptian husbands for my girls. Look at Hotep—and Zahra will soon wed an honorable Medjay." His eyes widened with a little gasp. "I could keep you alive and offer you to Nebiriraw as a peace offering. He could take you into his harem. You seemed at home in Thebes."

I remained silent, squeezing my eyes shut as I'd done when Zahra, Hotep, and I were children and Potabi asked us to clean waste pots or fast from favorite foods. Today, there were no requests. Only demands. But the same realization came.

I was his prisoner and had no choice but to obey.

FIFTY

He rescues me unharmed
from the battle waged against me,
even though many oppose me.

PSALM 55:18

Asenath

I stood at the back of the crowded throne room, Potabi at my left, living a nightmare. The silver pitcher in my hands held Canaan's finest wine, regarded as nectar from the gods by most Egyptians. Today, it was a weapon of death. Hodari would slip hemlock into the young pharaoh's goblet *after* his cupbearer had tasted and approved it. When the poison began its work, King Apophis and Potiphar would undoubtedly focus their concern on Yanassi. Hodari would move quickly, stealthily, to end the distracted king and his captain.

"Deep breaths, Nathy," Potabi whispered. "You're shaking."

"It will never work," I whispered. "Hodari can't best two trained soldiers."

"He'll have my help. I'm not trained, but I'm determined." Potabi pulled aside an ornately embroidered vestment at his waist, revealing a glimpse of a dagger's hilt.

"You'll never make it out of this throne room alive."

"I won't intervene unless I can appear the hero."

There was no logical scenario in which he could be the hero. "Potabi, we could simply offer the wine as a gift. Don't—"

His head turned sharply. "If I meet Anubis today, promise you'll provide for my afterlife."

"Anubis is a lie."

"Mistress Asenath." Pharaoh Yanassi's voice stole my attention. "It's a pleasure to see you. Come forward." Now a handsome seventeen-year-old, his bright smile pierced me. I exhaled a shuddering breath as Potabi and I started up the center aisle.

Memories of eight-year-old Yanassi at my wedding flashed through my mind. He'd wished to marry me himself. Queen Tani had been appalled. How could I serve the wine in my pitcher to that darling boy? My steps faltered, giving me an idea. I purposely stubbed my toe on the crimson carpet, lofting the tray and pitcher into the air as I stumbled forward.

The next moments seemed to happen in one slow motion after another. Onlookers inhaled a collective gasp as the silver vessel tipped slightly in the air. Potabi lunged with catlike quickness, grasping the pitcher, allowing the tray to clatter on the floor. The horrendous racket ended the suspension of time, awakening me to Potabi's lethal glare.

"Well done, Potiphera!" King Apophis chuckled. "I see you're still a master at forestalling disaster."

The throne room filled with laughter. Yanassi whispered something to his uncle. The two kings chuckled.

"He's mocked me for the last time," Potabi hissed. He shoved the pitcher into my hands, and we resumed our march. I was barely ten paces from the dais now, and my breaths came in short, quick gasps. How could I do this? I couldn't watch these men die. I couldn't help *kill* them!

"Think of your sons, Asenath," Potabi whispered. "If I nod to Hodari, you'll never see them again."

I looked up at Yanassi's captain and saw him focused on Potabi, waiting for a signal to take away my children—or worse. Refocusing on the kings, I forced my lips into a smile but couldn't stop their quaking.

Elohim, help me! What else can I do?

Was there anyone on the dais who could help me? Scribes, two cupbearers, the kings, and—Potiphar. He held my gaze. I blinked rapidly, as if fighting tears, hoping he'd notice something amiss. When his brows drew together and he cocked his head, I knew he'd perceived my distress. What if he drew attention to my angst? What if Hodari signaled someone to harm my boys? *Elohim, please! What do I do?*

Speak truth. The words came like a gentle breeze, leaving calm in their wake.

Potabi and I halted at the edge of the carpet. Potabi bowed, while I carefully crafted words. "I offer wine from Canaan with the blessing of my abi, whom you both know well."

"Wine from Canaan?" Yanassi's brows arched. "Paneah's homeland."

"Is the gift from Paneah or Potiphera?" Apophis asked, suspicion in his tone.

"The gift is from *Canaan*." I hoped my evasive answer would alert Potiphar. "As my kings may have heard, Paneah's brothers came from Canaan to buy grain."

"We've heard Zaphenath-Paneah cleared his courtroom to speak with them privately and then wept so loudly, he was heard by those returning to the grain booths."

"Yes, he . . ." *Speak truth.* "I also had a reunion of sorts when I discovered Potabi had returned to Avaris. He convinced me to leave Joseph with his brothers and deliver the wine myself."

"So the wine is a gift from Potiphera?" Apophis asked again.

"Does it matter?" Yanassi waved his cupbearer down the dais stairs. "If Paneah's brothers brought it from Canaan, I'm sure it's the finest in the land."

"Perhaps." Apophis's gaze lingered but gave way to a smile as he reclined on his throne. "After the cupbearers taste the wine, we'll celebrate Paneah's family reunion."

Potabi stepped aside as both royal tasters approached me with the kings' empty wine goblets. I poured each cup half full and watched as the tasters swirled it, sniffed it, and drank two gulps. They motioned to the timekeeper, who emptied a small cup of water into the royal clock.

Anyone could have counted to sixty, but it was more impressive to see the water drain from the official timepiece. Every eye focused on the cupbearers. The water level dropped quickly past each line on the bronze container at precisely the speed royal physicians had determined poison would begin its work. When the container emptied and both tasters remained unaffected, the audience cheered.

"Let's have some wine!" Yanassi shouted.

Hands trembling, I filled both goblets to the rim, hoping to dilute the hemlock Hodari added. The cupbearers returned to offer the wine to their pharaohs.

Had I not known Hodari sprinkled a small portion of poison into Yanassi's wine, I would never have noticed how slowly he passed the goblet to the young pharaoh. The kings raised their goblets and saluted the crowd.

"Wait!" Potiphar grasped Apophis's wrist, which startled both rulers and stopped them from drinking. "Forgive me," the older captain said, turning toward me. "Perhaps it's the paranoia of rooting out so many conspiracies, Mistress Asenath, but I'm still unclear as to the reasons Lord Paneah wouldn't bring the wine himself." He motioned toward someone behind us.

I turned and found Hami slicing through the crowd toward me. In a terrifying moment, I saw Hami's composure shatter. With a warrior's thrust, he shoved me aside and lunged toward the thrones. My body skidded across the floor. My head was on fire—throbbing pain. The throne room exploded into chaos. I heard a heartrending screech. A stampede raced to escape. I crawled toward the dais and pressed my back against it to avoid being trampled.

Metal clanged above me. Behind me. Shouts. Screams of men in pain. I hid my face. Covered my head. *Elohim, protect good men.* Panting. Praying. I whined in barely controlled panic.

Men shouted. Controlled urgency.

"Noooo!" An unmistakable death cry rent the air. "Yanassi, no!" Apophis sobbed. "Someone call a physician!"

Dread forced me upright, and a horrifyingly familiar sight lay before me. Bloodstained floor and bodies. I was instantly back in Memphis, emerging from beneath a temple altar. But this time I knew all the bodies that lay dead or wounded around me.

"Where is the physician?" With bloodied hands, Apophis clutched Yanassi to his chest, rocking.

Potiphar braced himself against the throne. "A physician won't help, my king. Your nephew is gone." A serious gash in Potiphar's side drained blood like an open wineskin.

Yanassi's death meant Hodari had grown impatient and used his dagger. I'd diluted the poison, but I still hadn't saved Yanassi's life— but neither had I caused it. The traitorous captain lay dead between two thrones, and Potabi lay facing his fellow conspirator, blood pooling around him.

I heard death's rattle in his chest and hurried up the steps. Leaning over him, I saw his color waning as his life spilled out. "Isis, my girl, your destiny . . . heal Egypt." He gasped for each breath. "You. Are. Isis. Incarnate."

I shook my head, refusing his final manipulation. "Only Elohim can heal."

His eyes widened into a distant stare. His ka left. The finality of it left me gasping. Sobbing. Death and pain all around me—again.

"Asenath, are you all right?" Potiphar leaned over me—and then stumbled. His eyes rolled back, and he collapsed.

"Potiphar!" I crawled toward him, but strong hands pulled me away.

Hami circled my waist and helped me stand. "You must answer to King Apophis, Mistress. Come."

We stood before Apophis, who still cradled Yanassi's body.

"How could you let Potiphera manipulate you?" His face hardened with tortured control.

"I had no choice, my king."

"Everyone has a choice!" he shouted.

I bowed my head and noticed my bloody hands. Potabi's blood. His madness had injured me for much of my life and, now, taken him from me. I had lost as much as anyone in this throne room. Lifting my head, I met the king's pain with my own. "Had I not complied, Hodari would have given a single nod to someone in your court, and my children would have been killed."

Apophis was on his feet, dagger drawn. "Who else?" he shouted. Every Medjay in the room stilled, his stony expression fixed on me.

"I don't know, my king, but some of the Medjays at Hodari's villa knew of the plan. Zahra is holding my sons captive under their protection."

"My wife's maid is involved?"

"She is, but Potabi controlled her whole life. He's the one to blame."

"I decide who's to blame." King Apophis looked down at the lifeless young man in his arms. "We'll discover who was waiting for Hodari's signal. Hodari's and Potiphera's punishment has only begun. They'll spend eternity wandering, as will everyone involved in this atrocity." He kissed Yanassi's forehead, then lifted his voice to address the guards still in the room. "I will now be called Pharaoh *Aqenenre*—Ra's great strength. Were it not for my god's great strength working through you, I would not have survived this slaughter. And only by Ra's great wisdom will I discover the measure of deception in my kingdom."

Potiphar groaned as two Medjays carried him away. *Elohim. Please let him be all right.*

"Asenath!" The king regained my focus. "Tell me what you know of the plot."

Shaking violently, I said, "Potabi planned to kill both you and Yanassi. Hodari and Zahra agreed to help because they were angry that Pharaoh Yanassi hadn't allowed them to marry. They meant to kill Potiphar because of his recommendation in the matter, but also because Potabi promised Hodari he'd become Pharaoh Nebiriraw's captain when both you and Yanassi were dead."

"Pharaoh Nebiriraw is involved?" Apophis's voice thundered in the near-empty hall.

"No, my king. Nebiriraw recognized Potabi's madness and refused to support the coup."

"Are there others?"

"Shedet's high priest leads a significant zealot population in the Faiyum, but even he realized Potabi's plans were futile and left early this morning." I summoned every drop of courage I possessed. "Since my ommi's death in Memphis, Potabi has wanted a united Egypt under a full-blooded Egyptian king."

Apophis sat hard on his throne. "The reason he was so adamant that you and I marry."

"Yes, my king. Potabi's hatred for the so-called Hyksos—forgive me, my king—focused on my husband and turned to madness. Today, he forced me to offer wine from Canaan in hopes that you would deem Paneah the mastermind and execute him as a traitor."

"My king!" A Medjay stood beside Potabi's body, holding a bloodstained papyrus scroll. "I found this tucked in the priest's belt."

Apophis motioned for a guard from his royal contingent to place a pillow on the dais. He reverently laid Yanassi's head on it before taking the message and reading it silently. With a weary sigh, he looked up and handed me the papyrus. "Potiphera confirms his madness from the underworld."

It read simply: *To the honorable and mighty Pharaoh Nebiriraw—should I die in my efforts to unite Egypt under your reign, I leave you this written request that you would take my daughter, Asenath—Isis Incarnate—into your harem and train my grandsons as priests of Amun-Ra.*

I squeezed my eyes shut as a shiver slithered down my spine. "Will you please send someone to rescue my sons?"

"May I go, my king?" Hami asked.

Apophis studied him. "Why aren't you with Paneah?"

"Lord Paneah ordered me to leave his presence at the same time Mistress Asenath left the villa." It was true but guarded truth.

"Please," I begged the king. "My boys know Hami. They might be frightened if anyone else barges in."

"Go," the king said. Hami dashed away with four Medjays accompanying him.

Apophis stared at me. "I still have many questions, Mistress Asenath."

My eyes wandered to the precious young king lying on the dais, not far from the two conspirators. "There are no answers that can dull this kind of pain." My chest ached with grief for Apophis and Queen Tani. "And nothing can absolve me, no matter how unwilling my part in it."

FIFTY-ONE

*Then [Joseph] threw his arms around his brother
Benjamin and wept, and Benjamin embraced
him, weeping. And he kissed all his brothers and
wept over them. Afterward his brothers talked
with him.*

GENESIS 45:14–15

Joseph

Eleven burly shepherds reclined around a table, telling stories of
their childhood as though Joseph had never been ostracized or left
Canaan in chains. He studied each face. Reuben, the oldest, was now
a grandfather. Simeon, whom Joseph had believed beyond redemption, bore an almost eerie meekness. He credited his solitary imprisonment and a morning spent with Asenath for his renewed
appreciation for family. Levi, whose name meant *attached,* had
somehow *de*tached from Simeon's poor influence and become his
own man. Judah displayed a strength of character far above any of
the others. He'd offered his life in exchange for Benjamin's. He would
never have done that for either of Rachel's sons twenty years ago.

Joseph glanced at his little brother, who sat at his right hand.
Hami had been right. The well-muscled young man was handsome.
He bore their ima's striking appearance.

Benjamin caught him staring. "You're the only one with eyes like mine," he said proudly.

Joseph circled the young man's neck, gently wrestling as they might have done for years—if he'd listened to Asenath and reconciled sooner.

Today, the brothers shared wine and bread, joy and sorrow. Conversations, long overdue, flowed like a river cleared of debris after years of neglect. And he'd finally convinced them to bring Abba and everything they owned back to Egypt for the remainder of the famine. *Thank You, Elohim, for changing all twelve of Jacob's stubborn sons today.*

The cedar doors burst open. "My lord, you must come!" Maahir shouted. "Pharaoh Yanassi is dead. Mistress Asenath is in custody."

"Custody?" Joseph sprinted toward him. "Is she injured?"

"Not yet."

Joseph heard the cryptic answer as he ran into the hall, down the staircase, and through the crowded palace complex. "Out of my way!" He ignored the pleas for grain rising around him. "Move!"

Elohim, protect my wife! He raced up the palace stairs three at a time and through the foyer. "Open the doors!" he shouted at the guards. Bystanders clogged the hall, slowing his entry. Unintelligible whispers ushered him through a slender opening, and he slipped inside the courtroom. The doors closed behind him. At the front edge of the crimson carpet, Hami stood between Asenath and Zahra. Zahra was in shackles. Asenath wept quietly, her eyes pleading when she saw Joseph.

King Apophis and Queen Hotep waited—pale and stone-faced—on twin thrones. Fear lengthened Joseph's strides. "Why is—" The question lodged in his throat when he glimpsed Potiphera and Hodari lying dead beside the counselors' benches.

Joseph approached his wife at the edge of the bloodied carpet. Hami lodged himself between Joseph and the two women he guarded. Confusion now conquered fear. He looked at Apophis. "My steward said our young pharaoh . . ." He swallowed hard, unable to say anything more.

Apophis took a moment, his features hardening. "Pharaoh Yanassi is in the temple, his ka protected by his patron god, Seth, while the sem priest embalms the flesh for his eternal journey."

"What happened to—"

"I will ask the questions, Paneah, and you will provide the answers I seek."

"Me?" Joseph suddenly realized Potiphar wasn't there to guard his king. Panic rose, but he dared not ask.

Apophis glared with a soldier's disdain. "How long have you known Potiphera was in Avaris?"

Joseph glanced at the corpse. "Just now."

"Did you send wine from Canaan as a gift to your pharaohs?"

Wine? What wine? "No . . ."

"When did your brothers first contact you?"

"My brothers?" Joseph swallowed hard. "They have nothing to do with—"

"Don't make me ask again, Vizier." King Apophis ground out the words through clenched teeth. Queen Hotep wiped tears, smearing what little cosmetics were left.

A chill ran through Joseph's veins. "Ten of my brothers came to Egypt last year but didn't recognize me. I arrested them under the *false* charge of spying on our grain systems."

"So, you admit your brothers are Hebrew spies."

"No, my king. I observed them in prison for three days. Convinced they were no threat, I released nine and kept the brother in custody that I believed to be most dangerous."

"I'm told your brothers have returned with an additional brother and you freed the one you admit is 'dangerous.' You've been feasting with them privately all morning. Have you been plotting—"

"No, King Apophis!" Joseph shouted but calmed at the fury of Apophis's threatening demeanor. "Forgive me, my king, but may I explain?"

Apophis barely nodded.

"Nine brothers returned to fulfill the condition of buying more grain and retrieving the imprisoned brother by bringing Benjamin, the only other son of my mother." Joseph lowered his head and voice, hoping the truth wouldn't condemn the brothers he'd just forgiven. "I tested their character today, to see if they'd changed, and I believe they have. They've become better men. Honest. Hardworking. Loyal to one another. And they mean no harm to Egypt."

Queen Hotep laid her hand on the king's arm, a silent signal of some kind.

"King Apophis, please," Joseph said, "I don't know what happened here, but I'm as anxious for justice as you are. Pharaoh Yanassi was like a son to me. And if something has happened to Captain Potiphar—" His voice broke, but he cleared his throat and continued, "I tell you with utmost certainty that neither my brothers nor I had any part in the atrocity that happened here."

"It was all Potiphera." Zahra's tremulous voice was like a rock scraping fine faience.

King Apophis looked at her. "How do you know?"

"Pharaoh Nebiriraw sent a message to Potiphera refusing to send support troops for today's coup. Yet Potiphera believed Nebiriraw would use his Theban army to stabilize Lower Egypt if both kings were killed in Avaris." Her face twisted in bitter emotion. "Both Nebiriraw and Shedet's high priest were wise enough to discern Potiphera's madness. Hodari and I were too blinded by hate."

"Why, Zahra?" Queen Hotep cried. "Was life in a palace so terrible? Is death better than being my friend?"

"Friend?" Zahra shouted. "I thought we were sisters—until you made me your servant. Now I have no one. Pharaoh Yanassi kept Hodari and me apart in this life, and your husband's punishment robs us of peace in the next."

"I've begged mercy for you," Hotep said through tears, "but you must show some remorse."

Zahra grew still, emotionless. "I want no mercy."

"Then you shall have none." Eyes narrowed, King Apophis turned his attention to Joseph. "Potiphar was severely injured, Lord

Vizier. Pushpa and my personal physician are tending his wounds. Their care is his best chance of recovery." He waved a dismissive hand at Hami, signaling Asenath's release.

She rushed into Joseph's arms, weeping. Joseph said, "Please, my king, would you explain to me what happened?"

"Potiphera, Hodari, and Zahra pooled their half-witted vengeance to contrive a plan to not only kill both kings, but to do it in a way that would make you the traitor so you'd be executed for treason. Thankfully, Ra protected one king, but Hodari's dagger found Yanassi's heart before I could stop him." He sniffed back emotion and added, "They coerced your unwilling wife to participate by threatening to harm your sons."

"Our sons?" Joseph turned to Asenath.

"They're safe," she whispered before his terror could fully bloom.

Apophis removed a cloth from his belt and pressed it against his eyes before continuing. "When Hodari lunged toward me, Potiphar blocked his blow. The priest raced up with a dagger and stabbed Potiphar, giving me time to kill Hodari. Were it not for Hami, Potiphar would be a dead man."

Joseph shot a glance at his captain. "Thank you for saving Potiphar." Then his attention shifted to Asenath. "I'm sorry our friend had to kill your abi."

Asenath lowered her head, and Hami whispered, "I have no regrets."

A new angst shot through Joseph. What was his wife feeling? Betrayal? Anger? Was Joseph partly to blame for today's violence? He stepped toward the throne. "My king, I knew Potiphera hated me and did nothing to reconcile. I knew Hodari and Zahra held a grudge against Potiphar and Pharaoh Yanassi. But I never imagined any of them would go to these lengths—"

"No, Paneah," Apophis said. "We can preempt a logical plan, but this was madness." The king held his gaze until Joseph nodded his assent.

"Is Asenath cleared of all wrongdoing?" Joseph asked.

The king nodded. "Yes. Take her home."

"Wait. Please." Asenath lifted her eyes to the king and queen. "I beg you. Spare Zahra's life."

"No!" Zahra shouted. "I don't want—"

"Silence!" Apophis glared at Zahra and then returned his focus to Asenath. She didn't flinch or look away when he addressed her. "Why would you intercede for the woman who held your sons hostage?"

"Because I've seen Elohim heal and change people. Some, like Potabi, are given many opportunities yet refuse every offer of healing balm. Others, like Joseph's brothers, commit terrible crimes, but Elohim softens and molds them with layers of decisions that make them new. Zahra has never had the luxury or responsibility of choices. She's always lived under Potabi's control. Since we married, Hotep and I have been given many freedoms to make our own choices, and we've chosen who we wished to be." Asenath lowered herself to one knee. "I beg you, King Apophis and Queen Hotep. Give my sister Zahra the opportunity to choose who she will be now that Potabi no longer controls her."

"I don't believe Zahra herself would have harmed the boys," Hotep said, "but the fact that she helped Hodari and Potiphera kill Yanassi . . ." She shook her head, unable to say more.

The king sighed. "As you can see, Paneah, Queen Hotep is biased toward the maid—as is your wife. They assure me Zahra is worthy of mercy because she'll change if given the chance. You and Asenath have said your brothers proved capable of change—perhaps finding some latent integrity because they share your bloodline, Lord Vizier." He leaned forward. "But I believe the guilty woman is cut from the same cloth as Potiphera, unable to change."

"She's not Potabi," Asenath pleaded.

Apophis's lips twitched with the declaration, "She will be punished by death for my nephew's death."

"Yes, please!" Zahra pleaded, "Let me die!"

King Apophis lifted both brows, studying Zahra with an unexpected pause. "If death is your desire, life in prison should be your torture."

Zahra crumpled to the floor, sobbing.

Asenath glanced at Joseph, hope blooming with color in her cheeks. "My king, may I speak once more?" Apophis sighed and waved her to continue. "Potabi claimed that I was Isis, the great healer, but Elohim alone can heal Zahra's inner wounds by personally demonstrating His love to her."

Apophis scowled. "No honorable god would deign to meet personally with that." He pointed at Zahra, who wept uncontrollably at Hami's feet. Hotep laid her hand on her husband's arm. "Show mercy, my love. Let Zahra live so Asenath and I may show her the love of true sisterhood without Potiphera's influence to poison her."

Apophis pulled away. Joseph had known the warrior king long enough to realize he desired vengeance as much as justice. Perhaps Elohim could satisfy his need for both.

"I stand as my God's witness," Joseph said. "I don't know if Zahra's character matches Potiphera's, but I know the prompting of Elohim. As certain as I was of the interpretations of Pharaoh Yanassi's dreams, I'm equally confident that Elohim can change Zahra. He will reveal Himself through Asenath's and Queen Hotep's love for her."

The king lifted a single brow. "You and your wife have made grand claims about your god's power to heal, Vizier." With barely a hesitation, King Apophis rose. "I will commute Zahra's execution to life in prison. If, within six months, the maid hasn't shown measurable improvement in character, I'll receive it as proof from almighty Ra that she shares Potiphera's irreparably damaged ka and that your Elohim has failed. The maid will be fed to the crocodiles—as Potiphera's and Hodari's bodies will be tonight at dusk."

Zahra wept quietly without acknowledging her final sentence.

Asenath turned to her sister on the throne. "Hotep, my queen, if King Apophis allows it, would you accompany me to visit Zahra in prison?"

"Please, my love." Hotep nestled close to her husband's side. "I wish to accompany Asenath."

Jaw muscles flexing, Apophis released a huff and nodded his permission. She and Asenath shared a resolved glance.

"Thank you, my king," Joseph said. Realizing the many challenges the coming days would bring, he added, "Our whole nation grieves at Pharaoh Yanassi's death. For the next seventy days, I'll send grain vouchers to the nomes for distribution so citizens need not travel while we observe the official mourning period."

"Thank you, Paneah. I—" Apophis cleared his throat. "I wasn't sure how we could provide grain and still honor my nephew. I appreciate your wisdom and flexibility." He offered his hand to Hotep. "Come, Wife. We should check on Tani." They retreated through the private exit at the back of the dais.

Joseph glanced at Hami. "Take Zahra to the prison below my villa. I'd rather she be there than below Hodari's villa."

"I'll do as you command, but you should know—it's Potiphar's villa now." A slight smile curved Hami's lips. "As it should be." Hami took Zahra's elbow, commencing their journey to the villa's prison.

Asenath's soft gasp stole Joseph's attention. She watched as Medjays dragged Potiphera's and Hodari's bloody corpses from the throne room. Asenath hid her face against Joseph's chest, the finality and savagery of her abi's death too horrifying. Asenath's grip around his waist tightened, but she didn't speak. What could he say to erase the awful images conjured by the brutal events and the king's verdict? Joseph whispered quiet assurances to his wife. "We'll visit Queen Tani, tell her we love her, then take our boys home. We can bring them back tomorrow if she—or you—needs the distraction." Asenath nodded and wiped her eyes. When she looked up, he added, "I need to speak with Apophis soon. I've asked my brothers to bring Abba back to Egypt—along with their families, the flocks, and herds. But they mustn't return before the seventy days of mourning for Pharaoh Yanassi has ended."

A sweet smile brightened her face. "Joseph! You've forgiven them completely?"

He nodded. "You were right, my love. Elohim *is* the Great Healer."

FIFTY-TWO

*Now Jacob sent Judah ahead of him to Joseph
to get directions to Goshen. . . . Joseph had his
chariot made ready and went to Goshen to meet
his father Israel.*

GENESIS 46:28–29

I waited at the top of our villa stairway at dawn, watching for Hotep, Pushpa, and Ahira to make their way across the palace complex. The official grieving period for Yanassi had ended yesterday, and though our hearts would take longer to mend, the urgency of new beginnings had never been greater.

"I'm not sure Zahra will ever change," I whispered into the morning silence. I'd never voiced my fears aloud and wouldn't say the words to Joseph. Two months of the six-month mercy period Apophis had given Zahra had passed with no visible improvement in her mood or disposition. If she continued like this, Zahra would be executed in four months.

When I returned from yesterday's visit to my sullen and silent sister, Joseph had offered brave words. "She'll come around, my love. Two months means nothing in a prison cell. Elohim created time so there is still a chance we could be awed by His sovereignty. He's never late, seldom early, and always follows His schedule, not ours. We must simply trust Him." His tone was even, his wisdom glib. Others might have been fooled, but I noted his flexing jaw muscles and the sheen of sweat across his brow. My husband was anxious, too, but we were both trying to apply Elohim's past faithfulness to our current dilemma.

The guenon left behind by Shedet's high priest was the only positive outcome of the whole awful ordeal. I cuddled her against my cheek, watching my three friends and their large retinue of Medjays cross the empty palace complex. Apophis had doubled all protection for his family and ours since Yanassi's murder.

"Here they come," I whispered. "They'll be so happy to see you." The little guenon must have seen her other ommis. She began squawking and wriggling in my hands. "Yes, yes, they're coming to see you." We'd kept her on a regular rotation of two days with each family, beginning at our villa, then to Hotep's, and then to Ahira and Pushpa's. I'd learned from the Faiyum guides that a guenon bonded quickly, so we hoped sharing the baby's care and taking her once a week to visit Zahra would maintain the bond I'd seen developing between them in Hodari's villa. But Zahra had refused to even touch the precious gift.

Last week she'd shouted, "You'll take her away the moment I start to love her!" Then she threw her bowl of gruel at Hotep. I understood her distrust. Potabi had often given gifts to tease us into attachment, then used our affection to control us.

I'd immediately taken Hotep, dripping with gruel, to my chamber. We'd washed her hair, changed her robe, and regained our calm before she returned to the palace. Had Apophis heard of Zahra's disrespect, he likely would have executed her immediately, regardless of the mercy period.

As my friends drew near, I looked into the monkey's golden eyes and stroked her silver-tipped fur. "You look almost identical to my Jendayi when Potabi brought her to the tower. My sisters and I fed her goat's milk and gruel every two hours—as we have you." But the happy memories couldn't remove the niggling doubts. Could Zahra care for her in a cell? How would this little one get the sunshine and activity she needed? Zahra likely remembered how we'd cared for Jendayi, but would she ever allow herself to nurture and love a monkey again? I shook my head, clearing the dismal thoughts. *Elohim, help me to be wise about the gift but also trust You to work out the details.* Zahra needed this little orphan as much as the guenon needed Zahra. And I needed to reach the hidden corners of my sister's heart—or in four months she would die.

"Ooh, there she is!" Three cooing women mounted our villa stairs, each entirely focused on a monkey no larger than a wine goblet. With their thirty Medjays trailing behind, Hotep, Pushpa, and Ahira surrounded us like a swarm of locusts.

"Today is the perfect day to try giving Zahra this precious gift again." Hotep took the guenon from me. "We can celebrate Yanassi's enjoyable afterlife and a new beginning for us all."

"We certainly hope so." Joseph's hand slipped around my waist, startling me.

I turned to face him. "What's—"

"Excuse me, ladies, may I take my wife aside for a moment?" His handsome smile still weakened my knees. My friends ignored him, enamored with the monkey.

I followed Joseph to a corner in the entrance hall, my stomach twisting when I saw his smile had faded. "What's wrong?"

He held me close, pressing his lips against my ear to whisper, "I received a message after you left our chamber this morning. My family arrived in Goshen last night. I need you to go with me to meet them."

I stepped back. "But Zahra . . ." I was torn between the two most important healings in my life. If Elohim didn't change Zahra, I'd lose a sister, but cultivating relationships with my new family was equally important. "I'll give Zahra the monkey and return right away."

"Asenath, hurry!" Hotep called. She and the others had already started down the hall toward the prison.

"Go on," he said, stealing a kiss before he released me. "I'll get everything ready for our short journey to Goshen."

I nodded and hurried to rejoin my friends, but my divided attention turned my head several times, glancing back to see Joseph and Hami exit toward the stables.

"May I carry her?" Ahira reached too quickly, and the startled monkey nipped her hand. "Ouch! She bit me!" Pushpa examined her thumb but found no blood.

Hotep tried to stifle a giggle. "Well, she's got Jendayi's temper." The mere mention of Potabi's gift drained her face of color.

"It's all right. Jendayi was the best gift Potabi ever gave us." I patted her arm. "I'm choosing to believe that some of his actions during those early years were motivated by true affection. He saved our lives in Memphis and initially meant to protect us. Perhaps Zahra will learn what real love is by protecting this little one."

"I'm proud of you for focusing on good memories," Pushpa said, her cheeks damp with tears. "My Potiphar's body is healing quicker than his spirit, but Elohim is at work. He'll work in Zahra's heart, too."

"I hope so," I whispered.

We walked in silence past the servants' quarters and finally reached the prison door. Both Pushpa and Ahira carried baskets of food—as always—and offered one to the guards before we continued down the stairs.

I always announced our arrival before we reached the bottom step. "Good morning, Ubaid!" The crusty old warden from Potiphar's villa had been transferred to ours in hopes that he'd be as kind to Zahra as he'd been to Joseph during his years in prison.

When we reached the main chamber, Ubaid was emerging from his chamber, smacking his lips and rubbing sleepy eyes. "Is it morning already?" He stretched his arms high overhead and yawned so wide, I thought he might swallow his own face. Not exactly the protocol greeting for Queen Hotep. His eyes widened when he saw the little guenon. "Well, good morning, beauty." Ubaid started toward the monkey, his hands outstretched. Both the monkey and the queen's Medjays protested, as they'd done every time he'd done it.

Pushpa salved his feelings by offering one of the baskets she carried. "Ahira and I brought enough food for you and Zahra to share with well-behaved prisoners."

Ubaid took the baskets from their arms, riffled through them, and thanked her. "No one bakes better bread than you, Mistress Pushpa, but I'm afraid it will take more than good food to help Zahra. You should all be prepared. She hasn't said a word or moved from the corner of her cell since you left yesterday." He reached into his chamber for a ring of wooden keys, then started down the torchlit hall of barracks cells. "I heard Lady Zahra was a chantress at Ra's temple. Everyone needs purpose. Maybe if she sang something, she'd feel better and brighten the whole prison."

We passed empty cells on both sides of the barracks hallway. The prisoners in this part of the prison were released for daily slave tasks as part of their sentence. The cellblock hallway on the opposite side was lined with small, dark rooms with straw-covered dirt floors where prisoners waited for execution. Joseph had been sequestered for months in Potiphar's cellblock, not knowing whether he'd be executed or live out his days in utter darkness—until Ubaid made him assistant warden. "Ubaid, have you considered making Zahra assistant warden as you did for Joseph?" I asked.

He cast a remorseful glance over his shoulder. "I already offered, Mistress, but she refuses to leave her cell." He stopped at the familiar last cell on the left with its wall of iron bars, wooden door in the middle, and—this time—a wraith huddled in the back corner.

"Zahra?" I pressed my face against the bars, but she didn't look up. Ubaid unlocked the door, and I rushed inside. But I stopped when Zahra lifted her head.

Today, I saw her differently. Sharp cheekbones and jutting brows framed cavernous eyes. Her hand brushed the wall, where she'd kept count of days. "Come to celebrate moving on with your lives, did you?" Her cracked lips bled with the effort, and the skin on her hand was translucent, blue veins like tree roots showing above the soil.

"We've come to offer a new life." Hotep placed the monkey beside her and then stepped back. The baby guenon trembled, huddling alone—much like Zahra.

She watched the creature and released a weak huff. "Why would you torture that creature with a lifetime in a prison cell? Take it away so I can die."

I turned away, shaking my head. *It's hopeless, Elohim.* I asked Ubaid, "How long since she's eaten?"

"Since she threw her gruel at the queen last week, but she's refused water since yesterday."

Until this moment, I hadn't realized Zahra could choose death. I remembered when I'd been so sick in the tower and with my first pregnancy from lack of sufficient food and water. I looked to Hotep, Pushpa, and Ahira for counsel. "What can we do?"

Pushpa nudged me toward my hopeless friend. "Try again, beloved."

I sat in the filth beside Zahra and gathered the monkey into my lap. "I saw the way this little one bonded with you when Shu brought her to Hodari's villa. You loved her and she loved you. We've kept her alive, but she's not ours. She's yours, Zahra, just like Jendayi was mine. This little girl is yours alone, someone you can love and who will love you."

Head bowed, Zahra sniffed and wiped her nose. "I don't deserve love. Not after what I've done."

"No," I said, "you don't."

Hotep gasped. "Asenath!"

"None of us deserve the kind of love Elohim offers."

Zahra looked up at me. "I don't believe in your god."

"He's very patient. He'll stay right here in this cell with you. I've told you dozens of times that Elohim is always with you. His presence never leaves, and He gives us reminders of His love through people and His creation. Every time this baby guenon shows how much she loves you, you'll know that it's Elohim who placed that love within her."

Hotep knelt on her other side. "Forgive us, Zahra, for not showing Elohim's love to you better."

Startled, I met the queen's eyes. "You've never used Elohim's name."

"I see a great difference in the legends of Egypt and the way your God loves. Perhaps if I'd embraced Elohim earlier . . . Zahra, I share the blame for what's happened to you, my sister."

"No one shares the blame," Zahra said. "My choices were my own." Her face twisted with grief. "I see no reason to stay alive if this hole is the entirety of my future."

"Zahra, name this monkey," I said, using a commanding tone. "Care for her. Love her." Then I remembered Ubaid's suggestion. "And sing for the prisoners who feel the same despair you feel. Your voice can give them hope and restore your purpose."

Ubaid stepped into the chamber. "I still need help keeping the prison records, Lady Zahra. Mistress Asenath stole my assistant warden, and I've never found a worthy replacement."

His levity broke through Zahra's stony shell. She reached for the monkey. "I will name you Ifa."

"*Love.* Perfect." I gave Hotep a wink. "I'm sure while you remind Zahra how we fed Jendayi, she'll also be ready to eat a little gruel herself." I pulled both friends into a sideways hug and stood to go. "I must be on my way. Joseph's family has arrived in Goshen, and I'm nervous about meeting his abi for the first time."

Zahra looked up, tucking little Ifa against her chest. "I hope Joseph's abi is someone who shows your god's love well."

Astounded at her profound words, I leaned over to kiss her forehead. "So do I, my friend." I hurried out of the cell and up the stairs with newfound hope that my sister would find healing, love, and purpose in Elohim's presence.

Hami waited for me at the villa entrance. "I'm here to escort you—immediately."

"Is everything all right?"

The Medjay's easy smile was a good sign. "Yes, but we must hurry. The vizier waits for you in his chariot."

"Chariot?" I tried to peer over the mountainous guards that now surrounded me but saw nothing but their backs and shoulders as we left the villa. Hami sliced through the crowded palace complex like the point of a spear. Breathless at his pace, I begged, "Hami, slow down."

Must I ride in Joseph's chariot? *Absolutely not!* I may have overcome my childhood nightmares of the Hyksos chariot invasion in Memphis, but I wasn't about to *ride* in one.

"She's here!" Hami shouted at the same moment I saw Joseph mounted on the vehicle I dreaded. Dressed in full regalia, Egypt's vizier was more stunning than his white stallions and golden chariot combined. I stopped three paces away, panting from the run and breathless at his smile.

"Potiphar said King Apophis was amenable to meeting my family, Asenath. I want you to be with me when I see Abba Jacob and tell him." The joy on his face was brighter than the sun. I studied the chariot more closely. Creaking each time the horses pranced, the glorified cart was dusty, and deep gouges marred the gilded wood. A mere object. Not so scary. I suddenly realized it was just a silly cart on wheels. How could I refuse?

"Come, my love." He offered his hand.

"Joseph, I . . ." The words drowned in a surge of fear—not of the chariot, but of meeting Prince Jacob. "What if your abi hates me because I was a priestess? Shouldn't your first meeting be untainted by my presence?"

He handed the reins to an attendant and stepped off the chariot to hold me in his arms. "You and I are free now. I'm no longer a slave, and you're no longer held captive by Potiphera's deceit. We cannot—will not—allow my family to become our master either. Without your persistent faith in Elohim to reconcile my family, this day would never have come. *That* is what Abba Jacob will know about my wife." He offered his hand to me again. "Come, my love. It's time you finally met Elohim's covenant bearer."

Swallowing hard, I accepted his hand and stepped into the chariot. My husband stood behind me and then tied a leather belt around his waist but not mine.

"Don't I get a belt?"

"I'm your belt." He slapped the reins, and I leaned back against his chest as the two white stallions raced toward my new family.

FIFTY-THREE

*Then Joseph brought his father Jacob in and
presented him before Pharaoh. After Jacob
blessed Pharaoh, Pharaoh asked him, "How
old are you?"*

GENESIS 47:7–8

Asenath

I stood with Joseph outside the palace courtroom with five of his
brothers and Prince Jacob, waiting to appear before Pharaoh. "King
Apophis will likely ask one question," Joseph said. "When he asks,
'What is your occupation?' answer *exactly* as I told you. Don't
improvise." He'd been schooling them since we left Goshen early
this morning.

I, on the other hand, was trying to forget the last time I visited
Pharaoh's court. The images of violence and dead bodies still rav-
aged my thoughts. Had they replaced the bloodstained carpet on
the center aisle?

"You're trembling, my dear." Abba Jacob patted my hand and
placed it on his forearm. "Are you afraid Pharaoh will deny Joseph's
request that we stay in Egypt or grant it?" Mischief danced in his
rheumy brown eyes.

I grinned at the jesting. "You know I want nothing more than for my sons and I to become part of your family."

"Joseph's sons are already part of my family—as are you." His lips quivered. "You have Rachel's beauty and Leah's wisdom. My son chose wisely."

"Thank you, Abba." He knew we had no choice in the matter, but I was flattered still.

The courtroom door opened, and the king's herald announced, "The vizier's family may enter."

"Ready?" Joseph asked.

I nodded, too nervous to speak. Two Medjays opened the doors, and I led his five brothers down a new crimson carpet amid a room full of whispers and pointing fingers. Not only were shepherds detestable to Egyptian nobility, but word had spread that Hebrews had taken up residence in Egypt's finest grazing land. The bias had been as obvious when Joseph and I arrived in Goshen. My sisters-in-law wanted nothing to do with me. However, Abba Jacob and my brothers-in-law assured me they'd warm immediately to Nasseh and Ephraim. *Elohim, I'm trusting You for complete healing.* On our next visit, I planned to wear wool robes and allow my boys to play with their cousins until they were caked with dust. Perhaps I'd even learn to spin wool.

"Mistress Asenath," Pharaoh said, one eyebrow raised. "Welcome. I expected my vizier to introduce his own family."

I stopped at the edge of the new crimson carpet, offering a respectful bow to the king, Queen Hotep, and Queen Tani, who I was surprised to see in public so soon after Yanassi's assassination. I glimpsed Potiphar standing beside the royal council, his wounds nearly healed but his arm still in a sling. Pushpa and Ahira were with him, and both gave me a subdued wave that settled my nerves. I returned my attention to King Apophis. "My family was once very small, Mighty King, but it's grown quite large since I married. I'm honored to introduce five of Zaphenath-Paneah's eleven brothers." I began with Judah and Reuben, two of Leah's sons, then presented Asher and Naphtali, sons born to Abba Jacob's third and fourth wives. "This handsome young man is Benjamin, the only brother from Paneah's ima, Rachel, Prince Jacob's second wife."

A grin softened Apophis's features. "Does your husband also plan to take four wives, Mistress Asenath?"

"Not if he intends to keep his first wife, my king."

Apophis's wry grin sobered as he examined Joseph's brothers. After an extended silence, he addressed Judah. "What is your occupation?"

Joseph had correctly guessed the king's opening question. The answer was obvious with the odor of sheep dung clinging to the brothers' robes. But King Apophis was testing their poise, not searching for information.

"Your servants are shepherds," Judah replied. "As were our abbas before us."

Not exactly the rehearsed answer but very close.

"We've come to Egypt for a time," Judah continued. "As you're aware, the famine is severe in Canaan, and your servants' flocks have no pasture. We humbly ask that you allow your servants to settle in Goshen—but only in Goshen, my king." Joseph's talkative brother bowed, as did the others.

I gawked at King Apophis, wondering if I should say something to intervene. But what? Had Judah said anything that Pharaoh might interpret as a threat? Joseph would know, but I didn't. He'd sent me with his brothers so he could introduce Abba Jacob afterward.

I held my breath while Apophis stared at Judah with an enigmatic smirk. Was he pleasantly disposed or preparing for verbal sparring?

"Zaphenath-Paneah and Prince Jacob of Canaan!" The herald's pronouncement from behind us snapped the tense silence. Joseph's brothers and I turned, as did everyone in the audience, to watch Egypt's vizier escort his aging, bent abba.

Jacob's gnarled hand gripped a shepherd's staff on which he leaned heavily. A long white beard had grown past his leather belt, and thinning white hair fell in disheveled strands over his shoulders and down his back. His mind was as sharp as a Medjay sword, but his body had betrayed him long ago. Joseph matched his abba's stuttered pace.

When they stood beside us, Joseph whispered to Judah, "You had to improvise, didn't you?"

"Congratulations, Lord Paneah." Apophis's tone held a tinge of challenge.

"For what exactly, my king?"

"For maintaining loyalty to your king while saving Egypt's Two Lands from certain disaster—despite all the injuries you've endured." Apophis rose, approached the edge of the dais, and motioned toward Potiphar.

One of the king's Medjays stepped from behind Potiphar and produced a large gold collar. I whispered to Abba Jacob, "It's the Gold of Praise, the highest military honor any soldier can earn." Potiphar, Hami, and King Apophis wore it but few others.

Potiphar took the solid-gold collar from his Medjay and approached my husband, sniffing back emotion. "I present you with this honor, Zaphenath-Paneah, as my vizier and my brother." He clasped the collar in back and then lowered to one knee before the Hebrew he had purchased as his slave. Soldiers and nobility joined Potiphar. Even Abba Jacob bowed to his son.

"Egypt is before you," Apophis said. "You've protected it as fiercely as any warrior, and you should settle your family in Goshen if that's where you want them." He lifted one brow. "And if any among them are better than my own stinking shepherds, put your brothers in charge of my livestock."

My husband's jaw muscle flexed as he fought for control. "Mighty Pharaoh, how can I express my gratitude—"

"May El Shaddai—Creator of all—bless your coming in and going out." Prince Jacob struggled to stand. Joseph and I helped him to his feet as he continued his blessing. "May Elohim protect you and provide for you even as you have shown the same kindness to my beloved son." He inclined his head to the king amid a silence so profound, beetles didn't dare crawl across the tiles.

Apophis appeared startled. His mouth opened and closed several times before words finally came. "How old are you?"

"My pilgrimage on this earth is only 130 years—few and difficult compared to my abbas before me."

"Few?" Apophis's brows shot up, and he turned to Joseph. "You didn't tell me your abi had passed the year of perfection."

"Forgive me, my king. It's not unusual for my family to live well past the 110th year. Great-Saba Abraham lived 175 years, and Saba Isaac until he was 180. Abba Jacob lives a covenant bearer's life, and he chose to share that blessing with you."

"Bless me again." Apophis's smile had turned to pleading. "I don't know your god, but I can't deny his power. Bless me, Prince Jacob, and may your family bless my land."

I stood in awe as Elohim's covenant bearer fulfilled Abraham's promise before my eyes. Perhaps even more astounding was when the king who had hoped to make me his wife invited my Hebrew husband and his family to a banquet in their honor—during a famine we would survive because of a God who blessed *all* nations.

Judah hugged me. Then Reuben. Then three more brothers of a family I now called my own. Finally, Abba Jacob gathered me into his arms and whispered, "Elohim has given Joseph back to me and added a daughter. Know that you have an abba who loves you, Asenath."

An abba who loves me. I'd yearned to hear those words and ached for Potabi's approval. Now Elohim defined my destiny, and His love was my strong tower. Whether in feast or famine, Joseph ben Jacob had shown me the only firm foundation—and, together, we'd teach our children to bear their blessings well.

AUTHOR'S NOTE

I love the fascinating culture of ancient Egypt, the splendor of its architecture, and the abundance of artifacts preserved by the hot, dry climate. However, there's one glaring frustration: sometimes I find *too much* information that leads to conflicting conclusions.

Though research is always my favorite aspect of writing biblical fiction, it's also when I'm most aware that I'm a *novelist*, not a biblical scholar or an archaeologist. I write the "might have beens" based on biblical truth, academic theories, and informed imagination. I read widely—books, scholarly articles/dissertations, maps, websites, etc.—and look for two or three experts whose names recur in footnotes and bibliographies. They become my authority for names, dates, and locations for a single book. The two experts I relied on most heavily for *In Feast or Famine* were Manfred Bietak and K. S. B. Ryholt.

Dating the Dynasties

My go-to scholars had nothing to say about Joseph specifically or his sojourn in Egypt. However, overall research described the Hyksos dynasty as foreign rulers whose ancestors had been driven out of Canaan by a wealthy Bedouin tribe. These Canaanites were thought to be Amorites (related to the Rephaim—see Deuteronomy 3:11) since Egyptian records describe them as Amu. Could the wealthy Bedouins who drove them out of Canaan have been Abraham and his descendants? My informed imagination interpreted Scripture's truth that way for this story:

> [On his deathbed, Jacob said to Joseph,] "And to you I give one more ridge of land than to your brothers, the ridge I took from the Amorites with my sword and my bow." (Genesis 48:22)

With each generation the "Amu" rose to higher-ranking positions in Egypt's government and eventually grew powerful enough to destroy the thirteenth dynasty of Egyptian pharaohs in Memphis. Egypt splintered into a fourteenth, and later sixteenth, dynasty in Thebes (Upper Egypt), with a simultaneous (and relatively short-lived) Abydos dynasty during the same time that the Hyksos fifteenth dynasty (Lower Egypt) established their capital in Avaris.

By the end of the seventeenth dynasty, Theban pharaohs conquered the Hyksos and united Upper and Lower Egypt again under one Egyptian ruler. (See the Author's Note in *Potiphar's Wife* for a fuller discussion of the dating and K. S. B. Ryholt's *Political Situation in Egypt During the Second Intermediate Period, c. 1800–1550 B.C.* for more historical background.)

Names, Dates, Locations—Oh My!

In 2012, I first dipped my toe into researching the Nile and was quickly drowning in scholarly debate and conflicting "facts." Extremely intelligent people disagree on pharaohs' names, dates of reign, and even city names and locations! Remember, my job is to write a novel, to create a *believable* world that remains true to Scripture, represents Egypt's overall history as accurately as possible, and spares my reader clunky technical facts that distract from the story.

For instance, during the Hyksos era, the ancient city of Thebes was likely called Waset. However, since most readers wouldn't be familiar with Waset, I refer to Upper Egypt's capital as Thebes. To measure traveling distances between cities, I used a single map with its legend. It may differ slightly from my 2013 and 2014 books, *The Pharaoh's Daughter* and *Miriam*, in which I used a different map.

Our best resource for Egyptian reigns is the Turin King List. Unfortunately, the portion recording Egypt's Second Intermediate Period (c. 1800–1550 B.C.), including the fifteenth dynasty of Hyksos kings, is damaged beyond recognition. There are only two recognizable Hyksos kings on the Turin King List: Khyan and Apophis. Though Yanassi was recorded on a stele as Khyan's son, he was never inaugurated as a pharaoh. Tani is recorded on a stele as Apophis's sister, but her role as Khyan's wife and Yanassi's ommi is purely fiction.

Experts "proved" a vast array of relationships between Sobekhotep/Djehuty/Sitmut by using information from various steles. Here's what I learned from all my studies: Someone married someone else's second cousin's aunt's brother-in-law's grandma's third cousin twice removed; then they all died. My trusted expert, Ryholt, lists the Theban kings in this order: Djehuty, Sobekhotep, Neferhotep, Monthhotepi, Nebiryraw. Notice the different name spellings. Were these different people or the same kings with varied spellings? I faced similar inconsistencies at every stage in the Egyptian research. So, I used the mortar of imagination with Ryholt's adapted building blocks to create what I hoped would be believable fiction.

Gods and Grace

The records of Egypt's gods are as varied as its pharaohs. Though Amun and Ra were historically separate sun gods that eventually evolved into a single god, Amun-Ra, my explanation of the way Potiphera made it happen is purely fiction. And there was never an attempt to add "El" to the name—but it sounded like something Potiphera might have done!

When I first began researching Asenath, I discovered an ancient short story titled "Joseph and Asenath." It details her life as a priestess, their courtship, her conversion to Elohim, and her efforts to secure her sons' future as part of Israel's twelve tribes. Most scholars agree the story was originally written as Jewish fiction between 200 B.C. and A.D. 200, intended to proselytize pagan worshippers to believe in the God of Abraham, Isaac, and Jacob. Later adaptations included Christian themes (bread, wine, and so on) but for the same purpose of evangelism.

Isn't it stunning that Elohim invited the daughter of an Egyptian priest to partake in His covenant blessing? She wasn't perfect or even the most likely candidate, but she was God's choice. Elohim—who is the same yesterday, today, and forever—still chooses the unlikely and those less than perfect to partake in His promises. Discover more about the God who chooses the undeserving at mesuandrews.com.

ACKNOWLEDGMENTS

My world gets pretty small when I'm on deadline. I breathe, eat, sleep, and dream whatever plotline, revisions, or edits come into my world. Few people can put up with that kind of intensity, and I'm so grateful for the amazing people who help me plow through it as well as those who occasionally remind me to take a break in the midst.

First, I'm so grateful to Lissa Halls-Johnson for her friendship and patience during both the content and line editing stages of this book. How many times did we feel like quitting? Many! But, thankfully, neither suggested it at the same time, so we made it! And I believe we've created another story about biblical characters who walked off the pages and into people's hearts.

Second, the team at WaterBrook continues to blow me away with their sweet mixture of professionalism and grace. On everything from the stunning cover to moving the release date to serve the best overall marketing plan, this team of God-honoring professionals finds new ways with each book to encourage me with kindness. What amazing people you are!

Third, the team behind the scenes—my assistant, Amanda Geaney, and my husband, Roy—may have the most difficult job of anyone. They see the underbelly of my writing life. Those ugly first drafts. My grumpy and unreasonable days. The times I want to throw my laptop into the mountain holler outside my back door (yep, we live in Appalachia—the land of knobs and hollers). Yet they cheer me on, pray for me constantly, and tell me hard truths when I need them most. I wouldn't want to do this writing thing without either of them.

Fourth, my beloved Biblical Family Forever (BFFs) and newsies. My BFFs is a group of women who have a heart for biblical fiction in general and a zeal for God's Word. Some in the group have been members since its inception in 2013, while others have been chosen to join us for this book. My newsies are open to any and all. My publisher calls them my "superfans"! I call them . . . amazing. The BFFs and newsies together become an army of committed readers. They have helped me spread the word about my books to others who might enjoy a deeper historical understanding of the real people in the Bible.

Finally, to my precious family, related by both blood and heart-strings: Thank you for sacrificing the amount of time we once had together so I can write full time. Writing is a calling, and your support makes it a joy.

ABOUT THE AUTHOR

MESU ANDREWS is the Christy Award–winning author of *Isaiah's Daughter,* whose deep understanding of and love for God's Word brings the biblical world alive for readers. Andrews lives in North Carolina with her husband, Roy. She stays connected with readers through newsie emails, fun blog posts, and frequent short stories. For more information, visit mesuandrews.com.

Egyptian Chronicles

Joseph, sold by his brothers and betrayed by Potiphar's wife, is redeemed by interpreting a young pharaoh's dreams. Promoted to Egypt's second-highest office, Joseph must shepherd the whole nation through fourteen years of feast and famine—while navigating a marriage to Asenath, the pagan priestess Pharaoh gives him.

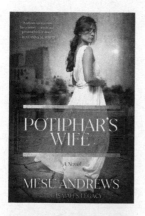

Abandoned. Rejected. Humiliated. One woman trapped in her Egyptian marriage longs to be free—and is willing to betray Joseph, her husband's good and godly servant, to do it.

Meet the pagan priest's daughter, who marries Joseph to change him, but later discovers she's part of Elohim's plan to change the world.

Treasures of the Nile

Pharaoh's daughter dares to defy the gods, drawing a Hebrew baby from the Nile and making the boy a prince of Egypt. Meet the prince, Moses, after he's exiled to Midian and returns to Egypt as an eighty-year-old man—and experience Israel's Exodus through his sister Miriam's eyes.

Pharaoh's daughter—the sister of King Tut—draws a Hebrew boy from the Nile and changes not only her life with her defiance but the future of nations.

See the Exodus through Miriam's eighty-six-year-old eyes. Having known only a life of slavery and the God named Elohim, how can Miriam accept her younger brother, Moses, who returns to Egypt after forty years, promising Israel's freedom and touting God's new name?

Prophets and Kings

Hephzibah is taken captive then marries her lifelong love, King Hezekiah. But when the fulfillment of the prophecy of her father, Isaiah, puts her son, King Manasseh, on Judah's throne, the repercussions of Manasseh's evil deeds echo for generations, leading to Daniel and his friends' exile to Babylon.

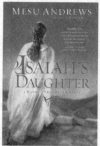

Follow the story of Hephzibah, from captive to queen, as she learns to trust Yahweh and the people He chose to love her.

Follow King Hezekiah and Queen Hephzibah's story through their son, King Manasseh, and witness Yahweh's power to redeem the evilest prodigal of all.

Experience the familiar stories of Daniel, Shadrach, Meshach, and Abednego through the eyes of Daniel's fictional wife and see Yahweh's power at work in world history.